ONLY W

ONLY WITH BLOOD

THÉRÈSE DOWN

LION FICTION

Published by Lion Fiction
an imprint of
Lion Hudson plc
Wilkinson House, Jordan Hill Road
Oxford OX2 8DR, England
www.lionhudson.com/fiction

ISBN 978 1 78264 135 3
e-ISBN 978 1 78264 136 0

First edition 2015

A catalogue record for this book is available from the British Library

Printed and bound in the UK, May 2015, LH26

For God, who makes all things possible, and for my children, James, Michael, and Grace, who never fail to inspire me.

ACKNOWLEDGMENTS

My thanks go to my colleague, Andrew Jackson, who helped me find the title of the book. And to Pam Rhodes, for all her encouragement.

"The altar of liberty totters when it is cemented only with blood."

Daniel O'Connell

CHAPTER ONE

It was cold. Frost stopped the breath of the land, seized the breath of those who moved upon it. Winter would come early and it would be harsh. Jack Flynn thanked God for a good harvest, for the cows would need early hay. Lately, he felt more keenly the pain of rheumatism in his hands. This creeping infirmity and a cough which daily grew fiercer were insistent reminders to Flynn that he could no longer put off marriage if he were to have sons to inherit his land. The alternative of selling to strangers the land his great-grandfather had purchased over a hundred years before was unthinkable. And so, this evening in 1943 at the age of forty-three, though he would rather have faced any kind of physical test of his courage, he put on his only suit and set off on foot towards the village of Dunane and the house of Malachai Brett, the matchmaker.

"Jack Flynn, come in, come in." Malachai Brett was a small, wizened man with a red nose from too much poteen and a cap and braces without which it was impossible to imagine him. His hands were raw and gnarled with years of picking rocks, handling baling twine and rough ploughshares, but their gestures were expansive and he greeted his visitor with a ready smile. He was, though, greatly puzzled by this visit from Jack Flynn, who, in thirty years of neighbourly acquaintance, Malachai had never seen down a pint or laugh out loud.

"Will you have a drop of the hard stuff with me, Jack? 'Twill drive out the cold."

"No."

"Of course, of course – 'tis early, right enough. Will you have tea?"

11

"No, no."

Jack shifted uneasily, spat into the open grate, then spoke. "I want to get hitched, Brett. I have enough money and land..." He could not go on. Malachai struggled to suppress an amazed guffaw but he checked himself – he had seen what a thump from Jack Flynn could do to a mocking face. He could not, however, think of anything to say in response to this most unexpected of announcements. After what seemed a long time, Jack turned to face the matchmaker, fully expecting to see him purple with suppressed laughter. Instead he found only a mildly bemused expression and Brett's eyes fixed on the hearth.

"Well?" barked Jack.

"Well," answered Malachai distantly. Then he seemed to arrive at definite thought. "Did you have anyone in mind?"

"That's what you're for!" came the gruff reply. The clock in the corner ticked smugly and the shadows grew longer as the early winter evening seeped across the village. Malachai busied himself adding coal to the fire, poking it into embers till it smoked and caught.

"Now, Jack, forgive me, but you're no young fella." Without turning to face him, Malachai registered the sharp rise of Jack's head and he continued quickly, "So we have to be careful – extra careful – about this match. You don't want an auld one that's no good for... breeding." Malachai met Jack's eye, risked a conspiratorial wink, regretted it, and moved on. "Now let's see... there's Nancy Madigan, over near Darcy's. She's not a bad catch – ten years in the convent at Cashmel and a fine pair of hips on her. I'd say she's good for a few years yet, Jack." Jack was startled at the image of Nancy Madigan swaying full-hipped through his milking parlour, stirring stew on his range with her wisps of carroty hair and plump, veined cheeks. People would say it was all he could get.

"She will not do."

"Ah, now, Jack," began Malachai slowly, beginning to relish a little Jack's discomfort and intrigued by the idea that Flynn was finally succumbing to carnal desire, "it never pays to be too hasty. Nancy's a good woman. She've a fine strong back on her and she'd make a fine mother. She've a hundred or two coming to her, too, when her auld fella goes – won't be long now."

"I don't want money. Who else?" The clock ticked itself to sleep. Malachai rose from his fireside chair, wound the clock, and lit a gas lamp.

"Is it a looker you're after, Jack?" Jack scowled more intently at the fire. "Well, now," continued Malachai, already seeing the incredulity on the faces of the other men as he related this extraordinary episode over a few pints at the local bar, "that's a different league altogether. Tell me, Jack, was it a young one you were looking for?"

"For crying out loud, Brett, will you stop your codding around!" Jack rose from his chair and rounded on Brett so that the matchmaker leapt backwards in alarm, dropping his taper. "You're like a dog sniffing round a heap of dung with your stupid questions. It's a simple enough request, isn't it?"

"Ah, now, Jack, calm down. It's not often I have to do all the asking! Usually, the man have someone in mind at least, or else it's the father who comes, looking for a match for his son." Malachai, seeing Jack's jaw clench, did his best to feign matter of factness but Jack did not miss the tremor in his hands as he retrieved the taper and put it back in its tin on the press. "Now I'm only trying to help you, Jack."

Flynn crossed the room and threw open the door with such force it smashed against the wall and made the little window pane shudder in its frame. In the doorway he turned.

"To hell wit' you, Malachai Brett! Sure what could the likes of you do for a real man, anyways?" With his pride momentarily restored by this show of bravado, Jack Flynn set off to his lonely farmhouse. The door shut, the fire roaring like laughter in its grate, Malachai hugged his knees in anticipation of relating this meatiest of events to his wife and sons when they returned from evening mass.

* * *

The following evening saw Malachai in his usual corner seat of the little bar in Dunane, surrounded by sceptical farmers. "I swear to ye, lads, he be after a woman to warm his old bones. She have to be good-looking, too."

"Did he mention any names?" asked one listener.

"He did not. I suggested Nancy Madigan, but he turned up his nose – 'She will not do!'" Malachai adopted Flynn's snarl, narrowed his eyes, and scowled at each farmer as Flynn had scowled at him the previous evening. The imitation was a good one, capturing the tight-lippedness and barely controlled fury which seemed always to set Flynn apart from his fellows. The listeners laughed.

"Who the hell would want to marry him anyway, the dirty auld beggar – and him past forty?" enjoined a younger man who would have liked the means to marry himself but was some way off yet.

An older man, married with several children, added, "Sure, would he know what to do with a woman, Brett? Could you show him?" More raucous laughter. A few became uncomfortable at the turn the conversation was taking and glanced nervously at the door as if Flynn could walk in at any moment, though he hadn't been known to do so in twenty years.

"Away wit' you, O'Riordan, you dirty dog," replied Malachai, determined to regain his position as respected narrator. "What he does wit' her is his own concern and none of mine."

"'Tis a skivvy Flynn is looking for – nothing else. He've no time for the rest of it," said another quietly, from the depths of his pint.

"Ah, he's not a bad-looking man now," mused Malachai. "A fine dancer and a handsome man in his youth."

"What?" The young man spoke again, inexplicably piqued by this turn of events. "Sure he've less hair than Malachai, now, and a scowl on his puss, boy, would stop a clock!" The company erupted in laughter at this petulant put-down and someone slapped the young man on the back.

"Don't worry, Dan – he've no chance against you in these races."

"He's big, mind," conceded the lugubrious man from his pint mug. "I wouldn't like to take him on."

A new voice carried clear above the others from the bar. "Have he much brass, do you think, Malachai?" The company turned to observe Mick Spillane, leaning against the bar and listening with increasing interest to the banter.

"Well, now, Mick," began Malachai in his best narrative tones, "he must have a fair few shillings in it for he've no one to feed except himself and he never drives a cow back home from market. That farm was paid for a long time ago. Then his auld fella must have left a tidy sum..."

There was a silence during which the older, weather-beaten men considered how well off they'd be without their families to feed. And in that moment, the germ of a plan took root in Mick Spillane's head. Mick had four daughters and no sons. Times were hard and two of the daughters were still at home. The elder, Maureen, was no looker and likely to take the veil. The youngest of his daughters, on the other hand, was a wilful one with a mane of dark hair and a brain beneath it which was causing Mick considerable consternation. She would not, she insisted, be married off to some ignorant culchie. She would, she declared, go to Dublin and study at Trinity. *She will and her foot!* thought Spillane and snorted into his pint. "Malachai," he said at last, resolutely wiping his mouth with the back of his hand and indicating outside with a jerk of his head, "a word."

In 1921, aged twenty-one, Jack Flynn had been part of a flying column which ambushed and killed four Black and Tans posted to the village of Cappawhite. The column had been instructed by Michael Collins himself, and by the time the ambush occurred, the men were as familiar with the press of a rifle as a ploughshare on their shoulders. That was the high point of Jack Flynn's life. Now in his forties, life was a maelstrom of labour in all weathers, long, lonely evenings and dark, quiet mornings. He had immersed himself in hard work, first intent on impressing his brutish father, then on making more money than any of his fellow farmers.

Immediately following the murders of the four "Tans", Jack imagined he had achieved heroic status in the village. His vicious temper, he was convinced, would be regarded as the mark of a Republican activist of the highest calibre. He half expected Michael Collins to knock on his door and recruit him to the cause. His inability to relate to anyone on a social level Jack chose to view as evidence of an intellect disdainful of trivia. But within a year, guilt had usurped the triumphalism he had felt following his part in the Cappawhite ambush. He woke sweating from nightmares in which he relived that night and heard with a clarity he could not consciously recall, the pleas for mercy and cries of terror uttered by the four men whose lives he and his comrades had extinguished. Alone and with no one to reassure him of his righteousness in dispatching enemy occupiers who had undoubtedly committed their own acts of atrocity, Jack grew increasingly saturnine and depressed. More than anything, he was ashamed that he had shot men in their beds. No matter how much he tried to justify to himself what he had done, he could not escape the fact that there was no bravery in killing men who could not defend themselves.

Jack threw himself entirely into hard work and abandoned all attempts at social intercourse. No one invited him to drink in the local bar, and, in spite of his good looks, no girl had the opportunity to soften the line of his mouth with a life-giving kiss. His only part in village life was when he drove his horse and cart to the chapel on Sunday mornings. He had never missed mass.

Jack never discovered exactly what had happened to his mother. She disappeared when he was a small child. His father, one still-black morning, had left for the fields as usual. Jack had listened to his sighs and curses as he heaved himself out of bed, the heavy tread of his boots to the ladder, the descending knock of boot on wood. Then there was silence, broken intermittently by the hiss of spilt water on the hob, the clatter of metal on metal as he made his tea and the bang as he set his tin mug upon the table. Finally, there was the resounding thud of the door slamming shut and the house shuddered into breath. But on this occasion, his mother did not quietly open Jack's door, tread lightly across his room, and part the curtains on the early morning. She did not turn to his bed, smiling broadly, and say in a half-whisper, "And how's my Jack? There's porridge and nice warm milk in it for good boys – come on downstairs now, pet." She did not bend to kiss him, her plait curling around the nape of her neck and falling against his face, tickling.

He had waited. He waited and waited until the sun clearly burst through the curtain gaps and he could hear the hens scratching and cackling in the yard. When the voice of Tom McCormack the dairyman called his father's name and asked him for the churns, Jack began to panic. This late and no sign of his mother! Leaping from his bed, he ran into her room. No sign. Heart thumping, he descended the ladder to the kitchen. It was cold. The range had not been stoked and the porridge can was still hanging in the corner. He reached for the door handle and heaved the heavy oak door towards himself. Then, using his right hand, he pulled himself around it to stand uncertainly in his night shift, not daring to cry out her name. No one noticed him. No one came. He turned and went back inside, pushing the great door away from himself and shutting out the metallic clangs of churns being hoisted onto Tom McCormack's cart, the gruff exchanges of his father and Tom Mac as they calculated the day's milk value.

Shivering with cold, Jack hauled himself up the ladder and climbed back into his bed, covering his head against the light. If he just waited long enough, she would come. He remembered his father, a few days later, on the only occasion of near-tenderness he could recall, roughly taking Jack on his knee and saying in a tone jarringly confidential, "Remember this, Jackie-boy, women are dirty, treacherous whoores and they rot a man's soul, d'you hear me, soneen?" Jack had nodded, wanting to disagree, to say that Mammy was not those things, but he did not dare. "Good boy," ended the brief homily and his father had ruffled his hair. Suddenly overcome with sorrow and disarmed by the moment of rare warmth, Jack had been unable to prevent the screwing up of his face and the outpouring of hot tears.

"When is my mammy coming back home?" He had hit the floor with a thud and began to bawl, his mouth a startled tunnel from which issued at once all his childish despair. Rivulets of snot poured with tears around the curves of his mouth and chin while his tiny chest heaved with the effort of drawing breath. "Mammy, Mammy!" he gasped again and again until his father roared, "Will you stop your wailing, you scut! Your mammy's not coming back, d'you hear me? She's not ever coming back, so get that through your thick skull. Get used to it." Jack had stopped calling, but, still sobbing, he pushed himself up on all fours, then to his feet. He crossed the kitchen to the ladder and the sanctuary of his bed. He never cried aloud for her again. Forty years later, as he walked his cows back to the field after milking, Jack spat at the memory. He had never dealt with the terrible grief at losing his mother so suddenly and inexplicably. It waited for him, just below consciousness. He often woke from dreams of abandonment.

Over the years, he had come close to hating her. He understood that somehow she was to blame for his fear of womankind. Now, Jack was sure that Brett would have told the whole parish of his wish to wed. He blushed in the biting wind and lashed at the nearest cow's hindquarters. Her startled lowing set all ears twitching, and the herd's heavy shoulders moved faster away from the man and towards the sanctuary of their frozen field.

CHAPTER ONE

* * *

Caitlin Spillane was seventeen when her father decided she would marry Jack Flynn. She was a beauty with a quick wit which caused her teachers to shake their heads in lamentation that she was not a boy, for surely it was a shame to waste such a brain. She had come top of all the pupils in the local school in her Intermediate Certificate examinations. Her bold assertions that she would try for a scholarship to Trinity College, Dublin, only made her mother laugh disparagingly. "You will do no such thing, Caitlin Spillane! Set your mind on simpler things. Farmers' daughters do not go away on their own to Dublin or England. Unless of course you'd like to be a nun, like Maureen?"

"I will not!" Caitlin would reply and toss her lush hair as if to defy the very notion that such beauty could be shorn and denied. She planned to consort with educated men – doctors and politicians, city men with suits and pocket watches and shiny shoes who had manners and washed themselves regularly. She would look at her father, at his filthy boots and the streaks of cow dung down his trousers, the baling twine keeping them up, and she would try to remember the last time he had washed more than his face and hands. He would catch her scowling at him in disgust when he spat in the fire or wiped his sleeve across a running nose.

"What are you scobbing at?" he'd demand gruffly, nonetheless reddening at her evident revulsion.

"Oh, nothing," she'd reply in a tone which left little doubt she meant precisely that.

At night, Caitlin would sit before the large mirror in the room she shared with her sister Maureen, and brush her long shiny hair. "Aren't you ashamed of yourself, preening in front of the mirror like an auld jackdaw?" chided Maureen irritably, hitting her pillow in a gesture which indicated her wish to sleep.

"Isn't jealousy a sin, Maureen?" came the tart reply, addressed still to the mirror.

"Who's jealous? Aren't you fierce proud now of yourself, for a culchie's daughter, Caitlin? A little humility wouldn't do you any harm, so it wouldn't. And pride cometh before a fall – don't forget that, miss high-and-mighty."

"Ah, cop onto yourself, Maureen. Read your Bible."

The milking over for another day, Jack eased off his boots and then sat contemplating the fire, a mug of strong tea in his hand. But this night, the sharp rap of hawthorn stick on oak jolted him from his choleric reverie. He was so unused to the idea of a visitor that he struggled to make sense of the sound which had shocked him. Wits gathered, he strode to the door and swung it open. Malachai Brett stood before him, obsequious but with the flint of an advantage in his eye. The big man blocked the doorway, light seeping around his heavy frame. "What the hell do you want, Brett?"

Undaunted, Malachai assumed the confidence of an important messenger. "Let me in, Jack," he said quietly. "I've some very interesting news for you." Jack, curious in spite of himself, stood back to admit the matchmaker. "This is cosy, now, Jack," continued Brett, surveying Jack's filthy kitchen.

"What do you want, Brett? Spit it out." Suddenly weary, Jack rubbed his forehead with an aching hand. The rheumatic pain in his knuckles was severe enough that even this movement caused him to wince.

"You recall our conversation the other day?" began Malachai, in as assertive a tone as he could manage, given the scowl on Flynn's face. "Ah, will you sit down, for the love of God, Jack, and hear what I have to say?" Jack sat heavily, eyeing Malachai all the while. "I've been doing a bit of discreet research, Jack, and I've found the very young one you'll want." Malachai allowed himself a wide grin which showed his sharp black and yellow teeth. Like an old fox, thought Jack.

"Who?"

"Caitlin Spillane – Mick Spillane's youngest. A rare young one. Sure she haven't left school yet, and she's fine looking, boy."

Jack struggled to remain calm. "I don't know her," he growled.

"Jack, Jack, you're a hard man! Have you not seen her? She be at mass every Sunday with Mick Spillane and the rest of them. She's a good girl, Jack – she've a fierce brain in her head, they say."

"It's not her brains I'm concerned with," Jack spat into the kitchen grate. "Can she cook? Can she clean? Can she milk a cow?" He rose, walked over to the centre of the room, and faced Malachai square on. "Can she keep her mouth shut and keep out of my way when she's not wanted? She won't be needing brains around here, Brett."

For the first time, Malachai started to appreciate the enormity of what he was doing. He could not proceed in making a present of this young girl to this tyrant. A joke was a joke and there were the makings of a very good next instalment of this compelling tale for the amusement of the men in the pub, but there was nothing funny about the turn things were taking. He would have no further part in the sacrifice. "Now, Jack," he began, getting slowly to his feet and making towards the door, not a little concerned that his progress may be impeded, "I'll leave you in peace, so. Obviously, I've made a mistake. She's not at all suitable. Sorry for the trouble, now. Good night."

Malachai's withdrawal of the girl could not have worked better to hook Jack once and for all if it had been planned. "Where are you going, Brett? I want more information!"

Malachai paused and half turned towards Flynn. "I wasn't entirely honest with you, Jack. I was trying to do Mick Spillane a favour, but to tell the truth, this young one is bad news. She've a sharp tongue on her and she's fierce proud and as vain! A man of your... stature wouldn't be bothered with a scut like that. I think Spillane is half afraid no one will want her, the mouth on her. I'm sorry, Jack. Good luck."

"I want to see her, Brett."

Malachai heard the determination in Jack's voice. Well, if Flynn and Spillane negotiated the dowry between themselves, at least Malachai would not get his commission. There was some relief in that.

"I don't think it's a good idea, Jack," replied Malachai with as much dignity and wisdom as he could convey in his tone. Then, with one hand on the door handle, he placed his cap on his head with the other. "Good night to you now, Jack." And he stepped outside.

"Go on, clear off, Brett!" shouted Jack after his back. "Who needs you, anyway? I'll see Spillane myself!"

For answer, Malachai did not turn around but raised his hand in acknowledgment, nodding sagely at the expected response. "Ah, well – God's will be done," he consoled himself quietly and, turning his collar up against the biting wind, quickened his pace home.

There had not been the feared reprisals after the Cappawhite ambush in 1921. The bodies were removed by Tipperary police around nine o'clock the following morning. They had discovered them at the barracks in the pitch dark of the previous night but fled home, terrified, lest they met the same fate. English soldiers arrived in Cappawhite about a week later, walked through the main street, and went into the bar in the evening, scrutinizing every man's face. None met their eyes. Those who had killed the Tans had come from a range of villages within a ten-mile radius of Cappawhite. Very few people could have said with any certainty who the men were who had pulled the triggers. And those who could would have died themselves before denouncing them.

At daybreak following the murders a group of silent villagers had climbed the hill to the Cappawhite barracks to see the corpses of the Black and Tans. Boys crossed their arms and contemplated the wounds, the glassy open eyes. Women covered their mouths and blessed themselves, whispered things to each other. Someone had fetched the priest from Dunane. Father Kinnealy, twenty-eight and inexperienced, had been in on the conspiracy from the start, burdened by a series of confessions before the murders. He paced up and down, making the sign of the cross over each dead man, fighting nausea but eager not to alienate his parishioners. The son of a Cashmel accountant, he was wholly unprepared for the rawness of rural life, yearned for the sanctuary of his books and the seminary study hall. One of the "Tans" was found fifty yards from the rest, his clenched fists full of scree. Someone had shot him in the gut and there was no telling how long it had taken him to die.

The night Malachai Brett brought news of Caitlin Spillane, Jack's nightmares began again. He woke sweating and rigid with fear from a horror which survived unconsciousness. He dreamt of babies, the slaughter of the innocents. They lay helpless in the road, chubby arms extended, hands dimpled as he had seen them in Madonna and Child pictures, but they had calves' heads and their eyes rolled in piteous fear. They were cold and naked and desperate to be comforted. At first Jack was beside himself with concern, maddened by his inability to help these calf-children, for he didn't have a clue how to bring them solace. He thought of bringing them hay but they needed milk. Where were their mothers? He could not provide them with sustenance. Where were their mothers? He looked around crazily, his ears full of the desperate bawling of the cow-children. A man approached. He wore boots and the customary drab garb of the farmer. He carried a pitchfork. Jack thought he was his father, but couldn't be sure. He might, he thought, be the cow-children's father. The man stood over the babies and raised his pitchfork. "What are you doing?" Jack cried, horrified at the man's intentions.

"It is for the best," the man had stated. "They're no use, as you can see." With that, he brought down the prongs of his pitchfork and, with one swift motion, impaled a cow-baby through the belly where it wriggled and screamed in agony.

"Stop, please, stop!" Jack had screamed, but the man pitched the child away behind him and set to killing the next. Blood ran over Jack's boots and down the road, and he was assailed by a terrible grief. He woke sobbing.

Caitlin Spillane played the accordion beautifully. The local boys would watch her long white fingers, sure and nimble as they pressed and spanned the keys. They coveted the way she looked at the keys as she played, as if she cared for them in the tenderest fashion. She played at local dances, but few of the young boys danced to the waltzes, jigs, and reels which flowed from Caitlin's accordion. They grouped awkwardly around her, hands in pockets, waiting for her to finish and occasionally plucking up the courage to ask her to dance. But Caitlin cared little for the longings of farmers' sons and labourers. Sometimes she danced with them, but on summer nights she was more likely to pack away her instrument, give it to her father for safekeeping, and leave the dance hall alone. She preferred to walk home rather than wait for her father to stop drinking and drive her there in his horse and cart. That way she could indulge her reveries in rare solitude and peace. Caitlin's disdain for ordinariness did not go unremarked by the local women. "Just look at that young one," they would whisper, watching her as she whirled absently across the floor in the awkward embrace of some red-faced ploughboy. "You'd think she was a queen, boy, the puss on her! Isn't vanity a terrible thing?"

"Sure 'tis. And her sister Maureen the quietest young one you'd ever come across and a grand girl wit' it."

"Give me Maureen any day of the week."

Caitlin knew their sentiments and did not care. She would be eighteen and sit her Leaving Certificate exams the following year. Then – then she would be free. She was quite sure she could win her scholarship to Trinity. She knew that it was practically unheard of for a girl, let alone a rural girl, to go to university but her grades would be so good they would not refuse her. She would read a science, become a doctor, find a cure for a tropical disease – leave forever the world of cows and farming. And the clothes she would wear! Fitted bodices and skirts, elegant gloves and shiny, pointed shoes. And then, who knew? Europe? America? A marriage of minds with a handsome doctor? She would swap her accordion for a harp or a piano, and an audience of farmers for genteel gatherings of cultured people.

Sunday, and Jack strode up the aisle of the village church to his usual pew on the right, near the altar. But this particular Sunday he did not stare stonily ahead for the duration of the service. He stole quick glances to his left, then behind him in an attempt to catch the sloping shoulders and thick, greying hair of Mick Spillane. He barely registered the uncertain nods of acknowledgment as his eyes scanned people's faces or the heads bending together to exchange surprised whispers at his uncharacteristic behaviour. When at last he located Spillane he scrutinized the two mantillaed heads to Spillane's left. Now, which one was Caitlin? The girls were of equal height and both followed the mass in their missals, holding the books open with white gloved hands. Jack gave up and looked ahead again. He realized at last that his behaviour would have attracted attention and everyone would know he was interested in the Spillanes. *Ah, to hell with them all!* he thought, though panic gripped him and his heart raced.

After mass, Jack made his way to the end of the pew with more haste than usual, genuflected and crossed himself stiffly, then strode with his heavy steps down the aisle and into the autumn sunlight. He remained standing outside the church, nodding cursorily when people saluted him as they filed past. When at last he saw Mick Spillane he swallowed hard and greeted him with, "Are you right?", his direct gaze leaving no doubt as to the intended recipient of his words.

"Jack – hullo there. Fine day."

Jack reddened, unable to make any more social headway let alone express his purpose in stopping Spillane in his tracks. Spillane looked puzzled for an instant. He moved first one shoulder then the other to let people file past him as he stopped before Flynn. Then realization dawned. Malachai Brett had said he would speak to Flynn about Caitlin. Mick hadn't bargained on being caught like this though, in public, not ten paces from his family, none of whom he had informed of the plan he was hatching to marry his youngest daughter to this man near his own age. Both men shuffled awkwardly. Spillane bent his head and spoke to Jack through barely parted lips.

"Is it Caitlin you're wanting to talk about? I haven't told her yet. Are you interested?" He looked up and searched the vivid, tormented eyes.

"I haven't seen her yet, have I?" came the uncomfortable reply. Mick thought for a moment, looked around briefly to ascertain the whereabouts of his daughter, then called to her.

"Caitlin, come here a second. Say nothing" – the last injunction to Jack, who hardly needed warning.

Caitlin, puzzled that her father should be talking to the miserable old devil Jack Flynn, took her leave of the school friends with whom she had been talking and approached her father. At once, Jack saw she was exceptionally pretty and she carried herself well – straight back, head up.

"What?" she said, nodding briefly to Jack then focusing on her father's face. From that one word, Jack picked up her lack of respect for Mick and he straightened his back, assuming a stern expression.

"When is the next ceilidh? Aren't you playing?" asked Mick.

"Yes. Why?"

"Isn't it enough that I'm asking?"

Jack coughed to give his breath an outlet. Caitlin frowned and searched her father's face for the meaning of this exchange but found only a warning in his eye to mind her manners.

"Next Saturday, at Dundrum," she said sullenly, turning her sulky gaze on Jack. She didn't know why she was being asked to perform in this way; her father knew well enough when the next ceilidh was, for he had already arranged to meet several people there. She watched a flush spread across Jack's face. He had never struck her as one to blush. For a second, Jack met her eyes and was startled by their brightness.

"Is it all right if I go now, da?" Caitlin asked, as politely as she could manage. Spillane was evidently pleased with his daughter's behaviour. A man must be seen as master of his household.

"You can." He did not catch the curl of her lip and the scorn in her eyes as she turned away from him but Jack did and he could not resist a smirk at Spillane's expense. When she nodded at Jack to take her leave he regarded her levelly, nodded back. How clear and blue her eyes were, how lustrous her hair as she tossed it over her shoulder and walked away. There was not much fear in her.

"Well?" enquired Spillane, with the confidence of a man parading stock at a market.

"She will do," said Jack, "but she's spirited. She needs a few jerks on the reins, boy." Spillane was surprised. Jack was shrewder than he thought.

"I wouldn't lie to you, now, Jack." Spillane became ingratiating. "She's got a… way with her all right, but nothing the right man can't cure. Sure, she's no match for the likes of you, Jack. No problem at all." He eyed Jack and watched with satisfaction as Flynn straightened up under the flattery. "Do we have a bargain?" he ventured.

"We do." And the two men shook hands, once, firmly, feeling the strength of each other's grip.

"I'll discuss terms with you later, so." Mick regarded his boots, put his hands in his pockets. "There're plenty would jump at Caitlin given half a chance, Jack. She's a rare young one. I hadn't thought of matching her now 'til Malachai said you might be interested. 'Tis a favour, really." He looked up. Jack narrowed his eyes and curled his lip.

"You'll get what she's worth." Jack walked away to where his horse was hitched, and mounted his cart. He began the drive home. Mick watched him go for a few seconds, then rubbed his hands in sudden excitement. He had solved several problems at once; he had become comfortably well off, he had avoided the possibility of having to waste money on some half-baked scheme cooked up by Caitlin to get educated – and he had finally shown her who was boss.

For the rest of that day, Caitlin Spillane moved through Jack's thoughts "like a fine filly", he decided, "a filly in need of a master". He drove his cows back to the field after milking, barely aware of the biting frost or the pain in his hands. The cows moved with a leisurely gait, the pungent warmth from their tightly packed bodies comforting in the darkness. Every now and then one of them would snort or low as if in need of reassurance in the pitch stillness. At the gate they paused patiently while Jack moved around them to open it, then they filed through as one. This night, Flynn felt keenly the loneliness he usually suppressed. As the last cow passed through the gate, he reached out with near tenderness to touch her rump. His cattle were indifferent to him and his welfare; he was part of their routine as they were part of his, yet there was comfort in that.

CHAPTER TWO

"Come on, now. Come on, wee Jack – no time for dawdling, darling – we must be back before dark to do your Daddy's tea." Jack ran to his mother, face screwed up against the sun, curls bobbing, hands outstretched. "Sure, you're too big to carry, Jack! How can Mammy carry a big boy like you?" Yet she lifted him all the same, using his momentum to whirl him off the ground and round twice in the air before she hugged him to her, crossing her arms under his backside. She kissed him once, twice, in the hollow of his neck, making his tummy tingle, and he squealed and chuckled in delight. "Come on, now, pet, let's hurry." She put him down, picked up her basket in her right hand, and grasped his soft hand with the other, which curled inside hers like a flower.

In the landscape between sleep and wakefulness, Jack followed himself and his mother down the road on a visit to his Aunt Maisie's house in a village called Golden, seven miles from Dunane. They walked and hitched rides from passing farmers, fortified by milk from a jar and soda bread, which she carried in her basket. He wondered why the village was called Golden, but his mother didn't know. She guessed it was because a beautiful lady had once lived there, who was the pride of the county, and she had long golden hair to her knees, which shone like the sun. All the men flocked to catch a glimpse of her, and her name was Mary. But it was just a guess, and she would smile at the wonder in his round eyes and how he squinted as he tried to look into her face in spite of the sun. "What happened to her?" he had asked as they were jostled in some donkey cart.

"Well, 'twas very sad, for Mary got sick and died when she was still a young one, and no one was able to marry her." But when she saw the distress on his face, she soothed him with promises that Mary with the gold hair was in heaven, and happy, for she was closer to the sun and with Jesus and all the angels.

She used to sing for him. She had a lilting, sweet voice, and she sang mournful ballads when he was tired. He would lie in his bed and watch her eyes. Sometimes they filled with tears, but she would clear them away and smile again. He loved to lose himself in the pictures conjured by her songs: of ladies weeping in fields of flowers and men on horses, riding away from love and into battle; children and maidens succumbed to untimely deaths or were exiled from the land they loved. But the one she loved most, she told him, was about a lady who was turned into a swan and doomed to live alone on the River Moyle, until Jesus allowed her soul to enter heaven. He dreaded that tune, for always it meant she was unhappy. But there were other days – like the ones when they went to Aunt Maisie's house – when she would be blithe and the songs would trip from her lips: light, rhythmic airs in which leprechauns schemed to keep their pots of gold or lovers conspired to meet by moonlight. She would pick him up and whirl him around and he felt happy that she was happy.

"You know what, Jack?" she would sometimes say. "You and I are songs. We are – everyone is."

"Yeh," he would answer, not understanding but eager to please her, and she would laugh, tousle his hair.

"One day, you'll understand. We all need someone to sing us, Jack. If no one sings us, sure we get forgotten about, we fade away. I'll never let that happen to you." How wistful she became, and he would frown, unable to follow her. "I'm going to sing you, like the beautiful song you are. And if you change, I'll learn you and sing you all over again. Sure we'll sing each other, you and me, will we?"

* * *

Aunt Maisie was his mother's aunt and kindly beneath her sharp tones and alarming jowls. Her husband was long dead and her children had moved away. She was enjoying her freedom. She made cakes which melted in your mouth, and blackberry jelly like Jack had never since tasted. She stood by her range, one brown-spotted hand holding the handle of the kettle with a tea towel as it came to the boil, the other gripping her ample right hip. When the tea was made and the bread jammed, the cake cut, his mother would sit and talk in low, unfinished sentences, mindful of Jack's presence. Sometimes she would begin to cry and Aunt Maisie would tut and pass her a handkerchief, saying, "Ah, now, pet, now pet." She would turn to Jack, wipe the jam from his cheeks, and distract him with bric-a-brac from worm-riddled drawers: yellow photographs of unsmiling men, old tobacco pipes, and prayer books with pictures of chubby angels rolling their bulging eyes heavenwards. Often, she would stuff one of the pipes with tobacco and light it with a match from the mantelpiece. He would watch her, fascinated, through clouds of rich smoke, as she rocked and nodded and soothed his mother until his eyes grew heavy and he slept on his mother's knee, comforted by her warmth, though still troubled at the sadness she kept for Aunt Maisie. One visit, the last one, he had awoken to hear Aunt Maisie urging his mother to come and live with her. Sure, wasn't there plenty of room for herself and the young lad – and the baby too, when it came? They'd be grand. And she could stay in the cottage when Maisie passed on, for the boys had their own houses now. He had come to quickly, turned to look upon the weary, bowed face of his mother, searching it for the meaning of these words. "So, you're awake, are you, pet? Did you have a good sleep?" Had he misheard? He continued to look curiously into his mother's face. She smiled at him, rubbed his head. "Ah, sure Maisie, how can I?" was all she said, and he rested his head against her breast once more, puzzled by the ways of these women.

A memory or a story he told himself? No, real enough.

Aunt Maisie had come to the house, once, after that last visit. His mother had flustered and turned red, wiping her hands repeatedly on her apron, hardly daring to look at Jack's father while she rushed around making tea, cutting bread. "Don't fuss, child." Maisie sat down at the table and parted her knees beneath her widow's dress, planting her walking stick firmly between them. She produced a pipe from somewhere beneath her shawl and to the horrified fascination of Jack's father had packed it leisurely and lit it, drawing the smoke with backward gulps through her puckered lips, like an ancient fish. She seemed oblivious to his incredulous stare and wholly unperturbed by its heat. Smoke curled around her head like conjured mists. He shifted uneasily because he could no longer see her face clearly. She glared at him and spoke through teeth which clasped her pipe stem. "How are you, Mairead?"

"Oh, grand, Aunt Maisie, very well," said his mother, dropping the lid of the teapot and bobbing after it as it wheeled giddily around the kitchen floor on its rim.

"You don't look very well to me." Jack had looked quickly towards his father, whose eyes were narrowing in suspicion of conspiracy. He wished Maisie would go away. Didn't she know what always happened? "Where did you get those bruises, child, on your face and arms? Sure you look like someone's been belting the life out of you, and you in your condition." Still, Maisie did not take her eyes from Jack's father's face. Jack looked at the farm dog, skulking under a chair, muzzle on its paws, eyes rolling from one voice to another. He wished he could crawl under a chair.

His mother seemed almost to have swooned. She sat down heavily, fighting for breath, her trembling right hand on her bosom, as though to steady her heart. She could not speak.

"How would you like to come home with me, Mairead?" Maisie continued. Jack saw his father's hands tighten into fists. The dog turned its head towards a wall, curled into a ball, feigned sleep. "Go and pack." There followed an agony of silence in which the dark forces of Maisie's and his father's fury gathered like storm clouds in the kitchen.

"Get out of my house, you old witch!" The first words spoken by his father brought a sort of relief, like the first crack of thunder in static air.

"I will go when Mairead has answered me and not before." Jack's father sprang to his feet and, with a sweep of his arm over the table, sent saucers spinning across the kitchen. They smashed in bright, white pieces. The dog whined, smacked its jowls, curled more tightly into itself.

"Sean, for God's sake!" His mother's plea was barely audible. She clutched at her swollen belly with eyes closed, dreaming this violence away.

"Get this creature – this, this… harpie out of my house or I swear to you, now, I'll wring her auld neck!" His father's voice had assumed a hysterical pitch. Yet, he did not advance on Maisie, who betrayed no feeling, her only concession to the physicality of things being a lowering of her pipe and an adjustment of the grip she had on her walking stick. Jack's father actually seemed wary of Maisie; she was old enough to be his mother. Maisie began to speak again. The steadiness of her voice made Jack's father seem like a child having a tantrum.

"Aren't you ashamed of yourself, carrying on like this in front of the child, and your wife about to have another? God help her! You know, it's men like you, Sean Flynn, are the scourge of Ireland. Ireland will be a bog, and that's all, with men like you in it! Nothing good – nothing good…" And here Maisie lost the evenness of tone she had preserved to that moment. She leaned on her stick, using it to lever herself to a standing position, before she continued, "… will ever come of Ireland until the likes of you learn how to treat a woman with respect!"

Jack's father danced closer to her, fists raised like a boxer. She did not move but jutted her chin towards him and banged the table with the side of her left hand, the pipe still gripped in its fist. "Give me a Sassenach any day, boy, for if they're soft as mud, they know how to look after a woman." Then she added loudly, "Are you coming wit' me, Mairead? I will not ask again." Jack moved towards his mother, distraught yet emboldened by Maisie's lack of fear. He had never seen anyone – let alone a woman – so unaffected by his father's fury.

"Go on! Get out, the pair o' ye, stinking whoores! To hell wit' you! And you too, huh?" He turned his fury on Jack, who now clung to his mother's skirt, staring dumbly at his father's mad eyes.

"Jack, pet, come wit' me. Come on to Maisie." Jack looked at his mother for the signal to obey, willed her to give it. It did not come.

"Mammy!" he insisted. Roused by his voice, she reached for him, held him close.

"We cannot come, Maisie. Go on, before it gets too dark."

"You're a fool, Mairead. He'll be the death of you and the child will be ruined. I'll go, so." And Maisie turned her back on all of them, then leaned on her stick to open the door. The dog made a dash for outdoors and freedom. Maisie climbed into her donkey cart and drove away.

Jack's father cursed and broke chairs into smithereens. He smashed photos of Jack's mother and ornaments she had brought with her from her girlhood, and he ground them to powder with the heels of his boots. He caught Jack's arm and hurled him across the kitchen, splitting his lip on the leg of the table, which finally got him what he wanted, some sort of defiance to justify the violence.

"For God's sake, Sean, leave the boy alone!" his mother shrieked and lurched from her chair after her son, wiping the blood from his face with her apron.

"Don't ever tell me what to do in my own house, you whoore, you – d'you hear me? Do you?" He menaced ever closer, spittle flying from his mouth, clenching his teeth. The first blow shook them both, knocking her sideways, and Jack sprawled on the floor with her. She had to curl into a ball on the floor to better protect her belly from his boot and Jack, having pushed himself onto all fours, watched as she cradled the unborn child.

Eventually, he left them alone and disappeared to the bar, "to clear his head of stinking women and the stench of treachery," he said. Jack and his mother clung to each other for a long time on the floor for fear he might change his mind and return. But something had hardened in Jack's heart against his mother. She should have taken him and gone with Maisie.

Mick Spillane decided not to tell Caitlin, or his wife, of the bargain he had struck with Jack Flynn, until terms were agreed. He was surprised at the ferocity of his anxiety every time he imagined breaking the news of her fate to Caitlin; there was no telling what she would do. And then he would become angry; she would do as she was damn well told. Yet he could not escape the feeling that he was doing something very wrong. He sat alone in his kitchen drinking poteen by the range, drowning memories of Caitlin as a girl, Caitlin on the day she got the results of her exams, Caitlin as she filled a room with accomplished music, the very voice, it seemed, of her youthful hopes and dreams. Then, with the determination of a murderer, he conjured images of Caitlin in her blackest moods, the set of her mouth, the defiant toss of her head, and worst of all, the contempt which made her blue eyes smoulder when he told her off. "Brazen scut!" he slurred aloud to himself and swigged at the poteen. "Good riddance to her." And he slumped into oblivion.

The days were grey and cold. A bitter wind cut through the milking parlour. Still October and there was not a leaf left on the trees and the cows flared their nostrils across an unyielding expanse of ice in the water trough. Every morning at six o'clock Jack was in the field, breaking the ice and opening the gate to his patient cows, herding them up the road to be milked. The pains in Jack's shoulders, in his back, and particularly in his hands were almost unbearable at times on these freezing mornings. He looked at his knuckles, raw with cold and barnacled with callouses, and fought the panic at not being able to straighten his fingers any more. How could these hands caress the flesh of a girl less than half his age? He thrust the thought from his mind. No details, just the blanket of duty, necessity. Abraham took him a handmaid when he needed a son. Jack would do likewise. The thought that he would have to talk to her terrified him as much as the thought of touching her. She was bright, so Malachai had said. But how sharp could a seventeen-year-old girl be? If she would only treat him well, that would be enough. And a little company in the evening. He imagined her rocking and singing quietly as she sewed something before the fire in the kitchen.

Jack had been bright. There had been none brighter in the village in his day. The likes of Spillane and Brett couldn't hold a candle to him. But his father had wanted him in the fields from dawn till dusk, ploughing furrows, making hay, sowing seed, picking rocks, digging trenches, harvesting beet, milking cows, rounding up calves for market. The chores were endless, the work merciless. In the end, so as not to miss school, Jack had risen an hour before his father, was in the fields by four, had done half a day's work by eight and was walking the two miles to the village school. As soon as he got in from school in the evening there was more work to do. He couldn't do his homework before seven in the evening and was usually so exhausted that he fell asleep on his books, filthy with sweat and dirt, his face often streaked with tears of frustration. And still, he did well in his Intermediate Certificate.

It was in the year that followed, studying for the Leaving Certificate, that he could no longer cope. It seemed his wit and ability to assimilate information in spite of obstruction had reached its limit. In order to succeed it was necessary to put in hours of hard work, grappling with close pages of fluent Latin and mathematical theories which could build new dimensions for his mind to explore if only he could be allowed time to fashion them. His father never said a word but his steely eye was enough to let Jack know any slacking on the farm would be noted. To ignore such warnings was to invite close-fisted blows of full force, or even a horse whip across the shoulders. Always the threat was the same: there would be no farm to inherit if Jack did not work on it. The thirst of the land must be slaked; the thirst for knowledge could dry up Jack's brain for all his father cared.

The truth was that his father was terrified of losing his farm. If his son left him for university, for a finer life, then who would look after the land? Who would plough the fields when he could no longer uncurl his misshapen hands? The purpose of the cycle was never questioned and happiness was no more a consideration to him than it was to his cows. And Jack never thought for a moment that he might really have a choice. He had dropped out of school, and although one concerned Christian brother had visited his father to express his regret, there was never a real hope that the boy would return. Jack poured his learning into the soil, reciting aloud Latin declensions and accounts of Punic wars, mathematical formulae and verses of poetry in Gaelic and English. The greedy furrows closed on and smothered them. He had been about Caitlin's age then. It was strange how now he could not remember how to distinguish one declension from another, could not now even vocalize thought with ease. He had learned to live silently, speaking only to communicate basic needs. Just like his father.

By seven o'clock, the milking was done and Jack stood in the yard, pumping water over his boots before going inside. It was dark and there was more frost in the air. Once inside he boiled a pan of water on the range, poured some of it into an enamel bowl, took a small mirror from a drawer in the press, and sat down at the table to shave. Several times he nicked himself with the barber's blade and cursed through a beard of soap. He eyed the thin wisps of greying hair as they fell across his forehead, and he recalled with sudden sadness his youthful good looks. How far they were from the weathered complexion and wrinkles he contemplated now! How would she like him for her husband, she who was so young and fresh? He cursed his age, the pain in his hands, and reflected that he and Caitlin might have been an ideal match were he twenty years younger. But he wasn't ready then. He was ready now. Well then, he must face with courage whatever this course would bring.

Caitlin stared into a mirror and brushed her long black hair, killing time while Maureen finished her evening chores, and then both were to ride together in a neighbour's cart to the Dundrum ceilidh. She was wearing her best dress, made by her mother years ago for her oldest sister's wedding. It was of cotton with a rather faded blue floral print and it had long sleeves, a loose round neck, and hung straight to her calves with a tie-back hanging at each side, to be made into a bow at the back. Maureen had one exactly the same. Caitlin pulled the bow tight to accentuate her flat belly, her small waist, then tied back her thick hair with a blue ribbon, so that it would not fall over her accordion and impede the dance of her fingers across the keys. As she stooped to lace her boots, then flung her shawl over her head and around her shoulders, she told herself that it would not be long before she swapped these poor clothes for finery. Descending the crude wooden stairs, she met Maureen.

"Hurry up, would you?" she instructed as they passed. "I'll be late."

"Well, you could always lend a hand, Caitlin. Did that occur to you?"

Caitlin did not answer. She did not really care if she was late. The music could start without her. She carried on into the kitchen where she leaned against the range. When Maureen came running down the stairs again, she too was wearing her blue floral dress, except that on Maureen the dress looked comfortable. She had removed her tie-backs and wore it straight, hiding her feminine curves lest they should inflame men to sinful thoughts. Maureen's plainness was made austere by her scraped-back hair. The contrast with Caitlin was striking.

"Ah, Maureen, take off the dress, will you? You know I'm playing tonight, sure, I don't want you in the same dress."

"Aren't you awful sure of yourself, that anyone will notice what you've on? You're not the Queen of Sheba, you know."

Caitlin pushed away from the range and thrust her face towards Maureen. "And you're not the Blessed Virgin, you know!" She mimicked her sister's prim tone. "Sure if you had any sort of chance with the men, you'd never be entering the convent." Even as she observed her sister crumple, Caitlin tried to analyse why it was they so hated each other.

"How dare you say such things to me, Caitlin Spillane! You are as cruel!" Maureen spat the words through tears. "You wait, Caitlin. The day is coming when you get your come-uppance, lady. 'Tis worse you're getting!"

"Yeh, yeh, Maureen." Caitlin leaned back against the range, feigned nonchalance. "Are you ready or what? Maher will be waiting."

"I'm not coming – isn't that what you wanted to hear?" announced Maureen, wiping tears from her eyes. "Go on your own. I'm not coming with you anywhere."

"Ah, now, Maureen, cop on!" But Maureen was running back upstairs and Caitlin heard their bedroom door slam shut. She would get in terrible trouble for this when Maureen spilled all to her parents – as she always did. Well, she had to go. Caitlin shrugged her shoulders, lifted her accordion, and went to the back door. Before she left, she turned and shouted in the direction of the stairs, "Are you coming? Pat Maher's below at the cross."

She hesitated for a few seconds, but when there was no response, she left. Lying face down on her bed, Maureen sobbed aloud as the door slammed.

"You're late – what kept you? Where's Maureen?" Mick Spillane approached his daughter as she rushed into the dance hall, flushed after her freezing donkey cart ride from Dunane to Dundrum.

"She decided not to come." Caitlin took off her shawl, moved away from her father. Mick followed her, suspecting another row between his daughters.

"Why didn't Maureen come?" he insisted. "Where's Maher?"

Caitlin lifted her accordion onto her shoulders, adjusted the weight, avoiding eye contact with Mick.

"She's tired. Maher's tying up his horse."

A fiddler, a flautist, and an ancient man with a bodhran were about to strike up a reel. They stopped as she approached and assisted her in mounting the platform. The gathering dancers clapped her arrival. Mick eyed her from halfway across the dance hall and thought to himself that this was the last time the little scut would rub poor Maureen's nose in it. He slurped his beer and turned away from the stage as his youngest daughter pressed the first chord of the opening reel.

Jack's cart bumped and rattled over the loose stones of the Dundrum road and his horse's ears moved like antennae in the dusk, picking up the strains of music which emanated from the dance hall ahead. Jack was reminded of the night at Cappawhite. That was the last time he had attended a ceilidh. Several of the men from the South Tipperary column had gathered at the Dundrum ceilidh and, on a few nods from the leaders, had taken their leave. Outside, they had climbed wordlessly into a hay wagon and felt under a large tarpaulin for their rifles. Under cover of darkness and a load of hay, they had passed an uncomfortable half an hour before the horse stopped and the driver banged on the side of the wagon – the signal for the all clear to dismount. Tonight Jack was as nervous as he had been then. In spite of the cold, his hands slipped on the leather reins. "Ho, there!" He urged his horse faster towards the music, anxious to get this over with.

He had decided to meet Spillane at the ceilidh in order to discuss terms and, at Spillane's suggestion, get a closer look at Caitlin without her suspecting she was the focus of his attention. He entered the dance hall to a lively jig, running a finger inside his starched collar as if he could lessen its grip. The dancers were becoming intoxicated by music and drink. Caitlin was enjoying herself, in spite of the enthusiastic stamping and the extravagant winks of her fellow musicians each time she looked towards them for a cue. When the jig was at its height, the dance floor a-spin with villagers, heads thrown back or inclined to the floor in the interests of dynamics, Mick Spillane downed the last mouthful of his pint, wiped his mouth, and walked over to greet his intended son-in-law.

"Are you right?"

Jack nodded, took the extended hand, squeezed it, let it drop.

"Well?"

"Will you have a drink, Jack?"

"Er, no t'anks. No." He nodded to Mrs Spillane, who could not prevent a raised eyebrow and a quick look askance at her husband. Jack Flynn never went to ceilidhs, and she was more than a little bemused at this late alliance of her husband with this antisocial loner. There was, historically, no love lost between them.

"We can't talk here, Jack. Will we step around to the bar?" But Jack was staring at the stage. The jig ended and Caitlin looked up from her accordion to acknowledge the clapping crowd. She smiled warmly. She was lovely to behold. *Good luck of her, boy,* Mick thought to himself, but he reached for a flask of poteen in his inside pocket and gulped 'til his throat was aflame.

Jack moved forward slowly. Caitlin spoke a few words with the band and they fell back, leaving her at the front of the stage. She fanned her accordion, pressed a major chord, and to everyone's delight began to sing a lively ballad. The dancers drew closer and began to clap; a few linked arms and span to the lilting rhythm. Her voice was clear and strong, the glissandos sure. Her confidence and beauty wove a web around her the men could not resist. The married ones watched her, savoured her youth and sweetness with each draught of beer they took, while the wide-eyed admiration of the boys made women nudge each other and nod at their mesmerized sons. Young girls stole glances at their partners and lost confidence momentarily in their own allure.

"Sure, wouldn't anyone get the attention if they sat on a stage and played the accordion?" they whispered to each other.

"Who is she, anyhow? Is she from Dundrum?"

"Dunane. That's Caitlin Spillane." Her name was associated with jealousy and longing, though she was oblivious to the stir she caused.

Jack took in every detail of her. The shining hair, the slope of her nose, the full lips. There was a healthy pink flush to her cheeks and her skin looked almost downy, it was so soft. And her eyes. Every now and then, she would look up from the accordion keys as she sang. Her eyes were a china blue and her lashes thick and black.

A sudden nausea assailed Jack. His collar was too tight; he was too warm. He had to get outside and get some air. Fifty yards or so from the hall was a fence and Jack leaned on it, resting his head on his forearms. On the clear cold air, strains of Caitlin singing "The Rose of Tralee" reached his ears and he breathed more softly to hear her. Raising his head, he tried to focus on the icy stars. Inside the dance hall, Caitlin finished singing to tumultuous applause. She bowed graciously and tapped out an introduction to "The Siege of Ennis", a rousing reel for which she was re-joined by the other musicians.

CHAPTER TWO

Mick Spillane was annoyed. Where the hell was Flynn? He was eager to agree terms, finish this transaction. He dared not think how it would be in the house between the promise and the wedding. He would think of that later. He caught sight of Malachai Brett, who was sitting at a table and drinking with his wife. Malachai returned his nod then looked away quickly. He had seen Flynn watching Caitlin, knew well what was transpiring. He wanted nothing to do with it. Mick found Jack outside.

"Well?"

"I will give you five hundred pounds, no more."

It was more than Mick had hoped for. He tightened his stomach muscles against the excitement. Five hundred pounds would see him comfortable for a long time.

"A good price," he stated, careful not to betray his surprise.

"It is what she is worth, is all."

"Grand. And when will the wedding be, Jack?"

"I don't know. I'll leave that to you."

"Right. Well. Shake?"

"Haven't we done that, Spillane? I said I would give you the money."

"Well…" Mick put his hands in his pockets, scuffed the dirt surface of the road with his boot. "Are you coming back inside? Have a drink at least to seal a bargain?"

"No. I'll away."

"Good luck, so, Jack – I'll be in touch."

Jack turned and walked towards his waiting horse and cart. It was done.

Miserable devil! thought Spillane, spitting on the road. He reached again for his poteen flask, shuddered from the heat of the liquor and the icy breeze which chilled him as he stood in his rolled-up shirt sleeves. How was he going to break this one to herself and Caitlin? Another swig. Ah, to hell with it! Wasn't a man the master in his own house? Spillane walked back up the road and towards the warmth and lights of the dance hall.

CHAPTER THREE

The ceilidh over, Caitlin and her mother rocked unevenly in the cart, which Mick drove home.

"You played grand tonight, pet. Didn't she, Mick?" Mrs Spillane could not see Caitlin raise her eyes to heaven at the appeal for her father's approval.

"Aye," was all Mick replied.

"What a pity Maureen never wanted to take up the music," Mrs Spillane mused.

"Sure, Maureen have her eyes on higher things." Mick accompanied his observation with a flick of his whip across his horse's rump.

"Maureen is a different young one altogether to Caitlin, Mick. There's no comparison."

Caitlin took satisfaction in the platitude because it irked her father, while wincing inwardly at her mother's failure to detect the illogicality therefore of her first statement. Mick just "hmphed" loudly, urging the horse on. They continued in silence for a while, the light and warmth of the ceilidh fading from their faces in the dank November night.

"Caitlin, I want you to start doing a few of Maureen's chores. You can start with the evening milking tomorrow," said Spillane with calculated evenness. She rallied at the assault, in spite of herself.

"That's Maureen's job! You know I have to study in the evenings! Why can't Maureen do it?" She shrugged off her mother's restraining touch in the darkness.

"Don't you, lady – don't you adopt that tone of voice with me! Maureen is to enter the convent soon and needs time to

45

prepare – 'tis a big step for her, and the least you can do is stop being selfish for once and help your sister."

"Selfish?" Caitlin's voice was tremulous with passion. "Who's selfish? Who's the one costing the earth with her dowry to the nuns while I have to work all hours for a scholarship and play at lousy ceilidhs for a few shillings here and there? Why don't you help me, like you help her? Why don't you help me be what I want to be?"

There was no reply. Mick stared ahead stiffly. The horse started at the sudden assault on the night's quietness and, unbidden, began to trot faster. Caitlin could not prevent the words which followed. "Now you're making me work instead of studying so that Saint Maureen can meditate in peace! It's not fair! You want to… punish me… for trying to get away – or something."

Mick was incensed at the bitterness in his daughter's voice and the astuteness of her accusations. He half stood in the driver's seat, twisting to aim his words at her. "Ah, cut the dramatics, will you, Caitlin? See how you snap like a bitch at a reasonable request. What the hell goes on in that head of yours? Cop on to yerself!" There was a pause. Mrs Spillane again reached for her daughter in the darkness, but this time she gripped Caitlin's forearm and squeezed it hard in warning.

Caitlin shook off her mother's hand as Mick began talking once more, the pitch of his voice rising as he gave vent to his scorn. "And while you live in my house, my girl, you'll obey me. Is that clear? You think of no one but yourself! All this blather about gadding off to Dublin and going to university. Your head is in the clouds, Caitlin, and you'd better realize that. You are not more important than the rest of us, and you will do what I say, when I say it, or by…" He checked himself; the horse was now very alarmed. "Whoa, there, whoa now." Spillane changed tone to soothe the animal. "… Or you can clear out of my house and keep yourself. Feel free – any time." If he kicked her out, she would never finish school. In spite of her fury, Caitlin remained quiet.

CHAPTER THREE

Mick relaxed a little when his daughter did not retort, and enjoyed some satisfaction in this reassertion of his role as head of the household. He thought of his wife, mute behind him, too simple to connive against him though she might like to. The idea came into his head to make use of her in his plans to marry Caitlin to Jack Flynn – and the sooner the better.

When they arrived home, Caitlin leapt off the cart and ran indoors, straight up the stairs, leaving her accordion in the cart for her mother to retrieve. She flung herself on her bed and sobbed into her pillow. Maureen smiled briefly in the darkness before turning over and falling into a deep sleep.

For the first time in many years, Jack whistled as he moved about his house getting ready for bed. He whistled "The Rose of Tralee" and flushed like a nervous boy. His head was full of the beautiful face of Caitlin Spillane, and he could barely stifle exclamations of glee at the thought she would soon be moving about this house, preparing the porridge kettle for the next morning, setting the fire with peat, sweeping the floor of the mud from his boots. Oh, dear God, it would be good to have a woman in the house.

Mick Spillane sighed as he rolled into bed beside his wife, his longjohns still on against the cold. He lay on his back and stared through the window on the opposite wall, watching a slither of moon struggle for life behind heavy clouds. There were no curtains on the windows, facing as they did acres of fields, and no one lay in bed after sunrise. Mick knew his wife was awake, though her back was to him. He knew she would be deeply troubled by the row with Caitlin and that she would have sensed something was on his mind, to do with his recent association with Flynn. He wished she had an opinion for once; wished that, when he broke the news of his bargain, she would discuss it with him, or lose her temper or beg him not to proceed – anything but the mute and passive protest he knew would be her reaction.

"I struck a bargain with Jack Flynn tonight," he said gruffly. The moon still had not reappeared.

"Did you?" Mrs Spillane pulled the blankets over her uppermost ear.

"He will give me five hundred pounds for Caitlin. You sort out the wedding – and tell Caitlin." The words out loud were surprisingly shocking. He turned onto his side so that husband and wife lay back to back. Mrs Spillane's eyes widened in the darkness. In spite of the confirmation of her worst fears, she could not help but calculate the differences such a sum would make to their lives.

"Have he that much put away?" she said at last, quietly, because something needed to be said. Mick scowled in the darkness.

"Make the arrangements, will you? And don't tell herself until everything's ready, OK?" He rose on his elbow to look over his shoulder, requiring acknowledgment.

"OK."

He wasn't surprised later to hear her stifling sobs, when she thought he was asleep.

The latest argument with her father made Caitlin more determined than ever to get out of Dunane. She set her jaw as she took on Maureen's chores but she did not argue and she did not shirk them. She began to have shapeless dreams of being abandoned and woke feeling panicked and alone. Could it be that they did not love her? Such thoughts were ridiculous, she consoled herself. A family's love must be taken for granted. Didn't she love them?

Mick watched his daughter and admired her strength of character. He told himself she was a lot like him and that was why they were always at odds. Well, she would need all the character she could muster where she was going. As she scoured the churns and washed down the milking shed, hair falling in strands across her face from her ponytail, wearing gum boots and her mother's old coat against the wet and the chill, he told himself she was made for this life and there was nothing wrong with it. She would have food in her belly and a roof over her head, and sure, didn't all women come to children in the end? What matter whose, or where, as long as they were fed? He told himself that hard work was a sure deterrent to pride and the devil, and he was saving his errant daughter from the temptations of easy living and the damnation her great vanity was sure to bring her. He did fear that her sharp tongue would land her in trouble with Jack Flynn, though. He knew how Flynn's father had beaten his wife and that Jack was no stranger to violence as a means of getting things done. But if he could refrain from belting the puss off of her at the worst of times, so should Flynn. Anyway, a slap now and then would do her no harm, if it came to it. She needed taking down a peg or two.

"There. Finished." Caitlin pushed her hair back from her face and stood panting with exertion, leaning on the huge milking shed broom.

Her father nodded. "Right, so," he replied, not unkindly, and she slopped away from him in her rubber boots, throwing the brush against the milking-shed wall as she did so. She consoled herself later in the kitchen, as she brought water to the boil for a wash, that she would never again be covered in cow dung after next August when the Leaving Certificate results came through. Then… then…

Donal Kelly rested a boot on the right shoulder of his spade, lifted the cloth cap from his head and, still holding it, used his sleeve to wipe away sweat from his brow. His thick, brown curls were matted with sweat, and, in spite of the biting early November chill, he pulled off the gloves he had borrowed from his father and which were moulded into fists from years of gripping a spade handle. He discarded them then yanked his jacket open, struggled free of it, and threw it on the ground next to his gloves. He had been digging and clearing ditches around his father's fields for hours – not something people usually did in November, for the ground was more sodden than ever and the relentless rain, cold, and damp of the Irish winter was not conducive to the work. But Donal's father had become ill in April and there was a backlog of heavy work to do if the farm was to be productive in the following year.

When Donal had managed to get home to help his father, from June 1943, he had spent the summer months digging turf and bringing in the hay and modest sugar beet crop, and so the annual clearing and re-digging of irrigation ditches around the crop fields had to wait. Without this work the fields would be sodden and unproductive, and the new crops, sown early in the spring, would rot in the ground.

Kelly sniffed, wiped his face again, screwed up his eyes, and peered into the heavy, wet fog which clung like mould to the boggy land. He pushed away the spade and it fell heavily. He leaned forward so that his hands braced his upper weight against his thighs and let his head drop low. In this position, he waited for his heart to return to a resting rhythm. He straightened up, clenching his eyes tight against the muscle pain, and leaned back to stretch his spine. Finally, he retrieved his coat and gloves, swung the spade onto his shoulder, and trod the squelching turf to higher ground where a patient, half-dozing donkey stood hitched to a cart. Grunting with the pain it caused his muscles and tendons, Donal put on his jacket and flung the spade onto the cart, levered himself with a swift movement onto the edge of it. "Move on," said Donal gruffly, and the donkey laid back its ears, straining forward at once with its load.

One April morning in 1943, Dan Kelly, Donal's father, had arisen at dawn to fetch the cows for milking and had collapsed in the kitchen. His daughters found him when they rose for school an hour later and could neither rouse nor move him. The doctor, when he came, helped them lift their father onto the mattress they brought downstairs for the purpose, and after a careful examination, had pronounced it was Dan's heart that was the problem. The doctor had advised that the sisters had a choice: they could drive their unconscious father by horse and cart the nineteen miles to the new hospital at Nenagh, or he could help them to get him into his 1935 Austin car and he could drive him to the hospital. But Dan was over six feet tall, and getting him into the back seat of the car would be no easy feat; the trauma of moving him in this way, and the position in which he would be forced to travel for forty bumpy minutes, might be fatal.

And so it was that Dan Kelly was transported to the hospital at Nenagh as fast as his ageing horse could manage, while the doctor went ahead of them to warn the hospital to be ready for an acute cardiac case. The oldest daughter, Jacintha, drove the horse, while her sister, Deirdre, tended her father where he lay prostrate in the cart.

At the time his father was hospitalized, Donal Kelly was in Belfast on an IRA assignment. Twenty years old and a mathematics teacher with a law scholarship for Cork University, Kelly had not been an obvious recruit to Republican activism. Had he been content to harbour an ideological zeal for Ireland's freedom from English oppression, he would have been well equipped for an illustrious legal career. Many influential and erudite Irish lawyers since Daniel O'Connell had shared such passion. What was prohibitive to the assumption of his scholarship place was that by the start of the university term in September 1942 Donal Kelly had committed several acts which, under the provisions of President de Valera's 1937 Constitution, might well have attracted the death penalty.

It was already dark before Donal arrived home but the donkey knew the way.

"Hello? Donal, is it you?" Deirdre's voice carried clear and bright above the damp darkness as she opened the cottage door onto the yard. There was a pause while she strained by the light from the open door to make out the donkey cart. In the stillness she heard the scuff of his boots and the occasional grate of a metal blade on tarmac as her brother moved away from the cart and crossed the yard to lean his spade against the outer wall of the house. The kitchen light was a welcome sight and Donal's spirits lifted a little as the aromatic melange of freshly baked bread, tea, and stew reached him on the damp, chill air. His sisters would have stoked the range and turned down his bed, ready for a warming pan between the sheets. But there was the milking to be done and the pigs to feed; he would not sleep for hours yet. When he was close enough to answer her without having to make the effort to raise his voice, Donal responded.

"Aye."

"Will I put the donkey away?"

"Aye."

And as her brother made for the kitchen door, Deirdre was already talking in soothing tones to the exhausted donkey and unhitching it from the cart, leading it to a freshly littered stall and a good feed of mashed turnips and hay.

Dan Kelly had arisen as though startled when his daughter had opened the door declaring she had heard something in the yard. It did not rest easy with him that he could not cut his own turf or dig his own ditches or that Donal had sacrificed a university place to help him out on the farm. He could not be sitting down reading a paper when his boy crossed the threshold, cold and exhausted from heavy, lone labour on his land.

"Are you right, son?" Dan's tone was concerned and affectionate.

"I'm fine, da. The ditches are good enough now to see us through sowing next year and to harvest – if it ever stops raining. We could do with another freeze."

"That's grand; that's great work, Donal. Sure we'll all help to keep them clear when the weather gets a bit warmer."

Donal sat down heavily at the table. Jacintha smiled at him and served him a steaming cup of tea. He nodded his thanks and wrapped his freezing hands around the mug. The warmth of the kitchen was a sanctuary against the latest bone-chilling, muscle-tearing day he had spent in the fields. Deirdre came in pink cheeked and smiling from tending the donkey.

"He has a bit of a sore where the harness has rubbed him," she announced, "but sure you're not going out again tomorrow, are you, Donny?" She directed this with the diminutive of his name to her brother but he did not answer her. His eyes were closed and the spoon with which he had begun to eat the stew Jacintha had served him was slowly tipping upwards on the rim of the bowl as his hand relaxed in sudden sleep. Both sisters and their father exchanged looks of pity. Jacintha approached her brother and touched his shoulder gently.

"Donal," she enquired quietly, "are you too tired for supper? Why don't you go on up to bed for a sleep? Deirdre and I will do the milking. Sure you can eat the stew later."

Her brother started. "No, no, I'm fine. Just give me a minute or two. I'll be right." He stood up, moved towards his jacket and gloves where they lay on a wooden chair inside the kitchen door.

"Ah, you're not going out again, Donal?" enquired Jacintha. "Sure, at least finish your supper!" But Donal was already opening the door onto the now freezing darkness.

"No. I'll away up and get the cows – it takes longer in the dark." And he was gone, the door shutting behind him.

"Curse this useless…" Dan flung his newspaper to the floor, leaned forward, and covered his face with his hands. "What sort of a man am I now?" His voice was muffled by his hands but the girls thought they detected a break in it which no one would have dared name aloud for the embarrassment it would bring. Deirdre kissed her father's head, ran to the back door, and grabbed her coat.

"I'll go and help him," she said. "Keep him company."

CHAPTER FOUR

Maureen Spillane was to enter the convent in the following January on the occasion of her nineteenth birthday. The preparations were almost as consuming and costly as those for a wedding. There were habits and tunics to be bought and thick black cardigans to be knitted for the cold convent in winter. There were new rosary beads, and missals with white marble-effect plastic covers, pairs of sensible black shoes and boots to be bought, in good leather, to last years. And Maureen needed books – tales of sainthood and Christian courage – to fill her mind with comfort in the darkness of her lonely cell for the half an hour she would have to collect her thoughts and wash herself by candlelight before lights out.

Caitlin watched these preparations and her mother's fawning ministrations to them with growing resentment. She wanted her mother to smooth down clothes between layers of tissue paper for her, in a trunk being prepared for a journey to Dublin. This preparation in black seemed morbid. What could it mean, to become a bride of Christ? Why marriage to Christ, who was celibate, unworldly? Was this bond really all the church believed women could understand? Marriage to a man incarnate or otherwise, it seemed to Caitlin, was a conspiracy to take the life from women.

One day in early November two nuns drove from a convent in Tipperary town to visit with Maureen and take tea, but the main purpose of their journey was to discuss her dowry – a donation to the convent made by all novices' families, to help towards their keep. Caitlin's mother had put on her best dress and washed her hair. Maureen and Caitlin were required to do the same. Mick sat in his only suit, twitching in discomfort, trying to remember manners. He kept running his hands through his slicked-back hair, feeling naked without it bushing up from his crown and sideways like a horse's forelock. Sister Mary Callasanctious and Sister Mary Rosario sat wreathed in smiles, though behind the thick lenses of her spectacles, Callasanctious's eyes were pinpricks and her jaw was angular, her mouth prim.

"Will you have some more cake, sisters?" asked Mrs Spillane sweetly.

"You're very kind, Missis," replied Sister Callasanctious, "but we won't, thank you." Sister Rosario, fat and busty with a moon-round face, blinked a little uncertainly and could not disguise her disappointment.

Mick Spillane, perched on the edge of his chair, knees threatening to split his trouser cloth, reached up a tobacco-stained pincer of forefinger and thumb and pulled on the tip of his nose. Feeling it give up an unexpected indelicacy, he held on to it while he rummaged in his trouser pocket with his other hand for a handkerchief. The nuns averted their eyes and seemed to search the carpet for a way to open the conversation. Sister Rosario was inspired.

"Tell me…" But a loud snort from Mick, who had found his hanky, blasted her words from their course. She smiled again. Mick mumbled an apology. Maureen squirmed with embarrassment, which was noted appreciatively by Sister Callasanctious. "Tell me," began Rosario again, "are you managing to find time to prepare yourself for your big step, Maureen?" Maureen smiled sweetly, nodded before she spoke.

"Oh yes, sister. I pray and meditate for at least a couple of hours a day now. And I read the Bible every evening."

"Oh, you must do that, my child," said Callasanctious. "After all, it is Jesus' voice, and the very one which has called you to be his handmaid. Listen well, Maureen, for he speaks clearly for those who will open their ears to hear him."

"I will, sister." Maureen was eager to please; a rapt look had settled on her face. Caitlin coughed to cover an involuntary sigh.

"Good girl, good girl. And have you everything else you'll need? We do without much, but woolly socks and a good vest you'll be needing for sure – isn't that right, sister?"

"Oh, indeed. Attend to the simple needs first, and then the mind is free to soar."

Mrs Spillane was anxious to show the nuns that her daughter would be well provided for. "We have her trunk all ready, sisters – I hope we haven't put too much in it, now! She'll be warm enough, and if she needs anything else, sure we'll visit her all we can – or she can write."

The sisters nodded, hopeful that Mrs Spillane would continue the present direction of the conversation to the indelicate matter of the dowry. They had to be back at the convent for Vespers. Mrs Spillane, however, was intent upon impressing the good sisters with the suitability of Maureen for convent life, and with the support her family had been giving to her vocation.

"And Maureen has been locking herself away every evening, lately, to say her prayers and prepare herself."

The sisters stifled sighs and smiled again in tolerance of this return to old ground. Mrs Spillane continued, turning to Caitlin, who was perched on the arm of her chair, looking obedient.

"Caitlin here is doing Maureen's little jobs to give her sister more time, aren't you, pet?"

Caitlin smiled. *Little jobs!* she thought. Just clearing a few little tons of cow manure and scouring a few little churns till they were spotless, twice a day; and then there were the little mountains of potatoes she had to peel every night for the dinner, and the little cows she had to fetch up and down the road at all hours for milking.

"Now isn't that grand?" said Sister Callasanctious approvingly. "Isn't she the good girl to help her sister? And will – Caitlin, is it? – will Caitlin be taking the veil, too?"

57

"No indeed," came the firm reply from the object of interest, simultaneously with a cynical guffaw from Mick.

Mrs Spillane reddened as she began, "Caitlin is…"

"I am going to university," Caitlin announced. "Trinity perhaps."

"Is that right?" Callasanctious's tone was mildly exclamatory. "Trinity, is it? Isn't that a brave thing for a girl, now?" She looked to Mick and Mrs Spillane in turn, saw the anger on his and the pained confusion on his wife's face, and sensed all was not well in the Spillane household. "Well, it's not unheard of. Sure, didn't Sister Xavier begin a degree up at Trinity, sister, a few years back?" continued Callasanctious.

"She did, sister – in theology. Sure, she'd her book half written – her thesis, is it?"

"Yes… that's right. She had." Callasanctious nodded, sipping her tea thoughtfully.

Mick's tea cup looked dainty and useless in his grip. *Like a gorilla at a tea party*, thought Callasanctious.

Caitlin, piqued by her parents' lack of response, spoke again. "Women do take degrees, you know!" she exclaimed, asserting her tone a little too boldly for Callasanctious's liking. "Women have been admitted to Trinity since the turn of the century."

"Indeed, yes." The nun lowered her eyes, sipped her tea, and continued, "But usually only the very privileged daughters of wealthy men and, of course, religious women like ourselves, who are academically gifted. They are sponsored by the church, naturally. But even so, the cost and the prolonged periods in the outer world are often… prohibitive, and I'm afraid, well, Sister Xavier had to discontinue her studies." She stole a sideways glance at Sister Rosario, who closed her eyes in knowledgeable agreement.

"There are scholarships – Sizars, they call them – for 'students of limited means'…" Caitlin broke off, aware of the pleading in her tone. She felt the frustration of a child who has nurtured a longing for a special toy or favour but realizes at last there is no hope of adult indulgence. She finished lamely, "I have read about them in school."

The nuns did not answer. Sister Callasanctious lifted her cup to her lips, stared unfocused over its rim. Sister Rosario smiled reassuringly at Mrs Spillane, as if Caitlin had said something embarrassing and the nun was keen to show she was not offended. Mick shifted irritably in his chair. He could not decide if he should be incensed by his daughter's implication that he was not well off; then it occurred to him that this might work in his favour, given the reason for the nuns' visit.

"Why…" Caitlin could hardly believe she was asking the question. She knew she was testing her father's tolerance. "Why did Sister Xavier 'have' to discontinue her studies?"

"What's that, dear?" Callasanctious's lips stretched to a tolerant smile, and she met Caitlin's earnest gaze with cold eyes.

"Why couldn't she finish her studies? Don't priests study for years and years in the seminary, learning Latin and maths, Greek and philosophy? Isn't the cost of that 'prohibitive'? Why did Sister Xavier have to stop?"

"Caitlin, that's enough, pet." Mrs Spillane tapped her daughter's trembling arm in rapid succession, as if she were communicating in code her anguished warning to beware her father's wrath. Caitlin heard and sat back, looked down at her fingers spread in supplication in thin air, and dropped her hands to her lap. Callasanctious said that nuns were hardly to be compared with priests: priests were the ministers of Christ, the intermediaries between the Holy Ghost and poor sinners. Nuns were mere handmaids to Jesus; they devoted their lives to humility and quiet prayer and had not the terrible burdens of the priests. The priests, she reflected finally, were the soldiers of Christ and it was for nuns to pray for their success.

Sister Rosario nodded and smiled and stared covetously at the last slice of cake, only averting her eyes in the interests of good manners just before it disappeared whole into Mick Spillane's mouth. Mick was animated, his colour high. He sat perched on the edge of his chair, listening to every word Callasanctious spoke and nodding vigorously. "Of course, of course!" he spluttered through fountains of crumbs.

Caitlin rose to her feet, trying not to be "dramatic", as her father liked to describe her thoughts and actions. In as dignified a fashion as she could manage, though her voice faltered, she pronounced, "I believe that if a woman has as good a brain as a man she should be allowed to use it." Maureen eyed her with amused contempt. The vainglorious Caitlin looked childish, ridiculous.

"Well, we think a lot of things when we're young, my child," said Callasanctious, bold with the support of the parents, "but modesty is a wonderful thing in a woman, dear. Humility is a godly thing, and if the lack of it makes a man proud and dangerous, in a woman..." She struggled for words which would belie the anger she now felt towards this brazen girl. She was not insensitive to the strength of family bonds and they had not yet discussed the dowry. She had registered the fine looks and the fire of this girl, and liked neither. She had seen it all before. God gave them pretty faces and they thought they owned the place. She continued, "In a woman, lack of humility is... destructive to the very fabric of society." She looked to Mick for his agreement, and he readily gave it, and both turned to Caitlin for a sign she was chastened. Caitlin left the room.

"Caitlin! Caitlin!" Mick was on his feet, his voice raised in embarrassed fury.

Callasanctious was gracious. "Let her go, dear Mr Spillane," she said soothingly, then added, "She will learn."

Mick said he was sorry for her rudeness, and thanked the sisters for their understanding.

"No, no! Not at all, not at all." They both waved away his discomfort. "Sure, don't we teach young girls? What can you tell us about them?"

The family and both nuns laughed a little and there was more pouring and drinking of tea. At last, Callasanctious could wait no longer. "Now, I am sorry to seem indelicate, but Sister Rosario and I must be back at the convent for Vespers…"

"Of course, of course, sisters – don't let us keep you, now. It was good of you to come," interrupted Mrs Spillane, getting to her feet.

There was nothing for it, clearly, but the most direct approach. "Now, Maureen's dowry…"

Upstairs, Caitlin sobbed into the eiderdown and fought the urge to scream in a childish venting of frustration and embarrassment. When finally she was still, she lay on her back, and as her heart quietened, she stared at the ceiling, feeling nothing. She heard the clock ticking on the wall, was aware of the light slanting through the curtains at the usual angle for this room at this time of day. It was very cold but she knew rather than felt the dank chill which pervaded the bedroom. It was as if she had finally been subsumed by the ordinariness of things. Snatches of words, exchanges with her father, relations of her dreams to her mother replayed in her head and she understood at last her impotence and that her words and dreams were absurd to those who heard them. Downstairs, sonorous, punctuated by Callasanctious's shrill interjections and Rosario's occasional fluttering laughter, her father's voice. Caitlin realized that if Mick said the word, she could emerge from this life like an imago from a cocoon. Maureen had his blessing and she would soon be gone. But without his permission and a considerable amount of his money, university may as well be Tir-na-nÓg.

Donal Kelly had achieved straight A grades in his Leaving Certificate and the Holy Ghost Fathers asked him to teach mathematics. He willingly complied, for the wages would be handy when he went up to university. Although he easily won a scholarship to study law at Cork University, Donal would need living expenses and his father was in no way able to help – which the Holy Ghost Fathers understood. It was in his first term as a maths teacher that Donal Kelly realized fully that, after years of schooling and farm work, he was free – free from the obligation to help his father with backbreaking labour and free of the heavy mantle of responsibility that came with primogeniture and his sex. In acceding to Donal's preference for academia over rurality, Dan Kelly had liberated his son. Teaching mathematics to rows of pale, silent boys was comparatively easy and enjoyable for the most part. Donal metamorphosed from student to teacher with remarkable facility, assuming authority as if it were the natural corollary of the high spiritedness and not infrequent insolence for which Donal was well known at Blackwell.

He became popular with most of the boys he taught, for he was not averse to the odd joke at the Holy Ghost Fathers' expense, or the sharing of an anecdote about his own experiences as a Blackwell scholar. But, if the laughter became raucous, Donal was quick to reassert order. He understood only too well how quickly his pupils would discredit him, given the opportunity. The uneasy, predatory tension between scholar and novice master was a sea necessarily captained with celerity, or disaster was certain. And as time went on, many came to fear Donal Kelly's sarcasm or sudden displays of temper, as he experimented with the disciplinary tools at a teacher's disposal. Donal wore his master's gown with panache – straight shoulders and a deliberate flourish of cloth as he turned corners. Always, his shoes were shining and he had his wayward curls cut to a manageable crop. The Holy Ghost Fathers nodded to him and smiled as he passed them on the corridors, their influence on his transformation undetected by Donal. But the priests had little influence on what happened to this young man outside the college walls. Although Donal had to be in his room in the seminary by no later than ten o'clock each night, there was time for recreation between the end of prep supervision and the nine fifty-five curfew. A short walk and he was in the heart of Cashmel town. One night a week, he did not have to supervise the boys' prep and was free to go into town straight after supper.

Tipperary County in the 1940s was a hotbed of IRA activity. In every bar, on every street corner, men with stony faces nodded and talked under their breath between pints of ale or pulls on cigarettes. Firm handshakes and prolonged eye contact confirmed clandestine arrangements or renewed fealties. Uniformed gardai patrolled the streets of Tipperary towns, banging truncheons against their leather boots with apparent nonchalance, smirking or pretending not to notice as the men they passed turned their backs or spat on the pavement.

When he assumed his teaching role in the autumn of 1941, after a summer's hard labour on his father's farm, it was as if Donal had emerged from a cocoon. Sometimes, as he sat alone in a Cashmel bar, or occasionally with a lay master from the college, someone would "casually" drop a back copy of *The Wolfe Tone Weekly* on his table. Banned in 1939 by de Valera's Fianna Fail government, penned largely by men subsequently interned in the Curragh, *The Wolfe Tone Weekly* endeavoured in urgent, passionate prose to educate a new generation of Irish people regarding their Fenian history. The appearance of underground pamphlets entitled *The Weekly War News* and *The Republican News* would occasion huddles of animated men in every Cashmel bar. They raised their voices in rebel ballads, banging their ale tankards in time to the illicit music of their hearts. But wherever such fervour ignited, it would not be long before a garda sergeant in full uniform would appear, accompanied by several officers whose job it was to douse Republican passion with icy stares and the threat of immediate arrest and internment without trial.

The first thing that was material in Donal Kelly's becoming a member of the IRA was the arrest of the landlord of O'Hallorahan's bar one night in February 1941. Donal and a colleague from Blackwell, a geography teacher of middle age, were chatting over a pint. It was a Saturday evening and Donal was enjoying a rare night off from supervisory study duties. Suddenly, six gardai crashed into the bar, batons raised in anticipation of resistance. Hollering orders to everyone to stay calm and remain still, they formed a barricade before the bar. The most senior of them was a huge and fierce sergeant. He had been relocated from County Clare to discover and destroy Tipperary's insurgent safe houses and paramilitary leaders. He announced to all that the landlord, Sean O'Hallorahan, was under arrest for harbouring and encouraging the dissemination of treasonable and seditious documents, in direct contravention of the Offences Against the State Act 1939.

There was an immediate chorus of protestation from O'Hallorahan's patrons. Several of them came towards the ring of gardai, fists clenched or wiping their mouths of the froth from hastily downed beer, squaring for a fight. Donal and his colleague got up uncertainly from their chairs and took cautious steps further into the bar room as men shouldered past them and towards the gardai. "Come out here, Sean O'Hallorahan," commanded the sergeant. "Come out and there will be no trouble. It will be worse for you…" He paused, turning from the bar to face the punters, now standing side by side and staring with silent menace at the gardai. "It will be worse for all of ye, if you do not come quietly, O'Hallorahan." There was no response from the landlord. He had disappeared, it seemed.

"Right, so!" announced the sergeant. "Don't say you weren't warned!" And with one swift movement he put a hand on the bar and levered himself onto and then over it. There was a sound of crashing and banging as bottles and glasses on the bar were sent flying. Then, the sergeant kicked in the door from the bar to the kitchen through which O'Hallorahan had absconded, locking it behind him.

This commotion was the signal for the men to attack. With a sound like a battle cry they launched themselves at the gardai. Donal watched with a mixture of terror and excitement as the men clashed with the officers. All was chaos. Blood and spit rose in sprays from the fray. Batons rained blows on bare heads, across faces, while fists and boots landed wherever there was an opportunity. Stools and chairs and tables smashed like toys as the combined weight of two or more grappling men landed on or crashed into them. The fight expanded to fill the bar. Donal and his friend were soon pressed against the furthest wall in a bid to remain uninvolved.

The geography teacher, slight of build and gentle of demeanour, raised his arms to cover his face, crouching as if to make himself even smaller. Others had joined the brawl – old men smashed bottles on the police officers' heads whenever they saw a chance, and the floor was slippery with blood and beer and shattered glass.

At last, a whistle pierced the ruckus. Gardai reinforcements arrived and waded in to save their colleagues from further injury and to apprehend the men who fought them. They were merciless with their batons. Right before his very eyes, not three feet from where he stood, Donal saw the face of a burly gard contort in a hateful grimace as he brought his baton down with full force on a young man's head. There was a sickening crack and then, like a marionette whose strings had suddenly been cut, the young man crumpled, blood flowing spontaneously from his nose and then his ears. As he fell, he half turned and hit the ground close to Donal, his pale blue eyes wide with incomprehension and then, in a second, they went blank, as if someone had switched off a light. As his head impacted the stone floor of O'Hallorahan's bar, some of the blood on his face was displaced and landed on Donal's black, shiny shoes.

Donal heard his own voice before he knew he would speak. "You've killed him!" he yelled at the top of his voice. "You've killed him!" The pitch of Donal's voice as much as the words themselves was enough to distract gardai and patrons alike from their combat. Within a minute, all was silent, and, panting, bleeding, sweating, the men turned as one to determine the source and truth of the terrible, anguished words. The young man, Davey Nunan, just nineteen, was indeed dead. The gard who had dealt the fatal blow was standing above the body, chest heaving, blinking at the corpse as if its blood and twistedness were surprises he could not comprehend.

"I didn't…" he began, his tone defensive, the words an effort through his laboured breathing. "I didn't hit him that hard." He looked wildly at the faces before him, searching each man's eyes for understanding or sympathy, but he was met only with hatred and fury or the confused gazes and lowered heads of his colleagues. He began to panic. "Sure, weren't we all at it, huh? Eh? Weren't we all here to stop the fighting? I did what I was told, is all!" He ended by shouting, turning on his heel to look behind him. Someone must surely support him!

"I saw exactly what you did!" The voice was Donal's. He was dimly aware of the timid tug on his jacket sleeve as the geography master pleaded mutely with him to keep quiet, but he could not stop himself. "He wasn't even fighting you! You just came from behind him and you smashed his head with your stick with full force – he didn't stand a chance!"

The gard was shaking his head, took a step towards Donal. Donal pushed away from the wall and came forward to meet him, eyes blazing into the policeman's frightened face. "Yes, you did!" he continued, raising his voice. He was shaking with fury and disgust. He had to step over the dead boy's head to get closer to the gard. "You murdered him!"

"No!" shouted back the officer. "No! I only did what I had to – I didn't hit him that hard." Someone pushed him roughly so he lurched forward and Donal was so close he could smell his breath. A gunshot split the terrible silence, which, in another second, would have re-erupted into calculatedly murderous violence. At gardai gunpoint, the crowd of grieving, angry drinkers fell back and the constabulary men regrouped.

"Move the body," commanded the sergeant. "O'Reilly," he addressed the gard who had killed Davey Nunan, "get out. Barracks. Now." Looking as if he would cry, O'Reilly obeyed. A few gardai followed him. Then, loudly, eyes burning with anger but not without sadness, the sergeant addressed the bloody, tattered men of O'Hallorahan's bar. "I warned you, time and again! You will not keep the law! Ye know full well that IRA activity is illegal and that it is our job – on the orders of the President of Ireland himself – to stop ye from plotting and rebel rousing and this…" He looked down as two gardai dragged Davey Nunan across the bar by his feet, leaving behind him a trail of blood, his pale blue eyes staring into the space above him. "This is what it leads to! Isn't there enough blood spilt, but ye want more?"

"You killed him!" shouted a man, pushing others out of the way to a place before the sergeant. "We did not."

"Is that right?" Unabashed, the sergeant returned the defiance but adjusted his tone a little. "Ye're innocent of blood spilling, are ye? You and I both know that in here, this minute, are several men who have killed and are plotting to do so again." He surveyed the men before him. "Don't be kidding yourselves that this is a holy war or that ye're justified in ambushing innocent men in the middle of the night or blowing up kids and women on the English mainland – aye! We know well what the IRA is planning and how ye shoot each other like dogs on the mere suspicion of treachery!"

He pulled from his back left pocket several rolled copies of *The Weekly War News* pamphlet, confiscated from O'Hallorahan's kitchen press, and waved them as if they were evidence his words were true. "I'd bet a few shillings there's men in here now who know well the whereabouts of George Plant – know fine well where Michael Devereux is, and his young wife breaking her heart over him. Honourable, are ye?" The sergeant raised his hand and wiped his face with it. The gesture was one of exhaustion. His shoulders seemed to drop. When he spoke again, his voice was flat. "If the likes of you boys have their way – with your 'Sabotage

Britain' campaign…" he unfurled the pamphlets, raised them, and exhibited the headline which referenced the IRA Chief of Staff's banner slogan for pursuing open aggression against England, "… there'll be a British soldier on every street corner of Ireland! Is that what ye want, is it? We know full well ye're colluding with Germany, dabbling in matters you are in no way able to handle – playing with fire! And until ye stop plotting and ambushing your own…" he became passionate again, raised his voice, and cast his eyes over the grim faces before him, "… ye're asking hell in all its fury to consume us! One more bomb in England, one more escapade with the likes of Plant or Hayes – and de Valera will not be able to stop the English from coming here in force to wipe you out. Is that what ye want, is it?"

There was no answer. Just mute hatred. The sergeant shook his head. Several officers still vigilantly monitoring the crowd, hands on guns or gripping their baton handles in readiness, moved slowly towards the door of the bar. "Go home," said the sergeant almost quietly. "Go home and mourn this boy's death. This bar will be closed till further notice. O'Hallorahan is on his way to the Curragh. Ye know well why."

Someone spat and the spittle hit the sergeant's left arm. He sighed heavily then stood tall and squared his shoulders once more. "Out!" he shouted. "I want this bar cleared and boarded up in five minutes." As Donal filed past him, the sergeant stopped him. "You," he said. "You saw what happened there?"

"I saw all right!" Donal returned, glowering at the policeman.

"What's your name and address?"

"Why?"

"Because you are a witness – why else? Don't leave here without giving this officer," and he paused to beckon over a gard, "your details."

Once out of the bar and standing on the pavement beneath a clear and starry sky, Donal closed his eyes and breathed heavily, dissipating with oxygen the dizziness he felt, the tightness of his chest. The geography master was throwing up behind him, retching repeatedly into the gutter. When at last he had finished, he came trembling back to Donal.

"What now?"

"Well, it's way past curfew," retorted Donal. "Can I sleep at your house?" For answer, the little man nodded, wiped his mouth with the back of his hand, and began to walk home, shaking his head and muttering things Donal could not discern.

CHAPTER FIVE

Jack had never really been ill, and so, at first, it was hard for him to identify the unusual way he felt on waking one morning in mid-November 1943. For a start, his limbs were heavy and reluctant, as though he had been drugged, and his head remained full of sleep after his eyes opened. But his chest was of most concern. He had a cough which had started out as just dry and irritating but had been growing steadily worse over the last few weeks. He had dismissed it as one of those things – people got coughs and colds in winter; you just got on with it. There was, however, a deviance about the way his chest felt this morning which was outside his experience of illness. There was a tightening and a pain like smouldering coals in his lungs. He sat up and the coughing started, a mighty spasm of his diaphragm he could not control. He concentrated on getting to the next breath, really feared he might not get there. The pain was agonizing. When finally the fit had passed, Jack lay back, trembling. What the hell was this, now?

His father had never been ill a day in his life, had never taken a holiday or missed a day's work in his sixty-five years. His death was sudden and quick. Sean Flynn had come downstairs one morning as usual. Jack had already left to get the cows for milking. Sean had knelt to mutter a rosary before the open fire in the kitchen, as was his custom, and wasn't halfway through his second decade when he had been seized by a massive heart attack and had fallen head first into the embers.

As Jack crossed the yard on his way back to the house at the end of the milking, he had noticed black smoke curling under

71

the door and hanging sleepily in the cold air. Running into the kitchen, he coughed and waved his arms to dispel the smoke, and tripped over his father's boots. Sean Flynn's head and upper torso smouldered on the fire, his right hand charred as it gripped the rim of the grate in a feeble attempt to avoid the fire; his left hand lay behind him like a hooked fish. Trying not to vomit in fear and revulsion, choking on smoke, Jack pulled him from the fire by his feet. Then he stumbled from the house and vomited profusely. When he had hitched the horse to the cart with trembling hands, he drove at top speed through the narrow lanes to the doctor's house on the other side of Dunane. The doctor had come and examined the body, sorted out the necessary paperwork, and made arrangements for the corpse to be removed from the house to the nearest hospital. There would be no open coffin wake for Sean Flynn.

As November drew on, Caitlin adopted a policy of passive resistance towards her family. If she could just keep her head down, avoid inciting anyone to anger, then perhaps her father would take pity on her. She would do all Maureen's chores if need be, she would study through the night if necessary, and she would not complain. Maybe then he would look more kindly on her desire to go to university.

Mick watched Caitlin perform her tasks around the house and farm, and scrutinized her face for a scowl, the curl of a lip, the movement of her mouth in a curse, but could detect none. She remained neutral, even cheerful, and though at first suspicious, he was soon convinced that Caitlin had learned something from her humiliating exchange with Sister Callasanctious. Perhaps now she would accept the yoke of her life with better grace.

Maureen, in the meantime, was growing holier. She seemed to transcend the banality of everyday life and assumed a beatific serenity which made Caitlin uneasy. Was this a game, too? Maureen's way of trying to convince the world she was happy?

CHAPTER FIVE

Caitlin could not afford to give it much thought, for it disturbed her tactical equanimity.

It was weeks now since Mick had told his wife of the betrothal of Caitlin to Jack Flynn and asked her to tell Caitlin. Mrs Spillane grew increasingly anxious at the duty he had placed upon her and would have dearly liked to ask him to change his mind about the whole thing, but she dared not provoke him. And she knew too well how much he was relying on the money from Flynn to furnish Maureen's dowry to the convent. The nuns wanted two hundred pounds, and Mrs Spillane was aware that Mick wanted a truck to replace their horse and cart. And there would still be at least two hundred pounds over! Five hundred pounds would transform their lives. But there never seemed a right time to devastate Caitlin with the annunciation of her fate.

As Maureen's entrance to the convent drew closer, Mrs Spillane occupied herself with the departure of that daughter and tried not to think of the other. However, it was precisely Maureen's imminent cloistering which provided the opportunity to get preparations underway for Caitlin's marriage to Jack Flynn. Mrs Spillane came up with the idea that she and Maureen should go and stay with Mrs Spillane's eldest sister and her husband, in Wexford. It would be a sort of farewell to the outside world for Maureen and a chance for her relatives to wish her well. Maureen would also be able to meditate and reflect more profoundly on the imminence of her vows in the quietness of a town house where she would be free from the chores and hardships of farming life, her mother explained to her.

"But Mammy, we haven't seen the Hickeys for years!"

"All the more reason, so." And Mrs Spillane climbed the ladder to the loft and passed down their suitcases to her excited daughters.

Caitlin would go with them, and while they were away, Father Kinnealy would read the necessary wedding banns at three consecutive Sunday masses. Of course, by the time they returned, the village would be abuzz with the prospect of so sensational a wedding, so Caitlin would have to be told as soon as she returned to Dunane. At least, though, there would be fewer weeks in which to watch her suffer.

Mick was less than pleased at the prospect of being left to fend for himself and the farm for over two weeks but he saw the logic. In any case, apart from the milking and feeding of pigs, there was comparatively little to do on the farm at the start of December.

Father Kinnealy nodded and raised an eyebrow occasionally as Mrs Spillane explained her husband's contract with Jack Flynn and asked him to read the wedding banns from the last Sunday in November. The priest preferred not to get embroiled in the private affairs of his parishioners; it brought him only heartache and a troubled conscience. He knew he should ask about the wisdom of such an alliance, especially given Caitlin's youth and potential, but he remained tight-lipped. A girl's duty was to her father, after all, and we all had, in any case, our crosses to bear. It was no picnic being the parish priest for Dunane, that was for sure.

Father Kinnealy, just twenty-eight when he had first been sent to Dunane in 1921, had sat for hours every Saturday since, in a small, dark confessional box, and listened to his parishioners – whose names he knew as soon as he heard their voices – confess their sins. Wife beating, child abuse, drunkenness, fornication, and murder had all been committed by the good people of Dunane, and he absolved them all for the asking. He had, though, spent untold hours discussing with his parishioners through an iron grille that wishing each other dead or envying neighbours to the point you steal from them or kill their livestock; lying, cheating, gossiping, cursing, lusting, and taking the Lord's name in vain were all mortal, and not venial, if you did them on purpose and kept on doing them. There wasn't much Father Kinnealy didn't know about everyone in his parish and a great deal he knew that he wished he did not. Now, what level of wilful sin was it that Mick Spillane and his simple wife were about to commit in the deception of their daughter into the sacred covenant of marriage? Dear God in heaven, was there no end to it?

"Missis," he had pronounced at last, trying to ignore the tearful eyes of Mrs Spillane, "are you telling me to read out banns for a marriage your daughter knows nothing about?" There was a long pause. Tears spilled onto Mrs Spillane's face. Her cheeks burned red with shame. She bit her lip and nodded. There was another long pause. "Do you not think you should tell her, now, what the three of ye're planning?"

Mrs Spillane looked even more desperate. "Sure how can I, Father? She'll go berserk! She thinks she's off to university in Dublin next year – sure we've no money for that, Father. Caitlin is a dreamer…"

"True enough," interrupted Father Kinnealy. "There's precious little cause for dreaming in these parts."

"Isn't it the truth, Father?" Mrs Spillane's tone indicated she had derived some encouragement from the priest's words. "Sure we do always be telling her!"

Father Kinnealy arose from the leather chair behind his desk. He sighed heavily and closed his eyes, bent backwards with his hands at the base of his spine, and thrust out his belly. Then he moved his shoulders up and down in a piston-like movement, his eyes scrunched up all the time and he was making little gasping noises every now and then, as if in pain. Mrs Spillane watched him, an expression of confused concern on her face. Finally, the priest rotated his head first one way then the other, the bones and sinews in his neck cracking as he stretched them. Then, he opened his eyes and looked at Mrs Spillane as if mildly surprised that she was still there.

"I suffer terribly with my back, Missis," he explained.

"I'm sorry to hear that, Father," responded Mrs Spillane. "Have you tried rubbing goose fat on it?"

"No. I have not." There was another silence. "When are you proposing this... wedding should take place?"

"As soon as possible, Father," Mrs Spillane rushed to explain, glad to be back on topic. She had almost forgotten if anything had been agreed and couldn't imagine what she would tell Mick when she got home. "After the banns, that is. You see, Caitlin is a wild young one, and..."

"Just let me know when you want the wedding – give me a week's notice, anyway," interrupted Father Kinnealy again, walking to his study door, opening it. He gestured her out and shut the door behind her. He did not want to hear of Caitlin's demolished dreams. As it was, he would be in for a sleepless night, and an overdose of whiskey would not quell the familiar, awful feeling that he was abetting something unholy. "Forgive them, Father, for they know not what they do," he said aloud and, reaching for his reading glasses, resumed his seat at the desk. But a few moments later he removed his glasses and folded his hands, rested his chin on them, and seemed to contemplate the space in front of him. "Can I plead that one?" he added softly.

Caitlin went obediently to Wexford, although it meant missing two weeks of school. At least she would not have to milk cows and scrub churns, for her aunt was married to a sergeant in the gardai and kept a modest but elegant town house. Caitlin would have ample opportunity to study. Best of all, her father would not be there. And when she came back, it would be Christmas, and then the New Year, 1944 – the one in which she would make her escape.

Twenty-four hours after leaving Dunane, Caitlin sat in her aunt's parlour, reading. The curtains were blood red and fell in rich folds from the pelmet to the floor. A cheery fire burned in the grate and elegant brass implements for stoking it hung from a stand on the marble hearth. There was a richly patterned wool rug on the floor, and the floral covered settee and leather armchairs were draped in hand-made lace coverlets. Caitlin, feet curled beneath her in a well-worn leather armchair, was comfortable and at ease. Outside, the occasional motor car passed by. This was civilization! No cows, no cold stone floors, and best of all, her aunt put hot water bottles in everyone's bed each evening before they retired. Such small comforts were luxurious to the country girls, who wore woollen socks and cardigans to bed at home in a bid to keep warm. Here, too, there were quilts stuffed with goose feathers!

"Maureen will be spoilt for the convent, Bridie," Mrs Spillane had said to her sister, revelling with her daughters in this warmth and these soft furnishings. The thing that caused her to marvel most of all when she visited her sister was that she could wear shoes all day, and never had to sink up to her ankles in manure and mud.

Sergeant Hickey, Bridie's husband, was a quiet, strong man of few words. He stood six feet four inches tall and his eyebrows were bushy with long hairs the consistency of a wiry dog's. He had white, beautifully manicured hands, the backs of which were covered in thick black hair, and black hair frothed through the "V" of his open collar in the evenings as he sat smoking his pipe. Caitlin adored his pensive manner and measured temperament. He was gentle with his wife and she was courteous to him. Mrs Spillane's heart filled with painful longing to see her sister so happy. And Bridie had four fine sons and a daughter. The sons had all done well for themselves; one was a doctor, and the daughter was married to the son of a family friend, also a policeman.

It was hard for Mrs Spillane not to curse the day Mick Spillane had made her blood race at a ceilidh in Dunane, whirling her around and telling her she was the best-looking young one at the dance. Her mother had warned her of the hardship of a farming life – had told her to follow the example of her elder sister and find herself a man whose trade would take her out of the cow dung – but how could she listen, with the headlong jig of desire making her blood dance? When she discovered she was pregnant just eight weeks after the wedding, Mrs Spillane was nonplussed. Marriage was not at all how she had imagined it would be. But after thirty years of it, Bridie touched her husband with a tenderness that spoke of love and consideration. Though she hardly understood it, Mrs Spillane was not sorry to introduce to this marital harmony a note of discord. When she confided in her sister that Caitlin was to be married to a local farmer old enough to be her father and as yet unknown to her, Bridie was appalled. She considered the whole business immoral and primitive.

"How could you make Caitlin marry an auld fella, Mary? Sure she deserves better than that. Is it Mick's idea?"

"Of course!" exclaimed Mrs Spillane. "You don't think it's mine, do you? I want Caitlin to be happy but once Mick has made up his mind… well, it's his house. And Caitlin is his daughter. That's the end of it, Bridie. He wants the money."

"How much?"

Mrs Spillane dropped her voice to a whisper. "Five hundred."

"Pounds?"

A quick nod confirmed the obvious.

"God between us and all harm, Mary, that's an awful lot of money!" Then she remembered her niece. "But ye're selling your daughter – ye can't put a price on her – and to an old man! A young one like Caitlin needs a fine young man – a good-looking man, not an auld fella." Bridie screwed up her face as if she had been asked to eat something unsavoury, at the thought of an old man ravaging her niece.

Mrs Spillane assumed a resolute expression. "She could do worse, Bridie. 'Tis a small price to pay for food in her belly and he'll be dead long before she is, sure. Then she'll have the place to herself and her children." There was a long pause while each woman considered Caitlin's fate.

"For goodness' sake, don't tell Conor," said Mrs Hickey, lowering her voice for fear her husband should hear through the parlour wall. "He'd hit the roof! He thinks the world of your girls, especially Caitlin."

A few days later, Bridie began to help Mrs Spillane adjust her own wedding dress to fit Caitlin, after the girls had gone to bed. Mrs Spillane sewed the slightly yellowed linen and hand-made lace along the seams, to make the bodice smaller, while her sister repaired tiny flaws and holes in the veil, casting a fine net across the bright patterns of her hearth rug while her niece slept soundly upstairs, weaving dreams of freedom.

One morning soon after Caitlin had gone away, Jack returned from repairing a fence in a distant field, to find a brown-suited man wearing a trilby hat and carrying a leather briefcase. The man had obviously knocked on the door and, finding no one home, was re-crossing the yard on his way back to his motor car. He looked up at the sound of Jack's boots on loose stones.

"Ah. Mr Flynn?" Jack nodded. "Mr Flynn, I'm Daniel Ryan, from Bord na Bainne. I'm afraid I have some bad news for you. I left a letter – under the door." All the time, the man was walking towards Jack, and he extended a soft white hand which nonetheless delivered a firm handshake. Jack stood square, squinted his eyes at the man, put his hands on his hips.

"Oh?" he said.

"Yes. You're aware the Bord has started to carry out random checks on the milk collected in all the main dairies – checks for quality?" Increasingly experienced in such encounters, Mr Ryan was unperturbed by Jack's surliness. He searched the farmer's eyes for understanding, and the slight impatience in the knit of his brows with the icy calm of his manner impressed Jack, who nodded. "Look, Mr Flynn, I'll come straight to the point. Recent tests show that milk coming in from your herd is infected with tuberculosis. I'm certain you understand how serious this is. I'm here to serve you with official notice, and to advise you that the dairy can accept no more milk from you until the TB has been eradicated."

"What?" Jack's interrogative was spoken as though the man had addressed him in a foreign tongue. Mr Ryan put his briefcase on the ground while he worked his fingers to the extremities of brown leather gloves.

"I'm sorry for you, Mr Flynn," Ryan said, looking kindly into Jack's eyes then stooping to pick up his case, producing his car keys from his jacket pocket. "A vet will come from the Bord to test the cows. It's a routine procedure. I'm afraid the cost will be yours initially, though it may be reclaimable later, under insurance. It must be one of our vets, though – that's regulation. Excuse me, now." The man pursed his lips momentarily in a sympathetic grimace, looked briefly once more at Jack, then walked away from him towards his car.

"When will he come?" asked Jack.

"As soon as possible – tomorrow perhaps," replied the official, not turning. When he got to his car, he added, "Oh, and you'll have to tip away your milk until you get the all-clear. Good luck, now, Mr Flynn." Daniel Ryan climbed into his vehicle, turned out of the yard, and started noisily up the lane. Even then, Jack did not make the connection between what he had just learned and the cough which immediately racked his frame until his tongue protruded. He gasped back air at last and crossed to the house, cursing through spittle and the searing pain in his lungs.

Donal Kelly had been interviewed at length by the gardai following the killing of Davey Nunan at O'Hallorahan's bar in February 1941, but as he was the only witness, his testimony would not stand up against that of the gard who killed Nunan and swore he had not meant to. The geography master who was with Donal at the time of the incident insisted he had seen nothing, for he had spent most of the fight hunkered down against the wall of the pub furthest from the bar, his elbows on his knees and forearms over his face, eyes tight shut. No one else could recall any precise details of the moments leading up to Nunan's death and the whole thing was assigned to accident and misadventure. Officer O'Reilly was transferred to Dublin. Donal's statement was filed, a full report made.

On the day Davey Nunan was buried, the streets of Cashmel overflowed with mourners from three counties. Provisional IRA men of high ranks turned out to fire a salute over the tricolor-draped coffin and the gardai looked the other way. There were scuffles and ballads and drunken shouting into the early hours of next morning, but the sheer numbers of gardai drafted in from Cork, Limerick, Wexford, and Kilkenny headquarters were prohibitive of rioting or more serious violence. Donal attended the funeral, and there the indignation he felt at the injustice of Nunan's death was consolidated into a virulent subversive Republicanism. Many handshakes and respectful cap-tippings were proffered in his honour as he followed the coffin and stood at the graveside. IRA men, aware of his bravery on the night of Nunan's death and in testifying against Officer O'Reilly, showed Donal their respects.

The next thing that was substantially decisive in causing Donal Kelly to join the IRA was the arrest of George Plant in October 1941. On the orders of Stephen Hayes, IRA Chief of Staff Officer at the time, "General" George Plant, a Tipperary man and official executioner of the 7th IRA battalion, bank robber, and ambusher of trains, executed a young man from Wexford, whose name was Michael Devereux.

Twenty-four-year-old Devereux, newly married and a father, was suspected of betraying to the gardai the whereabouts of an IRA weapons cache and so had to be shot. Plant did his duty and in spite of Devereux's pleas that he was innocent, put a bullet in his head at close range in a remote location on Slievenamon mountain in September 1940. It was to this paramilitary execution that the sergeant had referred on the night Nunan was killed in

O'Hallorahan's bar, for it was certain that many a South Tipperary household had afforded safe conduct, food, and shelter to George Plant following his murder of Devereux.

Ironically, it was the IRA's kidnapping and torture of the IRA leader Stephen Hayes, in the spring of 1941, that led to the exposition of Plant as Devereux's murderer. Hayes was accused of collusion with de Valera's government. At first he hotly and persistently denied the charge, but after two months of torture and interrogation by his own men, Hayes confessed to treason. He was about to be executed when he escaped and sought sanctuary with the Rathmines gardai.

A substantial part of Hayes' quid pro quo confession to the police included his admission that he had ordered George Plant to kill Michael Devereux, and Plant became the country's most wanted man. By the time he was arrested, Plant had garnered a legendary stature comparable with the one Dick Turpin must have enjoyed in eighteenth-century England.

O'Hallorahan's bar reopened eventually under the patronage of the previous landlord's daughter, Molly. Married to a Kildare lorry driver named Desmond Corcoran, but with no children, Molly ran her father's bar with stern eyes and tone which could nonetheless be tempted to sparkling and laughter. Her status as O'Hallorahan's daughter, and the respect she deserved as a married woman and landlord, kept the men in check most of the time. There was less cursing and more cap doffing in the bar of an evening.

"Well, what'll it be, young Donal?" asked Molly one rainy evening in October 1941, though she could not have been more than four years older than Donal.

"The usual, Molly, please." Donal shook the rain from his overcoat and tousled his hair to dislodge surplus water, as the landlady levered the ale pump towards her and expertly filled his tankard.

"Now," she said at last, placing the brimming mug before him on the bar, "twopence please."

Donal handed her the pennies and, lifting his pint to his mouth, looked over it and into the bar room for familiar faces. A few caught his notice at once and someone beckoned to him in an urgent manner. Frowning quizzically, Donal went to join his friends.

"Have you heard?" whispered John Tuohy as Donal approached.

"Heard what?"

"They've got Plant!" Tuohy was a small man with a mop of unruly black hair and bushy eyebrows beneath which his small brown eyes flashed and smouldered by turn. He seemed never to smile, but the extent to which he appeared ruminative indicated the relative sociability of his mood. At present, he was animated in a way people rarely encountered him.

"Who's got him?" asked Donal, too interested to discover the facts to be wary of appearing foolish.

"De Valera's got him!" spat Tuohy. "The gardai have got him! They picked him up last night. He's above in Dublin by now." Men close to them shook their heads and expressed their sadness.

"That whoore Hayes have a lot to answer for, boy," enjoined Pat Moran, a tall thin man with a large hooked nose and white hair which splayed from his cap as if in a bid for freedom. "If ever the boys get hold of him, now…"

"They hardly will," retorted Tuohy disgustedly, "for he've the full protection of the state."

"If you call prison the protection of the state," contributed Michael Flaherty – balding, fat, and genial but with a right hook no one would invite.

"I do!" Tuohy rounded on Flaherty. "They'll look after their own, so they will."

"And are you sure now, John, that Hayes is a guilty man? There's not much I wouldn't say after two months of beating and starving at the hands of the IRA top brass!" Flaherty again. Most within earshot lifted their pints to their mouths and contemplated the hypothetical horror of Hayes being the latest victim of IRA paranoia. After a moment or two, Tuohy rallied again.

"Of course he is! He's guilty as sin. Wasn't it he who told the gardai where the arms were below in Wexford then blamed poor Michael Devereux and had Plant shoot him?"

"That is speculation and nothing more." This time, the voice was new, sonorous, and everyone turned to the speaker. Joseph Morgan was a man of few words but generally considered to be intelligent and in possession of an insight bordering on the prophetic. Some said he was a senior IRA member but none knew anything for certain about Joe Morgan. His contribution was therefore weighed with respect, even by Tuohy.

"Do you not think Hayes is a traitor, Joe?" Tuohy's tone was incredulous.

Morgan "hmphed", downed the remainder of his pint, said nothing for a long while, then commented, "Well, let's hope he is, for if he is not what we have done does not bear thinking of and George Plant will pay for our folly with his life."

Donal was by now sufficiently informed to start asking sensible questions. "What'll happen to Plant now?"

"He will be tried by the Special Criminal Court," responded Morgan, "and it will not go well for him. Good night now, lads, I salute ye. I'm away." So saying, Joseph Morgan put on his cap, adjusted his collar so that it would afford him some protection from the driving autumn rain, and left.

"Where do you suppose he is off to, lads?" asked Tuohy, reverting to a more usually morose demeanour after the evening's first flush of excitement.

"Nobody knows," said Flaherty, "and it's better not to ask. I'll stand ye another beer, lads. Who's in?"

December 1943, and after a week in Wexford Caitlin was looking healthy and relaxed. She spent her days studying, making up for lost time, aware that on her return to Dunane her father would again set her to work about the farm and she would have precious little time for her books. In the evenings she would play her aunt's piano and the others would sing. And when they were tired of singing, Caitlin indulged her love of more classical fare and her relatives sat quietly in the firelight, each preoccupied with his or her own thoughts, to the accompaniment of music both foreign and beguiling to them. On fine days, there were bracing walks along the Wexford Quays and shopping trips to the town. Caitlin stole glances at the gentlemen who stepped in and out of the many offices and business premises along Wexford Main Street, and her heart fluttered with excitement at how much grander Dublin would be.

Maureen rarely left the house, preferring to remain in her room, reading the Bible, praying for guidance and courage, and becoming increasingly remote as the time for entering the convent drew near. Mrs Spillane and her sister watched the transformation of this girl into a bride of Christ, and were impressed by the awe and romance of it. Mr Hickey, however, often exhausted at night from dealing with drunken brawls, IRA insurgence, or scenes of domestic violence, grew unaccountably uncomfortable with this spectre at his dining table. He looked for relief to the rosy cheeks of Caitlin, whose freshness and good looks reminded him of his youth and made his pulse quicken a little. Caitlin always had a witticism or a canny observation on life to make everyone laugh or guffaw in surprise, where Maureen was maudlin, censorious.

"The intelligence of that young one!" he declared fondly of Caitlin one night, as he and Bridie undressed for bed. "The wit of her – and she not eighteen yet. Where does she get such… insight?" He turned to look at his wife, smiling broadly. But Bridie avoided his eyes, busying herself with folding and hanging her clothes.

"Where indeed?" she replied, then added under her breath, "Not from her parents, that's for sure." Conor made a face as if to say "What's eating you?" but he said nothing and she did not see. Some minutes later, as they climbed into bed and Conor reached out to turn off the bedside lamp, he added, grunting with the exertion of turning over to get comfortable, "She'll go far, that Caitlin – you can just feel it about her." Mrs Hickey stared silently into the darkness, heart pounding.

CHAPTER SIX

"If any one of you knows a just and lawful reason why these two should not be joined in marriage, then come and see me after the mass."

The chapel in Dunane village seemed to gasp and then whispers and exclamations erupted in every pew, as people turned to confirm with their neighbours what they had just heard. Malachai Brett's wife was as outraged as any there. She turned on her husband with a murderous expression and such vehemence that he instinctively inclined his body away from her.

"What's wrong with you?" he hissed at her.

"Did you do this?" she hissed back.

"I did not!" he exclaimed aloud, relief making the conviction ring in his voice.

"You didn't arrange this… this… marriage, did you?" She spat the words, still unconvinced.

"What's it to you who he marries?" Malachai lowered his voice again, acutely conscious that the eyes of the congregation would be on them, resenting his wife's public show of disrespect.

"'Tis a crime to let an auld fella like that have that young one – brazen though she is she doesn't deserve him!" retorted Mrs Brett, high colour and indignation making her even more frightening. Her words could now be plainly heard two pews to the front and back of them, for she could keep quiet no longer.

"Whissht!" instructed Malachai. "Amn't I after telling you that I did not have a hand in this?" His own voice matched his wife's in volume and there was more talk, everyone's voices becoming louder as they wondered anew how this thing came to be. Malachai lowered his eyes to his missal, and said quietly and with as much dignity as he could manage, "I'll thank you next time to listen to what I am saying." Mrs Brett curled her lip at him then forgot him as she turned around in the pew to exchange exclamations with a woman called Ellie Bergin who ran the grocer's shop in Dunane.

No one could think of a single lawful reason why Caitlin should not be joined to Jack Flynn, for they had not a clue how the proposed joining came to be and Caitlin was not around to ask. It was not likely that anyone would dare enquire of Flynn how he had managed to gain the hand in marriage of the most attractive girl for miles around. Mick Spillane stood alone in his pew and stared straight ahead. Even more determined to appear impervious to the commotion the announcement had caused was Jack, though it was all he could do to prevent himself turning around to Spillane and mouthing obscenities at him, for neither Mick nor his wife had considered it necessary to inform Jack of when, exactly, the banns would be read. Jack kneeled and buried his head in his hands, as if in prayer, and at last the congregation began to file out of the church. He toyed with the idea of approaching Father Kinnealy to discuss the forthcoming wedding but when he looked up, the church was empty, all the altar candles were blown out, and there was no sign of the priest. Jack emerged from the chapel to find Mick Spillane waiting uneasily for him.

"Well?" Mick tipped his cap, eyeing Jack with a wariness bordering fear – much as he had regarded him when they were at school together. Jack shot him his blackest look.

"Couldn't you tell me the banns were being read, couldn't you?" he growled as he continued walking. Mick followed, hands in pockets, really afraid Jack might turn and hit him at any moment.

"Sure I thought we'd agreed the arrangements were up to meself?" Jack said nothing, kept walking. "Well, have you a date in mind for the wedding, or will I go ahead and fix it?" Mick followed Flynn, raising his voice to be heard as the latter quickened his pace. Just before Jack was out of earshot, he turned.

"Just let me know when to turn up," he snarled, then placed his hat on his head and strode swiftly to his waiting horse and cart.

"What are you doing?" The man's voice was quiet, but it made the two women start as though he had suddenly shouted. Bridie looked askance at her sister across the waves of lace and linen. Mrs Spillane did not look up from her sewing.

"We are adjusting this dress to fit Caitlin," she answered steadily, then bent her head to bite the thread clear of the garment.

"What?" Mr Hickey looked puzzled, but half amused. "Is Caitlin to be married?" He looked at his wife, concerned by the panic in her eyes. She nodded, a look of guilty apology on her face. "Why didn't you say so?" asked Mr Hickey again, turning again to his sister-in-law.

"Bridie didn't think you'd like it," came the calm reply, and she stooped again to pick up the next bit of sewing. Mr Hickey looked concerned; the amusement had died from his face.

"Oh?" he said, fixing on his wife. Home unexpectedly early from a late shift, blocking the doorway in his full garda uniform, Sergeant Hickey appeared to his wife as criminals saw him. She rose from her chair, letting the veil fall to the floor. She looked briefly for assistance to her sister, but Mrs Spillane kept sewing. He couldn't touch her.

"Let's go upstairs," said Mrs Hickey, wringing her hands. Mr Hickey pushed away from the lintel and followed his wife across the hall to the staircase.

Well over an hour later, Mrs Spillane could still hear their raised voices and her sister's pleading through the wall which separated her room from theirs. She did feel a certain anxiety when she thought of her sister's anger against her following this episode, but the next day in any case was their last full day in Wexford, so it would be bearable. And Bridie could not say anything aloud for fear Caitlin would overhear. She would not risk the fracas that would cause. Mrs Spillane knew it was wicked to gloat at others' misfortunes, but if this was all Bridie and Conor had to contend with, they had an easy life! Let them try running a farm in all weathers, up to their knees in dung and cold mud, with nothing but daughters to help them. Then let them judge people on what they did with those daughters and what sacrifices had to be made to get a bit of money and comfort in their old age; then let them warm with considerate passion for each other! 'Twould do them no harm to taste a bit of someone else's reality. And putting a pillow over her uppermost ear, she fell asleep.

Jack Flynn watched as the milk ran in eager rivulets towards the drain. There could be no more heart-breaking work than this milking purely to relieve his cows. The dairyman had stopped calling. The vet had arrived and officiously taken blood from each cow, putting it into little bottles, each labelled with the number on a cow's ear tag. He would be in touch when the results were through – about two weeks. And so, each morning and evening, Jack milked his cows and poured the warm, white milk into the dirt runnels which ran to the drain, and he watched it gather twigs and soil as it disappeared into the ground. He marvelled grimly at its whiteness as though seeing it for the first time. How could this essence of life be carrying a disease fatal to man and beast?

Another Sunday and this time, when the banns were read, no one stirred. The silence seemed to be one of collective disapproval, but this was easier for Jack to bear than excited gossip. Disapproval made him resolute. He stood, head erect, eyes narrowed, but suddenly he was bent double with an unstoppable coughing fit which made him clutch the pew in front, and the priest could not continue until it was over. At last, he stood trembling, head bowed, leaning on his pew. Once more, Mick Spillane was waiting for him when he came out of the church.

"That's a nasty cough you have – you should see a doctor," ventured Mick. He had wanted to discuss terms again, in the light of the second banns being read. He had to be absolutely sure Jack would stick to his word and was good for the five hundred pounds. It would be too late for complaints about being short changed once vows had been exchanged.

"I don't need any doctor," muttered Jack. He was always irritated by Mick's presence. He didn't trust him. Mick shrugged.

"The wedding will be in January," he said. "You said to let you know." Jack was taken off guard. It was already December.

"January? Why so?"

"Why not?" responded Spillane. "Is there a reason to wait?" Jack could not think of one. "Will you be able to have the money by then?" ventured Spillane. Jack looked at him contemptuously then half smirked. Spillane was always angling, always conniving. He had been the same in school. Once, when they were no more than twelve or so, he had walked to school with him, and Spillane had kept up a relentless barrage of questions about the story they were supposed to have read for their Irish homework. Did Jack think it was any good? Didn't he think the ending was useless and what did Jack suppose this meant and that meant? It was not until they were in afternoon class and the Irish master – a terrifying man with moles on his face and yellow teeth – had hit Jack's desk with his cane and demanded to know why his homework was so similar to Mick Spillane's, that Jack realized he had been taken for a fool. Unable to tell the truth, for snitching was an unpardonable transgression among schoolboys, Jack remained mute and suffered two lashes of the master's cane across his open palms. He couldn't hold a pen or open a gate without wincing in pain for days afterwards.

"You will have your money, Spillane – have I not said so more than once?"

"All five hundred pounds? On the day?"

Jack smiled cynically into Spillane's pale grey eyes and held his gaze till the latter had to look away, then he turned his back once more and walked off. He wished to goodness he never had to look into those shifty eyes again.

Caitlin, Maureen, Mrs Spillane, and Bridie sat at the breakfast table on their final morning in Wexford. The wedding gown was finished and packed in Mrs Spillane's suitcase. This last meal was a sullen affair and all were preoccupied with their private thoughts. Maureen was pale and ate little. The journey back to Tipperary would conclude in a few weeks at the steps of the convent where she would finish her life, but the peace and apparent satisfaction this had afforded her earlier seemed to have deserted her. She and Caitlin barely exchanged glances these days. What was more, their growing antipathy seemed mirrored in a sudden cooling of amity between Aunt Bridie and their mother. On a few occasions during the last day or so in Wexford, Caitlin caught her aunt narrowing her eyes at her mother, while the latter assumed a nonchalance around her sister, approaching smugness. Neither spoke to the other unless it was necessary.

"What's wrong?" Caitlin finally broke the uneasy silence around the table. She had aimed her question at her aunt but it was her mother who answered.

"Nothing, Caitlin; nothing you need worry about." This reassurance elicited an incredulous snort from Bridie. Even Maureen surfaced from her reverie and began to observe the women around her. Caitlin frowned, looking to her mother, who warned her with a glare to mind her manners, keep quiet. Caitlin rolled her eyes and sighed. If her mother had argued with her aunt, so what? But could they not sort it out? For it was a shame that such a nice visit should end this way.

"Go upstairs now, girls, and pack." Her mother's voice again. "Now?" queried Caitlin. "Can't we do it later?"

"No. Now. We will go to mass here with your uncle and aunt and then your Uncle Conor will drive us to Waterford. We'll get the train to Limerick Junction this afternoon. There is only the one train on a Sunday. Your father already knows we'll be on it. He will meet us with the cart. Go on. Go and pack."

As they climbed the stairs, Maureen and Caitlin could hear the hissing reproaches of their aunt and the laconic replies of their mother, as the two women moved about the kitchen, clearing up. Their uncle had avoided the breakfast table. They could hear him clearing his throat in the living room and turning the pages of the Sunday papers he had risen early to purchase.

"I wonder what that's about?" whispered Caitlin, stopping on the stairs to try to make out the words her mother and aunt were exchanging.

"I'm sure it's none of our business, Caitlin," reproached Maureen, squeezing past her sister.

On the train home, Caitlin tried again to make sense of their unceremonious departure. More than anything, she had been very hurt by what she perceived as a sudden coldness towards her by her uncle, whom she had come to adore. He had stayed in the car when Bridie helped them carry their suitcases to the platform.

"Why didn't Uncle Conor come to the station?" she ventured, as her mother's eyes flitted to and fro, watching the scenery scud past the steam train's windows.

"Things go wrong in marriages, Caitlin. Even theirs," was all her mother said, without taking her eyes from the window. Then she drew her shawl over her head and around her face, indicating she no longer wished to speak.

On the third Sunday after Caitlin had left for Wexford, Mick Spillane stood alone in his pew and listened to the third and final banns being read for the marriage of his daughter to Jack Flynn. Across the church and towards the front stood Jack in his usual pew, staring straight ahead, nothing giving away that he had heard the priest's words but the working of his jaws as he clenched and unclenched his teeth. He felt the eyes of the congregation bore holes in his back but he shouldered his shame with apparent stoicism. One word of dissent was uttered above the silence, starting a short-lived wave of murmuring among the parishioners.

"Disgraceful!" said Mrs Brett, and Malachai rolled his eyes.

"Well, bow your heads for the final blessing," said the priest, stepping down from the pulpit and crossing to the altar. Jack stayed where he was until everyone had gone, this time not taking his eyes off the priest so he would not miss him. He was consumed with a need to speak to Father Kinnealy about this marriage but he did not know what he wanted to say. He felt he needed someone's blessing.

"Father Kinnealy."

"Yes, Jack? What can I do for you?" But the priest's tone and expression were incongruous with the generosity of his words.

"This wedding…" Jack could not go on.

"Yes?"

"January."

"Yes, that's right."

The priest contemplated Jack's consternation and was moved to pity this gruff man who had never missed a Sunday mass in all the years Father Kinnealy had been the parish priest, but to whom he had spoken only a handful of times. Jack could not raise his head; he seemed uncharacteristically vulnerable. As much as Father Kinnealy did not approve of this marriage and wished not to engage with it on any level other than that necessary to effect it, he sensed this man needed his help. He put down the brass candle snuffer on the credence table and prepared to hear what Jack Flynn had to say.

"How are you, Jack?" The priest's tone and his words were the kindest Jack Flynn had heard since his mother had disappeared. He could not look up. A terrible force was gathering in his chest and spreading into his throat and he was not sure what it was. It was different from the urge to cough.

"Fine, Father – thanks," Jack managed at last and shuffled uneasily.

"Good, good." Father Kinnealy was unsure how to proceed. "So, you are to marry Caitlin Spillane, Jack?"

At last, Jack recovered enough composure to look at the priest. When he did, his expression, thought Father Kinnealy, was more like that of a guilty schoolboy asking for clemency than a middle-aged man who had purchased a young bride without her knowledge.

"She's a grand lass, Caitlin; you're a lucky man, Jack." Jack smiled nervously, nodded. The priest continued, his tone of voice intended to give his words an unmistakable gravitas, "Will you look after her, Jack?" Father Kinnealy's eyes searched Jack's face.

"I will, Father." Jack's eyes filled with tears. He was horrified and sought instantly to wipe them away before they could spill. The gesture allowed Father Kinnealy to look away and spare Flynn's pride.

"Good man," he said, reaching once more for the candle snuffer. "Sure that's the best you can do. Good luck, now, Jack." And he moved away to resume the extinguishing of candles.

From the ninth to the eleventh of December 1941, George Plant was tried for the murder of Michael Devereux by the Special Criminal Court in Dublin. There was much rejoicing in O'Hallorahan's bar on the night of the eleventh, for Plant was found "not guilty" following the withdrawal of their statements by two IRA witnesses, Walsh and Davern, without whose testimonies there was no evidence. Tables and chairs were cleared in the bar and a man with an accordion played reels and jigs to which the patrons danced and sang. Several wives were fetched from home for "the craic" and even a few children, too young to be left alone and without older siblings who could mind them, were allowed by Molly Corcoran into the bar and she gave them sweets and lemonade.

"You were wrong about Plant, so, Joe." The voice was John Tuohy's. Joe Morgan, sitting on a bar stool, right elbow leaning on the bar and supporting the ale tankard in his hand, turned slowly to contemplate the glint of mockery in Tuohy's small eyes. He said nothing. "You said it would not go well for him – do you not remember, Joe?"

"I do."

Tuohy's face crumpled into an incredulous grimace. "But it has gone well for him, Joe – sure he's a free man! God is on our side!" Joseph Morgan sighed heavily, put down his pint.

"I have never professed to know the mind of God, Tuohy, or even if there is such a thing." He paused and turned on his stool to give the smaller man his full attention. "But I pride myself on knowing a little about the minds of men." He paused again, allowing his gaze to rest a fraction longer on Tuohy's than was friendly. Tuohy looked away, picked up his pint, swigged from it. "And de Valera will not – cannot – let Plant walk free from this." Tuohy finished his pint and replaced it on a table, shrugged. Taking his leave of Morgan, he moved towards the dancers, remarking to someone as he went that Joseph Morgan could be a miserable auld beggar.

Little heed that night was paid to the certainty that Plant had shot Michael Devereux without any sort of trial. The important thing seemed to be that Plant, who had only been following orders, had escaped his sentence, and de Valera's Special Criminal Court was outsmarted.

Donal drank and laughed and danced with the best of them. He was likely to miss the curfew again. He was in danger of losing his job at the college if he once more breached the Holy Ghost Fathers' requirements to be in his room by ten o'clock. Something had to be done. He could not countenance going back to his father's farm and leaving behind the camaraderie and the easiness of life he had come to love in Cashmel.

"Sure you can board here if you like," Molly said, having listened yet again to Donal's expounding on the difficulty he was having conforming to the Holy Ghost Fathers' curfew regulations.

"I am never," he slurred on this particularly celebratory evening, "never late for work. No matter what I drink or how late I am getting away, I am there…" He paused, envisaged the row of silent, clean faces before him for maths class at nine o'clock in the morning, and continued, "… ready and able to instruct my students in *Principia Mathematica*."

"What?" Molly laughed, raising her eyebrows and her tone in good-natured mockery.

"Maths!" exclaimed Donal. "I'm always there." He slurped his beer, put the tankard down, and ran a hand through his hair. Several men and women were trying to dance "The Siege of Ennis" in O'Hallorahan's bar. There wasn't enough room and furniture kept falling over, being righted amid general laughter and whooping. There was no sign of the gardai.

"Did you hear what I said, Donal?" Molly was leaning across the bar, shouting at him above the music and his inebriation.

"What was that?" he leaned towards her, turning his head so that his left ear could better receive her words.

"You can lodge here if you want; I'll charge you a shilling a week for board and lodging. How's that? We have a spare room and it's no bother to us if you stay – sure you're in here most evenings anyway!"

"Really?" Donal's eyes widened. He turned to look her in the face. "You mean it, Molly?"

"Of course I mean it, ya gobeen, ya! But would the Fathers let you, like? Can you keep your job and live outside the college?"

"Well, I can't see why not," retorted Donal. "Other masters do exactly that. I'll ask them!"

The Holy Ghost Fathers weighed up the irregularity of a Blackwell scholar's lodging outside the college gates, against the inconvenience of having to put up with his inability to observe curfew. They considered sacking him altogether but he was an excellent teacher, and if they dismissed him on grounds of misconduct, he would lose his scholarship to Cork University. This, agreed the Fathers, would be a tragedy, given the boy's potential and the opportunity to enhance Blackwell's reputation as a breeding ground of excellent scholars and the next generation of influential Irish men. So it was that Donal Kelly's freedom was increased further and he moved into lodgings above O'Hallorahan's bar in Cashmel, nestled in Tipperary IRA heartland, in 1941.

Late on the second Sunday of December 1943, Mrs Spillane was reinstalled in her house, scrubbing and blacking the range, cleaning the floor, and washing the dishes Mick had neglected to clean while she was away. The girls were busy unpacking their suitcases. Mick enquired for the first time after his wife's sojourn in Wexford and broached the subject of Caitlin's imminent wedding.

"Well?" he began. "How are all in Wexford?"

"Oh, they are well," she replied. "And you? Here?" She searched his face anxiously.

"The banns are read." Spillane crossed to an open fire at the far end of the kitchen, spat into it. "The wedding will be in January." He did not turn to look at his wife as he spoke, other than a cursory movement towards his left shoulder to indicate the direction his words should take. There was a pause during which Spillane watched the flames reclaim the coal on which he had lately spat and Mrs Spillane returned to blacking the range with greater fury than before. "Tell her," he added, his imperative finding its mark though Spillane's attention on the hearth was resolute. He thrust his hands in his pockets. "Tell her she will be married in January."

"It's too soon, Mick!" At last Mrs Spillane abandoned the range, threw her cloth on the floor, and sat down heavily in the nearest chair. She began to sob as he rounded on her and continued.

"It must be in January. That's when himself wants it. The whole village is talking about it. Tell her! I'm off to check on the cows."

Some minutes after the kitchen door had banged shut Mrs Spillane sighed and rose from her chair. She washed her hands until the waxy blacking was only a shadow then took off her apron as though the movement was ritual, laid the garment over the back of the chair, and slowly made for the stairs. Once in her bedroom, she lifted the altered wedding dress and veil from her suitcase and laid them on the bed. "Oh, my little girl! My little Caitlin!" she sobbed to herself. "Will you ever forgive us?" Then she blew her nose, breathed deeply, and shouted, "Caitlin, come here to me, will you?"

"What's the wedding dress for, Mammy?" asked Caitlin, smiling in a bemused fashion as she came into her parents' bedroom. "Is it yours?" and she came forward to finger the lace.

"No, Caitlin," replied her mother. "It is yours."

"What?" Caitlin half guffawed, her voice incredulous.

"I don't want any scenes. Your father and I... have decided... you are to be married, and that's all there is to it."

"Married? Are you mad?" Caitlin was backing away towards the door.

"Caitlin! I will not be spoken to like that! Your head is full of ridiculous notions – about Dublin, and university. It's all nonsense, do you hear me? Your place is here, in Dunane, and you'll live the life that's been good enough for your father... and me. We have no money to send you gallivanting off to Dublin, my girl, and that's no life for a young one! You heard Sister Callasanctious the other day." Mrs Spillane's voice had become shrill. Maureen came into the room, alarmed by her mother's tone and the volume at which she spoke.

"What is it, Mammy? What's happening?" Her eyes fell on the dress, then travelled to her sister where she stood in an attitude of utter horror, her hands covering her mouth. "What is wrong with you, Caitlin? What's going on?"

"Caitlin is getting married!" declared Mrs Spillane.

"Married? Who to?"

"Yes, Mammy..." Caitlin had dropped her hands and she spoke in low, almost vicious tones. "Tell us who Caitlin is going to marry!"

"She is – you are – to marry Jack Flynn." The voice was Mick's. He had been crossing the yard to rinse his boots under the outside tap, having fed the cows their hay and beet, when he heard his wife shouting. Guessing the cause of this unusual occurrence, he had hastened to support her. There was no telling what Caitlin would do.

"No!" Caitlin was at once raw fury. In an instant she recalled the strange meeting her father had engineered between herself and Flynn on the church steps and how Flynn had stared at her while she played the accordion at the Dundrum ceilidh. It all became clear.

"Caitlin! Pull yourself together," he said sternly. "There's no need for this carry on!"

"I hate you!" she screamed at him again. "How could you do this to me?"

"Ah, cut the dramatics, will you?" shouted Mick, though it was more difficult than he had imagined to hear his daughter say those words. He had to regain control. Caitlin's face was contorted in a grimace of undisguised loathing.

"I will never marry that filthy..." She could hardly breathe, paused, then continued, "...disgusting old man!"

Maureen had adopted Caitlin's earlier stance, hands covering her face, eyes wide with shock. Turning her head from her father to Caitlin, she could not disguise her horror.

"You will marry Jack Flynn," Mick said menacingly, walking towards Caitlin. "It is all arranged, and you will marry him in January!" Maureen gasped. He was right in front of Caitlin now. "You will be mistress of a good little farm – and some fine cows. The house is big, and worth a few bob. You will have food in your belly and he've plenty of money. You will be well provided for." Mick looked behind him, towards his wife. Her continual weeping infuriated him. Always, she was weak and pathetic. Maureen's gormlessness was very irritating, too. These useless, helpless women!

"Shut up!" he shouted at his wife. "Shut your stupid carry on and do something useful for once in your pathetic life, would ya? Help me out here! And you…" He turned back to Caitlin who contemplated him with an expression of passionate hatred. "You will do as you are told!" He finally lost his temper. "All this talk of gallivantin' off to Dublin and your fine airs and graces… It's all bull! Four daughters I have raised – four! No sons to help me, no money coming in – ye can't even roll a bloody milk churn or… or mend a fence, or…"

He was so enraged he could not go on. He paused, tried breathing through his nose in an effort to sound more in control, but couldn't manage it, for the breaths came too rapidly. "It's high time I had something for my years of back-breaking stinking grind, so it is, and there's no money for the likes of you, my lady, skidaddling off to un-i-ver-si-ty…" He sneered the last word, spinning it out, emphasizing each syllable.

"I will get a scholarship!" she screamed in his face. "I don't want your stinking money!" She was not dissatisfied by the effect of her outburst; he seemed to shrink a little at the invective. "You've always hated me!" she continued. "Couldn't wait to spoil everything for me, could you? You want to tie me down to this godforsaken place, and watch me drown in cow dung – just like her!" She pointed at her mother, who was now sitting on the end of her bed, hands over her ears and rocking quickly back and forth. "You make me sick! The pair of ye! Plotting and scheming behind my back, while I was saying how much I wanted to go to Dublin – be something…"

The enormity of the treachery was more than she could process. She had always suspected her parents could make her life very difficult and try to dissuade her from applying for a scholarship but she never dreamt they were capable of this. "I hate you both! I'll never forgive you as long as I live!"

The slap when it came was resounding and shocked all three women to the core. Caitlin reeled beneath its force and put out a hand to make contact with the wall and prevent herself from falling.

"That's enough!" Mick's voice was a bellow, an exasperated, primordial roar. "I will not be spoken to like that in my own house!" He advanced on his daughter, hand raised to hit her again.

"No, Daddy!" cried Maureen. Mrs Spillane was on her feet, reaching for the raised hand.

"Ah no, Mick, not that," she gasped. "Please, Mick, please." And he dropped his hand but pushed away his wife, who fell into the steadying arms of Maureen. All three women sobbed and cried loudly.

"I am the man of this house, and by God, I will be obeyed!" He spat as he spoke; his eyes seemed to bulge as they fixed on Caitlin. She cowered, turned her face to the wall. "You will be married and that is final. Do you hear me? Do you?" He advanced on her with the attitude a boxer adopts as he faces an opponent, one foot before the other, hands raised in a parrying attitude. Caitlin slid down the wall, covering her face with both arms. When she did not look up or challenge him further, he took a step back, chest heaving, hands trembling. He had never hit a woman before. "This is not the church, or… or some rich family with nothing else to do but send people off to dream their lives away at university!" He found a handkerchief in a trouser pocket, wiped his mouth, ran a hand through his hair. His voice approached its usual timbre. "This is a working farmer's family, with precious little to spare. Five bloody women I've fed all my life." He looked around to fix Maureen and Mrs Spillane with his words. They looked back at him, sniffing and sobbing in each other's arms. "And I have no money to fund a life of leisure for you, my lady. Do you hear what I'm saying?" At last, Caitlin tried to speak through her sobs, to defend herself, though still she did not look up.

"I'll get work – I'll keep myself."

Mick laughed mockingly. "And what'll you do? It's all we can do to persuade you to shift your backside into the milking parlour a couple of hours a day; how the hell are you going to work long and hard enough to earn your keep in Dublin? Have you any idea what you're talking about, have you? You're a girl, Caitlin! And you have no idea of the dangers awaiting young girls – especially in the city. It's all codology. Grow up, for pity's sake."

Later, Caitlin would wonder bitterly if this was what growing up really was: being forced to swallow someone else's reality; to feel it deaden the heat and quick of young blood, like an antidote to hope. He left the room and his boots on the stairs were like drums, or nails, or something else ultimately male, ultimately pitiless.

CHAPTER SEVEN

The night before his mother disappeared, Jack lay in bed listening to the hoarse wailing of his baby sister. She had been crying for hours.

"There's something wrong with her, Sean." His mother had pleaded several times with his father to hitch up the horse and get the doctor, but it was now after midnight and Flynn was already furious that he was getting no sleep. It was calving time and he was exhausted. To make matters worse, he had lost a cow that day during a difficult birth and the calf was not thriving either. It wouldn't suckle from its surrogate and she seemed uninterested in it. The loss of a good milking cow and a calf was a financial blow. The following day too there was a market in Thurles and he needed to get a trailer load of piglets there by no later than ten o'clock.

"For the love of God can't you just shut her up?" he bellowed. "I have to get some stinkin' sleep – unless you're getting up at half past four to milk the cows and take the bainbhs to market!"

The baby cried and cried. For a few seconds every now and then, it seemed she had stopped, but then she began to wail again. The intermittent nature of her crying was almost worse than if it had been constant, for each lull afforded Sean Flynn just enough hope that he might, finally, be able to sleep, only to be awoken again by a shrill scream as he dropped off.

In his bed across from his parents' room, Jack put his pillow over his head and whispered fervent prayers that God would make the baby stop. Please God, make the baby stop.

"Sean!" His mother was shouting. Jack sat up sharply, heart pounding more than ever. If she was shouting at his daddy there

105

was really something wrong and everything was going to get worse. She must never shout at his father! "Will you for pity's sake get out of the bed and fetch the doctor or take me to the doctor with this child, because I know there is something wrong with her!" There was an agonizing pause during which only the baby's screaming could be heard, but then there was a series of thumps and thuds as Jack's father sprang out of his bed and thundered his way across the room opposite to Jack's. What followed next had Jack whimpering in terror, "Mammy, Mammy!"

"Sean! What are you doing? Sean, give her back... Sean, what are you doing?" His mother was hysterical. From the sounds he heard, Jack knew his father had thumped downstairs.

The baby's crying reached a pitch it had not attained that night and was now coming from downstairs. Jack got out of bed, and though he was shaking with terror and a warm rivulet of urine was running down the inside of his leg, he opened his door and stepped cautiously onto the landing. He was all the time mouthing "Mammy, Mammy, Mammy", as though it were a charm against evil. His mother had almost flown down the wooden stairs to the kitchen. She was still screaming.

"Give her back to me, Sean. Sean!"

"Shut up – will you shut the hell up!" His father's voice was monstrous and it filled the house but Jack could not tell if his shouting was directed at the baby or his mother. The baby's screams were now no more than background noise.

Peeping over the banister at the top of the stairs, Jack could see some of the kitchen. His eyes widened with horror as his mother flew at his father and his father pushed her away from him with all his might so she reeled across the kitchen out of sight, her nightdress a flash of white. And in his other hand, Sean Flynn held aloft his tiny daughter by her clothing as though it were the scruff of her neck. Before Mairead Flynn could recover from her assault and make another bid for her baby, the child stopped crying. There was utter silence.

"Sean?" His mother's voice was quiet and there was such a tone to it, more frightening than her screams. Jack began to cry aloud. No one paid him any heed. "Sean?" When his mother spoke again it was louder and more urgent, but his father wasn't answering her.

"Ah no, ah no… ah, come on now… no, no, no!" His father's voice now, and it was impossible to tell why he was saying "no" over and over again and then his mother was screaming, just screaming, a howl of desperate, furious grief. Jack's own howls of terror added to the cacophony but a voice was missing. The baby girl did not cry again. Though he yelled and screamed at the top of his voice for her, Jack's mother did not come to him. Then he heard the outside door opening and slamming shut and he thought his father must have gone, at last, for the doctor, but when he quieted himself in a bid to find out what was happening, sobs still shuddering through him and tears still pouring down his face, it was his father crying below in the kitchen that he heard and there was not a sign or sound of his mother. Jack's sobs abated as his father's gathered force and he wept like a child.

Jack never saw his mother again. His father refused to talk of that night or its consequences. Jack only knew as he got older that his mother was wearing her nightdress when she left the house in the middle of the night, and she was carrying baby Irene in her arms. Now, just over forty years later, Jack lay in bed on his back and stared into the semi-darkness of early morning. He had awoken from a terrible dream and though its shapes and images were already indistinct, the feelings it had evoked were all too keen, and his heart was still pounding in spite of the breaths he was taking to steady it. Tears escaped the corners of his eyes and he closed his eyes, swallowed hard. And as he once more recalled that terrible night, he tried, as he had tried so many times before, to imagine what had happened to his mother and why she had never come back for him.

* * *

A few days after she had disappeared, the doctor had come. Jack was eating bread and butter at the big wooden table in the kitchen and his father was sitting by the range, picking dirt from under his nails with a knife. A knock came to the door and his father had thrown down the knife, leapt to his feet, and crossed the kitchen to the door in a second or two and swung it open. He had turned from the open door, walked slowly back to his chair, and sat down again, leaving the doctor to follow him in.

Jack had stopped chewing in spite of a hunk of bread in his mouth and sat watching the men. He could not understand what the doctor was saying and they kept their voices low. Jack's father nodded a lot, put his head in his hands. The doctor at one point reached out and put his hand on Jack's father's shoulder. Then he opened his brown bag and pulled out a piece of paper and a pen. Jack's father signed it and gave it back to him. After a few more minutes they stood up. Jack thought he heard the doctor say, "A terrible shame," and his father at one point had said quite clearly and loudly, "Her gut?" but as he lay in his bed recalling this shady encounter, Jack could only surmise that they had been talking about the baby and that the piece of paper must have been the death certificate. Not a word could he recall about his mother. The doctor had turned to Jack just before he left and asked him if he was "right", had tousled his hair and winked. Then he left and Jack's father sat in his chair for ages, head in his hands, before getting up and leaving the house, slamming the door behind him.

Almost as old now as his father was then, Jack felt his heart return to a normal rhythm but he felt the need to cough. He sat up quickly so he could manage the fit easier but the pain was terrible. He hacked and rasped for minutes and was exhausted by the time he could breathe again. And then, in the growing dawn light, he thought he detected something dark on the down-turned sheet that wasn't there before – an irregular shape in the half-light which he could not account for. Fumbling for the box of matches he kept on his bedside table, he lit one and used it to light the wick of a gas lamp, which was the only source of light for this room, other than the sun. As the lamp light gathered strength and spread outwards across the bed, Jack's heart lurched in shock, for his sheet was spotted in fresh, bright blood.

Caitlin's fate took up residence in the Spillanes' house like a black angel absorbing light and warmth. Mrs Spillane made a few tentative attempts to reach her daughter, but Caitlin hated her mother more than her father and shrugged off pity and remonstration with equal venom. They could do nothing that would hurt her more; there was a sort of grim freedom in that at least. She refused to eat, taking satisfaction in how worried this made her mother. Mick watched with concern the pallor which robbed Caitlin's cheeks of their colour. Sleeplessness dulled her beauty with shadows. He told himself she would rally in time, but at night he too lay sleepless and filled with guilt. Mrs Spillane cried and tossed and turned beside him, her movements sharp, as though she were irritated, and several times she turned suddenly towards him in the bed as though she would speak but never did. Maureen listened to her sister's sobbing each night, and pitied her. The idea of Caitlin – beautiful, talented, passionate Caitlin – married to the lugubrious and fearsome Jack Flynn was monstrous. Maureen even reached out to her sister, to console her as they lay side by side in the darkness, but her hand was met with stiff rejection. "Don't touch me" was all Caitlin said, and the accusation implicit in her words froze Maureen's compassion.

"I knew nothing about it, Caitlin – honestly."

"And you're destroyed by it, right?"

"What do you want me to say, Caitlin? Sure what can I do?"

There was no answer, and upset that Caitlin had rejected her sympathy, Maureen hardened against her sister once more. At least Caitlin might have children. Increasingly, the prospect of being childless was a cause of grief for Maureen. And what sympathy or concern had Caitlin ever expressed about that? What interest had she ever shown in Maureen's entrance to the convent?

On the fifth morning following the announcement of her fate, Caitlin descended the stairs to find Maureen and her mother putting up Christmas decorations in the parlour. They were chattering quietly together, and Caitlin heard them laugh at some remark Maureen made. Mrs Spillane turned, suddenly aware of Caitlin's presence.

"Hello, love," said Mrs Spillane. Maureen eyed her sister gravely, then turned back to the decorating. Caitlin did not answer. "Will you have some tea? Something to eat?" Caitlin regarded her mother with contempt, shook her head, and turned to leave the parlour.

"Caitlin!" Her mother's voice was sharp. Caitlin turned slowly to face her again. "That's enough, now! We've all suffered enough because of this. You are not going to spoil Christmas – your sister's last Christmas at home." Then more gently, "Things are not so bad. Just think, you'll have a house of your own soon, and you'll be…"

"What?" Caitlin interrupted her. "What will I be? Free, is that it? Can I refuse ever to milk another cow or scour another churn, because that's what I choose? Can I refuse to cook and clean and skivvy for a man I hate and can I stay out of his bed? Is that what you were going to say, Mammy?"

"Caitlin!" Mrs Spillane walked towards her daughter.

"You've condemned me to your life! Dancing to the tune of another filthy farmer. A skivvy – that's what you've made of me. I hope you're proud of yourself."

Mrs Spillane raised a warning finger and pursed her lips in anger. She took a step closer towards Caitlin and raised the forefinger to her daughter's face.

"Now, my girl. It is finished – do you hear me? We've all had enough of you! Just pull yourself together and stop pitying yourself. Life is what you make of it, Caitlin, and you can be a miserable little tinker or you can be gracious and accept what is your lot. We have precious few choices in this life, Caitlin, but how we live what's given to us is one of them. It's Christmas – think how our Lord bore his cross and remember that you have precious little to gripe about in comparison."

"I think you're mixing up Christmas with Easter," Caitlin retorted sarcastically, "but you have a point if you're trying to make analogies between my life and Christ's – you are crucifying me!" Caitlin's chest was heaving and in spite of her determination that it would not happen, hot tears spilled lavishly down her face so that it was hard for her to continue talking. "The difference is that there is no point to it!"

"Caitlin!" Maureen was shocked. "There's no need for blasphemy."

"Well done, there, Maureen," came Caitlin's response between sobs. "You're already sounding like a nun. All religion and no feeling. You'll fit in just perfect," she said, then turned from them and went towards the kitchen.

"Where are you going, Caitlin?" demanded her mother but Caitlin neither responded nor slowed her pace. She grabbed her coat from a hook behind the kitchen door and, flinging the door open, ran outside, though she had no idea where she would go.

Exactly two years earlier, Christmas Eve 1941, Donal Kelly was home in Golden. His sisters had made a real effort to put on a spread which would cheer up their father and celebrate Donal's homecoming. There was ham and bacon, for their father had slaughtered a young pig a month before. They had sold half of the animal to a local butcher but the rest they had smoke dried. There was a chicken too and cabbage and swede and roast potatoes. Tea, sugar, and butter were rationed, for they were in short supply during the war years, but they had their own eggs, thanks to the few chickens they kept. The girls had saved their sugar rations throughout October and November, had often gone without butter so that they would be able to make a fine sponge cake for Christmas Day with plenty of jam and fresh cream in it.

In the days leading up to Christmas, Donal exchanged his suit and shoes for the garb and boots of an Irish farmer and helped out with wood chopping, milking, and tending the pigs. The house was jovial and Mr Kelly was wreathed in smiles from morning to night, delighted to have his boy back home and helping him about the place. In the evenings, Donal would regale his family with stories of college life and teaching, making them howl with laughter at his imitations of Holy Ghost Fathers or foolish boys. He told them nothing of his increasing involvement with the IRA.

On Christmas Eve morning, Donal hitched the donkey to the cart and drove Deirdre into Golden village. There was just a post office and shop combined, a small bar, a butcher, and a shabby-looking barbershop in Golden's main street. There had been a grocer's but it had closed down in the Emergency declared by de Valera when world war broke out. Food rationing and the embargo on many imports meant there were no fruit or vegetables to be had which farmers did not grow themselves. Oranges and even apples were exotic now and Ireland reverted to the potatoes, cabbage, and swedes which had always been her staples. The tiny post office rarely had an up-to-date paper for sale. When there was a paper delivery to Golden it was a treat if they were just one day out of date. Those who could read well enough to follow the fluent prose and political arguments of *The Irish Press* or *The Irish Times* were mainly youngsters and uninterested in such things. Most got their news by mouth and hearsay, from fellas who could read and had an interest in the news at home and abroad, or who brought tales "from the field" to bars and late evening meetings in kitchens.

Deirdre collected the family's rations of tea and sugar from Mr Kiernan who ran the post office and handled the village post. Now, he distributed the rations for everyone in Golden, too.

Donal enquired of his wife, who served in the shop, if she had a newspaper.

"Wait now, and I'll see." Mrs Kiernan was small and round, of uniform width from her shoulders to her hips. She wore thick brown tights which wrinkled at the ankles, and the brown brogues of rural Irish women who were not otherwise in rubber boots. She rummaged beneath the counter, breathing heavily through her mouth with the exertion of bending, leaning one arm on her thighs to allow her to peer sideways into the recesses of the under counter shelf. "Wait a minute, now, and we'll see…" And then she reached one hand into the shelf and pulled out a single newspaper, a copy of *The Irish Times*. Mrs Kiernan straightened up with a grunt and narrowed her eyes to peer at the date of the paper, her mouth still open, experimenting with various distances from her face to aid ocular clarity.

"Can I help there, Mrs Kiernan?" asked Donal eventually, impatient to see the paper. He had had no news of the Plant affair since he had left Cashmel a week ago.

"Go on, so. Sure your young eyes might be better than my own." She passed the paper to him across the counter. Its date was the nineteenth of December. He told Mrs Kiernan.

"A recent one, then. I knew there was one of them in it." She looked pleased, nodded at him. "Do you want it?" Donal said he did.

"Give me a penny then, so."

"But Mrs Kiernan, it's almost a week out of date!"

"And there's plenty will have it if you don't want it," came the reply and Mrs Kiernan stretched out her hand for either the penny or the paper.

"Just one sec, now, Mrs K." Donal smiled charmingly at her, riffled quickly through the first few pages, scanning them up and down. His eye fell on a modest heading somewhere around page three and a brief column alluded to the Devereux murder trial's being inconclusive. There was no news. "No, you're all right, thanks. I don't want it after all. Sorry for your trouble now." Donal handed her back the paper with a wink. Mrs Kiernan hmphed and snatched it back.

"Sure it'll be grand for setting your fire this evening, Missis," added Donal cheerfully, "and a very happy Christmas to you."

As Joe Morgan had predicted in O'Hallorahan's on the night of the eleventh of December, George Plant had been rearrested and so had his accomplices, Walsh and Davern. In spite of the *nolle prosequi* Criminal Court verdict, Plant, Walsh, and Davern were detained in prison. As he and Deirdre climbed into the donkey cart and covered their laps with a thick woollen rug against the December chill, Donal nodded at his sister, but his eyes betrayed the anger he felt at what he considered was a terrible injustice.

"Are you all right, Donny?" enquired Deirdre, wondering what could have upset her brother in the fifteen minutes since she had last seen him.

"Fine," he replied. "Mrs Kiernan tried to rob me of the price of a paper and it was a week old."

"Did you buy it?"

"I did not! I read what I wanted real quick and gave it back to her – the cheek of it."

Deirdre laughed out loud that such a thing could have upset him so and Donal, taking the reins of the donkey cart and looking across at his sister, laughed with her and clicked the donkey forward.

"You'd better watch your back now, Donal," quipped Deirdre. "You're a marked man."

"Do you think she's slipping into her highway woman gear and galloping across country to cut us off at the pass?" Deirdre laughed afresh at the ludicrousness of her brother's question. "That'd be some outfit, boy," he went on. "Sure she'd look like one of them big fat bluebottles that get stuck in the windows."

"Donal!" Deirdre chided him. "That's very unkind, now," but she added, "I've never seen a fly that fat." And they laughed and joked all the way home.

Caitlin was to be married on the ninth of January 1944. Mick had decided that as the three banns had been read and the wedding was imminent, it was high time the couple met. Christmas Day seemed the obvious occasion for such an encounter. So, more nervous than he had been when he had first set off to Malachai Brett's house less than three months before, in search of a marriage match, Jack Flynn arrived on Christmas Day morning to pay his respects to his future in-laws, and to meet his wife to be.

He sat by the Spillanes' parlour fire looking fierce and scrubbed raw. His greying hair was moistened and combed back from his forehead, accentuating the hollows of his cheeks, the set of his jaw. His eyes burned and shifted beneath the bushes of his unkempt brows as if seeking an escape route. He sat on the edge of his seat, wringing his cap repeatedly in the space between his knees. Even the stretch of his breeches over his sharp knees looked threatening. Maureen noted the red spots along his starched collar line, and swallowed in sympathetic discomfort.

"Well, Jack," began Mick, cordially enough, "will you have a drop of the hard stuff?" He noted the loss of weight and the pallor of his neighbour's complexion, and put it down to hard work and worry about the wedding.

"Aye," mumbled Jack distractedly. It would be something to do, to hold a glass.

"Have you heard again from yer man from Bord na Bainne – Ryan?" Mick turned from the whiskey bottle, handed Jack his glass as he spoke. News of tuberculosis infection travelled fast in rural Ireland, and farms where it had been identified had to be named so that trade in livestock with the affected farmer would not result in spread of the disease. There were few catastrophes Irish farmers feared more than the sentence which followed the outbreak of TB in a herd. It could mean financial ruin, and this possibility had not escaped the attention of Mick Spillane, now that he had such a close interest in Jack Flynn's prosperity.

"No. After Christmas now."

"Do you think it's bad, Jack?"

Jack tried to focus on what Spillane was saying and once he had replayed the question in his head, realized it had been asked less from concern for his welfare than Spillane's own.

"I don't know, now. Sure, we'll see when the results are in."

"A terrible thing, Jack." Spillane shook his head. "A terrible thing for you." Jack swigged his whiskey. He hadn't had a drink in years. The fire in his throat made him gasp. Maureen almost sniggered as his eyes were flushed from their lairs in wide surprise.

"Will you have another, Jack?"

"Aye," gasped Jack and handed his empty glass for refilling. His belly warmed, and the heat which spread through his chest was strangely soothing of the fire he now carried with him everywhere.

"Well, hello, Jack." Mrs Spillane emerged from the kitchen, flushed and smiling, extending a hand in greeting. Jack did not rise. He tried clumsily to pass both his cap and glass to one hand, without success. "Ah, don't worry with all that," said Mrs Spillane, amused. "Sure, we're not strangers." He nodded cursorily; one side of his mouth twisted briefly in a sort of smile. He swigged his whiskey, more carefully this time. "And has Mick told you that Maureen here is to enter the convent in January? We're very proud of her, so we are." Mrs Spillane smiled at her daughter and waited for Jack to say something congratulatory. He said nothing, too strangled by the constraints of politeness to be able to converse. He nodded, slurped his whiskey, then lifted his index finger from the glass to insert it between his collar and throat. When he lowered it, Mick again replenished the glass, though he had begun to worry that an inebriated Jack Flynn could be a lot less than useful on this occasion. And it was only ten thirty in the morning. He was careful with the third measure.

"Where is Caitlin? Maureen, would you ever go and find her?" Mrs Spillane's voice was high and false. "That girl takes an age to dress herself – she's as vain, now!" Jack stared into his glass, squeezed his cap. Without looking up he felt Maureen move out of the parlour and heard her climb the stairs. He felt the exchange of anxious looks between Spillane and his wife and he cursed them silently for the dreadful fear in his belly. However, the fear was less insistent, more… abstract than it had been. *To hell wit them*, he thought, and the thought was accompanied by a sharp jerk upwards of his head, causing Mrs Spillane to jump. She laughed to cover her embarrassment. Jack fixed the Spillanes with a defiant glare and looked away again.

"Will you have Christmas dinner with us, Jack?" asked Mick with forced conviviality.

"Do," added Mrs Spillane. Both were relieved at the reply.

"No, no – thanks. I have plenty of stuff to eat back at the farm."

"Excuse me, now, Jack, a second. I have to tend the meat." Mrs Spillane left the room and shed a few hot tears as she lifted the kettle pan to check on her ham. Composure recovered, she returned to the tiny parlour. As she crossed the hall, Caitlin descended the stairs behind Maureen. She was pale and her hair was scraped back from her face in a severe knot. Her eyes were red and her mouth set. She held herself straight, though her eyes betrayed her fear. She looked for all the world like a princess on her way to a dragon.

"Well, now, and here she is," announced Mick, relieved to see his daughter at last, for he had found nothing else to say to Flynn, who seemed to feel no need to initiate conversation. Mick rose from his chair and indicated to his daughter to sit down. She assumed the edge of the seat, hands in her lap, studying the man opposite her with an increasingly fearless intensity. Jack glanced at her briefly, barely raising his eyes to her face.

"Well," he muttered. She said nothing. He focused on the ground, his heart pounding so that he felt dizzy, gripped his cap even tighter. He was far too immersed in his own terrifying ordeal to once consider hers. She watched his nervousness with growing anger. She scowled at his old man's hair and his furiously working raw-shaved jaw, the spreading redness of his throat. Mick saw the gathering fury in his daughter's expression and sought to diffuse the tension.

"Well, here's to ye both – a Happy Christmas!" And he gulped his whiskey. Jack could not return the toast, for all his concentration was spent in keeping his head and neck from trembling. Mick took his stubborn silence for shyness and decided to withdraw. Perhaps if they were left alone, they might talk.

"Maureen, go into the kitchen and help your mother with the dinner. I must go and make sure we have enough logs for tonight. 'Tis cold out there, boy!" And rising, he rubbed his hands together, laid a warning hand on his younger daughter's shoulder, and squeezed it tightly. She shrugged it off roughly. "Pour Jack another drink, there, Caitlin," he instructed before he left the room. "Make sure he feels welcome."

"Why are you doing this?" Each word was enunciated distinctly and carved itself on Jack's fuzzy brain with the knife edge of its contempt. He was shocked and looked at her almost beseechingly for a moment. But the hatred in her face steeled his heart.

"What?" he retorted, gruffly.

"Why are you… marrying me?" she hissed, thrusting her face forward, wanting to intimidate him. He searched his head for answers, but none presented itself, and he seemed to flounder, unable to make sense of the thoughts which shot by him. He looked at her again, embarrassed now; he felt very old. He stood up, felt the energy dissipate with movement, and his head cleared a little.

"I have a farm to run. So have your father. Both of us need… need…" What did he need from her? Good Lord above; he couldn't tell her. She waited. "I need a hand, and he need the money."

"What?" she almost cried out, then lowered her tone again so as not to bring her mother from the kitchen. "So, you want a skivvy and he's willing to sell me into slavery, is that right?" Jack couldn't answer. He paced the room like a beast emerging from the effects of a tranquillizer, sought to make sense through the whiskey and the years of silence and brutality. He wanted to comfort her, was full of the memory of her astonishing beauty on the night she had played the accordion, wanted to tell her how much he hoped she would be his… salvation, but he knew no words to calm or solicit. He struggled like a man in a foreign country. She spoke again. "So, how much is he getting for me, hmm? What am I worth?" He felt her rise from her chair and approach him. He crushed his eyes closed in desperation for a moment, then looked into her face.

"Ask him that."

"Leave me be," she hissed, coming nearer. "Don't make me marry you. You're an old man, for goodness' sake. It's, it's… disgusting!" Jack watched her face contort with contempt, and the fire in her eyes leapt to his, as a flame from one roof to another.

"Don't kid yerself too much, now, missie," he hissed back at her, leaning forward to do so. She was forced to take a step backwards so as not to make physical contact with him. "You're not the be all and end all! You've a strong back and can milk a cow and clean a house and that'll do for me. As far as I'm concerned this is a… transaction, nothing more, so don't be codding yerself about anything, anything… else." Now he was determined to erase from her mind any thought that he wanted her for carnal purposes. He was filled with the righteous indignation of his forty-three years of perfect chastity. "There's nothing… disgusting," he spat the word, imitating her contempt, "about me, let me assure you." He looked at her a moment longer and could tolerate no more. He walked past her, out of the parlour and, finding the back door, threw it open and strode into the dark December afternoon. Mrs Spillane came rushing from the kitchen at the sound of the door slamming shut.

"Where's Jack?" she asked, bewildered.

"He's gone," came the tart reply, "and he will not be coming back." And Caitlin ascended regally to her bedroom.

Back at home, Jack reproached himself in an agony of shame and frustration. What was he doing, what was he doing? He sank to his knees in fervent prayer, begging God to guide him, the Blessed Virgin to soothe him. Finally, he curled his joined hands in a vice-like grip and beat his forehead with them. He would not marry her. To hell with the bargain! He would manage alone. Then he felt the pain in his chest ignite and his lungs seemed to erupt. It had never been so bad. He rolled helplessly on the floor, convulsed in a relentless spasm of pain that gave birth to cough after cough. As he gasped and retched, he put his hand to his mouth. When he took it away, there was blood at the base of his index finger and it ran thickly towards his palm. He contemplated it in wonder, then panic seized him again. What was wrong with him? But even as he asked, he knew it could be nothing other than tuberculosis. When Jack eventually rose to his feet, it was with one thought on his mind. He would take Caitlin Spillane to the altar, and soon. She was now the only chance he had of making sense of anything he had ever done or believed.

CHAPTER EIGHT

Three days after Christmas, just after Jack had finished eating his lunch and was having a cup of tea in his kitchen, there was a knock on the door.

"Yes!" he shouted, getting to his feet and glowering at the door. The letter from the Environment Department had arrived before Christmas, telling him an appointed vet would be arriving on this day.

"Mr Flynn?" the vet greeted him, letting himself in. "I'm glad to find you in. Michael Brennan, Bord na Bainne vet. I believe you're expecting me?" Jack said nothing but eyed the sergeant standing behind the vet. The sergeant coughed into a fist.

"Well, Jack," he said. The two had gone to school together. The vet explained the gard's presence.

"Sergeant Locke is required by law to accompany me. The eradication of TB from herds is official business, Mr Flynn. May I?" Jack watched the two men approach the kitchen table and the vet put his briefcase on it. Jack did not like the big sergeant in his kitchen, the shiny buttons on his uniform and the way he squared his shoulders. He knew why he was there all right. Many a farmer could not tolerate the enforced destruction of his cattle; the law man was there primarily to protect the vet. In this role, Locke was an antagonism to Flynn before the results of the tests were made known to him.

The vet delved into his briefcase for papers. "I'll get straight to the point." Jack still said nothing. "Four of your cows are tubercular and must be destroyed immediately. The rest must be re-tested before you get the all clear. I'm sorry." Jack muttered something incomprehensible and sat down heavily again. When he did not accept the test results the vet was handing to him, the vet placed the papers on the table. "Have you anyone to help you with this – rounding them up and… disposing of them afterwards?" Jack shook his head.

The vet saw the sadness beneath Jack's features. As both a veterinarian and a man, he could not remain stoical in these circumstances, although he had served such notices many times. And he never underestimated the impact such news had on these hardworking men, whose herds were their lives. "Are your cattle insured against TB, Mr Flynn?" he asked kindly. Jack sighed heavily and nodded. The market value compensation for each cow he would receive, though, would hardly make up for the backbreaking, heart-wrenching business of milking his herd of twelve cows twice a day for three weeks, the loss of the calves the four tubercular cows were carrying, the untold gallons of milk he had watched run into the drain and would continue to watch run into the drain until he got the "all clear"; the loss of revenue that the sudden destruction of a third of his milking herd would mean, and the feed he had lavished on the four pregnant, infected cows to keep them well nourished. And then there was the genuine grief at having to destroy animals he cared for.

The cows were all grazing peacefully as the three men approached the first field. It was a crisp fine day, though the sun was indistinct in the pale sky. Some animals lifted their heads to inspect the men as they came through the gate, and their ears moved back and forward as if they were trying to make sense of the departure from routine. It was not milking time. The vet had a clipboard, attached to which was a piece of paper bearing the typed ear tag numbers of the diseased cows. Jack carried a large can of kerosene, as instructed by the vet. Jack moved among his cows, soothing them, stroking their hides as he passed them, keeping them as calm as possible. Some became skittish and lunged away from the herd but then trotted back. Mainly, though, they were compliant, for they knew Jack and had no reason to fear him. He quickly identified the infected cows, slipping a rope halter over one near to him, while pointing out another for the vet to rope.

In about fifteen minutes the four cows had been led away from the herd and taken through a gate at the bottom of the field into a separate, fallow field. Here they were tied to a fence.

"I suggest you bring one animal at a time to me," he said. "I'll stand over there, away from the fence or any trees. When it's done, you'll need to burn them. Have you the kerosene?"

Jack pointed to the can where it rested against the fence.

"Right. I'll need to see the fire set before I leave. Let's get this over and done with, shall we?" And he reached out, gently squeezed Jack's right upper arm, walked away, and took up position. "OK," shouted the vet, having loaded his gun and reached a suitable spot for the slaughter. "Let's have the first one." Jack untied the first heifer and led her towards the vet. The dull report of the gun at such close range was even more shocking than he had anticipated. The cow's legs gave way and she crashed to the ground, tongue lolling. He had some trouble leading the second cow after that. She fought him, eyes rolling, chucking her head back repeatedly. The scent of blood, the sharp report of the gun, the tension and unease of the man leading her, as well as the irregularity of the whole proceeding, was frightening her.

"Come on, there, girl; come on, now," said Flynn, coaxing the heifer gently. His hand trembled on the lead rope. The sense that he was betraying the animal was overwhelming. At last, it was done. The four cows lay in variously grotesque positions close to or even partially on top of each other. The grass beneath and around them was slippery with their blood. The vet looked sombre and pale. He put the safety catch on his gun and replaced it in a holster he had tied around his waist.

"Get the kerosene, Mr Flynn," he instructed softly. Jack fetched the fuel. "Now, douse them all well and as evenly as you can." Sergeant Locke had walked back to the road and leaned on the gate of the first field. This was a sorry business. He had no desire to witness it at close range. Jack poured the kerosene over his cows and tried to ignore the small movements beneath their hides as their calves kicked. Then, hand shaking so that it was difficult to do – and it took a few attempts – he struck a match and let it fall, then ran backwards quickly as the kerosene ignited. Within seconds, the fire was an inferno. The men watched it consume the cattle for a moment, and then the vet said, "I need blood samples from the remaining cows. Can you bring them to the milking parlour?" Jack had not spoken a word since the slaughter began and still, without answer, he strode away from the vet, pushed open the gate between the fields, and began herding his remaining cows towards the road.

The vet walked with the sergeant. Jack, weary past expression, drove his cows ahead of them. His chest was threatening to erupt in a coughing fit and he was glad at how fast the day was darkening so no one would see the blood he coughed up. He quickly pulled a huge handkerchief from his pocket in readiness. The horror of leading his cows to such wasteful slaughter and the death throes of their calves had affected him terribly. The gunshots had brought back to sharp relief memories of a night over twenty years ago, when he and several other men in a Tipperary flying column had ambushed a gardai and Black and Tan barracks, firing bullets into the darkness where men lay sleeping and unable to defend themselves.

Once in the milking parlour the cows went to their stalls and waited to be milked. The four empty stalls were recriminations. As he turned the handle of a crude generator the milking parlour was lit with unsteady, dim light, created by huge batteries at a few points on shelves along two walls. He started to cough and cough as he turned the handle, covering his mouth as best he could with his free hand, but at last he had to stop turning and lean against the milking parlour wall. The vet looked towards Jack intermittently as he drew blood from a cow's neck, withdrew the syringe, and squirted the blood into a sample bottle. As he pulled a pen from behind his ear and wrote the ear tag number on the bottle label, he shouted over the noise of the generator and the lowing cows, "You will need to get yourself checked, Mr Flynn. Have you had that cough for long?"

Jack pushed himself away from the wall and turned towards the vet, making a dismissive, waving gesture. The sergeant, who had been leaning against a wall in the parlour, stepped outside. When at last he could speak, Jack made a monumental effort to breathe evenly, ignore the pain. He stuffed his filthy handkerchief deeply into his pocket.

"No, no," he said, "'tis the kerosene and the smoke – and I've had a bit of flu, like."

"Nonetheless," insisted the vet, "please see a doctor, Mr Flynn. Can't be too careful. There's a high chance you've been drinking tubercular milk."

Sergeant Locke said he should be getting off, if that was OK. Nodding, the vet thanked him for his help. Of all the duties he had to perform as a Tipperary town police officer, the Bord na Bainne official business was the worst. It was boring, upsetting, and very possibly hazardous to health. He wasn't sure how you caught TB but he was taking no chances. The vet smiled to himself as he dropped a used hypodermic syringe into a tin, removed another from a sterile package, attached a new needle, and inserted it into another cow's neck. The chances of bovine TB contamination other than by repeated ingestion of infected milk or frequent intimate contact with a diseased person were minimal, and in all his years of practice, he had never heard of a vet contracting TB by testing for it or associating with farmers. But he had no more need of the gard.

Back in the kitchen, Jack signed papers. The vet explained that the test results for the blood he had just taken would be through in two weeks' time. Provided the remaining animals were now infection free, he would have to come back and re-test the cows in two months' time. If they were still free of infection, then the herd would get its TB free status back and Jack could start selling milk to the dairy again. If, however, any more became infected, Jack might like to consider slaughtering all eight remaining cows and starting again, rather than waiting for re-test after re-test, milking twice a day for no income, and bringing calves to birth which would immediately be destroyed.

For a less well-off farmer, such news might have spelt ruin. But for Jack, the only child of a single man and single himself till now, he had enough saved to cushion him from this blow. If need be, he would slaughter his cows and use the compensation to buy another herd. In the meantime, he would manage. The five hundred pounds he had promised Spillane, however, now seemed a great deal of money. He would need to take urgent stock of his assets if he was going to keep Caitlin Spillane.

Donal Kelly returned to Cashmel a few days after Christmas 1941. Reinstalled in his new digs above O'Hallorahan's bar, he was glad to be away from the harsh life of his father's farm and it was a luxury he never failed to appreciate, waking in clean sheets at eight o'clock each morning. Particularly decadent was New Year's Day. He was so tired from dancing and carousing into the small hours and so hung-over that he had slept in till ten o'clock, awakened by Molly's banging and clattering of glasses as she prepared to open the bar.

"Well," she said, blowing a stray curl out of her eyes and pausing in her rolling of an ale barrel to its position beneath a pump. "The dead arose and appeared to many!"

"Stop," said Donal. "I've never slept as long in my life." He looked genuinely ashamed.

"Well, no harm once in a while, eh? And it was great New Year's Eve craic, wasn't it? Give us a hand with this barrel now you're here – it needs to be lifted onto that stool so the hose can reach the pump."

Once the new barrel was set up, the glasses and tankards arranged on the shelves behind the bar, Molly went into the kitchen and filled the kettle, shouting back to Donal as she did so that if he wanted breakfast he could get it himself. There was plenty of bread and jam in; she had cooked for her husband before he left for the depot in Cashmel and she was not going to cook again. But Donal wasn't listening to her. He was reading with mounting fury an article in that morning's paper, which Desmond Corcoran had left on the bar for whoever might want it when the pub opened.

In a column towards the bottom right, on the front page, was a report that de Valera had issued an Emergency Powers Order, effective thirtieth of December 1941. This allowed, even retrospectively, that a military court had the power to discard the ordinary laws of evidence binding a civil court, which prevented retrial on previously submitted but rescinded evidence and "if a statement was made voluntarily, lawfully… then at any stage of the trial the prosecution may read such a statement as evidence".

"No!" shouted Donal. "He can't do that!"

"What's that?" shouted Molly from the kitchen, turning off a tap so she could hear him. When there was no answer, she came through to the bar, wiping her hands on a tea towel. Seeing Donal white with fury and gripping the paper before his face, she frowned in concern. "What's the matter, Donal?"

"De Valera! That…" Remembering his host, he tempered his language. He looked at Molly with such passion, she feared he would cry.

"What's he done? What?"

"He's passed some…" Donal struggled to articulate concisely the effect of the Order and get her to understand its obvious implications for George Plant. "Here," he said, passing her the paper and stabbing the article with a forefinger. "Read it, Molly." He jumped from his bar stool and swept past her then up the stairs to his room, grabbed his coat from a hook on the back of the door, and immediately turned around and down the stairs again, two at a time. In the bar, Molly was still trying to read the article and work out why Donal was quite so moved as he flew past her, drew the bolt on the outside door, and flung it open. He was gone before she could comprehend anything much.

Joseph Morgan and Donal had become friends of sorts, and once or twice on a Sunday afternoon, after a lunchtime pint, Donal had walked into town with Joe as far as the latter's house, then on into the countryside outside Cashmel. Donal still missed the fresh air and tranquillity of open land, and the freedom he enjoyed now that he was not confined by college walls and duties meant he could walk for miles whenever the weather permitted. Now, he ran through the streets of Cashmel to the small house on the town's outskirts, where Joe Morgan lived alone. Beyond the huddle of terraced houses on Joe's road, the only source of light or warmth apart from the sun was kerosene and batteries, but Joe's house was connected to the town's electricity grid. As the older man opened his front door, yellow electric light in a dingy hallway made the vapid January morning seem vibrant and healthy by comparison. Somewhere in the house, a radio broadcast a man's voice, sententious and grave in effect, and cigarette smoke groped for release at the open door.

"Donal!" Joe was not unpleasantly surprised to see the young man on his doorstep.

"Can I come in, Joe?"

Morgan stood aside and Donal noted with private amusement the big man's shabby slippers and the diamond patterns on his socks.

"What's the matter?" asked Joe, noting Donal's agitation.

"Have you seen today's paper?"

"I have."

"Well, what do you think?"

"Of what, precisely?" Joe was suspicious of Donal's sudden

political fervour but the look in his eye was more interested than aggressive.

"Of de Valera's Emergency Powers Order!" shouted Donal. "Sure he's going to use it to nail Plant and Davern and Walsh, isn't he?"

Joe stared at Donal – the way he bit his lip and how his chest heaved with emotion. He had to be certain, though.

"What's it to you?"

"What?" Donal's tone was incredulous. He ran both hands through his hair, half turned as if looking for something in the room, then looked back at Joe, almost desperately. "What do you mean, Joe? Don't you care? I thought you of all people would care! I thought you..." When still Joe stared at him, unmoving, Donal made a noise which indicated his incredulity. Shaking his head, he said simply, "I thought it was a big deal; I thought you would, too."

At last Joe spoke. "It is – and I do. Come into the kitchen. I have it on the radio." As they entered the dingy kitchen an announcement was being read by the man whose voice Donal had heard earlier. Joe raised his hand as if anticipating an interruption by Donal:

... will give military courts the jurisdiction under the Order, amending the 1939 Emergency Powers Act, and enables a military court to reconsider trial evidence – even retrospectively – if it believes such action is justified in the defence of Ireland's sovereignty. The new order, stated President de Valera, is constitutional under Article 28:3:3 which grants the state special powers "in time of war or armed rebellion". President de Valera added that the rejection of a Habeas Corpus defence by George Plant's legal team is also

constitutional, according to Article 40:4:5,
which provides that a military court may
override a Habeas Corpus defence in "a state of
war or military rebellion", where the release of a
prisoner might endanger the state. He reminded
the Dail of the statement he made when suing
for America's support in the establishment of
a Free State, following World War I, that the
sovereign Irish Republic was founded in 1919
"… not by poison gas and bombing planes and
liquid fire and tanks and all the implements of
modern warfare, but functioning by the will of
the people…"

"How is this justice?" sneered Donal. "Sure, when was disregard of the double jeopardy defence justice in any democratic nation, can you tell me? Dress it up how you like." Shaking his head, Joe looked sadly into Donal's earnest and intelligent face. He was struck by its youth and the passion in his eyes. He had seen it many times and long ago, most often in a mirror.

"De Valera is fierce clever, you know," he said slowly. "A mathematician, like yourself." Donal frowned and shrugged at the extraneous nature of the comment; he knew that. "He knows fine well what he's doing. He will stop at nothing to get rid of the IRA and keep Ireland neutral in this war – even if it means temporary martial law. He's prepared to go that far, believe me."

"How do you know, Joe?" asked Donal, then wondered if the question were insulting, assuming as it did that Joe must be uneducated. He coloured, stammered something like an apology.

"No offence taken," said Joe. "I know how I seem – one of the local lads, cap and a pint? And I am, true enough. But I wasn't always a warehouse supervisor in Cashmel. Sit down." Joe indicated a chair at his kitchen table. He sat down with

Donal, smiled at him. "I had a good education – like yourself. But I got involved in politics, read Marx on my own terms – not filtered by academics with Catholic agendas. I hooked up with some anti-treaty fellas in the twenties…" Here he paused, looked meaningfully at Donal, and continued, "De Valera was on the right side, then, boy." Donal did not respond, swallowed hard. "Have a cup of tea." Joe got up, filled and plugged in an electric kettle, then reached for a packet of cigarettes, lit one, and inhaled deeply. He leaned against the sink while he waited for the kettle to boil, crossed one leg in front of the other and began to outline a political career spanning almost two decades, at which Donal was astounded.

"When Dev first came to power in 1918, he was President of Sinn Fein, not Fianna Fail. The IRA was the official army of the Republic, ratified by the first Dail in 1919, and Michael Collins was Minister for Finance. They were my heroes, boy!" Joe's face lit with fond remembrance, his tone buoyant. His words and thoughts came fluently, astonishingly at odds with the laconic, wary persona he presented nightly at O'Hallorahan's bar. "When Dev went to America in 1919 to whip up USA support and recognition for a free and democratic Ireland, I was right behind him – though I was just a kid of eighteen or so." He smiled at Donal, continuing, "In a way, I followed him – literally, I think – sort of retraced his steps almost in a pilgrimage, once I'd found a way to get to America a few years later."

"You were in America? I'd love to go to America," interrupted Donal. "What did you do out there, Joe?"

"Well… I'm getting there… The main reason I left was things got… sticky here in the twenties – Collins was assassinated." He paused again, looking down. "When Collins signed that treaty, boy, I tell you…" The kettle boiled and Joe spooned tea into a pot, poured on the boiling water, replaced the teapot lid. "It cannot be denied that there were plenty at the time who said Michael Collins' signing of that treaty with England was a ruse, a means of lulling the English into a false sense of security – and of getting weapons – but how could you tell? To us, it looked like betrayal of de Valera and everything we had fought for…" Joe trailed off, seemingly lost in sadness.

"Weapons?" Donal was incredulous.

"What?"

"You said the English gave Collins weapons?"

"Yes indeed," answered Joe, pouring tea into two mugs, adding milk, placing a mug of tea before Donal, and indicating the sugar bowl in which a teaspoon stood upright. "The British trusted Collins, feared de Valera. They gave guns and ammunition to Collins so he could defend the Irish Free State against Dev and the IRA. There's irony for you now, eh?" But Joe wasn't smiling. He looked angry.

"Did you meet Collins, Joe?" Donal's question was met with a slight frown and knitting of brows. Joe sighed, and as he did so, he pulled out a chair opposite Donal and sat down at the table.

"I did. Loads of us knew him. Sure I was hanging around with fellas who were active from sixteen, in flying columns. Michael Collins, Sean Treacy, Dan Breen trained many a column in Tipperary." He paused again, sipped his tea, and continued, "Breen and Treacy were Tipperary boys, as you know. I knew them fairly well – speaking terms, like. And Collins was often this way. That was why it was such an almighty shock when he signed that bloody treaty pledging allegiance to England! It was only later – too much later – that we found out he was plotting all the while to turn their own guns against them."

"What?"

"It turned out that a few months before he was shot, Collins had ordered the IRA to kidnap a load of Northern Protestants. The lads kept about forty of them in safe houses in the South for ages – as hostages, like. Then there was a load of cross-border raids and attacks on the USC."

"USC?"

"Ulster Special Constabulary. There were fierce riots up North and about thirty people killed in the crossfire – many of our own. But it turns out that about forty USC were killed by the IRA – on Collins' orders!"

"So why was he shot?" Donal was shocked almost past belief at what he was hearing; had Collins really played such a dangerous double bluff of both Dail and British government?

"Because it was not – or could not be – generally known that a Dail minister and pledger of allegiance to the British – the man who had agreed to the partition of Ireland into North and South – was still an IRA activist and giving orders to the IRA!" Joe exclaimed, exasperated, his hands flailing as he spoke. Donal was undeterred by Joe's agitated tone. His hunger for a first-hand account of his country's recent political history was more compelling than any fear he had of possible rebuke.

"Did de Valera know about this?"

"Now that," said Joe, half smiling at Donal's fearlessness and adjusting his tone, "is the sixty-four thousand dollar question. One thing is for sure: when Dev got back from America in 1920, Collins was a lot more powerful – and dangerous – than when he'd left him. And by then, de Valera was talking of constitutional revision and freedom through democracy and negotiation. Looking back, it was clear Dev was turning soft."

"Who shot Collins, do you think, Joe?" Here, there was a very long pause. Joe sipped his tea and seemed to contemplate the table.

"Who indeed," he snapped, but then added, "That's when I went to America. I knew a chap who wanted someone to courier a package personally to a businessman in New York, no questions, and I grabbed my opportunity. The package fitted nicely in the lining of my bag. I never knew what it was. I never took my eyes off that bag the whole journey, boy – it was my pillow at night time. When I got off that ship I had four pounds and ten shillings in my pocket and the name and address of the businessman. The man got me a job as a bellhop in a smallish hotel on Seventh Avenue – I thought I was the bee's knees! And the place was full of Irish lads. The craic was something else, boy." Donal smiled widely, fascinated by this man to whom he had been instinctively drawn, whom he had watched with curiosity night after night in O'Hallorahan's bar, sipping his pint and measuring the world's revolutions with quiet, grey eyes.

"I joined a union," Joe went on. "I wasn't much older than you are now. We thought we could change the world, defeat capitalism, give the working man back his dignity... then the slump. Wall Street crashed. There's nothing philosophical about starvation – you can lose all the metaphorical chains you want, but dropping hunger is not an act of will." Joe sighed, closed his eyes, and rubbed his forehead for a moment.

"What happened?"

"I lost my job. The hotel closed down. Intellect and youth were small recompense for a rumbling belly. And I half froze to death in the winter of 1930. I worked my passage to England on a liner, sharing a tiny cabin with three other fellas below decks, with a food ration that would insult a sparrow. We stole what we could from the leftovers of the great and glamorous above decks. Nothing really changes, eh?"

"And you came back here? To Cashmel?"

"Eventually. I worked for a while in London, on building sites, but times were almost as hard as they were in New York, and the construction industry ground to a virtual halt. I came home via Dublin. Worked there awhile." Joe seemed to have come back to the present and a more usually guarded evasiveness. He looked directly at Donal. "When de Valera was elected President of Ireland in January 1932, he wasn't happier than I was – even though by then he was leading Fianna Fail and had relegated Sinn Fein to the Opposition."

"And now?" Donal was fascinated to discover Joe's feelings towards de Valera on this New Year's Day, ten years on. As

CHAPTER EIGHT

Prime Minister he had imprisoned thousands of IRA men in the Curragh and executed many, and was now squaring up to add Plant to the list.

"How far do you want to be trusted?" Joe's earnestness, the sudden alteration in his demeanour, and the challenge in his eyes as they held Donal's, took the younger man off guard.

"What do you mean?" faltered Donal.

"Exactly what I say." Joe's eyes were steely. The monotonous drone of the news announcer had been replaced by orchestrated traditional music; a lurching jig on strings filled the silence. "You came here hot and bothered about de Valera. How hot and bothered are you, is the question? How far might you go to do something about it, if you had the chance?" Donal did not shrink from Joe's steely scrutiny. He nodded briefly. "Are you sure?" Donal nodded again. Joe extended his right hand, still not taking his eyes from Donal's. Donal lifted his hand and the two men were joined in a firm handshake. "Right, so," Joe pronounced. "Right so."

CHAPTER NINE

On Sunday the third of January 1944, Caitlin refused to go to mass and Mick Spillane did not put up much of a fight, for he feared a scene if anyone tried to speak with her about the forthcoming wedding or if there were an awkward encounter with Flynn. He had not had an opportunity to speak with Flynn since Christmas Day and was half afraid to do so, given how Caitlin had treated him. He was seriously concerned that the deal would now be off and Jack would not want his rude and disobedient daughter. And so, as on Sundays gone by, Mick Spillane waited nervously outside the church for Jack to emerge after mass. It was raining and cold. Most pulled coats over their heads and ran for their carts or hastened on foot to their homes in the village. Maureen and Mrs Spillane lurked just inside the church doors and stood close together for warmth. Mick's cap was small protection from the heavy rain and he plunged his hands into his trouser pockets, hunched his shoulders as he paced outside the church. He did not want his wife or daughter to hear what transpired between himself and Flynn – whatever its nature.

"How're you, Jack?" Mick raised his voice above the rain as he walked quickly towards his neighbour when the latter emerged from the narthex. Jack turned, eyed Spillane with more weariness than irritation and stopped walking. "I wasn't sure now, how things stood... you know... with last week and all," Spillane said blinking away drops from his cap peak. He was shocked at how pale Jack was and how the shadows under his eyes made them look sunken.

"They are as they were, Spillane." Jack spoke quietly so that Mick had to use his powers of deduction as much as his hearing to get the sense of what he'd said.

"So, it's still on for Saturday?"

Jack nodded, keeping his mouth tightly closed to suppress a couple of insistent coughs. He had to get home, out of this rain. Spillane looked relieved for a moment, then spoke again.

"That's great, Jack, great," he said. "I hear you had to slaughter a few cows above?" Mick squinted through the rain at Jack's face with an expression he hoped was sympathetic, then carried on as Jack began to turn away from him. "Only... only, a thing like that could knock a man's finances, now... change things."

"It changes nothing, Spillane."

"Grand, grand." Mick nodded, smiled. "The wedding's at nine o'clock," he added. As Jack began to walk towards his horse, which stood hitched and tethered to a nearby fence, head down against the driving rain, Spillane shouted after him, "See you there, so – nine o'clock."

Jack did not turn. He raised a hand in a gesture which acknowledged the words and, reaching his horse, climbed into the cart. Mrs Spillane and Maureen ran into the rain and urged Mick to hurry home.

When the Spillanes burst through their door to a warm kitchen and the smell of simmering bacon and potatoes, Caitlin was in her room, reading. She put down the book when she heard their voices and then slowly got off the bed, stood up, and waited uncertainly for any sound which might indicate someone was coming upstairs. After a considerable pause and no approaching steps, she moved cautiously to the door and opened it, then headed for the stairs. She had to know if she were really free of this arrangement her father had made to sell her to Jack Flynn. She knew Mick would have spoken with Flynn after mass.

CHAPTER NINE

When they saw her coming down, Maureen and Mrs Spillane nodded and smiled to her but went into the kitchen and busied themselves with the preparation of lunch. There was bound to be another scene. At the foot of the stairs, Caitlin, pale, thin, eyed her father, watching him stamp his feet to dispel surplus rainwater from his clothing and stimulate blood circulation to his feet. He looked at his daughter briefly, threw his cap onto a chair, shook his head, and ran his hands through his unruly hair, blowing out hard.

"It's stinking weather out there today, so it is," he remarked. "I'm frozen!"

"Well?" said Caitlin softly, never taking her eyes from him.

"Well what?"

"You know fine well what I mean," she responded, her heart beating so fast she felt unsteady and gripped the banister rail.

"What did you expect? That your tantrum had ruined everything, is that it? Is that what you're waiting for me to say? Well it did not. You are to be married next Saturday, and that's final."

Caitlin did not answer him. She stared at him levelly for a moment and then turned around and ascended the stairs to her room, closed the door quietly. Mick frowned to himself in confusion and shrugged. Perhaps she had finally accepted things.

"Is the dinner ready?" he shouted to his wife. "I'm ravenous."

"Is Caitlin coming down for dinner?" enquired Mrs Spillane timidly, as her husband entered the kitchen.

"Leave her be," he said. "Sure she'll hardly starve."

Mrs Spillane drained the potatoes of water, closed her eyes, and sighed. She wondered if Caitlin would do just that rather than as she was told.

When Jack got home from mass he had no appetite. He had a temperature and his health had not been helped by the rigours of milking. Though he did not have to rise quite so early these days,

139

for the dairyman did not call on schedule any more to pick up his churns, he still had to get his animals to the milking parlour by eight o'clock at the latest or they would be uncomfortable, and the last thing he needed on top of the TB crisis was an outbreak of mastitis in the herd. By the end of February, though, the drudgery of milking would cease, either because his cows were within a couple of months of calving or because he would have them slaughtered.

He reached out a trembling hand for his mug of tea. He had to use both hands to lift it steadily to his mouth, and it hurt his rheumatic fingers to straighten them on cold, rainy days like this. Flynn reflected that no matter the cause, the end of milking for that year would be a blessed relief. The rain fell with increased ferocity, slamming against the windows as if it were angry they were there. Jack shivered feverously and sipped his strong, sweet tea. He could not summon feeling at the thought that by the same time next Sunday, he would be married. The notion was as hard to grasp as the certainty that one day, he would be dead.

On the twelfth of February 1942, Plant, Walsh and Davern were retried before a military court for the murder of Michael Devereux. On the twenty-fourth of February, Walsh's and Davern's previously withdrawn statements were readmitted and stood as evidence that Devereux had been drawn deliberately into a web of drama and deceit enabled by a whole cast of players. They had pretended to him that he was a suspect for the murder of a senior IRA officer – no less than the commanding officer of Devereux's own Wexford IRA battalion, Thomas Cullimore. The IRA Chief of Staff Officer himself, Stephen Hayes, gave the order – it was alleged – for Devereux to be assassinated. Plant had persuaded Devereux that he needed to abandon his wife and child in Wexford, drive through the night to an IRA safe house in Tipperary, and lie low to avoid being arrested for Cullimore's "death". Plant and Walsh and Davern pretended all the while to be Devereux's friends, but after three days of intimate contact,

Plant shot Devereux within minutes of suddenly accusing him of treachery. He used a gun borrowed for the purpose from a man in Carrick-on-Suir, to whom Davern returned it once Devereux's body was hidden.

It was heard again how Devereux had pleaded for his life, protesting vehemently that if they just gave him time, he could prove he was innocent of the charge that he had revealed the whereabouts of IRA weapons to the gardai. But he was given no opportunity to defend himself. His young wife and infant child next saw him when his remains were unearthed a year later and removed to Wexford for burial.

Davern was tricked into revealing the location of Devereux's body by a garda detective working under cover, a Sergeant Dennis O'Brien. On the twenty-seventh of February 1942, the military court reached its decision after just forty-five minutes of deliberation. All three men – Walsh, Davern, and Plant – were condemned to death.

The atmosphere in O'Hallorahan's bar was muted and grim when the verdicts reached the radios and newspapers of Cashmel. Outside the streets were icy, and remnants of snow froze in the gutters and along the edges of the road. There was no moon, as if she were sensitive to the mood which hung over the town, and Cashmel was lost in darkness. Even here, there was a strict curfew forbidding the lighting of streets or the appearance of light from houses, as German planes aiming for Northern Ireland or England had been known to bomb Eire by mistake. The Luftwaffe killed thirty-four people in Dublin following one such error. Joe Morgan, Donal, John Tuohy, Pat Moran, and Michael Flaherty sat around a table drinking their ale, apparently mesmerized by the roaring fire, which Molly fed with turf briquettes and logs.

After a long silence, Tuohy spoke. "'Tis a disgrace of the highest order, so it is, to try a man twice. Sure what the hell is de Valera thinking?"

"De Valera knows exactly what he's doing," replied Joe Morgan. "Not even the supreme court can object to a Government Order under Dev's Emergency legislation. That trumps case law and all the niceties of jurisprudence. There wasn't a thing the defence could do."

"I cannot understand that." Donal spoke ruminatively, shaking his head slowly, not taking his eyes from the fire. "How can hundreds of years of case law be overturned in a split second? Sure I've a scholarship to study law at Cork University starting next September. I don't think I'll bother! What's the point?" He looked away from the fire and turned to Joe as if seeking agreement in principle. Joe sighed, sipped his beer, replaced his tankard on the table, and contemplated it for a few seconds.

"It is a terrible but true thing that to conform to the constitutional legislation of this so-called Free State today, is to betray natural justice. This has never been so clear as it is this night." He looked meaningfully at Donal, held his gaze for a moment, then turned to the fire again.

When Donal returned to contemplation of the flames, he was greatly troubled. His comments regarding his scholarship and its futility had not been in earnest. For the first time, he felt the full weight of his late apprenticeship to a life in shadows.

"Mammy! Mammy, come quick – Caitlin is gone!"

Maureen's voice was shrill with alarm. Both Mrs Spillane and Mick raced for the stairs, she ceding to him reluctantly where they met at the bottom, and when they reached the girls' bedroom, it was indeed apparent that Caitlin had taken her leave of the house, through the bedroom window. Clothes and personal effects were thrown haphazardly on the floor and across the bed in her haste to pack for a journey they could only guess at.

The sash window stood open and Mick leaned out of it, cursing roundly and loudly as he strained to see past the rain and gathering afternoon darkness. The road was just visible across the small yard from this vantage point but there was no sign of Caitlin. She had obviously hung from the ledge then dropped the ten feet or so to the ground and had been sufficiently uninjured to get away. And so it was that – having just got dry and warm before the range, having settled down with a pipe and a full belly to read the Sunday paper – Mick Spillane put on his damp coat and his boots and made for the barn.

He had tethered his horse there and given him hay rather than send him out into the relentless rain. The cart stood dripping, resting on its shafts. The horse stopped munching hay, strands protruding from each side of its mouth, and eyed the man suspiciously. His ears went back as it seemed his worst fears were confirmed and the man began roughly throwing on his driving harness, pushing him backwards between the shafts and fumbling with the still damp leather harness to hitch him. And then Spillane was urging the horse out of the barn and across the yard and slapping his rump with the reins to make him canter up the road, spraying mud and water in all directions, towards the nearest railway station at Limerick Junction. Here, he assumed, Caitlin was heading. She had banked on it.

About two miles up the road in the opposite direction was Maher's farm. Maher and his family were resting after their Sunday meal and enjoying the luxury of being able to relax for a few hours in the long week. By contrast, Caitlin was very busy in their barn, hitching their pony to the small trap they used for shopping trips. She wasn't sure about her immediate destination other than she intended to drive Maher's pony and trap as far away from Dunane as it was reasonable and humane to ask the beast to travel.

The rain suddenly reduced in ferocity to a sullen drumming on the pony's hide and Caitlin no longer had to squint to see the road. Maher's silver grey pony trotted and cantered smartly till they came to a village called Golden, around seven miles or so from Dunane. Caitlin wore woollen gloves but they were sodden and her hands were cold. The January afternoon was dark, and as the rain abated, the evening chill announced itself in a stiff breeze which lifted the pony's mane and stung Caitlin's cheeks. They adopted a more leisurely gait through the almost deserted village. A woman opened a door briefly and put out a cat, revealing for a moment a warm, yellow glow from the open fire and lamplight in her front room. There was a small bar at the far end of the main street, and although its windows were blacked out Caitlin could hear strains of accordion music and an indistinct fuddle of combined voices as she passed it by. All else was silence except for the hooves of the pony and the whir and occasional squeak of the buggy wheels.

George Plant was executed in Portlaoise jail on the fifth of March 1942. Davern's and Walsh's sentences were commuted to imprisonment. Stephen Hayes, IRA defector to the forces of the Free State, following two months of torture by his own men, was sentenced to five years' penal servitude by the Special Criminal Court.

"Well, he must have spilled his guts, boy," remarked Joe darkly on a sullen early summer evening, soon after Hayes's sentence was made public. Donal and he were in his kitchen, a frequent meeting place when privacy was of the essence. "Sure, given what he did… five years?"

A clock ticked dully on the wall above the sink as the shadows lengthened and the sun suddenly lost its grip on the horizon and sank. Joe got up from his stool, pulled down the blackout blinds, and pressed the light switch. A sickly orange bar of light was roused to flickering service, managing full power after two minutes or so.

"De Valera executed a couple of our lads in 1940 for colluding with Germany – lads working with Hayes – Harte and McGrath, IRA leaders."

"Hayes was colluding with Germany?"

Joe nodded, raised his eyebrows, and looked at Donal directly. Then, reaching out to an ashtray as he exhaled smoke, he jabbed the butt of his cigarette into it to extinguish it.

"We had absolutely no chance of overthrowing the Free State, let alone England, on our own," Joe retorted as if Donal had suggested otherwise. "How the hell were we supposed to arm ourselves when Dev was doing a vault face and beginning to clamp down on us the way he did?"

"We?" said Donal. "You helped Hayes?"

"By 1940," said Joe more quietly, "Dev was every bit the statesman, wanted no more truck with the IRA – was determined to put behind him once and for all his old associations, and the rhetoric was high, boy. 'Lay down your arms,' he was saying in the Dail. 'Put away those means of striving for freedom which allow the English to name you terrorists and invite their scorn.'" Joe imitated de Valera's sententious, nasal voice and tone and Donal laughed. "Or words to that effect," finished Joe, half smiling. Then his smile died. "I had started to hate him."

There was a long silence. "You're shocked about the Germany thing. I don't blame you. But those of us who disapproved of the more right-wing leanings of our comrades had a choice. We could split – sabotaging any small chance the IRA had of a successful military coup in Ireland – or we could wait until victory was ours by any means, straighten out the politics afterwards."

"But," Donal strove for words to phrase his incredulity. "But... Hitler, Joe?"

Joe sighed heavily. It was almost as if he hardly knew how or lacked the energy to articulate the meandering apologetics which had resulted in the alliance of a Communist IRA faction with the policies and actions of their Fascist brothers. He plumped for defensive forthrightness. "Donal, the IRA has always been willing to whore itself out to any enemy of England if it gains us a foothold. And is that so terrible? It was James Connolly himself – a great man and a Marxist – who said, 'England's difficulty is

Ireland's opportunity.' Sure, even Wolfe Tone joined the French army to help Napoleon against the British and get them out of Ireland." Joe was more animated now, summoning the rhetoric he had once delivered in small, smoky rooms in Dublin to placate outraged Republican Communists when they discovered that Sean Russell, the IRA Chief of Staff in 1940, had gone to Berlin to train with Hitler's Abwehr in the deployment of explosives.

"Sure, Roger Casement went to Berlin in 1914 to get help with establishing the Irish Brigade," went on Joe, but the light in his eyes had died again, inconstant as fealties and the orangey electric bar which lit his kitchen. "Russell's attempt to enlist Hitler's support was just the latest desperate bid by Irish men to rid themselves of the English menace – which even O'Connell called 'the sole and blighting curse of this country'." Donal could not remember much about Daniel O'Connell. "And that was strong stuff from a pacifist, and a patsy of the Catholic Church – like Dev has turned out to be! Sure where did pacifism ever get us? Can you tell me that?" Joe looked challengingly at Donal.

The latter's face was screwed into a frown. He was trying to remember something impressive about Daniel O'Connell. "Didn't O'Connell get the emancipation of Catholics in Ireland?" he ventured, looking uncertainly at Joe "… persuade the British to let Catholics vote and get good jobs and stuff like that? I remember my history teacher called him… what was it… 'The Liberator'. He used to say O'Connell 'singlehandedly delivered the Irish nation of spiritual oppression by the English – and all without shedding a drop of blood'." Pleased he had recalled something useful, Donal was unprepared for the curled lip and derisory stare with which Joe fixed him, just before he ignored him.

"Those of us whose strain of Republicanism runs back through the likes of Pearse and Connolly, to Wolf Tone, deplore Hitler and his stinking Nazism. But the only way to oppose Hitler full on is by hitching ourselves to the British, and that is wholly unacceptable! Sure, even Stalin is in bed with Churchill now," he added bitterly. Joe shook his head, the fervour coming back. "The only way – the only way to gather any sort of meaningful force against the British, Donal, is to remain united – in spite of our own domestic or ideological differences, and then, as I said, we can sort things out – afterwards."

"What, like whether we run to France or Germany or Russia, you mean, when we need help?"

There was an unmistakable menace in Joe's tone which was at odds with the words he said when he spoke again. "Have a cup of tea now, for the road – I won't offer you anything stronger, for we both have an early start." With his back to Donal as he made the tea, Joe continued talking. "Stephen Hayes," he said, pouring boiling water onto tea leaves in a pot, "was a friend of mine."

"What?" Donal's tone was incredulous.

"Yes, indeed. And I'll tell you one thing, Donal." Joe picked up the teapot and agitated it to encourage infusion of tea by the boiling water. "I don't think for a moment that Hayes passed information about IRA activity to the gardai."

Donal was astonished. "So you don't think Hayes betrayed Plant?"

"Not at all."

"How so?"

"I think Hayes gave Plant the order to kill Devereux, all right. But I do not think he told the gardai where our lads were hiding or where the safe houses were or where we were storing arms. Not for one second."

"Then why…"

"Why did the IRA arrest him and torture him?" Donal nodded. "Why indeed. We're all looking for someone to blame, Donal. There are those who think he failed us with the Germans, that he got Harte and McGrath executed." Joe poured milk into two mugs and poured tea onto the milk, then passed a mug to Donal. "The gardai and Dev's Special Forces are getting cleverer.

Sure most of those boys are ex-IRA, like de Valera! They know how we think, how we operate. They don't need IRA top brass informants to give them clues. Hayes was a scapegoat, is all. Who do you blame when everything you believe in starts to go bad, disappear?"

"So," began Donal, taking his tea and placing it on Joe's small, wooden table, "if the IRA hadn't tortured Hayes…"

"Then no one would ever have found out about Plant shooting Devereux. That's right."

"But how can you be sure?"

"I can't be one hundred per cent," admitted Joe, still standing against the sink, folding his arms carefully so as not to spill the mug of tea he held in his hand. "But I'd be willing to bet anything Stephen Hayes was innocent. Sure, think about it – why would he ask Plant to kill Devereux for treachery then betray the IRA himself? He's the leader of the IRA."

"I dunno," responded Donal. "There's many say he was using Devereux as a scapegoat for his own betrayal – blaming him, like."

"The Stephen Hayes I know – the man who led the IRA after Sean Russell died on a U-boat off the coast of Galway – the man I helped devise Plan Kathleen…" He stopped and put his tea down so he could gesticulate to emphasize his words. "Sure, right up to August of 1940, Hayes was meeting with Germans in Dublin to organize an anti-British offensive in the North." Here, Joe paused to let Donal appreciate the full impact of his words. "It is not likely he turned traitor by the time Plant pulled that trigger and killed Devereux – a month later – is it? Think about it."

Donal was trying. He enquired quietly, "What's 'Plan Kathleen'?"

The clock proclaimed it was almost ten o'clock. Donal had a half-mile walk back to his digs at O'Hallorahan's bar. He wanted to go home but he had to know the extent of Morgan's involvement with the IRA. He had to know how binding was the covenant to which he had lately sealed.

"Like I said," answered Joe, picking up his mug once more, "Hayes was working with the Germans. Fifty thousand German troops would arrive by submarine to the Derry coast, attack the British troops, establish a base in the North. We get rid of England, and Germany gets strategic control of Northern ports and a foothold into England." Donal's heart was thudding. He had a headache which had come on suddenly and was quite acute on the right side of his head.

"I take it the plan failed?" he managed, without the slightest attempt at humour.

"It did. Sure there were too many 'if' factors and de Valera is working with the British, without a doubt. He is letting them use Irish ports and harbours along the west coast right up to Derry – and it's pretty obvious the RAF is being allowed to use Irish airspace from Galway to Fermanagh – every day. What chance of a U-boat invasion?" Joe stared at Donal, not a trace of friendship in his expression. "You're wondering how I know all this, eh?" he asked, staring at Donal. "How could Joe Morgan, sitting nights at O'Hallorahan's bar, downing pints with the lads, know all this stuff, eh?"

Donal was actually wondering why he felt entirely powerless to get off his stool, announce his headache, and leave. "De Valera is the traitor here, Donal – not Stephen Hayes," went on Joe, quietly, more certain now that his novice was paying close attention. "And now, there are forty thousand American troops headquartered in Derry! How the hell does that happen in a neutral country, Donal, can you tell me that?" Joe's icy tone and the interrogative with which he had concluded this last utterance were an unmistakable challenge. Could Donal belittle this information in a witty, pat corollary? "Plan Kathleen was Ireland's last hope. It was expedient that we all got behind it. And in the light of Germany's invasion of Russia, it was the right decision." Joe paused, staring at Donal, who remained quiet. He was trying, under the older man's intense scrutiny, to retain a neutral expression. "And now that this... Plant affair..." Joe spat the words and looked away from Donal, something like anxiety crossing his face in the moment before he shifted his gaze to the kitchen floor. "This business with Hayes being tortured and then running to de Valera for help..." Joe looked back at Donal and this time there was a flicker of appeal in his expression, like an SOS signal. "Well, who knows which of us is next, eh?"

When Donal finally left Joe's house and heard the door shut against the still June night, his heart was much heavier than it had been on arrival, for now it shared the burden of a man's secret fear.

CHAPTER TEN

Donal's first IRA assignment had been straightforward enough. When the summer holidays began in mid-June of 1942, Joe got him a job at the warehouse in Cashmel, loading and unloading whatever needed to be transported to wherever it was required, from Monaghan to Bantry. Molly Corcoran's husband, Desmond, often ran errands for the IRA, passing on messages to people who worked on the farms and in the depots to which he hauled his freight. Donal's first job was to ride with Desmond, help him load and unload the freight, but more importantly, deliver a verbal message to a man called Eamonn McGinty who worked in a grain depot in Mullingar. The message was simply, "The dance is on for seven thirty on Saturday night and it's reels not jigs." On no account was Donal to write down the message. Donal had no idea what the message meant and Joe made him repeat it till it was word perfect, emphasizing that the precise order of the words was of vital importance. McGinty pretended he hadn't heard the message, then pulled on his right ear three times to indicate he had. Desmond and Joe bought drinks for Donal that night back at O'Hallorahan's bar, and said he had been initiated into the brotherhood with flying colours. When Donal mentioned later that evening that he should really be back in Golden, helping his father with the farm, Joe and Des exchanged glances and the latter stood up, shook Donal's hand, and said he was off to bed; there was a lorry already loaded with flour and potatoes and he had to be in a warehouse in Cork city by nine the next morning.

When Desmond had gone, Donal explained in detail why it was necessary for him to go home. Last year's calves would have

151

gone to market and this year's would be newly born. Milking would be in full swing again and it was a lot harder when there were new calves around. And then there were the pigs; they would all have farrowed by now and the bainbhs would soon need to be crated up and taken on the cart to market. There was turf to dig and fences to reinforce. And in August, there was the making of hay – backbreaking work. Donal had always been there to help his father from June through to September, the busiest part of the farming year. Joe occasionally nodded in apparent sympathy and laughed at times as Donal expounded on the challenges of farming. When Donal asked what was funny, he remarked that he could not imagine him shovelling manure or feeding pigs, so used was he to seeing him in his suit and shiny shoes. But then Joe got serious and said that he was sorry but it was out of the question that Donal should go home. He had obligations to his country now which overrode those to his father, and indeed would honour his father more in their exercise than if he went home to dig turf.

For the first time since he had associated closely with Joe, Donal became really angry. His colour rose and he took a large gulp of his beer. "You cannot prevent me from going home, Joe!" he said, trying to control his voice so that it did not draw attention to them. "I am not a prisoner here. My father needs me. Isn't it enough that I am away through the rest of the year? All through the winter he milks and feeds the animals on his own. I have two sisters – they work hard but they're at school and they cannot help him with turf digging and hay making like I can. He needs me, Joe. I am going home. I have to." Joe had been sipping his beer, his expression neutral throughout Donal's speech, but when Donal had finished, he put down his tankard and turned to meet the young man's flashing eyes.

The younger man was shocked at how steely and dark Joe's became in the instant they met his. When he spoke, Joe's voice was low and authoritative. "I don't think you fully understand what you have signed up for here, Kelly. Everything else in your life is secondary to the cause. And there is a new countrywide movement in operation – a Northern offensive and you are needed. Dev has locked most of us away and so every man on the ground is an essential soldier. You cannot go home because it is highly likely that next week you will be in Fermanagh." Joe raised a finger to his lips as Donal frowned and leaned forward suddenly, as if he were about to speak. Joe took his cap from the table in front of him and put it on his head, downed his pint, and stood up. "Oh, and it might interest you to buy a paper on Sunday morning, Donal. Good night, now." And just before he left, he put his hand on Donal's shoulder. "You did well today, son. I'm proud of you."

The Sunday papers all shared a front page story: three gardai barracks had been ambushed by IRA terrorists in an apparently synchronized plan at seven thirty on Saturday evening. "The IRA claimed responsibility for the attacks," Donal read, "in an anonymous note, sent to the Garda Siochana Headquarters in Dublin. It alleged the attacks were in reprisal for the execution of George Plant, shot to death in Portlaoise jail on March the fifth, following his conviction for the murder of Michael Devereux. The note," went on the report, "accused the gardai of treachery against their fellow Republicans. The three barracks in Kilkenny, Tipperary, and Dublin were attacked in an operation codenamed 'The Dance'. There were no fatalities but three gardai and an IRA man were seriously injured. The violence followed the Finglas Road shooting in April this year, also attributed to the IRA and in reprisal for Plant's execution."

Donal realized at once that the Thompson machine guns used in the barracks attack outside Dublin had been transported in the sacks of grain on the lorry in which he had travelled with Des Corcoran to Mullingar. He discovered later that if his message had advised of jigs, rather than reels, the guns would have been sticks of gelignite and the operation would have been a different one altogether from that needed to shoot people.

The Sunday press shook in Donal's hands so that he could hardly read the print. He leaned against a wall outside the post office, trying to comprehend that he had played a material part in this event of national importance. Donal folded the paper and began walking back to O'Hallorahan's. The full implications of the errand he had run, in order to be "blooded" into the IRA, hit home. He was a criminal of the first order. In one swift movement, he had metamorphosed from a naïve boy and potential upholder of the Eire Constitution by due process of the law, to an enemy of the state. He was as guilty – by association – of the barracks attacks as the men who had pulled the triggers. If any of those gardai died, he was an accessory to murder. There was no going back now. He would never be a lawyer. He was doomed to live a life in shadows and half-truths. Secrecy would be his refuge for as long as he lived; he would be peeping from it henceforth, a fugitive from both justice and the fear of treachery. He entered his room and lay on his bed, covering his face with both hands. What had he done? What had he allowed Joe Morgan to do to him?

On the day his father suffered a massive heart attack, in April of 1943, Donal was holding a machine gun, a cloth tied across his lower face to conceal his identity. He was on lookout, crouching behind a row of seats in a Belfast cinema, half listening to Hugh McAteer, the new IRA Chief of Staff, as he read aloud the Proclamation of Irish Independence to a surprised and captive audience. The Declaration had originally been read by Patrick Pearse outside the GPO on Sackville Street in Dublin, 1916, and had marked the beginning of Ireland's constitutional independence. McAteer, however, was on the run following a jail break and needed all the backup the illegal IRA could muster, to ensure he was not rearrested during the minutes-long gesture.

CHAPTER TEN

When Donal said again, in Spring 1943, that he wanted to go home to help his father on the farm, there was no objection from his regional battalion officer, Joe Morgan.

Caitlin was very hungry. It was more or less a permanent state these days. She had refused to eat with her family since they had betrayed her, and when the hunger was most acute, she cut herself slices of bread or sawed bits of meat from whatever was left in the press after the others had eaten. Before she had run away, she had had a chance to furnish herself with a little buttered bread, a few bits from the ham, and a couple of the potatoes she had been left to boil while her family was at mass that morning. She wrapped it all in newspaper and put it in her bag. Soon, she would need to eat and think about resting for the night. The question was where and what would she do with Maher's pony when she had finished with him?

It was getting colder and darker by the minute, it seemed. The road out of Golden led to a crossroads. There was a large signpost which pointed in three directions and which Caitlin had to dismount to discern in the half light. Straight ahead to Cashmel for twelve miles, left to Thurles for eighteen miles, and right to Cahir for fourteen miles. All were significant towns with railway stations. But it would take at least two hours with a tired pony to reach any of them, and it was easy to get lost along winding roads in the dark. The reality of what she was doing hit home and she was afraid. Fighting tears but determined she could not go back now, Caitlin remounted the buggy and set off at a trot in the direction of Cashmel. She would stop at the first farm she came to and sneak into their barn for the night. She had already written a note which said "I belong to Pat Maher of Dunane", which she intended to slip under the pony's halter when she left him somewhere he would be safe and quickly found. The difficulty was how to ride across someone's land, or even their yard, in a trap, without being detected.

Half a mile along the Cashmel road, as it led away from Golden, Caitlin came to a small farmhouse. It was close to the road, its yard accessed via a frontage without a gate. The wind was now whipping up into something like a storm and snatches of icy rain slapped into Caitlin's face. As she jumped from the buggy at the side of the road, unhitched the pony from the trap with fingers clumsy in wet wool, Caitlin realized the noisy wind would be a good cover for any hoof falls or sounds of movement which might otherwise betray them on a still Sunday evening.

Once he was unhitched, Caitlin led the pony away from the buggy, which she left dipped forward and resting on its shafts against the hedge. Bag in one hand, cheek strap of the pony harness in the other, Caitlin stole across the yard of the apparently sleeping house, for its windows were all blacked out. Putting her bag down, standing on a piece of trailing harness to prevent the pony from wandering, she lifted the heavy wooden latch to the barn and the door immediately yawned towards her. With some difficulty, and grateful now for the wind which almost snatched the door from her, making the pony start, Caitlin dropped her bag and soothed the animal as she led him around the door to the inky darkness and quiet must of the barn. There was another animal in there – a donkey, for it snorted and brayed in alarm at the intrusion. Caitlin soothed and cajoled the donkey to be still, let go of the pony, and went back for her bag, pulling the barn door closed after her.

As her eyes adjusted she could make out the bulks of the animals. The pony had found the donkey's manger and water and was helping himself. Caitlin could smell mashed beet and she could tell by feel and smell that there was plenty of hay in the manger. The pony would be all right at least. She wished she could remove his harness, but it would be folly to attempt it in this darkness and it was wiser to tether him to something lest he stumble over machinery or some other obstacle in the barn. She followed the harness reins to their ends and groped for the legs of the heavy wooden manger, tied the reins slackly around two of them, and made gingerly for the recesses of the barn and the stooks of hay she could now make out in the gloom. A few times she fell over rows of turf footings but, on reaching the hay, squeezed between a few stooks and pulled from them enough to cover herself. She fumbled in her bag for her food and reflected that at least she would be safe from detection that night. At first light, she would put the note under the pony's headband and set out on foot for Cashmel and the train station. She would hitch and walk the twelve miles. She would buy breakfast in the town and then a ticket to Dublin. She had almost four pounds, saved up from ceilidhs and birthdays and Christmases, for precisely this journey – though she had not thought her escape to Dublin would be so dramatic a flight.

And so it was that early the following morning, on Monday the fourth of January 1944, Donal Kelly's path crossed with that of Caitlin Spillane.

"Jack!" Spillane was banging on Jack's door. It was blowing a gale and pitch dark. Mick had driven to Limerick Junction and back and there was no sign of Caitlin. It was possible she was hiding in a field or a ditch to avoid him as his cart clattered up and down the main Cashmel to Limerick road through Dunane, but if that were the case, then she had not got to the train station and that was the main thing. No one had seen her. There had not been a train to anywhere from Limerick Junction after two o'clock that Sunday. Spillane had banged at the station master's house, much as he was now banging on Jack Flynn's door, and animatedly related the flight of his daughter to the astonished man and his wife. Such gossip would be abroad in both counties in no time. It was getting on for eight o'clock at night. Jack came coughing and angry to his door, pulling his braces onto his shoulders, cursing loudly. He had been in bed and fast asleep.

"Jack…" Spillane was breathless. "Can I come in a second?"

"What the hell, Spillane?" Jack did not stand aside to allow his neighbour egress. An icy wind blasted into Jack's chest, almost knocking Spillane off balance where he stood, one foot on the lintel.

"For the love of God, Flynn, let me in!" There was an urgency in Spillane's voice which did not invite further remonstrance. Flynn got out of the way. Once the door was shut, Spillane agitatedly smoothed his chaotic hair, eyes red and wild with tiredness and worry. "It's Caitlin, Jack," he started, voice almost breaking. "She's gone!"

"What?"

"She's gone – run away! I don't know where the hell she is."

"When?" Jack saw Spillane's distress but he was far more interested in the whereabouts of Caitlin.

"Five – six hours ago, maybe longer. She went out of her window while we were all downstairs."

Jack frowned, put his hands on his hips, studied the floor as if for inspiration. "Was she on foot?"

"What? Yes," said Spillane. "She was. The horse is outside. I have been to Limerick Junction and back."

"Why?"

"Why?" Spillane did not try to disguise his irritation at the question. "Because she's always gobbing off about going to Dublin, that's why!"

"What's in Dublin?"

"Does it matter, Flynn?"

"Yes."

Spillane was exasperated. "University! She's always going on about going to Trinity and getting a degree. Codology, Flynn. Sure we've no money for that lark and she's all dreams. Caitlin is a dreamer, always has been. She have her head in the clouds and you may as well know…" he trailed off. The point of the visit was to inform Jack of Caitlin's flight. There were only six days left to the wedding. Jack dropped his arms by his side. He walked to his kitchen table, pulled out a chair, and sat down heavily.

"She'll hardly have gone in the direction you would look first, Spillane," he said quietly, feeling as though he was going to cough. He fought the urge and his upper body convulsed in two rapid spasms.

"Well, where the hell else would she have gone, so?" Spillane was still angry, his voice raised. It wasn't clear with what, precisely, he was angry: himself, his daughter, or Flynn.

"I don't know, Spillane, but there's more than one way of getting to Dublin. And she can hardly go to university with no money and no qualifications, can she? Where else might she go?"

Spillane paced Flynn's kitchen. He smoothed his hair and shook his head in a gesture of hopelessness. He stopped and looked at Flynn. "She has relatives in Wexford but she'd hardly go there."

"Why not?"

"Because she was there before Christmas, and she has found out since that they knew about the wedding and didn't tell her. And she'd be afraid they'd make her come back."

Jack leaned forward till his elbows were resting on his thighs. He held his head in his hands and fought the urge to cough, but wasn't as successful as previously. Neither man talked for a long while. The kitchen range was still warm. As Mick calmed down, he was overcome with tiredness. He sat down and undid a few buttons of his soaked coat.

"She will not have got far, Spillane," said Jack finally. "She will be found."

"How can you be sure, Jack?" Mick looked towards Flynn and his expression was now more hopeful than annoyed. "What if something's happened her?"

"What would happen to her in these parts in six hours?" Flynn had raised his head and was looking directly at Mick. "She'll be hiding."

"Where?"

"How the hell should I know, Spillane! Sure if I knew, she would not be hiding very well now, would she?"

159

"My daughter is gone, Flynn!" Spillane matched the sudden rise in volume and tightening of tone. "She is my child and I am wondering where the hell she might be, what could have happened her – aren't you worried, now? You're marrying her in a few days!"

Jack looked levelly at Mick. "What are you more worried about, eh? The money or your daughter?" Spillane's eyes widened with apparent fury. Jack continued to regard him, unfazed. "Unless she has been spirited away by tinkers, there is not a place around here where a young one can hide for long and not much to happen her in a few hours. She is in someone's barn or a hayloft, or else she has hitched a ride to a town and is looking for digs. But she is alone and will draw attention. Her only chance of getting to Dublin or anywhere she can be anonymous is to board a train tomorrow. If not Limerick Junction then further afield – Tipperary, Cashmel, Thurles."

"Well, how do you suggest we stop her?"

"Use a telephone, Spillane. Ring the gardai. Get them to be on the alert – and ring the stations too. Go up to Mary above in the post office and ask her to put a call through to Sean Carmody tonight. He'll be on the case straight away."

"Do you think?"

"I do," added Jack. "Sure when was the last time Sean Carmody had a missing person case? He's lucky if the gard's hut in Dunane has more to do than stop Malachai Brett getting on his bicycle after a skinful." Mick jumped up, pulled his cap from his jacket pocket, and put it on his head. His eyes were hopeful and almost tearful with gratitude.

"I'll do that, Jack – thanks very much, now." He began to leave, rethought it, crossed the kitchen, and held his hand out to Jack. The latter looked up at him, allowed his frown to soften slightly, lowered his head, and extended his right hand.

A few moments later, the clatter of hooves and the rumble of wheels on concrete announced Mick was pulling out of Jack's yard at speed. Jack could cough freely, his shoulders hunching against the pain in his chest.

At around five o'clock in the morning, someone's cockerel crowed the world awake. Caitlin had fallen into a deep sleep at some stage after feeling for a long time she would never sleep because she was so cold and the hay was so prickly. She stirred now, opened her eyes, and lay still, trying to work out where she was. She remembered she was in someone's barn and that Maher's pony was in the barn too, sat up, and struggled to see the animal above the hay stooks. It was still too dark to see clearly and would be for another two hours, but if this farm was at all like her own, the farmer would be up and making tea just after cock crow. She had to move fast. There was one slice of bread and butter left, wrapped up in newspaper. She unpeeled the newsprint from the butter as best she could in the darkness and ate the bread hurriedly. Then she felt in her bag for the piece of paper on which she had written the name and location of the pony's owner and got up from the hay, aching and shivering with cold. The pony and Kelly's donkey had become acquainted overnight and stood close together, noses inclined towards each other. The pony tossed its head and snorted as Caitlin inserted the paper under his browband and kissed his nose. "Thank you, pony," she whispered and was just feeling her way with tentative steps across the barn to the door, when she heard footsteps. The barn door swung open.

A beam of battery torchlight spotlit the floor in front of the open door. The sudden noises, Caitlin's startled movements, and the light all worried the pony, which whinnied nervously. The beam of light lifted immediately in search of the source of the noise, for its origin was a life form wholly unexpected in Dan Kelly's barn.

"What the...?" Donal Kelly exclaimed, at the discovery of a horse in his barn at five fifteen in the morning, when all he'd wanted was turf for the fire. But it was less surprising than what followed, for not far from the horse was the silhouette of a woman, and his torch beam next fell on her face. She raised an arm to shield her eyes from its light. "Who the hell are you?" he demanded.

Caitlin did not know what to say. Donal trained the torch on her. She kept her arm over her face but she watched beneath it for a chance to dart past the man as he slowly approached. "What are you doing in my barn?" he demanded, though he was busy trying to reconcile his immediate suspicion she was a thief with her depositing of a horse next to his donkey. Suddenly, Caitlin saw her chance and lunged forward, as there was now a large enough gap between the man and the open door for her to get behind him and keep running. But he was quick and leapt to the left as she sought to dodge him. He collided with her and she was knocked off balance, stumbling into the darkness of the barn and falling over footings of turf. Still she said nothing.

That the girl might be dangerous had occurred to Donal, and if he were very honest in the telling of the story afterwards, he would have admitted that he had imagined the ignominy of being seriously injured by a girl in a barn, after the life and death scrapes he had survived with the IRA. In the moments of silence which followed Caitlin's evasion of him, Donal had to decide whether it would be better to treat her roughly or go for cajoling. He could shut the barn door and wait till it was light. "If you don't show yourself right now, I'll lock you in this barn and call the gardai," he shouted, all the while prying into the recesses of the barn with his torchlight. "Up to you. There's no other way out." The bluff worked. After a moment or two, Caitlin got up. She had been hiding behind crates of potatoes. Waiting for the torch to find her, she stood blinking as Donal fixed the beam on her face.

"Who are you?" he asked, more gently.

"It doesn't matter who I am," she replied. "Please just let me go. I have taken nothing. I want nothing. Just let me go."

"What were you doing in this barn?" Donal took a few cautious steps towards her. She was young, that much was clear. And she had thick, dark hair which fell about her shoulders in profusion. Her voice was assured. If she had been afraid, she was recovering composure fast. He was interested now beyond the need to establish her reason for trespassing.

"I was sleeping – that is all," she replied. "It was wet and I was cold. I couldn't get further."

"Where are you going?" he asked, all the while slowly walking towards her. Caitlin had to think quickly. If she were rude he could get rough and trap her, call the gardai. She could not be honest with him, for he would surely stop her or tell someone to come and get her.

"I am trying to get to Limerick," she said. "I have an aunt there – she's sick."

"Why didn't you knock on the door and ask us for help?" Donal was now standing before her, his torchlight etching the contours of her pale face from the darkness.

"Sure why would I disturb ye in the night – and the wind and rain?" she responded. "I only needed a bed. I had food." Donal stared at her. Even in the garish light of the torch it was clear she was pretty.

"Come in for some tea," he said gently. "Get warm, have something to eat." Caitlin hesitated a moment.

"I will," she said. "Thank you. Would you ever get the light out of my eyes? Please?" Donal lowered the torch and offered her his hand.

"Here," he said, "take my hand. There's a lot of stuff to fall over around here." In no hurry to risk physical ensnarement, Caitlin avoided his outstretched arm and came forward as confidently as she could, tripping over potatoes and extending her hands to steady herself, touching the man and pulling away as if burnt.

"Wait now till I get a few briquettes for the fire," he said and walked away from her. He stooped towards the turf footings to his right, putting the torch on the ground. As he did so, Caitlin bolted past him and out of the open door, into the dark January morning.

Once on the road, she crossed it and made for the ditch, crouching low, heart hammering. She heard him shouting, but after a while he walked away from her and all was quiet. She crept along the sodden ditch, cold seeping through her clothes and through her skin to her very bones. Her woollen gloves were in the bag she wore strapped across her body, but as she fumbled for them, her fingers met their sodden limpness and pulled away. She scrambled out of the ditch and through a hedge into a field. She would tramp through the grass parallel with the Cashmel road for as long as she could to avoid easy detection.

As dawn's pallor began to rub out the black morning, Donal Kelly lifted the pony trap away from the hedge and, standing between the shafts, pulled it into his father's yard. Then he went into the barn and considered the pony. Why had she run off without her trap? How was she going to get to Limerick without it? He stroked the animal's smooth silver flank, soothed it with his voice. When he finally fondled its head, his fingers met with the paper beneath the animal's forelock. He pulled out the paper and shone his torch on it: "I BELONG TO PAT MAHER OF DUNANE," he read aloud. Then he muttered to himself, "Well, I'll be…"

It was with a potent mixture of relief and indignation that Pat Maher threw open his kitchen door some five hours later, as the clatter of hooves in his yard announced the return of his pony and trap, driven by a girl and followed closely by a young man driving a donkey and cart.

"Flynn, Flynn!" Mick Spillane arrived in Flynn's yard once more, the day after Caitlin absconded. His eyes were bright with happiness. "We've found Caitlin!"

Jack was pumping water over his rubber boots in his yard to get the worst of the cow manure and mud off them before he went in for a cup of tea and a break. He stopped as Mick's horse reached him and turned to face Spillane where he sat grinning in his cart.

"Where was she?" he asked, pushing a strand of straggly grey hair from his eyes.

"She was at Limerick Junction, boy! She'd taken Maher's pony and trap and travelled half the county to get there." Jack turned back to the pump, looked at both boots, decided they were clean enough.

"Have you nothing to say?" demanded Spillane. "Are you bothered about this girl at all now, Jack?"

Sighing and turning again to Spillane, Jack replied, "She is found, Spillane; the wedding will happen. Is there more you want?"

"You could show that you care a damn about my daughter!" Mick's horse champed its bit and stamped skittishly at the tone of his voice.

"Is that what you expect, Spillane?" Jack's own features darkened with anger as he spoke. "Is it? That I should care about her? And will you stop the wedding if I don't?"

Mick eyed Jack furiously from the vantage point of his cart, steadying his horse. "Perhaps I will!" he shouted.

Jack made a face that suggested that seemed reasonable enough, and nodded, saying, "OK, so if that's what you want." He began to walk towards his front door.

"Well, is it on or off?" bellowed Mick. "There's only five days to go, Flynn!"

At his door, Jack watched Spillane turn his horse so that he could exit the yard but twist on his seat to look back. "Well?" he shouted.

"I'll be there, Spillane," answered Jack, "and so will you." He went into his house and shut the door.

* * *

It had taken Caitlin hours to walk and hitch donkey cart rides to Cashmel. She had made straight for the station on arrival in the town. There was a small café beside the station where she had bought fried eggs, bacon, and bread and a mug of steaming tea. Ravenously, she had consumed her breakfast and then gone into the outside toilet behind the café and straightened her clothing as best she could, brushed her hair, and washed her face in a small basin. Then she had headed for the station, heart thumping with fear and excitement. She had no definite idea of what she would do when she got to Dublin. She would find a job of some sort; beyond that she could not plan. At the station, she went to the ticket office and asked for a single ticket to Dublin. "Sure there's no trains from here to Dublin, alannah," replied the woman behind the glass. "You'd have to go from Limerick Junction. That is the only place in Tipperary you can get a train to Dublin."

Caitlin looked in disbelief at the woman, tears springing to her eyes. The woman got down from her stool and exited the ticket office, came around to the front, and stood before Caitlin. She was wearing a dress with a thick coat over it and she had on woollen gloves with no fingers in them. Her grey hair was pinned back to a knot behind her head. She looked pityingly at Caitlin. "Is it Dublin you have to get to, pet?" Caitlin nodded, tears flowing down her face. She sniffed and lifted a hand to wipe her face. "Here, here, pet," said the woman, delving beneath her coat to a pocket in her dress. "Take this," she said, offering Caitlin a handkerchief. "'Tis clean," she added. "I only put it in yesterday." Caitlin was past caring. She blew her nose and tried to recover her composure. "Is it important, like," the woman prodded, "getting to Dublin?"

Caitlin sniffed again. She didn't know what to do with the handkerchief and offered it to the woman, who took it and put it back in her pocket. "Where can I go from here?" she managed at last.

"What?" The woman looked puzzled.

"Where do trains from here go to?"

"Well, they go to Limerick Junction," said the woman, "or the other way, to Waterford."

"Then I can get a train to Limerick Junction and from there get a train to Dublin?" Caitlin asked, returning hope evident in her voice.

"Yes, pet," said the woman. "You could do that, right enough. Is it relatives you have in Dublin?"

Caitlin wanted the woman to go back into the ticket office and stop asking her questions. She already felt far too conspicuous.

"Yes – a sick aunt," she replied. "And I have to get there quick – before she dies."

"Oh!" The old woman gasped and her eyes widened. "Isn't that a terrible thing for you!" She showed no signs of going back to the office. "What age is she, your aunt?"

"Sixty-two. Please, can you give me a ticket to Limerick Junction? I'm in sort of a hurry," pleaded Caitlin.

"I can," complied the woman. "Give me a second, now." She turned away, reappearing a few moments later behind the glass.

After a torturous ten minutes, Caitlin finally had in her hand a ticket to Limerick Junction. An hour later and she was on the train, heart once more filled with anxious anticipation of a future alone in the capital city.

But when she enquired of the station master's wife who worked in the ticket office of Limerick Junction how much a ticket to Dublin might be and when the next train was, the woman asked Caitlin to "hold on a minute now" and left the booth. When she returned, it was with her husband.

"So, you're wanting to go to Dublin, are you?"

"Yes," said Caitlin, instantly on her guard.

"Why might that be?"

"What?" asked Caitlin, indignantly. "What does it matter?"

"Well," replied the station master, "a young girl, on her own, off to Dublin… doesn't happen every day."

"I am visiting an aunt," said Caitlin flatly.

"Ah," said the station master, looking knowingly at her. "An aunt, is it?"

Caitlin said nothing, though her quick breathing and facial expression were close to betraying her fear and mounting anger. Why could she not purchase a train ticket without this ceaseless interrogation? All the while, the station master's wife stared at her, arms crossed.

"The next train to Dublin is not for another hour," said the station master. "Sit yourself over there now." He nodded towards a bench on the platform. "Do you want a cup of tea?"

"No! Thank you," said Caitlin. "I want a ticket. Please."

"Have you the money?" asked the station master.

"I do, of course!"

"Right so, then I'll bring your ticket over in a little while. You've plenty of time." He walked away; his wife smiled at Caitlin briefly, nodded, and followed him.

"That's her," he said to his wife as they got out of Caitlin's earshot. "Ring the gard in Dunane."

And so it was that Sergeant Carmody, Mick Spillane in the passenger seat of his car, got to Limerick Junction well before the Dublin train and took Caitlin home.

CHAPTER ELEVEN

"If anyone knows just or lawful impediment why these two may not be joined in holy matrimony, let him speak now or forever hold his peace."

Rain drizzled down the windows of the Dunane chapel. Only one window was of coloured glass, an arched one behind the altar, depicting the Virgin Mary standing on a snake, eyes heavenward, holding out her hands as if in supplication. No one spoke. Jack coughed, doing his best to mute the sound. Anyone who might object to this wedding wasn't there. Maureen stood pale and serene in her flowery blue dress and a best coat handed down by two sisters before her. She was the closest thing to a bridesmaid Caitlin had. She had followed her sister up the aisle, holding a small bunch of artificial flowers which Mrs Spillane had found in a trunk in the loft. There were no fresh flowers to be had in Tipperary in wartime January.

Caitlin had refused to hold Mick's arm as he had accompanied her awkwardly to the altar. He was shaven, hair slicked back, wearing the only suit he owned. The waistcoat no longer fitted him and, some time ago, Mrs Spillane had added a bit of elastic to the waist band. Jack waited for his bride at the altar. He did not look at her until Father Kinnealy pronounced them man and wife and even then it was a fleeting, burning steal of a glance. Caitlin did not lift her veil nor look anywhere but straight ahead. Caitlin's two oldest sisters had not been told about the wedding until Christmas, and both had been issued with strict instructions – underlined and in capitals on their Christmas cards – not to speak with Caitlin about it. Neither had responded. Mrs Spillane cried quietly into a handkerchief as the wedding party turned silently from the altar and headed for the door.

"Will you come back to the house for a bit of breakfast, Father?" she offered through her tears as the priest saw them into the narthex.

"No, thanks, Missis," he declined. "The housekeeper has my breakfast all made, now. Good luck."

Outside in the drizzling rain, Caitlin hitched up her dress, pulling away her arm from her father's hand as he offered to help her climb onto Jack's cart. Her mother handed her a blanket while Mick loaded onto Flynn's cart a bulging suitcase full of Caitlin's clothes and a second bag full of other possessions. Once he had the horse's reins in his hand, Jack reached into an inner pocket of his jacket and pulled out an envelope. He threw it to Spillane, who caught it, nodded wordlessly, and shoved it into his own inner pocket. If Caitlin detected what they were doing she did not betray it. Ignoring her mother's pleas to say goodbye or come and visit soon, ignoring Maureen's quiet wishes of good luck, Caitlin drew the blanket around her shoulders and continued to stare straight ahead. Jack clicked on the horse, and the cart pulled away from the church.

Never so bedraggled and desultory a bride and groom reached their married home after a wedding. Jack drove the cart as close as it was possible to his front door then dismounted. He unloaded Caitlin's luggage and took it into the kitchen. She remained on the cart several moments after it had become essential for her to dismount, the blanket around her shoulders and over her head against the rain. Jack said nothing, standing at his horse's head and stroking the animal's face, waiting. At last Caitlin got down. Jack did not attempt to help her, for he had noted well her earlier disdain for Spillane's help. As she backed down the two steps of the cart to the yard, Jack noted how the frothing lace of her hem was swallowed by mud and his heart was filled with pity for the girl who wore it. And so, Caitlin entered Jack Flynn's kitchen, as his wife.

He had made some effort to address the cumulative effect of years of grime and neglect on the sink, the range, the walls and floor. But Jack had never scrubbed or blacked a range, scoured pots or washed a floor, and neither had his father before him; so the wet rags he had applied to various surfaces had only served to make arcs in the dirt or had not disturbed the grease which had hardened to a black crust on the range. The floor was cursorily swept only when the mud on it had dried sufficiently to allow this and, at present, was distinguishable from the yard outside only in the depth and consistency of the dirt which covered it. The absence of electricity was familiar to Caitlin as no one this far outside Tipperary or Limerick towns was on the grid. In any case, the soft light from the several kerosene lamps placed strategically around the kitchen was merciful; it was impossible for Caitlin to appreciate the full extent of the filth in the kitchen on that sullen January morning.

She stood beside her cases, pulling the damp blanket tight around her shoulders and shivering with cold. Jack could not think what to say or do to alleviate the tension or bring comfort.

"I'll make some tea," he announced at last, lifting the griddle cover and placing the kettle on the hob. Caitlin said nothing but watched his self-conscious movements, how he avoided looking at her, how he stood, hands on hips, back to her, watching the kettle warm. She let the blanket drop and her hands hung by her sides. It was very cold in Flynn's kitchen. There was no sign that he had prepared anything for her to eat. She looked down her body from the bodice of her dress to the mud-heavy hem and could not understand that it was hers. Her presence in this scene, where she stood in a wedding dress, married to a man as old as her father, was the result of little more than consciousness. She was alive elsewhere, in a dream. She did not want tea. More than anything, she wanted to get out of the dress.

"Where am I supposed to put my things?"

Jack spun around as if shocked, and looked at her. Indeed, she was like a ghost, standing in her white dress, long dark hair clinging damply to her shoulders, her face an impression of beauty in the lamplight. For a moment, he could not think how to answer her. And then he moved towards her, picked up the suitcase, and said only, "I'll show you." He crossed the kitchen to the wooden stairs, heaved the case in front of him, and began to climb. Caitlin took a few steps after him, then stopped. She did not want to be upstairs with him. She waited for Jack to descend. He picked up her bag and re-crossed the kitchen, took it upstairs, came down again. The kettle hissed and spat on the hob as the water boiled. While Jack tended to the tea making, Caitlin lifted her dress and climbed upstairs.

From the narrow landing stretched a short passageway in worn boards and on either side was a room. The door to the room on the left was shut and the other stood open on flickering lamplight. She approached the one on the right as if to certain execution. There was a double bed, but apart from a narrow wardrobe in one corner, a wooden chair, and some shelves on the wall, the room was empty. There was no sign of male habitation – no clothes strewn on the floor, no boots – and the room smelt damp but no distinctive male odours were detectable. And it was relatively clean; the floorboards had been swept and were discernible, not caked in layers of trodden grime like the rest of the house, as far as she could tell. Flynn had set a fire in the iron grate and had put her suitcase and bag on one side of the bed. Cautiously, Caitlin approached the bed, then doubled back and shut the door.

Downstairs, Jack made two cups of tea then sat at the kitchen table, unable to lift his mug for the tremor in his hands and the distraction of his thoughts. What the hell happened now? The situation was as unreal to him as it was to Caitlin. He had willed this to happen, and now he was clueless to direct things further. On his wall was an ancient wooden clock which had hung there as long as he could recall. It needed winding each evening and was the only way, apart from the crowing of cocks and nuances of light in darkness, that he could tell time in his house. As he sat at his table listening to Caitlin moving around in the room upstairs, Jack marvelled for the first time at how loudly it ticked.

The tea was cold when Caitlin came downstairs again, dressed in one of her old frocks and hair tied back, a thick woollen jumper over her dress. She was frowning. The feeling of detachment had subsided a little and the old resentment and anger were returning. She observed him, slumped and awkward, unable to hold her gaze, and contempt was unsluiced in her breast.

"Well, what now?" she challenged. Startled by the invective in her tone, Jack stiffened.

"What?"

"What now?" she repeated, louder. "Well, you surely had a plan for what we do now?" When he didn't answer, Caitlin grew bolder, began to give vent to her fury and grief. "But no, actually, it doesn't even look like you made any plans for today, does it?" He frowned darkly, the familiar pain and urge to cough becoming intense as he lifted his head to meet her eyes. "This house is a filthy tip, so it is!" She was almost shouting. "And there's not even a bit of food ready – is there any food here at all? Is this what you think I should live like, is it? Are you waiting for me to start cooking and skivvying from the moment I set foot in the place, is that it?" Jack fought the urge to put his hands over his ears. He was so stupid! Why hadn't he thought to prepare some breakfast, get some fresh bread in? What had he been thinking? He was so nervous and so ill, had so little appetite himself, and was so unused to caring for anyone other than himself that these simple demonstrations of comfort had not even occurred to him. He leapt to his feet, knocking his chair backwards so it almost fell. Unable to answer her, he strode across the kitchen and went outside. It was only eleven o'clock in the morning. He would drive to Dunane and buy food. It was, in any case, a blessed relief to be doing something.

* * *

173

In the days after Caitlin's appearance in his father's barn, Donal Kelly could not get her out of his head. The story Pat Maher had told when he and Deirdre had returned his pony was remarkable in every way. The farmer up the road, a Mick Spillane, had matched his seventeen-year-old daughter to another farmer his own age for a tidy sum of money, though Maher did not know how much. The girl had stolen Maher's pony in a bid to escape her fate. Maher couldn't be precise about the wedding date, though he knew all three banns had been read, so it could be any time. He asked Deirdre whether she was the girl, got closer, and squinted at her. She assured him she was not. On their way back to Golden in their donkey cart, Donal and Deirdre had discussed the horror they would feel if either was matched in this way against his or her will. However, the practice itself was not shocking to them, for it was still common enough. Deirdre was less than a year younger than Caitlin, pretty with light chestnut hair and her father's blue eyes. She empathized particularly.

"Sure how could anyone sell his own daughter like that?" she wondered aloud as they bumped in the cart and took turns to walk, in order to rest the donkey. "Daddy would never do that to Jacintha or me."

"No, he would not," agreed Donal, "but it's not a bad idea, now."

"What?"

"Well, it would certainly get me out of a fix," added Donal, then grinned at her. Increasingly, he was applying himself to the problem of how to get away from life on his father's farm, not least of all because the shadows from the secrets he inhabited were rolling over it like storm clouds. But the dependence on his help not only of Dan Kelly but of Deirdre and Jacintha also, was an anchor to Golden.

He wondered if the pretty girl he had found in his father's barn had managed to get away, though where she thought she was going on foot, in the January cold and darkness, he could not imagine. Perhaps she had relatives or even a lover who would conspire to liberate her from the marriage her father had arranged? As he lay in bed in the minutes between turning out the light and falling into exhausted sleep, Donal tried to remember any glimpses he had caught of Caitlin Spillane on that morning. Apart from an impression of beauty and courage he could recall nothing clearly. If he had known what she was doing, he mused, he would have helped her. He knew plenty of people across many counties from Tipperary to the North who would have taken her in if Donal had asked them; IRA safe houses masquerading as ordinary homes, occupied by apparently ordinary people who were well used to harbouring fugitives. He might have got to know her. A spirited, rebellious beauty with a mane of black hair emerged from the dim recesses of his father's barn and stepped into the light of Donal's imagination; a fitting partner indeed for a young man forced to flit from shadow to shadow by night, yoked and bent to the routine of his father's farm by day. "Where are you now, Caitlin Spillane?" he had asked aloud of the darkness at the same time that Caitlin, captured, had cried herself to sleep next to Maureen.

When Jack got back from Dunane on his wedding day, he brought in from the cart a sack he had been given in the post office shop. It contained his butter and sugar rations, two loaves of bread, potatoes, bacon, cabbage, and a quart of milk, for he could drink none of his own. He had also bought a pot of jam and a few sweets – things he would never have contemplated buying as a rule, but he thought Caitlin might like them. He tipped the contents of the sack carefully onto the table and was disappointed she was not in the kitchen to see.

The house was very quiet and cold. The clock ticked in the semi darkness, for the lamps had burned low, then out, and the range had not been stoked. Afraid she had run away again, Jack climbed the stairs with heavy tread and walked determinedly to the room he had prepared for Caitlin's arrival. He knocked on the door. After a few seconds, there was a sullen response and Jack closed his eyes in relief.

"What?"

"I've bought food," he said through the door, but he couldn't go on. He had wanted to add, "Come and eat something", but the imperative seemed too indelicate. He could not trust his tone, so unused was he to modulating utterances to elicit cooperation. His world was one where short declaratives and imperatives issued to beasts mainly sufficed to get things done. There was no answer to his announcement. He felt foolish outside her door, was about to turn away but was suddenly irritated. She had been here the whole time and the range was almost out, the lamps unlit.

"The range is cold, below." There was another silence and then he heard the bed springs creak as they gave up Caitlin's weight. She opened the door and stared at him resentfully. The rebuke implicit in the statement about the range had stirred her; she knew better than to ignore such remarks if she did not want trouble. Jack took a step back so she could emerge from the room and she passed him, made for the stairs.

While Jack coughed and moved around the gloomy kitchen, putting away groceries and filling the kettle, Caitlin trimmed the lamp wicks and topped up the kerosene from a can Jack kept under the sink. Then she fuelled the embers of the range with briquettes of turf and sticks until it was roaring gamely once more and the kitchen began to warm up. Mechanically, Caitlin brought the peelings pail to the table and sat down to peel potatoes, prepare cabbage. There was a joint of bacon already in the press and she sliced it and lay the pieces on a plate, which she first scrubbed as best she could using water made hot by the kettle. She put the potatoes on to boil, placed the plate over the mouth of the kettle pan, and put another plate over the meat so it would warm through. The cabbage would go in with the potatoes when they were half cooked. She sliced soda bread and put the butter on the table. She was ravenously hungry.

CHAPTER ELEVEN

Jack watched his new wife moving around the kitchen and marvelled at her dexterity, her youth and good looks. He could hardly take in that this lovely girl was in his house, making his dinner. Caitlin glowered at him, reddening under his scrutiny, and he looked away quickly, coughed his way to the kettle, made more tea. The thing she feared more than anything else seemed to be taking shape as the afternoon wore on. The dark angel of the annunciation seemed to have followed her here and was metamorphosing into something even more sinister in the shadows and corners of Flynn's house.

They ate in silence. When he had finished, Jack pushed away from the table, announcing that he was off to get his cows for milking. Caitlin was hugely relieved, for she had barely been able to chew and swallow her food in his presence; she planned to wolf the remains of her dinner and eat some of the bread and jam.

"Do you know anyone in Dunane?" The night before Caitlin's wedding, Donal was in a safe house halfway between Dunane and Cashmel. A man named Michael Kilty, a prosperous farmer and main supplier of the depot in Cashmel where Joe Morgan and Des Corcoran worked, had picked up Donal in his car. Des and Joe had come with him.

"I know a few farmers out that way, all right," replied Michael. "Why?"

"Do you know a Spillane?"

"I do – shifty yoke, would skin you as soon as look at you, boy. I have sold him pigs a few times – he'd try anything to get the price down. Told me once a sow was 'squinty-looking' and wanted a fiver off." Michael hmphed and topped up his poteen, knocked it back.

"Squinty-looking?" echoed Donal with amused incredulity. Joe Morgan laughed and shook his head. "Was she, though?"

"What?" Kilty put down his glass and fixed Donal with a look of mock indignation. "A finer looking sow you never beheld! I almost fell in love with her that day, boy, I looked so long and deep into her eyes. It fair broke my heart to sell her to that runt Spillane." The men laughed. The door opened, and a young, ruddy-cheeked man came in. He removed his cap and nodded to the woman of the house, who smiled and gestured to the table where Joe, Donal, Michael, and Des sat. They made room for him.

"How're ya, Pat?" Joe greeted the young man, slapping him on the back as he sat down. "So it's just Conor we're waiting on now, then? Will he be long, Missis?" The woman whose house it was answered that her husband had business to settle with a man in Clogheen, from whom he was planning to buy a horse. If the deal involved much drinking, there was no telling when Conor Rourke might be home.

The meeting was to discuss IRA tactics in the continuing campaign against English occupation of the North and to effect the overthrow of de Valera's Free State government. Hugh McAteer, the IRA Chief of Staff, had escaped from Derry jail in March 1943 by tunnelling out with twenty other men. They had surfaced like moles in a Derry back garden as a family sat down to their breakfast. A few weeks later, McAteer had mounted "The Broadway Cinema Operation" on the Falls Road, Belfast, at which Donal had been present. But by the time of this meeting between Joe and a few members of the revised Tipperary flying column, in January 1944, McAteer was recaptured and languishing in a Belfast jail. Joe Morgan and other senior IRA leaders now took their orders from McAteer's replacement, Charlie Kerins.

Kerins' distinguished service record included the murder of Detective Sergeant Denis O'Brien in September 1942 – the detective who had fooled Paddy Davern into revealing the whereabouts of Michael Devereux's body in June 1941. Kerins had mown down O'Brien with a machine gun as he left his house to go to work, then cycled past as the policeman's wife cradled her dying husband in her arms. Since then, the IRA Chief of Staff

CHAPTER ELEVEN

Officer had been robbing factories and committing whatever crimes were necessary to arm and organize the dwindling numbers of Irish men who reported to him. Kerins was holed up in a safe house in Waterford but due to move. Joe Morgan was key in ensuring the Chief of Staff's safety and in taking instructions from him to effect the next IRA cross-border attack. Tonight's meeting was seminal in the formulation of a plan.

"How're ye, lads?" At last, Conor Rourke came home. Ruddy faced from too much drink as well as the stinging wind, he nodded a little sheepishly to each man at his kitchen table. His wife took one look at his complexion, glowered at him, removed from the table the one empty glass, and began making tea. Rourke avoided her eye, didn't argue.

"Sorry there, now, lads," he began as he sat down with them. "That man drives a hard bargain."

"Did you buy his horse?" asked Donal.

"I did."

"Does it squint?" rejoined Joe and the men laughed. Rourke looked confused. His wife all but slammed a cup of tea in front of him so that the liquid lurched from one side of the mug to another. The men exchanged glances, stopped laughing. "To business," pronounced Joe, "if you're capable, Rourke, you dog, ya."

There was a moment's silence while each man marshalled his thoughts, came under command. Rourke's wife went upstairs to bed and slammed shut her door. "End of February or beginning of March – date to be decided – we make our way in two legs to Roscommon and then on to Buncrana. On the command, we cross the border to Derry where we meet up with a few of the lads who got out of jail with McAteer last year. Waterford and Kilkenny columns will be going via Dublin to Dundalk, then on to Belfast."

"What's the MO, Joe?" asked Donal. "Can we know what we're to do?"

"No details yet." Joe shook his head, glanced briefly at the table as though gathering thought, then looked at each man in turn. He continued, "But this is a big push, lads. McAteer is on hunger strike. We need to do everything we can to support him and the boys back inside. Kerins will travel with the Waterford lads as far as Dublin and I'll meet him there. The rest of ye will wait for us in a safe house in Roscommon. We'll travel up to Buncrana in separate vehicles. Michael, you'll take your car. Des, you and Pat will travel up in a lorry as if ye were on a depot run."

"Is there just us in it, Joe?" Pat wanted to know.

"No, no," said Joe impatiently. "There's more of us. You will see when we get to Buncrana."

Pat O'Meara was clearly very uneasy about the whole thing. Just nineteen, Pat was the youngest son of ageing parents and least likely to inherit on their deaths, for his four brothers – two of whom were married – would make sure they got their shares of the farm sale when their father died. The most he could hope for was a labouring job on another farm or maybe manual work in a factory or depot. Tall and good looking, with a shock of blonde hair rare in Tipperary, Pat had been an easy recruit to the IRA, for there was not much in his life to look forward to and little prospect of marriage. Even if he had been courageous enough to approach a girl with a view to courtship, he could not envisage a time when poverty would not prevent the trading of his dreams for something more solid. The IRA, on the other hand, gladly exchanged dreams of heroism and intellects seduced by rhetoric, for guns, explosives, and chances to kill people. When it finally came, the weight of a gun in the hands was the ultimate challenge to abstract notions of allegiance. Pat was now confronted for the first time with the reality of his pledge to the IRA. Donal watched him swallow hard – how he shifted in his chair to relieve mounting nervous tension – and remembered well the moment his own bluff was called. There was a silence. The kitchen range was quiet, its embers sleepy. A wind whistled past the windows and made them shudder in their frames.

"I'll give ye a lift back, lads," offered Michael Kilty.

"Will we just wait, so?" asked Conor, rubbing his face tiredly and stifling a yawn. "What's the word?"

"'Holiday'," came the reply and the others looked at him askance. "Sure doesn't everyone go to the seaside on their holidays?"

"I've never seen the sea," said Pat wistfully. "Will we see it, Joe?"

"It'll be hard to miss in Buncrana, Pat," replied Joe. "When ye's get the signal, someone will find you and tell you ye're off on your holidays and give you a date. Be ready for the knock on the door. We'll see you in Roscommon. Good luck, now."

In the car back to Dunane, Donal sat with Des in the back, for which he was grateful. Des hardly ever talked. Stockily built, always with a neat haircut, clean shaven face, and clean shirt, he watched the world and listened to how it went without much comment. Donal had often amused himself with the thought that Molly Corcoran spoke enough for both of them. Joe and Michael talked quietly in front. Donal was less occupied with thoughts of what might await him in Derry at the end of February than with how he might liberate Caitlin Spillane from her fate and perhaps entice her to a life of covert vigilantism.

When he had finished the milking Jack washed off the worst of the mud from his boots under the stream of icy water from the outside tap then made for his kitchen. That this was his wedding day and Caitlin Spillane was his wife would not be real to him. He had existed so long in solitude he could not emerge from the state of mind necessary to endure it. He observed the tremor in his hand and noted how red and old looking his fingers were. The anxiety that arose in spite of himself as he turned the door handle was as out of his control to quell as joy was his to summon. That she was actually there when he went in, scrubbing and scouring the sink with a brush, was almost absurd to him.

"This place is disgusting!" she snapped without turning around as the door banged shut. "How could you live like this?" She was scrubbing furiously, leaning on the brush and pushing it forwards and backwards in a froth of carbolic suds. He stood and watched her, not yet reacting to the rebuke. "What's more amazing, though," she shouted, the momentum of the brushing movements increasing with the fury in her voice, "is how the hell you expected me to live like this!" Throwing the brush down hard in the ceramic sink, she turned on him. Her eyes were swollen with crying but the anger shone blackly in them. She had twisted her hair and pinned it up.

Wisps of it fell across her face, stuck to her wet cheeks. She lifted a hand and used the back of it to push away hair from her eyes. Her dress was spattered with suds and streaked with grime. In spite of her evident hatred for him, Jack's heart filled with compassion for her. "Have you nothing to say?" She was sobbing with such ferocity that she could barely get the words out. "Is this what you wanted?" She stood before him, arms outstretched. He closed his eyes and shook his head slowly. He was going to cough. There was nothing he could do to stop the tidal wave of convulsions which racked him and the pain was more than he could stand.

Caitlin's sobs reduced in ferocity and her expression changed from one of intense hatred to horrified curiosity as she watched Jack stagger backwards in an effort to remain standing as the coughing fit possessed him. He reached behind him like a blind man for a chair he knew must be close but his hand flailed wildly and he could not find the chair. Turning, he fell against the table and bent over it, his knees buckling, all his weight on his arms, coughing and coughing. Caitlin took a few tentative steps towards him. She could form no words of comfort or concern, only watch him retch and cough and then, to her horror, an eruption of bright blood came from his mouth and spattered like paint across the table. Her hands flew to her mouth and her eyes widened above them as Flynn cried out in distress, a sound more like an animal's than a man. And then he slumped slowly, falling backwards from the table onto the floor as his legs gave way.

He lay quite still. Was he dead? Caitlin moved as if suddenly released from something and hunkered down at his head. His eyes were closed and there was a rivulet of blood running from the corner of his mouth to the floor. He was breathing but he was not conscious. She got up, ran to the sink, and seizing the scrubbing brush, re-crossed the kitchen to the table and began scrubbing at the blood. Then she raced back to the sink and ran the bloody suds under the tap, went back to the table, and continued scrubbing until there was no trace of blood left on the wood.

Flynn stirred. He coughed briefly a few times, opened his eyes, and remained staring ahead for a moment as if trying to remember where he was. He moved as quickly as he could to right himself, pushing onto his hands and knees and then onto his feet. He was trembling violently. Taking his handkerchief from his pocket he wiped his mouth. Unable to look at her or respond to her terse enquiry as to whether he was all right, he crossed the kitchen as if he were drunk and made for the stairs. A minute or so later Caitlin heard a door slam shut and then all was silence. As the evening shadows found her then melded in darkness, Caitlin dropped the scrubbing brush and bent her head. Hot tears spilled in profusion down her face.

An hour or so after that, Donal Kelly tied his donkey to a post and patted its rump as he walked away from the cart and towards the bar in Dunane's main street. It had taken him two hours in the cold to get there from Golden. The bar was lit by battery and generator but the light flickered as much as the flames from the myriad kerosene lamps which supported it in case the generator broke down. Men nodded to him as he came in and he nodded back, pressing his lips together in a tight smile.

Only with Blood

"What will it be?" asked Jim Fogarty the landlord. Fogarty's red, fleshy face was kindly and his small blue eyes twinkled at Donal from their beds of wrinkles.

"A pint," said Donal, smiling back. Then, as the barman levered the pump and filled his glass, he added, "There's a good crowd in tonight." Indeed, the little bar was occupied almost to capacity and there was an air of excitement, voices raised above the usual lugubrious timbres of tired men taking solace in alcohol and each other at the end of a hard day.

"Aye," said Jim, serving Donal his brimming pint of ale. "There was a wedding in the village today, so there was." Donal's heart lurched.

"A wedding?"

"Aye – the bride's father is treating everyone to a pint." Jim nodded to a ruddy-faced man with wild hair who, as if on cue, was the subject of a simultaneous toast. He raised his tankard in response and then bowed in mock gratitude.

"What's his name?" asked Donal distantly, never taking his eyes from the cheering men and the object of their attention.

"That's Mick Spillane," said Jim, looking at the young man with curiosity. "Why? Do you know him?"

Donal shook his head, not turning to meet the landlord's eyes. He drank his pint quickly, avoiding conversation, then slipped out of the bar into the January evening. He could not understand why it was that his heart was quite so stricken and why it should be that life seemed to have shifted on its axis in a moment. The donkey was too tired to make the journey back to Golden straight away. Donal would give it a half-hour's rest then walk and lead it back home. What the hell had he been thinking?

CHAPTER TWELVE

On the Sunday morning after her wedding day, Caitlin woke to the crowing of a cockerel as usual, but there was something unusual about her physical orientation in the darkness as well as an absence of familiarity which gave her consciousness no context. She lay still for a few seconds, then her heart lurched as she made all the connections. She sat up, wide awake. The house was silent.

Getting out of bed, she tiptoed to the window. There was still a sliver of moon in the sky. To her right was discernible the dark stretch of the barn, and straight ahead, a small tree whose black branches stretched westward as if it would escape the merciless battery of winds which made it stunted and forlorn in its fallow field. Caitlin drew her knitted bed-shawl close around her shoulders. What now? What now? The question repeated itself in her head and she was powerless to answer. It was as though everything important had been excised from her heart and brain and both stood idle and shocked. Her feet were very cold, and by the time she climbed back into the bed, the sheets had lost their warmth. It was too cold to snow, she imagined her mother saying. Tears welled unbidden at the thought of her mother and then there was almost intolerable grief as Caitlin contemplated anew this most bitter of betrayals – that of her mother, in the sacrificing of Caitlin's life to this pointlessness.

She stopped crying suddenly when the creak of bedsprings and then heavy tread on floorboards announced Flynn was up. She heard the steady metallic hiss as he urinated into a metal pot and closed her eyes in disgust. If he ever, ever came near her...

In a few minutes, he was coughing and sighing his way past her door and then on to the stairs, descending to the kitchen. He didn't hesitate in his morning routine, didn't call to her. She lay still and listened to him fill then boil the kettle, saw bread, pour tea. In less than twenty minutes from the first sounds which had announced he was conscious, he had left the house and slammed the door. Caitlin lay on her back in the growing dawn light and wondered what she was supposed to do.

Jack did not have to get out of bed at five o'clock on Sunday morning. He could have remained warm and resting for another two hours before getting up to fetch his cows for milking, but he had been awake most of the night. He was mortified with embarrassment following his worst ever coughing attack in front of Caitlin and he had spent most of the night in a swelter of self-recrimination. Why hadn't he controlled himself? Falling down on the floor like that in front of her! He had so wanted to say something of comfort to her. It had upset him terribly to see her so forlorn and distressed, covered in grime and eyes swollen with crying. On more than one occasion, he had contemplated crossing the landing to her room, knocking gently, and whispering to her in the darkness that everything would be all right, she would see. But he could no more have done that than forgive himself for his clumsy, stupid neglect in not welcoming her properly to her new home. What the hell had he done? He thrust his arthritic hands into his pockets and walked faster up the road to his cows, lowering his mouth into the collar of his coat to avoid breathing in the freezing air which so hurt his lungs. Why, he enquired angrily of himself, had no one stopped him? It was possible he was mad when he bargained for the hand in marriage of Caitlin Spillane a few months ago, but if that were the case, why had no one stopped him? It had been all too easy to acquire her, to net her as though she were a young bird unused to flight. Now, what could he do to keep the bird from dying in its cage?

CHAPTER TWELVE

As he pushed open the gate to the first field where his eight remaining cows were huddled together against the cold, he wondered how he had ever thought Caitlin Spillane might bear him a son. He knew he would never, ever be able to touch her. Once in the milking parlour, Jack cranked up the generator, coughing and wincing at the pain in his hands. Then he set about the awful, mechanical business of hand milking his cows to relieve the fullness of their udders, pouring away the warm milk into runnels leading to a drain, watching it steam and glow dully in the widening morning light.

He did not expect to find Caitlin up by the time he returned to his house and was as shy as a schoolboy to discover she was not only up but the range was roaring fiercely against the January cold and the lamps were all lit. There was fresh tea in the pot and slices of bread on the table. Caitlin was standing against the sink, hair pulled back severely from her pale face and her arms folded. She stared at him levelly, and when he looked towards her, as if she had been waiting for his return, she began to speak. Her voice was matter of fact but there was a tremor in it and she paused a couple of times to clear her throat.

"I have been thinking," she said. Jack's eyebrows raised involuntarily and he stood, back to the range, held his arms slightly away from his body, and fanned his bent fingers as well as he could to warm his hands. He said nothing while she paused to gather her thoughts. "We have to work out what to do… now." She could not mention marriage. "I know you have paid money for me." She could not keep the bitterness from her tone and he reddened, lowered his head. He really couldn't stand another round of recrimination. His heart beat thickly against his ribs and he tried to breathe deeply to calm it but the effort of inhaling enough air was so painful that he was distracted from her as she spoke again. "And I will clean your house and cook for you." He raised his head and looked at her, trying to keep as neutral an expression as he could through the pain in his chest and his

187

surprise. "But please…" She could not articulate her desire to remain separate from him physically. She was afraid of the words, the very allusion to any marital intimacy with him, and also, she feared physical punishment for her boldness. She had to control her revulsion and remain calm if this bargain were to appease him. "I can see you are ill," she went on at last, "and I can get a doctor." Jack frowned irritably. He moved away from the range and lowered his face in embarrassment. She continued quickly, "… or take care of you myself; I don't mind milking cows or cleaning out the milking parlour, stuff like that – if I have to. And I can chop wood and do shopping, all the things I'm guessing you need a hand with…" Jack sat down at the table and looked at her, put his elbows on the table and rested his nose on his joined knuckles. Her arms folded tightly at her chest, Caitlin struggled for her words, crying as she spoke them. "But please… Mr Flynn…" The formality of the address struck him like a stone. "Please don't… sleep with me!" She had said it. She covered her face with her hands and sobbed into them. Jack sighed, listened to the flames crackling their way through the wood, hissing through the turf in the range. The clock ticked loudly in the ensuing silence as if trying to make the point it was indifferent, hadn't heard what had just been said. Suddenly, he stood up. The grate of wood on the stone floor caused Caitlin to look up sharply and the alarm on her face told of her fear that he would hit her.

"Come with me," he commanded, not un-gently. When she stared at him in wide-eyed terror he added, "Not for that!" He carried on to the stairs, climbed them. A few seconds later, Caitlin followed. "This room," said Jack, as Caitlin gingerly stepped over the threshold of her bedroom, "is yours." He pointed at the wooden shelves nailed to the wall opposite the window. "I put those shelves up a few days ago," he added, "for books."

Caitlin looked at him, frowning in confusion. His eye fell on the second bag which Spillane had thrown onto the cart after the wedding the previous day. She had not touched it. He crossed to where it lay at the foot of the bed and pulled it towards him. Caitlin did not protest as he unzipped it and then marvelled at what he pulled from it. Textbooks and exercise books were dragged from the bag and spread from it in profusion on the bedroom floor. "I asked Spillane to put these in with your things," said Jack, grunting with the effort of standing up straight again. "You can put them on the shelves."

"Why?"

"Well, aren't you always going on about studying?"

"Well, yes," spluttered Caitlin, "but I hardly thought I could do that... now!"

"Why can't you?" asked Flynn, blushing, yet becoming bolder at the dawning realization on Caitlin's face. She stared at him. Was this some sort of cruel trick, some sort of counter bargain to the one she had just tried to make? He would let her study in return for... "You can still go to school, finish your exams, can't you? What's to stop you?" Caitlin still could not speak. "I can take you – in the cart – after milking. I can pick you up before milking in the evening. No need to walk. It's two miles from here, the school."

"I don't understand," Caitlin managed at last. "Why would you do that?" Jack thought, but words deserted him. The idea had slowly evolved in his head as his illness grew worse and had crystallized when she had run away and Spillane had said how she yearned for university. He knew how hard a thing it was to give up studying. He shrugged, moved towards the door, and she stood aside to let him pass. When she re-joined him in the kitchen a few minutes later, Caitlin was emboldened to press home her earlier request.

"What about... what I said earlier?" she asked quietly. Flynn stifled a few coughs. At last he answered her.

"You can put that idea out of your head – for good." The tears which sprang then to Caitlin's eyes were of unbridled relief and gratitude.

* * *

Donal Kelly was unusually grumpy as he set about fetching his father's cows on the day after Caitlin Spillane's wedding. He told himself what happened in Dunane village and to people he did not know was none of his business. But the lovely young girl he had encountered, who was so desperate to escape the slavery her father intended for her, would not leave his thoughts. He was filled with a growing anger and something akin to grief that she had been so snared. God alone knew what state she was in that very morning, he thought, as he walked up the road to get his father's cows.

He called to the cows so gruffly that they did not respond at first, but took only a few hesitant steps towards him then stopped, flaring their nostrils and twitching their ears to discern the nature of the threat implicit in the man's angry tone and demeanour. He opened the gate wide and stood back, whistling to them to come through. Eventually, they moved forward, eager to be relieved of the pressure in their udders.

When Donal got back to the milking shed his father was waiting for him and had started up the generator so that the building was lit by growing bulb light.

"I can handle this, Daddy, go on inside," said Donal impatiently. He said the same thing most mornings out of concern for his father's health, but this morning, his tone was terse and bordering on disrespectful.

"Sure I can milk a cow, Donal – it's one thing I can help with – don't wish that away from me." But Dan watched his son's lowering face and sharp movements with some concern. "Is there something wrong?" Dan Kelly hooked the chains in place behind each cow on the left-hand side of the milking shed. When all four were confined, he waited for Donal to fetch the gleaming milking pails from hooks on the wall and pass one to him.

"Nah, no," replied Donal, picking up two milking stools, handing one to Dan. "Nothing's wrong." He crossed to the cows on the right of the shed and sat down beside one, pressed his head against her warm flank, and started milking. Dan shook his head then did likewise. There was much, he feared, which troubled his son and it disturbed him greatly that a large part of it was likely to stem from the fact that farming life was not what Donal Kelly had chosen.

When the dairyman had been and gone, taking with him the two churns of fresh milk which the Kellys' small herd yielded twice a day, Donal sat in the warm kitchen while Deirdre and Jacintha laughed and chatted as they prepared breakfast. Porridge with cream skimmed from their own milk and sprinkled sparely with sugar steamed on the table, and eggs were frying on the range, their spitting confined to the pan by an upturned plate. Fresh sliced bread and butter was laid out ready for the eggs, and mugs of steaming tea were duly served to the men as they sat down.

"That's grand, girls!" said Dan, beaming at his daughters.

"You say that every day, Daddy," said Deirdre, putting her arms around her father's neck and kissing his head. He patted her arm and nodded.

"Sure you're grand every day." Deirdre joined in on the last words and they laughed. Jacintha watched Donal, however. He seemed miles away and there was a preoccupied look on his face which the family had come to respect as meaning he was not to be teased or disturbed. All of them were grateful that he had given up so much to be at home.

"Listen, Daddy," announced Donal suddenly as he finished his breakfast and stood up. "I'm away out for a few hours."

"Will the pigs be all right, Donal?" was his father's anxious response.

"I'll feed the pigs," volunteered Deirdre straight away. "Sure there's plenty of time before mass." She smiled at Donal as he struggled into his coat and took his cap from a hook on the back of the kitchen door. He smiled back at her as he opened the door onto the grey day.

Donal's donkey cart arrived in Dunane in time for mass, as he knew it would. The little bell in the church belfry stopped chiming as if suddenly choked, and the altar boy whose turn it was to ring it raced for the stairs and the relative warmth of the sacristy. Many turned to look at the handsome young man who removed his cap from an unruly mop of brown curls and took a place in a pew at the back of the church. Father Kinnealy and the altar boy emerged from the sacristy in their vestments, and, fingers still half frozen, the altar boy preceded the priest to the altar, candle held in both hands. Donal Kelly tried to ignore the curious glances backwards as the women in particular attempted to work out who he was and what he might be doing at mass in Dunane. He wasn't sure himself what he was doing. It had been years since he had willingly attended mass. He had had no choice when he was a Blackwell scholar and then a master living in the seminary, but as soon as he had taken up lodgings at O'Hallorahan's, he had never set foot in a church.

He was waiting for a glimpse of Caitlin Spillane and her new husband. Why, exactly, he was not sure. He was not the only one who wanted to see Caitlin Flynn. The whole village, the Spillanes included, were curious to see Caitlin enter the church as Jack's wife. They imagined what must surely have transpired on the wedding night and could only think that, somehow, the trauma of it would show in Caitlin's face and demeanour. Mrs Brett was ready with her most vicious and disapproving sneer, which she planned to deliver to Jack Flynn's back as he passed her by. She might even risk an audible "disgraceful" if there was no chance he would look back and catch her.

Mrs Spillane's heart fluttered quickly at the thought of seeing her daughter. She had lain awake most of the night with the sheets over her head, crying at the thoughts of what Caitlin must be going through. Still, she had consoled herself, it was always worse to start with; you got used to anything after a while. Mick Spillane was very hung-over and had barely managed to milk his cows that morning. He could think of little else but going back to bed for an hour or so when he got home. Maureen and herself could feed the pigs. He did want confirmation that Caitlin had survived her ordeal, but his continuing inebriation was just the distraction he needed from images of Jack Flynn with his daughter. He might go drinking again that night. All were disappointed, however, for when Jack Flynn came into the church, coughing his way up the aisle and assuming his usual pew at the front, he was alone.

"Geeney-mack," whispered one young girl to her friend, "he's kilt her!" And they both blessed themselves, exchanging wide-eyed looks.

Jack looked neither right nor left, and Donal knew exactly who he was from the sudden eruptions of mutterings and nudges and looks towards the tall, greying man who arrived last to mass. Throughout the service, Donal stared at Jack's back and hated him. He made up his mind that, married or not, Caitlin Spillane was to be rescued. Indeed, reasoned Donal, the act would be all the more heroic, for the victim would have lost all hope of deliverance.

When Jack eventually emerged from the church, he nodded cursorily to the Spillanes, who had huddled together to wait for him on the top step. Then he walked on as though they were nothing to him. The young man who suddenly pushed himself away from the railing at the bottom of the steps and stared at him was less easy to ignore. Flynn met the stranger's flashing brown eyes and frowned at him, enquiring who he was and what he wanted with a quizzical knitting of his brows and narrowing of eyes. No words were spoken, and after a moment Donal let his eyes slide from Jack's and turned slowly away. He would remember that face.

"Who do you suppose that is, now?" Spillane's voice was startlingly close. At Mrs Spillane's insistence, he had followed

Jack to enquire of Caitlin and had watched with great interest the encounter between Jack and Donal. Jack ignored him and strode off quickly in the direction of his horse. As far as he was concerned, any necessity to communicate with Spillane had terminated the moment he had handed him that envelope.

When Caitlin Flynn assumed her usual classroom desk after the Christmas break, there was a stir throughout the school. No one had expected her to return. The nun calling the register missed her off, paused, and looked at Caitlin when the register was concluded. Caitlin met her gaze, waited, and the nun said eventually, "Caitlin."

"Present, Sister."

Never before had a girl returned to school after marriage. In fact, it had been some years since a school-aged girl had married in Dunane. Times were very hard and the war made them harder. Those who could afford to marry at all were few and far between and the men who could afford it, middle aged. And, though matchmaking was familiar still, like many traditions, it was slowly being replaced by more civilized ways of getting things done. Halfway through the day, the head teacher, Sister Mary Francis, asked to speak with Caitlin in her office.

"Sure it's even in the Constitution, Caitlin, that a woman's place is in the home," she said, thrusting her hands into opposite sleeves of her habit and resting her elbows on her desk as she leaned forward. Caitlin stood before the nun and considered her words.

"But you work, Sister," she said sweetly.

"I am not married, child," retorted the nun, sitting back stiffly and frowning.

"And if my... husband," Caitlin reddened at the word, "wishes me to continue at school, then what does the Constitution say?"

Sister Francis looked perplexed. Her mouth pursed and her eyebrows seemed to dive behind her spectacle rims as she bowed her head to consult her thoughts.

"This is most irregular, child," she said at last. "I shall have to speak to Father Kinnealy." And the nun picked up a pen and wrote something on a piece of paper. Caitlin waited uncertainly. "Off you go," said Sister Francis at last, eyeing Caitlin from the depths of her spectacles.

"Ah, let her alone, Sister," said Father Kinnealy. "Sure if Jack Flynn doesn't mind his wife going to school, what harm?" The priest was sitting behind his desk. In order to see Sister Francis clearly he pushed his reading glasses up his face till they clung to his forehead. "The Constitution only says married women should not be obliged to work, Sister. It doesn't say they can't. And Caitlin Spillane has lost enough already, God knows. It's very good of Jack, so it is, to let her go to school. Good man, himself."

Sister Mary Francis looked unconvinced but said nothing. The priest's authority was above question. Father Kinnealy made to get up to show the nun out of his office. He had a sermon to prepare and it would be lunchtime in about forty minutes. His housekeeper, Mrs Finnegan, had promised him a nice beef pie. As he rose from his chair, he winced, his hand flying to the base of his spine.

"Do you ever get a bad back, Sister?" Father Kinnealy squinted at her from a face contorted with pain. She shook her head.

"No, Father, I can't say I do – praise God."

"Aren't you fortunate?" he rejoined. "I think the divil himself rides around on mine." Sister Francis blessed herself, muttered her thanks, and took her leave as Father Kinnealy pulled his glasses down to the bridge of his nose, sighed, and went back to his sermon.

"I have good news for you, Mr Flynn." Mr Ryan, the official from Bord na Bainne, smiled widely as he stood before Jack on the threshold of his house. "Rather surprisingly, if I'm honest, your remaining cows are all tuberculosis free, and within a week or so, you will get official notification of the reinstatement of your farm's tubercular free status." Jack closed his eyes and visibly relaxed in relief. "Always a pleasure to bring good news to hard-working men like yourself, Mr Flynn," added Mr Ryan graciously. "Get them out of their usual field, though. It is imperative you graze them on new pasture – to be certain the bacterium has died away on the old. Can you do that?" Jack assured the official that compliance was no problem; he had several fields. "Good luck, now," Mr Ryan said, as he tipped the rim of his trilby hat with a gloved hand and turned to retrace his steps to his motorcar. As he did so, Caitlin came into the yard. She had been feeding the horse where he was tethered in the barn, for he had become a little lame lately. Jack was treating a swollen fetlock with hot poultices as a prelude to calling the vet.

"Who was that?" asked Caitlin and Flynn told her, explaining how for weeks he had been tipping away his milk, waiting for the all clear. Showing little interest, she went past him into the kitchen.

It was more than a fortnight after the wedding. Relieved of her greatest fear, Caitlin applied herself to her studies as never before. She had no idea where they might lead her but they had never been so important. One day, she thought, one day, she would make her bid for freedom. For now, she just had to keep her head down and stay out of trouble. Slowly, seeds of her dreams began to germinate again. If she could just get good results in her Leaving Certificate, then…

She had started well enough in the keeping of her promise to clean the house and take care of Flynn. In the first wave of gratitude that he would not touch her, she chipped away for hours at the baked-on grime of the range, scrubbed and scoured till it was almost clean, then coated its surface with waxy blacking to stop it rusting beneath the endless spillages of water from pots and kettles. She washed the floor until the stone flags were discernible beneath the dirt and she kept the range going all day, emptying the ash can, stoking it, fuelling it, adjusting the flue to maintain an even temperature and fuel consumption. She cooked and shopped.

It seemed there was little curtailment necessary in the quantities and extent of the groceries and cleaning products she was allowed to purchase. Flynn handed her ample amounts of money and she rarely brought him change. She bought new lamps and threw away the ancient, blackened ones which barely lit the kitchen or her bedroom. She even washed clothes and sheets, hauling bucket after bucket of water heated on the range and pouring it into a metal wash tub in the yard, soaking the garments and sheets in lye soap, pummelling them with a wash pole. She would not consider scrubbing Flynn's clothes and sheets on a washboard. She found an old mangle in the barn and wrung the washing till it could be draped across chairs in the kitchen and a line which Flynn strung from hooks in the kitchen walls. Not since his mother had lived in the house had Jack seen a washing line in the kitchen.

But the lye soap and the scrubbing of pans, the blacking of the range, and constant immersion of Caitlin's hands in water made them sore and red. The housework was laborious and unending. No sooner it seemed had she cleaned the floor than Flynn, unused to taking off his boots before entering the house, trod mud and cow manure over it from door to sink. It irritated Caitlin beyond tolerance that he did not wash his hands before he sat down to eat and that he left his filthy cap on at the table. His coughing drove her to distraction. The handkerchief, stained with blood and dirt which he used to wipe his mouth, disgusted her utterly.

For his part, though Jack was grateful for the cleanliness and warmth of his house, he was concerned at how profligate Caitlin was with his money. They did not need a tablecloth or new knives and plates. He could not chop wood fast enough or bring in enough turf from the barn to fuel the range. The extra work was arduous to him in his failing health. He could barely cope with the milking, and though she saw how he suffered, Caitlin did not offer to help him with that. In the evenings, she shunned his company and remained in her room. When he came in from milking in the morning, chest on fire with pain and hands locked agonizingly with rheumatism, she was waiting impatiently for him to take her to school, scrubbed clean, well rested and well fed. She seemed to tolerate his eating of breakfast, looking often at the wall clock as if to remind him that he needed to fetch the horse and hitch it to the cart. She never offered to hitch the horse herself. Neither spoke on the way to and from the school and Caitlin never thanked him for the trouble he took to make sure she did not have to walk in the rain or the snow or the mud – as he had always done when he was a boy.

On the Saturday morning following Mr Ryan's visit, Jack came in from milking the cows and there was no sign of Caitlin. The range had not been stoked since first light and there was no tea brewing, no bread on the table. He moved to the foot of the stairs and called, "Hey, Caitlin? Are you up there?" There was no answer.

Panicking a little, he climbed the stairs and knocked on her bedroom door. No response. He turned the handle and pushed open the door. She was not in her room. His heart lurched and he was immediately bent double in a coughing fit. When he had recovered, he descended the stairs as quickly as he could. What to do? Had she run away again? In the moment he thought she might have deserted him, he realized how much he had come to need her, how grateful beyond his capacity to express he was that this lovely young girl dwelt in his house, how much just the look of her reminded him of his mother.

"Caitlin?" he shouted, trying not to sound too gruff, for she might hear and be alarmed. "Caitlin?" It was certain she was not in the house.

CHAPTER TWELVE

Almost crying, Jack went out again into the bitter day, looked around wildly. Where could she have gone? The horse! He moved, as quickly as the pain in his chest would allow, to the barn. There his heart almost stopped in his breast as his worst fears were confirmed. The horse was gone. Dear God, she had left him! Anger, humiliation that she had so fooled him, rushed through him like swirling waters. Grief rose like a sword from his heart's depths and pierced it. "Caitlin!" he roared, but there was no answer and nothing to do but return to his cold and empty kitchen and wait.

That she might have returned to her father caused Jack agonies of humiliation. He would be the laughing stock of Dunane in no time. And as he sat, rocking with anxiety, fear after agonizing fear rolled over him like waves and whipped his thoughts to a black storm. She would tell everyone that he hadn't touched her. He would be ridiculed by the likes of Brett and the others who drank nightly in the bar. He could imagine only too well the relish with which Brett would relate again how Jack had come to him seeking a wife, and now he had a fine young wife, he had no clue what to do with her! Jack got to his feet and roared his anguish till it seemed the walls of his house must begin to crack. Even the pain in his chest and the blood which erupted as he fell, coughing, to his knees could not prevent the primal sound. It had a life of its own, seeming to derive its energy from decades of pain and the dredging up of grief which Caitlin's abandonment of him had set in motion. And when he could roar no more, he slumped, head bowed and bloody lengths of drool trailing from the abject drop of his jaw. Even when he heard the sound of hooves and cart wheels and a girl's voice urging a horse to "whoa there", he did not think it could be Caitlin.

It was at least ten minutes before she came into the kitchen, having unhitched the horse, fed, and watered him. The kitchen was dark and cold. As her eyes adjusted, Caitlin could make out Flynn standing by the range. There was something wrong, that much was evident.

199

"It's fierce cold in here." There was accusation in her tone.

Through the stupor in which his rage had left him, Flynn struggled to make sense of that. He searched the fog inside his head for a step to clarity, made unsteadily for it, felt for the next. Was she annoyed with him for letting the range go out? There was a long silence, during which Caitlin avoided the range in spite of her last observation, for Flynn had not moved away from it and did not seem concerned that it was all but dead. She busied herself with lighting lamps and then lifted a shopping bag, and something else of considerable weight, from the floor onto the kitchen table.

"Where have you been?" Flynn's voice was low and there was in its timbre a menace she had not hitherto experienced.

"I went into Dunane," she answered, defensiveness already colouring her tone, "and bought a few things – for dinner like, and some more soap. We needed soap." There was no answer. "Can I not leave the house, is that it?"

Flynn was unable to prevent the fury uncoiling again in his breast but now it was precise and venomous.

"You will not take my horse and go careering off wherever the hell you please!" he roared. Caitlin was transfixed with fear. In the gathering lamplight, he walked slowly towards her. "And where the hell, may I ask, missie, did you get the money for… for shopping?" He sneered the last word, gesturing sharply at the bag on the table. "There's enough stinking food in the place to feed an army! Do you think you can just spend my money as you damn well please, do you?" He was face to face with her and his eyes were terrifying. He was unshaven and gaunt and his breath stank. Blood had crusted around his mouth and soaked into his shirt. Caitlin could not prevent the grimace of disgust which crumpled her face, and she took a step back from him. His arms were stiff at his sides, his fists clenched. He breathed heavily through closed mouth as he shadowed her steps, trying to stop the coughing and aware his breath was foul. She turned her head to one side.

"Well?" he roared.

Suddenly, Caitlin turned to face him. Her eyes flashed back at his and her face contorted in anger. "Well what?" she shouted. "I had a few shillings left in my purse from the last shopping trip, if it's the money you're mad about! And if you must know, I wanted to pick up my accordion from home."

If he could have been placated by the defence of her shopping and her explanation for the money it necessitated, the last piece of information and her use of the word "home" could not have been calculated more precisely to undo the balm.

"You what?" he erupted again. "You took my horse and cart to Spillane's house? You scut! Did you buy him a bit of shopping too, eh? Is that the plan, is it? To feed the likes of Mick Spillane with my money – as if he hadn't got enough out of me!"

Caitlin could not think of how to respond to what seemed stark madness. Even in his worst temper, Spillane had never approached the unsluiced vitriol of this man's wrath. She covered her face. The gesture checked Flynn for a moment; it seemed familiar. But the thumping of his heart and the rage unleashed in his head could not easily be appeased without a sacrifice. He turned away from her and strode to the table, then lifted the accordion roughly and it fanned in apparent alarm, discordant notes falling from it like confetti. Caitlin took away her hands and looked in horror as Flynn held aloft her instrument by one strap.

"Ah, please don't… please don't damage the accordion," she begged, tears rolling freely down her cheeks. "I just want to play it sometimes is all… I missed it." She came towards him, one hand over her mouth, the other outstretched in a gesture of supplication and request. Flynn tightened his grip on the accordion and lifted it higher. His eyes widened and his teeth clenched in an expression which seemed the precursor to dashing the instrument to the floor. But Caitlin fell to her knees before him and joined her hands in something like prayer. "Please, please don't," she cried.

Jack looked at the accordion – at his hand and the ferocity of the grip upon the leather strap – and lowered it. Caitlin greedily gathered her instrument to herself, pressing the bellows together and cradling it as though it were a child.

"Never," he shouted, but less wrathfully, "touch my horse again or spend my stinking money without my permission! Is that clear?" But Caitlin was kneeling on the floor sobbing, bent over the accordion and rocking with it gently. Jack strode across the kitchen and flung open the door. Just before he went through it, he turned back to her. "And from now on, you will go to mass on a Sunday."

Forlorn beyond his ability to process, Flynn walked up the road to his cow field. Another man might have sought solace in the bar. Leaning on the gate, Jack watched his cows moving about their new field, cropping the sparse January grass, unconcerned by his presence. It seemed to Jack that life had played upon him a cruel trick and that he would leave it as he had started, abandoned and alone. He knew enough to know there was no cure for TB and no respite he could take to prolong his life, for who would run the farm? Jack leaned on his gate, bowed his head, and contemplated the shivering grass, felt the small shifts of his boots on loose stones.

He tried to break through the barrier grown thick over the merciless wring of years, between sensibility and the instinct to survive. Somewhere, always, he had the impression of a small boy behind a door, who could not reach the handle but who lived in hope that one day he would be strong enough to let himself out to a world of light and freedom. Or else, someone would come and push the door wide open as if it were weightless and light would come flooding in, the way it did when his mother parted the curtains in the mornings. But no one had come.

Jack reflected now that he had known the key to his freedom was deep in his father's pocket, and no amount of book learning or fine language would ever have induced Sean Flynn to relinquish his hold on his son. It was hard now to think of words with which to name the things he understood. The ancient Irish Celts, he had learned once in classics, had introduced soap to the Greeks. Someone had sniggered and asked why they didn't make more use of it. And it was true enough; as far back as Jack could remember, life had been filthy. There was little reason to wash your clothes or yourself when all you did was trudge through mud and manure. Even in the summer, the work was sweaty and there was endless digging: digging for turf or to make ditches so the fields weren't sodden in the frequent rain and the crops didn't rot in the ground; digging to put in fence posts; digging to plant things, and when you had planted them, there was digging to get them up out of the ground. It seemed to Jack that all his years had been a bending to the earth, and soon she would fold him into herself entirely.

The only clear memories he had from learning were anchored like buoys in the swift, dark current of his life. Wolfe Tone's French galleys with their bloated sails, spilling ink blue uniforms and light snaring bayonets onto the sandy shores and grey marram grass of Buncrana; Brian Boru in warrior dress at the battle of Clontarf, fighting against Mael Morda mac Murchada, King of Leinster, and the army of Vikings Mael Morda had enlisted to challenge Boru for monarchy of All Ireland.

History was Jack's favourite lesson. He learned that Brian Boru had died saying his prayers in a tent. A cowardly Viking mercenary called Brodir had slain the almighty king when he had no chance of defending himself. It had made Jack so angry! That was no way for a warrior to die, on his knees with his eyes closed.

"The good news, boys and girls," professed his teacher, Mr Carolan, "was that the great King Brian Boruma mac Cennetig would have gone straight to our Lord and the Blessed Virgin in heaven, for he was 'taken at his prayers'." Jack was not consoled by the image of Brian, his spear in hand and mane of flying red hair, floating around with angels and a lady in blue clothes.

Remembering it now, though, he tried to imagine the light which everyone said you saw as you approached heaven. But his hands were freezing and his heart, receiving again its reservoir of sadness, sank heavily in his chest as the colourless day sighed into darkness. He opened the gate. He may as well milk the cows now. No point going down the road to come back up again.

That evening, as Caitlin cried herself to sleep in the pitch darkness of a moonless room and Jack sat guilt-ridden and ruminative by the range, Donal Kelly caused a stir by walking into the bar in Dunane. Mick Spillane was particularly intrigued to know who this young man was, for he recognized him straight away as the same who had wordlessly confronted Jack Flynn after mass a couple of Sundays before. Approaching Donal, Spillane extended his hand. Knowing who he was, the younger man hesitated half a second then returned the gesture. They shook hands.

"Well?" said Mick. "We've seen you hereabouts a few times now. Where are you from?"

"Golden," replied Donal, turning as he did so to pay Jim Fogarty for his pint.

"Golden?" Mick waited for Donal to turn back to him. "That's a fair few miles up the road, now," said Spillane. Donal looked down and smiled to himself. "Ah, hah!" exclaimed Spillane triumphantly. "It's a young one you be after, am I right, eh?"

Donal nodded again and allowed himself to laugh at the irony. "Indeed," he admitted.

"Well, now, and who is she?" Mick sipped his pint, smiling at Donal in what he assumed was a fatherly fashion.

"Ah, now, I'd rather not say." Donal affected coyness and Mick winked conspiratorially at him. What a pity, he thought in that moment, that Maureen was so bloodless. Sure this was a fine young man by any standard and he had a good strong back on him – would be helpful around the farm.

"Come and have a drink with us," urged Spillane. "What did you say your name was?"

"I didn't." There was a pause and Mick stopped again to look at Donal with amused confusion. "Kelly – Donal Kelly."

"Kelly up at Golden? Sure I know your father well," said Mick. "Have seen him plenty of times at the markets above in Tipp and Cashmel. Is he well? Sure didn't we hear he was after having a heart attack?"

Donal became very serious. "That's right. He's not too bad now."

Mick squinted and bit his lower lip as if trying to recall something else to impress Donal.

"And weren't you above in Blackwell – a teacher, was it?"

"I was," confirmed Donal, "but the old man needs me at home now."

Mick nodded and his eyes became serious. "Aren't you the grand son, now?" Then, turning to the men who had all ceased to talk and were watching Mick and Donal, he said, "This is Dan Kelly's boy. Make room there, lads, for he's planning to make himself at home in Dunane by the sounds of things."

CHAPTER THIRTEEN

"The horse is lame," announced Jack when he came in from milking the following Monday morning. "His leg is worse. You will have to walk to school." He could not look at her, such was his shame. But at the same time, his irritation was growing with what he regarded as Caitlin's slovenliness around the place. He understood that she was feeling sorry for herself and that life was a disappointment for her, but what about him? She had said she would look after him. Most of the time, she stayed in her room and it was all she could do it seemed to put a meal on the table or clear up after it.

Caitlin looked at Jack with an expression of sneering disbelief, though she was careful to ensure he did not see it. She walked quickly across the kitchen and out of the door. It was raining and cold. The thought of walking the two miles to school filled her with despondency. It would take her at least forty minutes in her rubber boots and the rain and the mud. She would be soaked. But her suspicion that Flynn had exaggerated the horse's lameness out of spite following their row was soon allayed. She was shocked at how swollen the horse's fetlock was. He stood with his weight on three legs, his painful foot dangling from the fetlock joint, the tip of its hoof just touching the ground. At her arrival, the horse turned and whinnied softly. Well, there was nothing for it – she would have to walk.

Within a few minutes, Caitlin had changed her shoes for boots and wrapped a shawl around her chest and head. She put on woollen gloves and picked up her bag, then left the house without a word to Flynn. When she arrived at school, Caitlin

207

was cold and bedraggled, like most of the children who daily walked to school. At the back of the classrooms, throughout the winter, were placed large paraffin heaters; the children hung their coats on pegs behind them. They arranged their soaked gloves along a bench which ran under the pegs and lingered as long as they could near the source of warmth before the handheld bell signalled the start of class.

Since her marriage, the five other pupils in Caitlin's class, four of them boys, had become awkward around her. She had always been renowned for her intelligence, and as the girls with whom Caitlin had started infant class dropped out of school to help at home on farms or seek paid employment in dairies, shops, or as maids, she had become increasingly aloof and isolated. There was only one other girl still at school at seventeen, Nuala Kenny. Nuala was exceptionally intelligent with a wiry mane of flaming hair which resisted all attempts to restrain it. She had bushy blonde eyebrows and freckles which seemed to halt like full tide at the boundaries of her spectacles. When Nuala removed her glasses to clean them, the paleness around her eyes was astonishing, and her blue eyes seemed small and vulnerable. Hardly friends – more comrades in adversity – Nuala and Caitlin sat together in class but competed fiercely with the boys and each other.

On this morning, as Caitlin unwrapped her shawl and removed her wet gloves, laying them out on the bench in the hope they would be dry by three o'clock, Nuala approached her in a state of rare excitement.

"Have you seen the dreamboat they've brought in to teach maths?"

Caitlin was not interested, too preoccupied with her sorrows and freezing fingers to care for gossip. She shook her head distractedly, did not turn to face Nuala. "Caitlin, he's an out and out doll! Apparently, his father has a farm in Golden but he's sick so Mr Kelly came home to help him out but it turns out he's brilliant at maths – went to Blackwell and taught maths there –

and he'll be teaching the young ones here part time, so he can still help his father." Smoothing her hair, Caitlin turned to regard her classmate's bright eyes and ruddy cheeks. The rims of Nuala's glasses were pink and she had a habit of pushing the frames up her nose with her right third finger.

"Well," said Caitlin, and could think of nothing to add. At the sight of Caitlin's pale face and lacklustre eyes, Nuala remembered, to her embarrassment, that she was a married woman now.

"Ah, sorry, there," she muttered, her excited flush deepening to red. "I didn't think, sorry." Sister Mary Francis rang the hand bell and the children in the playground ran into the school. Within minutes, all was silence and Caitlin took her place behind her desk, lifted its lid, and removed a geography textbook. She turned to page seventy-three and a chapter entitled "The Ruhr Valley" in perfect synch with Nuala and the four boys in Leaving Cert class.

"Begin reading please, Conor Fahey." Sister Mary de Ricci's crisp imperative began the lesson.

"I don't like the look of that pastern, Mr Flynn." Jack had walked into Dunane and asked Mary in the post office to put a call through to the vet in Tipperary. Without his horse, he was stranded. This was not such a problem when he had his health, but now that walking anywhere was an effort, Jack needed to know if his horse would get better and when. Though it pained him to spend money on a vet, he had no choice. The fetlock swelling was not responding to the poultice or hosing down treatment he had been applying to the leg. Caitlin's decision to use the horse without his permission had not helped. The animal needed complete rest. "He's getting on a bit now," said the vet, still palpating the fetlock joint, feeling for the tell-tale bony growth around the lower pastern joint and finding it. The horse flinched, stamped his foot. "OK, old boy, OK," soothed the vet, straightening up. "This horse has a nasty case of osteoarthritis," he pronounced, "and unless he gets several weeks of rest – maybe months – so the swelling can subside and he can avoid stressing the joint, I'm afraid the outlook is not good."

Jack cursed, passed a hand over his face in consternation. How the hell was he supposed to get by without a horse? Walking into Dunane and back in the cold rain had been a terrible strain on his chest. How would he make it to mass on a Sunday or get shopping? And how would Caitlin like it, walking to and from school every day? He particularly had not wanted her to do that. It was only two miles but it was hard enough in the wet and cold and the dark. He had been pleased to be able to offer her the lift. And how would he get feed up the road to his cows, or pigs to market, without a horse and cart? How would he dig turf in the spring and bring it home? How would he get hay from the fields to the barn? Even as he stood beside the vet and contemplated his animal, more and more ways in which his mobility and commercial survival were compromised occurred to Jack. A badly lame horse was no good to him.

"I can inject him now, for the pain," said the vet, "and to reduce the swelling a little. But if you want this animal to pull a cart again, you will have to rest him – totally – for a long time. We've caught the condition at an early stage, but this sort of thing doesn't go away. There's no guarantee he won't go lame again within days of use. You have a hard decision to make, now, Mr Flynn. How old is he?"

Flynn had to think hard. He bought the horse as a youngster and trained him to pull a cart. He had always been a good-natured and willing beast. Flynn could remember being fit and strong and in his prime, trotting fast through summer lanes to mass, proud of the way the light shifted on the horse's black, glossy coat. He recalled working as one with his animal as they turned furrows of earth, Jack guiding the bulk and will of the animal as it pulled the ploughshare up and down the sugar beet and potato fields all day. He had never given it a name.

CHAPTER THIRTEEN

"He's fourteen or thereabouts," answered Flynn solemnly. As if the horse sensed the seriousness of the trouble he was in, he turned to look at Jack, snorted, and bobbed his head. Jack stepped forward and rested a hand on the animal's broad, strong back, then slipped his hand beneath his mane and followed the warm line of his neck from shoulder to poll. The vet saw the affection in the gesture and sighed. This was never easy, the weighing of sentiment against economy. Everyone had a living to earn. Farm animals were beasts of burden or production. He awaited the verdict, prepared for what he might have to do.

"I will need a new horse." Jack's words were barely audible. "That will be expensive." The vet nodded. "Is there any sort of a chance he might be good for riding?" asked Jack suddenly. "Nothing too strenuous, like. Maybe for a woman?" The vet raised his eyebrows and considered the request.

"If you can afford to keep this horse and look after him, then I don't see why he couldn't recover enough for light work of that sort – with a woman on his back."

Jack smiled, patting the horse's neck. "Then that's what we'll do," he said. "That's what we'll do."

"And you'll buy another horse?"

Jack nodded. "Aye. Nothing fancy." The vet smiled and shook Jack's hand.

Caitlin sighed as she emerged from school and Flynn was not there with the cart. Much as she loathed her husband, she remembered how grateful she had been when he said she could continue at school and it was a luxury indeed to be delivered and picked up each day. School finished at three o'clock in the winter, but the sky was dark grey and the few houses visible from the road outside the school house were already blacking out their windows. The nuns who ran the school pulled out of the gates in their shiny car and away to their convent in Tipperary nine or so miles away. This had become a National school in the last five years. The Christian brothers in Dunane had aged and declined in numbers till it was no longer economical to maintain a seminary there. The Presentation convent in Tipperary was secure enough and there were several nuns young enough to take over the job. The state paid them and the lay teachers they employed, and subsidised the purchase of a car.

This afternoon, close behind the nuns' car came another – that of the science master, Jim Fennessey. What remained of Mr Fennessey's once curly black hair was a ring around his pate. He had bulbous features and a fleshy lower lip which hung open most of the time as if too heavy to lift. He had lived in England for years before the war broke out, coming home to his widowed mother in Cappagreen when it did so. He intended to sit out the war, teaching science and keeping his mother company in the little shop she kept on Cappagreen Main Street, eight miles from Dunane. Mr Fennessey was not married but rumour had it that he was courting, for some had seen him cruising about the country lanes in his little Austin car, a lady in the passenger seat. In the passenger seat now was Donal Kelly. As Jim drove past Caitlin, he raised his hand in a salute of acknowledgment.

"Who's that?" asked Donal, turning his head to watch the girl until the car left her well behind.

"That's Caitlin Spillane – no," Jim corrected himself, "Caitlin Flynn. Her father recently married her off to an old fella – got a tidy sum for her by all accounts. At least he lets her continue at school, which is most unusual. The girl is fiercely intelligent. Much good will it do her now. Primitive as hell but sure, what can you do? We're called to enlighten the natives not change the world, my friend. One step at a time." Donal said nothing but changing the world was exactly what he had in mind.

Mick Spillane had been very willing to tell all and sundry in the Dunane bar how Caitlin was getting on as Jack Flynn's wife.

"Sure he's letting her finish school," he boasted, "and he takes her there every day, picks her up in the evening."

"Boy, he have it bad!" smirked one of the men, and others shook their heads, laughed.

"And what'll she do with all that learning, do you think Spillane?" asked another. "And she married to Jack Flynn." Mick shrugged, staring contemplatively over the rim of his pint as he raised it to his lips and lowered it again.

"Search me."

"But it's a good way of placating her, all right," added Malachai Brett. "She has little else now to look forward to, I'd say."

And so the conversation had turned to education. Donal had listened attentively as Mick recounted Caitlin's dreams of university and how ridiculous the very notion was. "Aren't you a maths teacher, Donal?" Spillane had asked again, enjoying his position as storyteller and centre of attention – and glad to be able to turn the conversation from Caitlin if people were going to get maudlin.

"I was," confirmed Donal.

"They need a maths teacher above at the school," interjected Sean O'Riordan. "Sister Michael is retiring – dying more like, the age of her – and they have no one to teach maths to the small ones. The wife was telling me the other day, for our grandchildren are at the school." All eyes rested on Donal. It was interesting news, he admitted. But he couldn't go to work in Dunane each day in a donkey cart.

"Sure Fennessey lives out your way – Cappagreen. Couldn't he give you a lift?" suggested Malachai Brett. "He have to drive right past your neck of the woods to get here."

"God love you, Brett, but you're still a great matchmaker, eh?" quipped Spillane. "Will we drink to him, boys, will we?" Jim Fogarty stood to attention at the pump, readying himself for the next round.

* * *

213

If Dan Kelly was less than happy that Donal had taken a part-time teaching job in Dunane he did not say so. Jacintha had left school and was biding her time till she could look for work in Cashmel or Limerick or Tipperary. She could not leave her father while he was so ill and Deirdre was still at school. The girls did not welcome the prospect of the extra work they would need to shoulder while Donal taught maths three days a week, but, like their father, they said nothing. Donal's sacrifice of a university place was a burden they all lived with and none could reasonably resent his taking advantage of this opportunity. "I can still do the morning milking," he had pronounced, "and I'll be home in time to do it in the evening. And the money's good. A pound a week for a few hours. Sure that's the bills paid, lads, at least."

When Caitlin had gone home to pick up her accordion, her mother came out of the house wiping her hands on her apron at the sound of the horse's hooves in the yard. When she recognized her daughter, Mrs Spillane threw her hands in the air and cried out in joy. When Caitlin got down from the cart, Mrs Spillane pulled her to herself and squeezed her tightly. When at last she looked into Caitlin's face, Mrs Spillane's bright blue eyes were awash with tears. "You are so thin, alannah! And so pale! Caitlin, are you eating at all?" Moved beyond any expectation and unwilling to signal even a fraction of the tumult she felt, Caitlin stared dumbly at her mother and did not respond. "Come inside, Caitlin," urged Mrs Spillane. "Come in and have a bite to eat, for the love of God."

When she felt she could speak without dissolving in tears or screaming in fury, Caitlin said simply, "I am not hungry. I only came for my accordion." Tears spilled down her mother's face as she turned away and went back to her house.

It was harder for Caitlin to cross this threshold than it had been to step across Flynn's on the wedding morning. The kitchen was just as she remembered it – and why wouldn't it be? It was only three weeks or so since she had left it. But in that time, such changes had been wrought in Caitlin's heart and so complete had been the severance from her former life and expectations, that she felt like a traveller who returns to her place of origin to discover that it had forgotten her the moment she left it. The passage of time was irrelevant. Caitlin had not been sent into the world with the blessings of her people but sold to it, all rights and fealties waived. There was now such a gulf between her and the woman she beheld that a lifetime of weeping could not breach it.

It wasn't even, she thought to herself, a question of forgiveness; the notion was abstract to Caitlin, for the weight of the sorrow she carried was numbing of finer thought and feeling. She was vaguely aware that a very small cloud, no bigger than a hand, was somewhere behind her, white in a black sky. She supposed it was hope – something vestigial in any case. But she dared not look for it in case she was wrong and the sky was all lowering, rolling storm.

No, it was not that Caitlin could never imagine forgiving her family for their betrayal; more that she could never imagine feeling anything for any of them again. The amorphous sorrow at their loss, however, was as much beyond her control to avoid as the small white cloud was hers to determine. Caitlin inhabited a land of shadows – not dead but not quite alive either. She was someone else's dream, an idea someone had had to enhance his own life, but the price he was willing to pay for her shadow had cost the world her heart and soul. Somewhere, she slept like a princess in a fairy tale, pale and pure, awaiting a life-giving kiss. But unless the ogre himself became a handsome prince, what chance was there of rescue now?

"Will you fetch my accordion, please?" Caitlin had asked of her mother.

"I will, of course. Wait there a minute, now, Caitlin." And Mrs Spillane left the kettle warming on the hob and went upstairs. Caitlin envisaged the hallway, the bedroom door as her mother approached it; she followed her in imagination to the room Caitlin had shared with Maureen and, ten years ago, with two other sisters besides. Maureen. Caitlin imagined her sister must by now have entered the convent. She felt nothing at the thought. It couldn't be worse than her own life. In many ways, she reflected with an ironic smirk, their lives were similar: chaste, confined, austere, pointless.

Some minutes later Mrs Spillane reappeared with the accordion and a few cardigans and pairs of socks which Maureen had left behind. "Take these with you, alannah," said Mrs Spillane brightly. "Sure, Maureen have no use of them now she's in the convent above in Tipperary." Caitlin said nothing as she watched her mother fold the clothes on top of the musical instrument. "We took her up there the other day," went on Mrs Spillane, apparently undaunted by Caitlin's silence, "in your father's new truck."

Caitlin frowned. "What?"

"Yes," confirmed her mother, beaming with excitement at the revelation and Caitlin's interest. "He bought himself a second-hand truck – a red one…" And she stopped; her face fell. Caitlin got up, pushed the clothes off her accordion, and picked it up. She needed to leave before the hot tears started flowing.

"Sit up straight, Kenny." Donal took to teaching again far more naturally and willingly than he had resumed farm work. Farming to Donal was being yoked to the earth and, very specifically, a small patch of Tipperary. He wanted to travel and experience all life had to offer in light, clean shoes. Increasingly, all things Irish were weighing him down, including his covenant with the IRA. It was clear to him – as he knew it was clear to Joe Morgan – that a few hundred men were never going to bring down de Valera's government or drive Churchill's England from the North, before or after the war. Donal was formulating a plan. After the next campaign – Operation Holiday – he would find a way to abscond. Ireland was neutral, so in theory his passport could take him anywhere. He longed to go to America but would start by travelling to another neutral country – Switzerland or Sweden, perhaps.

He would find a job teaching English or even mathematics to English-speaking Swiss students whose parents had plenty of money. And when the time was right, he would pursue his studies. He knew that if he deserted the IRA it was not likely it would ever be safe to return to Ireland. At least, he could not envisage a time when the likes of Joe Morgan and the men he worked for would turn a blind eye to betrayal. But that was all right with Donal. He would earn enough money to send some home and never tell his family where he was. He would convince his father to sell the farm and so set his sisters free. Donal knew that neither Deirdre nor Jacintha wanted to endure farming life a moment longer than they needed to. Perhaps he would send for them all when he was settled. Perhaps Jacintha would marry soon and look after his father. If the farm was sold and she had a dowry, that was possible.

"I said, Kenny, sit up straight!" Donal's class of nine- and ten-year-olds was restless and bored. He had them working through a section of algebraic equations in a maths textbook. Seamus Kenny was a chubby, freckly boy who had not inherited the genes which made his sister, Nuala, so intelligent. He was more interested by far in fishing and catching insects and chasing bainbhs to make them squeal. His father was one of the few farmers in Tipperary to rear sheep instead of cattle – a shrewd move in many ways, for the labour was far less intensive and there was more call for wool now the war was on and clothing was at such a premium. Seamus loved his father's sheep dogs, Tess and Jack, and was often in trouble for rambling away with them on long walks, usually to rivers and ponds and fast-running streams where he could swim and fish and throw stones into the water.

"Sorry, sir," said Kenny on his second rebuke. "I was thinking of something interesting."

The class giggled nervously, but instead of getting angry, Donal said only, "I know what you mean, Seamus; I know what you mean." The last thought Donal had had before admonishing Kenny for his slumped posture and sleepy face was that it might be a very fine adventure indeed to whisk Caitlin Spillane away from the drudge and servitude of her existence, to a place of blue sky and bright sunshine; a place where the cows wore bells around their necks and the only evidence they were milked was the bars of creamy Swiss chocolate he would buy for Caitlin.

Donal had seen Caitlin a few times now, around the school. She was very pale and thin but there was no mistaking her beauty. She wore her thick, black hair tied back, and she always looked preoccupied and serious. She seemed to shun the society of other students and a couple of times he had seen her at lunchtime in the Leaving Cert classroom, perched a distance from the other students, absently eating a piece of bread. She didn't even look up when he had asked the students if they had seen Mr Fennessey – his ruse for putting his head around the door. Nuala Kenny's beaming face and slow blush he had noted and raised an eyebrow in amusement. He had to find a way of making meaningful contact with Caitlin Flynn.

"That, Spillane, is a very fine truck," affirmed Padraic O'Riordan. Jim Flaherty the landlord, Malachai Brett, and all the usual patrons of the Dunane bar agreed. It was a Saturday evening in the second week of February. Donal Kelly had persuaded Jim Fennessey to give him a lift into Dunane "for a pint", promising his colleague that if the bar was too rough for him or he got too uncomfortable, they would leave.

"Come on, Jim," Donal had urged the reluctant science teacher, "live a little, would ya? Come and have a pint with the men – you might enjoy it." Jim was very unsure about that. Happy in his mother's company and firmly attached to a spinster called Bridie, whom he had met through his mother, Mr

CHAPTER THIRTEEN

Fennessey was not a drinking man. He liked to read books about scientific discoveries and planets and, though he would never have admitted it to Donal, shared a love of cooking with Bridie which often meant he spent the weekend in her kitchen, baking bread and rolling pastry to make jam or treacle tarts. They joined together their sugar and butter rations for the purpose and then brought their confections to Jim's mother, covered with freshly laundered cloths and revealed with a magician's panache. The old lady would always exclaim and clap her hands and there would be smiles all around. Jim's idea of living a little was a nice bit of stew with fresh bread, tart and cream for pudding, and gentle conversation with his mother and Bridie about life in Cappagreen and the perennial subject of the priest's vestments. They always looked so snowy white, because Bridie and Mrs Murphy down the road took turns to bleach, starch, and iron them.

And didn't Bridie always used to make a lovely job of the flower arranging in the church at Cappagreen, before the war? When there was free trade across the Northern border and by sea from England, it was possible to find a range of fresh flowers out of season in a few Tipperary shops. Occasionally, if there was a wedding or a funeral, Bridie would go up on the train from Limerick Junction to Cashmel and bring back irises or roses, lilies and gypsophila, and spend hours tying them with ribbon in small bunches to pews, arranging them in vases before the altar. Father O'Neill was always happy to pay, for the chapel at Cappagreen was as fresh as a bride for days after the ceremony. But there was no money for that now and no flowers to be had either. Such memories were sources of light and fragrance in February blacked-out evenings and kindled hope for the future. Bridie Farrell was forty and thin with crooked teeth and dark-rimmed glasses but in her Jim had found a caring and attentive companion. And importantly, his mother already loved her like a daughter. It was likely he would marry Bridie in Cappagreen chapel and, one day after the war, perhaps when his mother passed away, he would take her back to Surrey suburbia from whence he returned in 1939.

But Donal had needed a lift into Dunane. He could not again make the fourteen-mile round trip on a donkey cart. It wasn't fair on the beast and it was uncomfortable and tedious beyond belief. Not only that, but picking your way along pitch-black roads and stony boreens late at night in a donkey cart, after a skinful of ale, was perilous. A fella could fall asleep in the hours it took the donkey to cover seven miles and end up only God – and the donkey – knew where.

Without effective transport, a village seven miles away was practically out of bounds, another life. If Donal was going to effect his scheme to spirit away Caitlin Flynn and escape, he needed a plan. And increasingly, it seemed to Donal, Mick Spillane was central to any that might just work. Any man who would sell his daughter would be easily manipulated and it wasn't hard to work out what was important to him.

"It is indeed a very fine truck," gloated Spillane, toasting his own good fortune and slurping his pint. *Well worth a daughter*, thought Donal cynically as he smiled and raised his own pint in salute.

"Drink up there, Jim," urged Donal quietly, for Jim was sweaty and uncomfortable in his white shirt and ironed trousers. The farmers eyed him wryly and exchanged glances. Fennessey was not of their ilk. He had clean, manicured fingernails, and the gut which hung over his leather belt as heavily as his lower lip dropped told of indolence and self-indulgence. He was as out of place in their world as they would have been in his classroom or at one of the London scientific conventions he used to attend.

"I'd quite like to go home soon, Donal," said Jim quietly, making an effort to get close enough to Donal's ear so that his words wouldn't be heard and perceived as rude. The men shook their heads and smirked at the sought intimacy and Jim's exclusion of them and Donal was embarrassed.

CHAPTER THIRTEEN

"Just a little while longer, Jim, OK?" he reassured his colleague. "I just need a little more time here." The older man frowned.

Then Donal had an idea. "Jim has to get off home, lads. So, as he's my only way home, I'll have to go with him, unfortunately." And Donal downed his pint and wiped his mouth with the back of his hand. Jim reddened, his lip hanging lower than ever.

"But ye've just got here!" Spillane was genuinely disappointed. He liked the cut of Donal Kelly; he was like the son he had never had, looking after his poor ill father that way. And it had occurred to Spillane that there might be mileage in getting acquainted with a young fella in line to inherit a farm from an ailing man, especially when that young fella didn't seem all that interested in the farm.

As Donal shrugged and assumed a sad but philosophical expression, picked up his jacket from a stool and started to put it on, Mick put a restraining hand on the young man's shoulder.

"I'll take you home in my truck," he announced. There were cheers of approval and jeers of mock derision at Spillane's great pride in his vehicle.

"Will you, Mick?" Donal looked surprised and delighted. "Well, I'll get the next round in, so!" He slipped off his jacket sleeve. The jacket crumpled on the bar stool as Jim nodded awkwardly to Donal and hastily took his leave.

"Daddy, we have been invited to lunch next Sunday, with the Spillanes over at Dunane," announced Donal to his father the next morning during milking. Dan Kelly stopped milking, sat up straight on his stool, and frowned as he searched his memory.

"Mick Spillane, is it?" he asked. "Wiry fella with mad hair he can hardly get his cap over?" Donal laughed a little at the description, confirmed it was correct. There was a brief moment during which all that could be heard were jets of milk hitting the pails. The warm smell of milk mingled with the aroma of manure and the straw which littered the milking parlour floor. "Be careful of that fella, Donal," said Dan at last. "He's a sly one, I'd say.

Always trying to knock down the price of anything at market or sell you something for more than it's worth. I won't come, son. You go, if you want."

Donal nodded at the expected response. "Right so, Daddy, but I said I'd ask, like." There was another pause.

"How did you come across Spillane, Donal?"

"In the bar at Dunane."

"And do you like him?"

"Not really. But sure, it's only polite to accept an invitation. He's picking me up in time for mass."

Dan pushed his head away from his cow's flank in order to look at his son. "Mass? You're going to mass?"

Donal did not look up from his milking. "Well, it was all part of the invitation. As I said, I'm being polite."

Dan went back to milking his cow but there was something in the back of his mind about a Spillane girl. Wasn't the girl Donal had found in the barn a while back a Spillane? And hadn't she been running away from a marriage match? He would have to ask Deirdre for the details. Something here wasn't right.

A little more than a month after the wedding and the world was adjusting, it seemed to Caitlin, to assimilate her status as Mrs Jack Flynn. The change in its landscape wrought by the seismic nature of the event was now a landmark. Life went on. Apart from emerging to stoke the range or empty its ash tray, prepare meals, and perform light housework duties, Caitlin spent the weekends in her room, watching the rain and the sky. Her window onto the back field was a study in greyness and precipitation cycles. She estimated the ferocity of the wind by watching how peacefully or fitfully the little black tree slept through the bleak winter.

Without the constant interruptions from her parents and Maureen which had characterized busy family life on a farm, Caitlin could read for hours, complete her homework in silence, and – in the third week of her removal to Flynn's house – she even started to sleep better than she had at home. She was free of Maureen's snoring and shifting in the bed and was not disturbed by her sister's early rising to meditate and pray. And, increasingly convinced that Flynn would keep his word and not touch her, she began to eat well. She told herself that it would not be possible to perform to her best ability in her exams if she were undernourished, and, in any case, when the time came to escape, she would have to be fit and healthy, with her wits about her. She had learned that much.

Late afternoon of the third Saturday in February, Flynn returned to the house having tended to his horse. He had made the animal very comfortable in the barn, deeply littering the floor around him with straw so that he might be tempted to lie down and take the weight off his feet entirely. He was feeding him hay and no sugar beet on the vet's advice and grazing him during daylight hours, for it was essential he got some exercise and good grass. In a week or so, the horse would need his hooves clipped and to be re-shod and led at least a mile or two a day around the roads.

As Jack entered the kitchen he was arrested by music. Spellbinding, an air in a minor key had slipped down the stairs and swirled in the kitchen like a graceful ghost. Jack stood transfixed, gratefully aware on a less conscious level of the warmth from the roaring range and the aromas of bacon and cabbage escaping the pot on the hob. He realized, in a moment, this was the very melody his mother used to sing when she was sad and which used to bring tears to her eyes.

He swallowed hard, closed his eyes, and allowed the music to caress him. When it was finished, he took off his coat and cap and made for the stairs. Almost reverently, after a brief hesitation, Jack knocked gently on Caitlin's door. She had heard him approach and was sitting perfectly still on the edge of her

223

bed, facing the window. Embracing her accordion, Caitlin turned her head towards the door. What did he want? She had made his dinner and cleaned the kitchen.

"Yes?"

There was no immediate response, but then the door opened gently. Caitlin altered her posture so that she could see him.

"What was that tune?" he asked almost shyly, awkward in the doorway as though he feared her.

"The one I just played?" He nodded. "'Silent, O Moyle'."

In spite of his nervousness, Flynn was transported by the title to a vivid memory of his mother's voice. But he could not have been more than three years old and the impression of familiarity he had now would not harden to remembrance, for the words had meant nothing at the time; only the sound of them was familiar.

"Do you know the words?" His voice was softer than Caitlin could have imagined him capable of. She was uncomfortable with the intimacy of this exchange. She was certainly not going to sing for him.

"I have them written down," she said, "somewhere." She turned away from him.

"The horse is going to need a lot of care," he announced, reverting to his usual imperative tone. "You can do that. He'll need feeding with hay every evening and bedding down for the night, mucking out. Next week, you'll have to walk him around the lanes for a mile or so a day. Vet's orders."

Caitlin did not respond but her head jerked upwards and she stared ahead, allowing the defiance and resentment to harden her eyes, for he could not see her face.

Flynn watched her a moment longer, withdrew a little, and was about to shut the door but he stopped, adding, "Oh, and don't forget – mass tomorrow."

"And how are we supposed to get there without a horse?" she rounded on him.

CHAPTER THIRTEEN

"We will walk! How else?" And he shut the door with much less regard than he had used to open it.

CHAPTER FOURTEEN

The congregation at mass in Dunane on the fourth Sunday of the month had their attention held by more than Father Kinnealy's ministrations. In truth, he was a lot less able to compete for it than usual, given the unfair distractions represented by the presence at mass of Caitlin Flynn and Donal Kelly. "What in blazes is going on?" wondered Mrs Brett to her husband. "Who is that young fella with Spillane?"

"Isn't he the new teacher above in the school?" replied her husband, turning his head to follow the direction of his wife's aquiline glare.

"What's he doing with Spillane?" she persisted, never taking her eyes from Donal Kelly's smiling face and how Mick was making a show of laughing and talking with him.

"How should I know?" Malachai observed his wife's pale blue eyes, which often struck him as being a lot like his pigs' eyes, but her eyelashes weren't as long. She pursed her lips in irritation and untrained her gaze to look at him.

"Do you know anything?" she sniped.

"I do," said Malachai, assuming a long-suffering expression. "More than you, I can assure you, because I keep my gob shut and mind my own business."

"In the name of the Father and of the Son and of the Holy Spirit." The congregation ceased to talk and rose to its feet as Father Kinnealy intoned the introductory rites.

"Amen!" said Mrs Brett loudly, with a sideways glance and a sneer at Malachai.

227

"The grace of our Lord Jesus Christ and the love of God, and the communion of the Holy Spirit be with you all…"

Jack and Caitlin stood apart in the first pew and both stared fixedly at the priest, trying not to think about the people staring at and whispering about them. Donal Kelly stood between Mick Spillane and his wife a few pews behind them, Donal looking more handsome than ever in a brown suit and brogues, his curly hair washed and silky.

"Oh, geeney, he's gorgeous," sighed Nuala Kenny to her friend Majella Clutterbuck, daughter of the local blacksmith. Majella, with short dark hair and china blue eyes, was a year younger than Nuala. She was an only child and had her own horse, which was a cause of much envy among her school friends and much speculation among her neighbours about the relative wealth of her parents. The imminence of Majella's removal to a boarding convent school in Adare, Limerick, so she could get riding tuition at a stables in nearby Lisaleen, did nothing to ease social relations. And Majella's mother had dyed blonde hair and wasn't in the least bit fat, while her father was dark and lean and would have been handsome, in most women's opinion, if he trimmed his eyebrows and prolific nose hair. The Clutterbucks had a strange way of talking, as if they knew that a broad Tipperary accent might hinder their social mobility, but where they thought they were going was altogether a mystery. Majella pushed back the edge of her lace mantilla and peered coolly at the man in the pew across the aisle and halfway up from where she stood. She would rather, she decided with an arch of a fine eyebrow, have her horse.

Donal strained as inconspicuously as he could to keep Caitlin's back and bowed head in view, noting how far away from Flynn she stood and pitying her at the same time as anger filled his heart anew at the injustice she had suffered. The thought that Flynn might have already impregnated her had occurred to him, but while it filled Donal with anguish it fuelled his resolve. It was urgent and imperative that he act soon. They would think what to do with a baby if and when that time came.

"May almighty God forgive us our sins, have mercy on us and lead us to eternal life."

"Amen," said everyone. The priest led them as one into the "Gloria".

There was no chance that Spillane was going to let Jack Flynn ignore him after mass this Sunday. And indeed, Jack was intrigued to see with Mick the young man who had wordlessly accosted him a few Sundays ago. Caitlin too was astounded to encounter the new maths teacher chatting amiably on the church steps with her parents.

"Jack! Jack!" shouted Mick as his daughter and her husband emerged from the narthex. "How are ye?" Several of the congregation milled and affected conversation at the foot of the steps to see how this meeting would pan out, eyes sliding from their neighbours' faces and up the steps as they spoke. Neither Jack nor Caitlin moved to join Spillane's party, so Mick beckoned to Donal and Mrs Spillane to follow him and walked across to his son-in-law.

"Do ye know this young man, now?" He beamed at his daughter and Jack, looked from one to the other. Both glowered at him. Undeterred, Spillane introduced Donal to Caitlin then Jack.

Donal fixed his eyes on Caitlin's pale and puzzled face, marvelling at the beauty of her eyes, and said, "I know Caitlin; sure I teach at her school."

There was something about the tone of his voice and in his proximity which made Caitlin contemplate Donal Kelly anew. In the brief time she had to acknowledge him the thought occurred that Kelly's familiarity had origins outside or beyond the school. She stared into his liquid brown eyes and tried to place him in any other context, but could not. Jack thought several things, none of them hospitable. He remembered the aggression of this man when he was yet a stranger to him and thought now, as he watched Kelly greet his wife, that he knew its source. He drew himself up as straight as he could and stared darkly at Donal. Mick watched the exchange with some amusement but stepped in. His plan was to re-establish contact with Caitlin and introduce her to his new friend and possible business partner. It would not go unnoticed, he thought smugly, that he had made acquaintance with the smart new maths teacher. He was counting on Jack's ignoring him and, particularly, Caitlin's unwillingness to cause a scene in public and before one of her teachers. Then he would move on and make a show of ushering Donal into his shiny red truck while most of Dunane's population looked on.

Mick had had a chat with a few men in the bar and it seemed Dan Kelly was getting no better after a huge heart attack months earlier. Kelly had two daughters after Donal, and it was anyone's guess what would happen to the small farm he was endeavouring to keep. Now that Mick's daughters had all left home and he was comfortably well off, he was thinking of expanding his herd and hiring a lad to help around the place. Dan Kelly's cows at a good price might be a starting point. Apparently oblivious to the extreme awkwardness of the situation he had engineered, Spillane turned to his daughter.

"Are you right, Caitlin? Sure, you're looking well." She did not respond but regarded him coldly. "Anyhows," Spillane rushed on, "it's grand to see the two of ye. Are your cows all right now, Jack? I heard you had to destroy a few. Terrible business." Mick's mercurial face assumed an expression of concern and he shook his head. "Donal's father is Dan Kelly of Golden," he added, brightening again. Jack regarded the young man and Donal returned his scrutiny. Dan Kelly always seemed to avoid Jack at markets. He did not know the man.

"Will ye come to us for lunch?" Mrs Spillane's small voice crept into the conversation and held everyone's attention as though it were a mouse running into a circle of cats. That would certainly make the prospect of lunch with Mick Spillane and his wife more interesting, thought Donal.

"No," said Caitlin straight away. "We have to get going. We've no horse and must walk."

"No horse?" Spillane was glad to change the subject but was, in any case, genuinely shocked. He may have lately acquired a truck, but even now, life without a horse was not an option to a serious farmer. You couldn't plough fields with a truck.

"It's lame," said Flynn.

"Sure I can give ye a lift home in the truck!" he beamed, turning his head to indicate the vehicle where it was parked, half on half off the pavement at the bottom of the church steps. He could drop Jack and Caitlin off then bring back Donal Kelly. That way, there was no chance that an unpleasant mood would spoil the impression he wanted to create at lunch.

"Ah, no, Mick," pleaded Mrs Spillane, less timidly, then looked imploringly at Caitlin. "Sure there's plenty of food below. More than enough for the five of us."

"We cannot," said Jack decisively, calculating immediately that Kelly was a lunch guest. "We have food above. Good luck." And he began to walk away. Caitlin glanced after him then back at the truck. She didn't want to walk the two miles up the road to Flynn's farm.

"Give us a lift, so," she said loudly enough to her father so that Flynn would hear. He stopped in his tracks and turned around. He was weary and his chest hurt. A ride home might not be a bad idea. Spillane dropped the tailgate and Jack and Donal climbed in, taking a seat on opposite edges of the truck bed. Mrs Spillane and Caitlin climbed into the front. Although Mrs Spillane cried and pleaded, Caitlin was obdurate. She was in no way ready to eat with her parents – particularly with a school teacher looking on. She was mortally embarrassed by the whole idea and just wanted to get back to the solitude and quietness of her room. Jack at first ignored Donal Kelly, but as the latter continued to stare at him, he returned the young man's cool and steady gaze with mounting ire.

"What's the matter with you, Kelly?" he shouted at last above the rumble and judder of the truck. The two men were forced to grip the sides of the truck with both hands and plant their feet squarely on the bed floor to maintain their balance.

"Me?" answered Donal, never taking his eyes from Jack's face. "There's nothing wrong with me, Mr Flynn."

"Well, keep your scobbing to yourself, then," retorted Jack, and began to cough, so that he was forced to remove a hand to cover his mouth and was almost thrown headlong into the rear window of the cabin. Donal smirked and looked away. No real problem here, he thought. In a few minutes, Spillane pulled into Flynn's yard. It was starting to rain. Donal leapt out ahead of Jack and waited for Caitlin to descend from the cabin.

Mick rolled his window down and shouted to Jack, "If it's a horse you're wanting, you could buy mine at a good price. I have the truck now and was thinking of buying a heavier horse, just for the ploughing, like."

Caitlin looked at Jack, blinking against the rain. Her father's chestnut, she knew, did not much like the plough, for Spillane had often come in swearing at the perversity of the animal and the swervy lines in his field which wasted precious sowing space because the horse would not drive straight. But it was a good carriage horse and only eight years old. He could be trained to be less skittish at the plough, with a more expert master. "I will think about that, Spillane," answered Jack. "How much?"

Donal climbed into the cabin next to Mrs Spillane and watched Caitlin make for the shelter of the doorway. Mrs Spillane sniffed and blew into her handkerchief and tutted repeatedly to herself but Donal had eyes and ears only for the girl before him. He was irritated by the windscreen wipers which Spillane had set in motion, for the rain was now driving against the glass and, with the wipers, was obscuring his view.

"Fifteen pounds," said Spillane, "because you're family now."

"I will think about it," answered Jack and walked away from the truck towards his house. Just before she disappeared inside, Caitlin turned to look at the place she knew Donal Kelly sat, for she had been keenly aware the whole time that he was staring at her. At last, her curiosity was aroused.

Donal timed his confession perfectly. Mrs Spillane had killed a chicken in his honour and served it roasted. They needed fewer eggs in any case, now that Maureen and Caitlin were gone. For dessert, she had baked a rich porter cake, using up the last of her precious raisins from Christmas. Goodness alone knew when she would be able to buy more, for fruit dried and fresh was a scarcity since the war broke out. She served it with cream.

"That was a marvellous dinner, Missis," said Donal, arching his back and caressing his belly. "Thanks very much." And he winked at her.

"Oh, that's a pleasure." Mrs Spillane simpered and coloured slightly. He really was a very good-looking, polite young man, she thought as she reached for his dessert plate. And her next thought was of Caitlin in bed with that old goat. She closed her eyes quickly on the image, turned away from the table, and made for the sink. Mick was delighted.

"It was grand, Mary, so it was," he confirmed. "Do ye's eat well above in Golden?"

"We do," replied Donal. "I have two sisters who can cook very well."

"Ah," said Mick, nodding. "What ages are they?"

"Jacintha is nineteen now and Deirdre is going on seventeen."

"Ah," said Mick again knowingly, not taking his eyes from Donal's face. "I suppose they're wanting to get married – move off the farm, is it?"

Donal smiled and looked down briefly before he answered. "I couldn't say, now. My father has need of them."

233

"Of course he does, of course he does," said Mick. "Is he doing better – Dan?"

"He is," affirmed Donal. "I do the heavy work but he milks and does jobs around the place."

Mick nodded. "It must be hard, though, I'd say, keeping everything going between the two of ye and you have your teaching and all."

Donal inclined his head to one side. "It is, all right, Mick. I can't lie to you, now. I have often wondered if we should sell up, and…"

"Have you?" Mick interrupted. "A big decision, but if it's for the best – sure your health comes first, Donal. What's the point of anything if your health is gone?" Donal nodded as if he were considering the wisdom of Mick's words. After a brief pause, while Mrs Spillane placed a teapot and her best cups on the table, Donal spoke again and both she and Mick paid especial attention.

"Can I be very honest with you both? Can I?"

"Of course!"

"Of course you can, pet." Mick and Mrs Spillane responded at once and together.

"It's kind of hard to say and I am not sure how ye'll take it." Donal frowned and looked at the table as though he were about to announce bad news.

"What is it, son?" urged Mick. Mrs Spillane covered her mouth with a hand and braced herself for more tragedy. Donal suddenly looked up and stared intensely into Mick's eyes.

"Do you remember that night I came into the bar below in Dunane and I walked out again real quick?"

"The first time – I do," said Mick, frowning, trying to anticipate what was coming and failing entirely.

"Then I came back again another night," went on Donal, "and you asked me if I was seeing a young one?"

Mick's expression lightened. Donal was going to ask him to

help out with a match – speak to someone about the availability of a daughter. He sat back and smiled. "Well, there was – there is – a girl I like all right." Mrs Spillane did not remove her hand but her eyebrows rose as high as they could go and her eyes told her intrigue.

"Spit it out, Donal! Sure if I can help you, I will." Mick winked, reached towards Donal, and slapped him on the shoulder.

Donal looked at Mrs Spillane and then to Mick, swallowing hard. "It's Caitlin." Mrs Spillane gasped.

"Caitlin?" exclaimed Mick. "Sure Caitlin is married, Donal – you saw that for yourself today!"

"I know that, Mick! Sure how do you think I found out? I came to the bar in Dunane that first night in search of someone who knew her and discovered ye were all celebrating her marriage!"

"Oh!" Mrs Spillane removed her hand at last and sat down heavily on the nearest chair. What a plethora of possibilities was unleashed in her head in that instant.

"And that is why," said Mick slowly, "you started towards Jack Flynn on that Sunday, on the steps outside the church."

"It is," admitted Donal, looking down again and nodding. "I could not help myself."

A cock crowed somewhere. Mrs Spillane ached with regret and grief that her daughter might have been sitting beside this fine young man as his wife, if only they'd waited – if only her stupid, headstrong, greedy husband had not rushed everyone into that horrible marriage for five hundred stinking pounds. She stared at Mick and could not disguise her fury. Mick stood up and pushed away from the table, rubbed his face, and turned his back on them.

"There," said Donal, getting up. "I have made ye all angry and upset – and after that lovely meal. I am very sorry. I should not have said anything. I'll go. No need to drive me," he added, crossing the kitchen and retrieving his jacket from a hook in the back door. "I'll walk."

"You'll do no such thing," said Mick. "Sit down, will you, and have some tea. It's a shock, is all." Donal hesitated and looked at Mrs Spillane, who smiled at him and nodded her agreement that he should resume his seat at the table. She poured him some tea. Mick was thinking as fast as he could.

"How did you know Caitlin at all?" he asked, standing behind his chair and leaning on the back of it.

"Sure she hid in our barn," came the reply. "When she tried to run away, like – before the wedding." Again there was general shock and gasping from Mrs Spillane. "I found her when I went out to get turf for the range. She ran off and left a pony behind. She'd put a note in its harness." Donal paused and appeared to be trying to remember what the note had said, though he remembered it vividly. "'I belong to Pat Maher of Dunane', it said."

"So it did!" exclaimed Mick. "It did! And was it you brought back the pony?"

"It was. Myself and Deirdre, my sister."

"Incredible!" said Mrs Spillane, eyes filling with tears again.

"Incredible!" echoed Mick. "Maher is losing it, boy," he added animatedly, tapping his forehead. "He couldn't remember who had brought back his horse. Just said it was a girl and a young fella. Sure we had no clue it was you!"

Donal sat still and contemplated the grooves and marks in the wood of the table. He waited for the full effect of his narrative to sink in; waited for an outcome he had planned but could not be sure of. How many times had Caitlin sat at this table, he wondered while he waited. How many of the grooves in it were there because she had slipped with a knife as a child buttering bread or because she had placed something on it too roughly? He passed the flat of his hand over the edge of the table. It was almost a shock when Mick spoke again.

"It is a great pity things turned out as they did, but she is married now and that is that."

CHAPTER FOURTEEN

"There is nothing to be done," said Donal. "I just wanted to let you know… in the interests of honesty, like, as we're becoming friends." And he smiled at Mick and then Mrs Spillane, whose watery eyes smiled back at him above her handkerchief.

"Wait, now," said Mick, a note of suspicion in his voice. "Is that why you took the teaching job at her school, is it?"

"Well," said Donal, "not entirely. Sure I am a maths teacher and the pay is good. Was I supposed to not take the job because he let her carry on at school? Sure who would ever have thought he would do that?"

"Fair play, fair play," said Mick, raising a placatory hand. "It's just that this is a shock, boy."

"It's fate, that's what it is!" cried Mrs Spillane. "Poor, poor Caitlin!" And she got up from the table and left the room, unable to stem the sobs any longer and burning with hatred for her stupid, stupid husband. The kitchen was quiet. The clock ticked sleepily. Late afternoon. Soon, it would be dark and time to milk the cows.

"I think I'd better go," said Donal, getting up again.

"I'll drive you home, son," said Mick. "Come on."

"Funny, that," said Donal.

"What?"

"You called me 'son', there, Mick." Mick said nothing. He watched Donal put on his jacket, fetched his own jacket from the back of the door, and checked that his keys were in the right pocket.

"I did," he said at last, looking almost sorrowfully at Donal.

"You know," went on the younger man as Mick opened the door and stood aside for his guest to go through it, "I was thinking all the way through lunch how different things could have been if I had met Caitlin first." Then, seeing Mick's face darken in a frown, he added quickly, "Of course, I don't blame you for what you did, like." Donal stopped walking and put a reassuring hand on Mick's shoulder. "I can perfectly understand it. Times are hard and hard times need hard decisions, right? A real man doesn't let sentiment get in the way of business, no sir." They proceeded to

237

the truck. Donal waited till Mick was in and had leaned across and opened the passenger door from the inside. He climbed in, and continued, "Only I was thinking – imagine if I had met her first and you and I had chatted, like, and I had said if I marry Caitlin, the two of us would run the two farms together – like father and son, is all."

Mick started the engine, turned the wheel slowly, and the truck rolled towards the entrance to the yard. He looked right and left, pulled out.

"That would have been grand," he said quietly.

"'Cause imagine, now, Mick..." Donal warmed to his narrative. "I could have helped you out here as well as above, and when..." He paused, struggling against the genuine sorrow which pricked his heart. "When my auld fella... well, then I would have the whole farm and you would have a son – and I would have a father still. Think, Mick, if Caitlin and I had kids, sure you and I would have ensured our farms were kept in the family!"

Mick drove on quietly. It was hard to tell how he was reacting. Donal turned to look at the countryside speeding past the passenger window, allowing his words to sink into Mick's thoughts.

"I didn't think you were too interested in farming, now, Donal," said Mick at length, looking briefly sideways at his passenger.

"Well, I would be if I were married to your daughter and thought I had a family here!"

When Mick pulled into Dan Kelly's yard he noted its neatness; how the cobbles of the yard were swept and its perimeters weed and grass free. The barn was painted black and shone against corrosive winds and rain. The window frames of the little house were clean and painted white.

"Thanks, Mick," said Donal as he got down from the truck. "I'm sorry now if I upset you. Say sorry to your wife for me."

"Not at all, Donal. Sure we'll see you again."

"I'm not sure about that now, Mick," said Donal.

"Oh?"

"I am not sure I can go on working at the school, like, and seeing her… every day." Mick pursed his lips and shook his head, struck the steering wheel with his hand. "And even if I wanted to carry on, sure it's the divil's own job getting to Dunane. Without Fennessey's car, I'd be stranded. We don't have a horse here – just a donkey."

"Is that right?" asked Mick. "No horse?"

"There was no need of a horse after Daddy got ill. He was an old thing anyways and not fit for hard work any more. We sold him to the knacker's yard. Sure the old man couldn't plough after the heart attack anyway. The donkey does fine well for turf cutting and messages. The girls can get in and out of Golden easy enough. We're close enough they can walk to school and mass. What need of a horse?"

"So ye won't be planting any crops, either?"

"Nah." Donal leaned on the passenger door frame and bent down to look at Mick through the open door. "We'll stick to grass and hay, keep things simple. Sure we can load a fair few stooks on the donkey cart. The girls will help me carry in the rest."

"A horse would get you to Dunane in an hour, easily."

"It would, but sure horses are expensive, Mick."

"It would pay for itself with ploughing. If you had one, you could get a crop or two in the ground in a month's time."

"Too many uncertainties," replied Donal. "But a horse would be handy all right for getting about. We are truly stuck out here."

"Leave it with me," said Mick, decisively. "All the best now, Donal."

Donal slammed shut the truck door and bent again to wave goodbye through the glass of the passenger window. Mick swerved away in an arc, pulled out of the yard, and was gone.

"That," said Donal aloud to himself, "is one shameless man."

* * *

"That was a long lunch, son," remarked Dan as Donal came whistling through the door.

"It was, Daddy, but I'm home now. Give me a few secs and I'll away and get the cows." Dan put down the paper he was reading and watched his son leap from the floor to the second step of the stairs.

"Jacintha," Dan said.

"Yeh?" Jacintha had just cleaned the kitchen, stoked the range, and emptied a bucket of slops into the pig trough. She entered the kitchen flushed and breathless. She was tall and, Dan considered, too skinny. She wore her hair up all the time and it exposed the protruding bones of her neck and upper spine. But she had her mother's chestnut hair, with a hint of red in it, and her mother's round, hazel eyes. If she would just fatten up a bit and let her hair loose once in a while, she'd be lovely.

"Do you know the Spillanes up at Dunane?"

"Spillane?" Jacintha frowned. She put down her bucket and used her lower lip to direct a breath upwards so that it displaced a lock of hair which had fallen over her right eye. "The name is familiar all right, wait…" Dan continued to look at his daughter over the top of his reading glasses. "There was a Caitlin Spillane, played the accordion at dances – Dundrum and Cappagreen – but I don't know if she's the same Spillanes, now."

"Is she a looker?"

"Why?" asked Jacintha, smiling quizzically at her father, using her foot to shift the slop bucket to its corner. She crossed the kitchen to wash her hands as she waited for his response. When none came, she carried on, drying her hands on a towel and replacing it on the bar of the range. "Yes, she's a fine-looking young one. Why, Daddy?"

"Is she married?"

"I haven't a clue! I doubt it – sure she's only Deirdre's age or thereabouts. Why?"

"Where's Deirdre?"

"Upstairs doing her homework – will I get her?" Dan nodded and Deirdre duly appeared.

"Yes, Daddy, what is it?"

"You remember that young one Donal found in the barn – the one who was to be married against her will?"

"Yep."

"Was she not a Spillane?"

"I think so now – I can't remember. Will I get Donal?"

"No, no, leave him be. I was just curious."

"Is that it?"

Dan lifted up his paper again. "It is – thank you."

Deirdre and Jacintha exchanged puzzled glances, then went about their business.

CHAPTER FIFTEEN

One late afternoon halfway through the last week of February, Caitlin started her walk home from school. Preoccupied as usual with the difficulties of her life and various academic problems such as a new history essay and her frustration with advanced trigonometry, she did not heed the sound of hooves as they caught up with her.

"Caitlin!" A man's voice demanded her attention. She stopped. She was astonished to see Donal Kelly driving her father's horse and cart. He stopped beside her, smiling broadly. "Get up," he said. "I'll give you a lift home." She frowned at him, shook her head. "Come on," he insisted, patting the seat beside him. "Sure I won't bite!" The horse tossed its head and seemed to paw the road in its eagerness to be off.

"Why have you got my father's horse?"

"He brought him along to the school for me to try – see whether he suits me and how long it takes to get home in the cart."

Caitlin tried to make sense of the news. "But I thought he was selling him to…" What did she call Jack Flynn? "My husband" was out of the question.

"He was," replied Donal, matter of factly. "But I made him a better offer." He grinned at her, winked. "Come on, Caitlin, you can tell me all about the horse and how he goes." Still hesitating, Caitlin looked ahead at the road as it stretched away from Dunane. There was something very wrong about all of this, she felt, but she had been so badly wronged herself, why should she care? She moved to the cart and climbed up, sat beside Donal. He

243

clicked-on the chestnut, which lurched forward. "He's a flighty one," laughed Donal, struggling for control of the animal. "Very different from a donkey, boy!" he said, as they trotted full pelt away from the village.

They passed many children; several stopped to stare at their maths teacher flashing past them in a cart pulled by a sprightly chestnut horse. The girl beside him looked like Caitlin Spillane. Why would that be? More curious than the children was Jim Fennessey, who had to slow behind them and then overtake carefully in his Austin car. *What the jumping Jupiter was Kelly up to?* he wondered for the umpteenth time. He decided, as he pulled away, to have nothing more to do with him.

Jack emerged from his kitchen and was about to feed his few pigs before he brought in his horse for the night. The sows were about to farrow and there would soon be bainbhs to get to market. He had stopped milking now, for his cows were dry and would not yield again till they next calved, from early April. Jack wondered if his horse would be fit to pull a cart load of crated piglets to market in a couple of months' time. These thoughts occupied him as Donal Kelly erupted into his yard and barely persuaded Spillane's horse to stop before it knocked Jack off his feet.

"What the…?" Jack exclaimed, leaping out of the way.

"Whoa! Steady there!" ordered Donal, and the chestnut, sweating and chomping at its bit, finally consented to stand. Jack could make little sense of the scene before him. Caitlin got down from the cart and stood awkwardly in the yard. Donal smiled broadly at her and tipped his head at Jack in greeting.

"Is that Spillane's horse?" asked Jack.

"It is – well," responded Donal, "not really. He says if I like him, I can buy him. And I like him! He's spirited, boy, but that suits me. Sure, who would want to break his spirit? Or anyone's?"

"Spillane promised that horse to me!" shouted Jack, coming forward and dropping the bucket he had been carrying as if he had forgotten it. Pig nuts fanned across the muddy ground as the pail hit stone. Jack caught the horse's bridle and held on tight. The horse shied and stepped back in alarm, fighting for its head.

"Well, as I recall," retorted Donal, "no bargain was concluded. He gave you a price and you said you would think about it. I made him a better offer." Jack was furious, desperate to get at the young man in the cart.

"Get down here, you brazen little scut, and we'll see what you have to offer!" he shouted. The horse was beside itself with anxiety; it tried to rear, snorting in its alarm.

"Let go of my horse, Flynn," scowled Donal, matching Jack's fury with his own. "You cannot buy and bully your way through everything. You think you can buy people and horses and make everyone do what you want, is that it?"

Jack could not let go of the horse in case Kelly got away and he could not climb into the cart to get at him unless he let go. In an agony of frustration he roared, "Get down off that cart, Kelly, and we'll see how much of a man you are!"

"You are an idiot, Flynn!" Donal shouted back at him. "An impotent, stupid old man who has met his match. If I get down off this cart I will probably kill you. Thank your lucky stars I do not – though it would give me great pleasure, I can assure you. Now let go of my horse before I run you down!" Donal let out such a roar and slapped the reins so hard on the chestnut's rump that the animal, in complete terror, lunged forward and Jack was forced to let go of its head and dive for cover, sprawling helplessly in the mud of the yard. Turning pointedly to Caitlin, fixing her with a meaningful look and nodding his departure, Donal Kelly left Flynn's yard with a deafening clatter and more vocal encouragement to the horse, which hardly needed it. For a few seconds, they could be heard galloping up the road towards Golden.

When at last silence resumed, Caitlin looked towards Jack. He had not moved. He lay face down and inert.

"Hey," she called to him, "are you all right?" She still could not say his name. He didn't answer her. She ran across the yard and hunkered down at his head. He was barely conscious. His eyes were half open as though he had just woken up and his mouth was open. A thin rivulet of blood and spittle oozed from one corner into the mud. "Come on," she urged. "Get up." But Flynn did not move. His eyes continued to stare lazily into the space to his right and his breath came in rasps. Caitlin stood up and half shouted half screamed in frustration. She could not leave him here, face down in the mud. But she could not move him. Maher! Halfway between here and her father's farm was Pat Maher's house. She would run there and get help. Caitlin ran the mile or so to Maher's house. He emerged from his tea chewing soda bread and staring at her as if she reminded him of someone. What was left of his snow white hair stuck out at odd angles and his braces were shiny with years of dirt.

"What?" he asked when she had breathlessly garbled her story. She could not start again.

"Will you come quick! Get your pony or your horse and come quick, for the love of God. There's been an accident above at Flynn's."

"Flynn's?" Maher squinted at her, wiped his mouth. "An accident?"

"Yes!" said Caitlin. "It's serious and he needs a doctor. We have no horse. Will you please get yours and take me back up there?"

"I know you," said Maher at last, craning his neck forward and peering at her.

"There's no time for this now, Pat!" shouted Caitlin, unwilling to get into a row about the stolen pony. She was very relieved when Maggie Maher came to the door.

"What's all the noise?" asked Maggie, peering around her husband's shoulder. "Caitlin! What's the matter?"

"It's Jack Flynn," explained Caitlin again. "He's had a fall,

Maggie, and I think it's serious. We have no horse – it's lame – I can't get him up. He needs a doctor."

"For the love of Mike, Pat," admonished Maggie, "will you quit gawping at the child and hitch the horse to the cart!" Maher complied at once, scratching his left buttock as he ambled away, muttering to himself. "Michael!" shouted Maggie over her shoulder, and within seconds an overweight man of about twenty appeared at the door.

"Yes, Ma? Hello, Caitlin," he grinned at his neighbour. His mother scolded him.

"Never mind hello – go on up with your father and help Caitlin get Jack Flynn off the ground."

"Eh?" Michael looked puzzled and stared open-mouthed at his mother, breathing thickly over his half protruding tongue.

"Just do what I say," snapped Maggie. "Or rather, do as Caitlin tells you." Michael turned to Caitlin again and grinned.

"Hello, Caitlin."

"Oh, for the love of Pete!" Maggie rolled her eyes at Caitlin and folded her arms. She looked impatiently up the yard towards the field at the end of it, from which Maher had just led his heavy grey horse.

"Go on up and help your father hitch that horse to the cart, will you? He's as likely, now, to hitch it to the buggy – go on."

Flynn was still on the ground when they reached him half an hour later. "I should have covered him over with something!" exclaimed Caitlin aloud as they entered the yard. She leapt from the cart and hunkered down at Jack's head again. His eyes were closed but he was still breathing. The sight of the prostrate man seemed to jolt both Maher and his son to sense. Between them they lifted him and each took an arm and a leg. Caitlin opened the door.

"Where shall we put him, Missis?" asked Maher, struggling for breath. Jack had grown thin since his illness had become serious but he was still a considerable dead weight.

"Can you get him up the stairs?" asked Caitlin. Maher and his son looked at the stairs, estimating the likelihood of success.

"We can try," said Pat. "Come on, Mikie." Lowering Flynn's legs, putting their shoulders under his armpits, they made for the stairs. Following Caitlin's instructions, they half lifted, half dragged him to his room. There, they dropped him heavily onto his back on his bed and he stirred fitfully. His eyes rolled open for a second, but he did not wake.

"He's in a bad way," observed Pat, while Michael leaned against the door frame and caught his breath, mouth wide open. "Will I get the doctor?" Caitlin fought the urge to roll her eyes.

"Yes please, Pat; would you do that?" she said.

While she waited for the doctor, Caitlin washed Flynn's face of mud and blood and cleaned his hands. She could not have undressed him even if she were able to move him, but she covered him with blankets from her own room. "Now what?" she asked herself yet again. She drew up the wooden chair over which Flynn threw his clothes each night, sat beside the bed, and folded her hands in her lap. She could not decide what to think of Donal Kelly. With his good looks, youth, and fine brain as well as his apparent courage, he had appeared like a champion – but one who had missed his cue. And much as Caitlin loathed Flynn and the situation to which he had brought her, she had not enjoyed watching him thrown onto his face in the mud. What part her father was playing in all this she could only guess, but Flynn was right about one thing – that horse should have been his.

And so, Caitlin sat quietly at Flynn's bedside, unable to think or feel her way past the trauma of the last hour or so, her head full of memories of the chestnut horse flailing and lunging in the yard, Donal Kelly's brown curly hair flying backwards in the wind as he rose to his feet to enable him to bring the reins down harder on the rump of the terrified horse. She looked at Flynn, his chest rising and falling rapidly beneath the blanket, listened to the rasp and catch of every breath he took. It occurred to her that he was lucky he had any breath at all after that.

"He is gravely ill, I'm afraid." Doctor Bergin unhooked his stethoscope from his neck and packed it away in his leather bag. Pat and Michael Maher had driven to his home in Pallas Green where his surgery served villages within a ten-mile radius. Surgery had been over for the day, and Doctor Bergin had been looking forward to a trip with his wife to the new Excel cinema in Tipperary. Then an old man had turned up on his doorstep, cap in hand, and had said he must come quick, that Jack Flynn had had a fall.

"Who is Jack Flynn and where is he?" the doctor had asked, immediately irritated by what sounded like a complete kibosh on his plans. The irritation was not diminished by the old man's apparent inability to answer either question. Eventually, the doctor had established that he needed to go to Dunane and find a man called Jack Flynn who owned the farm up the road.

"Up the road from where?" the doctor had asked, perceiving the need to be patient.

"From where I live," came the reply.

"And where is that?"

"Dunane – on the Golden road."

"Ah. At least now I know which end of the village to aim for, eh?" The doctor had enough information. There couldn't be more than three farms on the road out of Dunane to Golden. He'd find it. He apologized to his wife for their spoilt evening, put his jacket back on, and, grabbing his emergency bag, headed for his car.

"Was it the accident, doctor?" asked Caitlin.

"Well, the fall didn't help – I gather he fell? How did that happen?"

Caitlin wasn't sure what to say. She wasn't sure if what she had seen truly was an accident. As she had sat waiting the hour from the Mahers' departure till the doctor's arrival, she had not been able to come to a decision.

"He was thrown, by a horse."

"I see, well, no bones broken as far as I can tell," said Doctor Bergin. "It is not the fall itself which has made him so ill." Caitlin looked at the doctor with an expression of relief.

"I presume you are his daughter?" She coloured, looked down quickly. "You are his wife?" The doctor could not keep the incredulity out of his voice. "And you do not know what is wrong with him?" Caitlin still did not look up. Her cheeks were burning. She shook her head. "He has tuberculosis – and it is very advanced. This man has not more than a few weeks to live." Caitlin met his eyes, her own wide with shock. "Why these men carry on till they drop is a mystery to me. I've seen it several times. Is it pride?" he seemed to be wondering to himself. He looked at Flynn's sunken face and open mouth, listened to the rattle in the man's chest, which seemed to fill the room. "He has probably had this disease for several months – although he may not have begun to suffer badly till quite recently." Doctor Bergin studied Caitlin, folding his hands across his midriff as though he were a headmaster asking her name and form. "How long have you been married to him?"

"About seven weeks." A horrific thought struck her. "Is it catching?"

"TB? Certainly – if it is Mycobacterium tuberculosis." Caitlin's hand flew to her mouth and she backed to the chair, sat down. "You will need an examination and tests straight away, Mrs Flynn." He pitied her; she was so young. What the hell did these people think they were doing? When, in God's name, were they going to come out of the Dark Ages? "However," and his voice was kindly now, "if it is Mycobacterium bovis that has made your husband so ill, it is hardly ever passed from person to person. He will in all likelihood have contracted it a long time ago from drinking tubercular milk."

"He had cows slaughtered a while back – he's just got the all clear to start milking again!" blurted Caitlin.

CHAPTER FIFTEEN

"And you married him seven weeks ago?" Caitlin nodded quickly, doing her best to wipe away tears. "I am sorry to be indelicate, Mrs Flynn, but in the interests only of your health, is there any chance you may be with child?"

"No!" she said emphatically. "He has never touched me." She rummaged in her sleeve and pulled out a handkerchief, blew her nose.

"Really?" he seemed pleased. "Well then, it is not likely you are infected. You are young and strong. There is little point in my examining you now. You will need to get yourself to the hospital at Nenagh. I shall write you a letter of urgent referral." He opened his briefcase again, took out a pad and pen, and began writing hastily. "Give them this," he said, handing her the letter. "They will conduct a number of tests to detect the presence or otherwise of TB and determine, if it shows up, what strain it is. I have taken spittle and mucus samples from your husband. I'll get them to the hospital laboratory myself. Can you get to Nenagh tomorrow?" Caitlin nodded. She would have to miss school and ask her father to take her in his truck. "Excellent. Now," continued the doctor, looking again at Flynn, "let me tell you how to look after this man." He told her to feed him with soup and give him plenty of water. She was to wash her hands after every occasion on which she touched him or the cutlery and dishes he used. She was to buy at least a gallon of Lysol disinfectant when she went up to Nenagh and cleanse everything thoroughly which came into contact with Flynn.

"If you are not infected, Mrs Flynn," he assured her, "it is quite easy to ensure you remain infection free. People have been nursing tubercular patients for many years now. Very seldom indeed has there been a case of cross contamination, to my knowledge." He picked up his bag, made for the stairs. "Keep him warm and as comfortable as possible. Have you anyone to help you? It is no small job, to nurse a man to his death."

"I am not sure," said Caitlin. The reality of her situation would not settle.

She had read *Alice in Wonderland* when she was a child. Her Aunt Bridie and Uncle Conor in Wexford had given the story to her oldest sister, Finnuala, as a birthday present, before Caitlin was even born. As she followed the doctor down the dark stairwell and listened to his instructions on how to nurse the man who had just married her against her will, Caitlin was reminded of how Alice had found herself in the middle of bizarre and sinister events with no apparent reason or coherence. Unlike Alice's, however, Caitlin's life was all too real, with no plot to make eventual sense of the world at whose centre she seemed to be.

When they reached the kitchen and the doctor was about to take his leave, he turned and looked at her again, his watery eyes and doughy jowls intent on making forceful and clear his last instructions. "I warn you, Mrs Flynn, at the end, there is much blood. Do not get close to him at that stage without covering your mouth – use a handkerchief or tea towel; perhaps rip up a sheet." He stared at her for a while after he had finished talking. She looked frail and terrified and very young. "I will ask Nenagh to send you a nurse to check on things in a week or so."

The arrangement regarding the horse, which Mick and Donal had contrived, was that Donal would use the horse to get to and from work for a week, then decide if he wanted to buy him and the cart for the same price as had been quoted to Flynn for the horse alone.

"Your need is greater, Donal," said Mick. "Sure Flynn have a bucket load of money. You have nothing. He can buy himself any horse he likes."

Each morning of the three days a week Donal worked at the school, he would unhitch the horse and leave him in Spillane's barn, pick him up each afternoon when he had finished teaching, and drive back to Golden. On the second afternoon of the arrangement, Donal was accosted by a highly excited Mick Spillane as he crossed the yard to the barn.

"Come in!" instructed Spillane in a harsh whisper, as if he might be overheard by someone other than his pigs. "Come in till I tell you the news!" As soon as the door was shut Mick spoke. "Sit down, Donal – you might want to be sitting down when you hear this!" Donal complied. "Jack Flynn is dying." The younger man seemed to pale. He swallowed hard, said nothing. "I took Caitlin to the hospital above in Nenagh yesterday – we were there all day, boy." Spillane put one hand on his hip, leaned on the kitchen table with the other, and shook his head.

"What's wrong with him?"

Mick looked at Donal. A glint of mischievousness took the edge off his otherwise grave announcement: "He has TB – only weeks to live!" Kelly breathed deeply, looked less tense. There was a long pause in which each man considered the consequences and possibilities of the news. Then a sudden thought occurred to Donal.

"Is Caitlin OK?"

"Ah, now," said Spillane. "They are pretty sure she is. They think Flynn have a kind of TB that comes from cows. It's very hard for people to pass it on to other people, like. Sure he had a few cows slaughtered by Bord na Bainne a few weeks back."

Donal nodded. There was another pause. "Here's what we'll do, Mick," he said. "Will you sit down?"

"Oh, hello, Donal!" Mrs Spillane's tone betrayed her delight upon seeing the young teacher at her table. "Do you like the horse?" She leaned on the back of a chair and smiled into his eyes.

"The horse is grand, Missis," he replied, smiling.

"Mary, go on out and feed the pigs," said Mick. "I want a word with Donal."

"I've just fed the pigs!" retorted Mrs Spillane. "Amn't I just after coming in from feeding the pigs?"

"Well… check on the horse. Donal will drive him home in a while… hitch him up, will ya?"

"What? I can't lift that cart to the harness!"

"What can you do? Think of something you can do and go and do it!" Donal looked down throughout the exchange and bit his lip. As Mrs Spillane was about to turn and leave the kitchen and Mick was still facing her, Donal glanced up and winked. Her hurt expression dissolved into smiles again.

"It's lovely to see you, Donal," she said, then glared at her husband and left. Mick sat down.

"What about this, Mick," began Donal again, staring earnestly into Spillane's narrow blue eyes. "We both want the same thing, right?" Mick nodded, looked serious, but he was not entirely sure what they wanted. "I want Caitlin, and I'm guessing you want a son-in-law who is strong and healthy and can help you about the place." Mick nodded more confidently. "Well," said Donal, "what if – now I'm just thinking on the spot here, Mick, OK? What if I were to move in here…" Mick frowned and sat back. "Wait, listen – I could walk to work each morning, see a lot more of Caitlin. Sure if he's that sick and I'm just down the road…" Mick grinned.

"I see that, now," he said. "Go on."

"Well, the way I see it," continued Donal, "you can't lose. You already have the money Flynn gave you for Caitlin and if you hook up with me, you'll end up with another farm. And until I inherit my own place, sure I'll help you run this one. Once Flynn is dead, won't Caitlin get his farm?" Mick's eyes almost popped out of his head. Donal pressed home. "You could be a very rich man, now, in a short period of time, but you'll never manage three farms on your own and you don't want Caitlin getting in the way of things." Mick stopped smiling. Caitlin had not spoken more than a few words to him all day at the hospital. She had ignored any attempt he made at conversation, staring away from him as if he were not with her. She hadn't even said thank you when he had dropped her off home. Still a scut. "Forgive me, now, Mick, if this seems out of order, but I don't think Caitlin is all that fond of you at the moment." He stopped and searched Mick's eyes, which had grown stern and distant. Donal put a comforting hand over one of Mick's and patted it.

"What shall we do?"

"Well, leave Caitlin to me," said Donal. "Once she's with me, she'll forgive and forget – let you manage Flynn's farm because I'll be persuading her, like. But this is not just family stuff, Mick." Donal sat back, assuming a serious expression. "You and I are businessmen." Mick frowned slightly. "I'm a maths teacher – sure who better to work out sums and figures and come up with a business plan? If we are running three farms between us, we'll need one."

Mick smiled again. "But how can we make this work, Donal?"

"Very shrewd, there, Mick. Now listen, I suggest we show our commitment by… oh, I don't know, pledging certain things."

"What things?"

"Well, if I move in here, work for nothing on your farm – just board and lodging – how about you pay for a young lad to help my father? I know just the fella. He'll work for next to nothing and he can stay in my room above. I'll use your horse to check on my place now and again. I don't want wages." Donal ensured Mick appreciated the importance of this, then moved on. "I'll be pledging my word and good will by living here. After all, if I don't get Caitlin, we have no deal." He waited for Mick to appreciate how key were his charms to Mick's acquisition of great wealth and the establishment of a dynasty. "Living here will allow me to work on her – essential to the whole thing."

"And what do I have to do? Just give that young fella a bit of wages, is it?"

"A bit more, Mick. Sure the lad I'm thinking of will work for pennies a week and his board. If I'm willing to sacrifice my home to show my good faith, now, how about a down payment?"

"A down payment? To who? You?"

"I don't think that's an unreasonable request now, Mick."

Donal leaned back in his chair, put his hands in his pockets. "As you said earlier, I have very little – gave up a university education and the prospect of great money in the law, to come home and help my poor father." Donal paused, stared sadly at the table. "And I have three days' work a week above at the school, is all. And here I am, willing to work for you, Mick, because I think you are my future, and I think I am yours. I am willing to devote my muscle and brains to making the two of us the richest men in Tipperary. Think, Mick, three farms! And I hope I'll provide for myself and you sons and heirs to all our hard work. What do you say?"

"How much?"

Donal thrust out his lower lip and raised his eyebrows, seeming to consider for the first time what a reasonable sum might be to seal such a contract.

"A hundred and fifty pounds?"

Mick's eyes widened in shock. "That's a helluvalot of money!" he exclaimed. "What do you want that for?"

"I disagree, Mick," said Donal calmly. "As an investment, it's a mere bagatelle."

"A what?"

"A small amount. I'll use some of it to help my father – get him a horse. Sure we have to do all we can to keep things going on the farm above, while we plan. We're not ready to run all three. The rest of the money I'll put away – think about how I can improve the livestock and the way we do things. Consider it an investment, Mick." Seeing Spillane's incredulous gaze soften a little, Donal pressed home. "Have you any idea how much money we stand to make from this arrangement, Mick? Thousands! And if Flynn is dying, sure we can start to rake it in in a few months! And," Donal smiled warmly at Spillane, "you'll be getting me for nothing. Milking will kick off again in six weeks or so. There's sowing to be done and pigs to get to market, ditches and turf to dig. Imagine what it would be like if you didn't have all that to do on your own, Mick! Sure God love you, but you're not getting younger. I'll look after you like you were my own father."

Mick remained silent, his eyes fixed on Donal. The stillness of his exterior belied the growing excitement and dawning joy in his heart. Donal Kelly seemed to be the answer to every prayer Mick had uttered or thought in the last few years.

"Of course, if you're not interested, we'll leave it. It would be a shame, but I'd just go back to my own farm, leave your horse, and give up my teaching job, for I cannot stand to see Caitlin three days a week with no prospect of having her. I'll need to get her out of my head." And he stood up.

"A hundred and fifty?" said Mick. Donal beamed at him. "And you'll move in straight away – help out straight away?" Donal nodded. "We have a deal." Mick too rose to his feet, extended his hand, and Donal shook it firmly.

"A great decision, Mick," said Donal. "You're a true businessman and a great man altogether."

"I'll have the money for you in a couple of days," said Mick, "after you've moved in. Cash, is it?"

"It is. I'll pack up a few things tonight."

Donal and Mick crossed the yard to the barn. Mrs Spillane was in there, littering the temporary pig enclosures with straw, ready for the farrowing sows who snorted and snuffled in a small field off the yard. She nodded again and smiled at Donal. "The horse is fed and watered," she said. "He'll just need a bit of hay tonight."

"That's grand, Missis," said Donal. "Thanks for everything, now."

"Go in and make the dinner, would ya?" Spillane issued the command as he slipped the driving harness onto the horse, backed the animal between the shafts of the cart where it waited in the centre of the barn. She tutted, climbed out of a pig pen, and muttered her way back to the kitchen. When the horse was hitched and Donal had assumed his seat in the cart, Mick patted the animal's neck and looked up at Donal. "Tell me," he said, "what would you have done if I hadn't told you Flynn was dying?"

Donal nodded as if he had expected the question. "Well, Mick, let's just say it's as well for all concerned that he's dying of natural causes. Good luck." And he clicked-on the horse, rolled out of the barn. Mick removed his cap, scratched his head through his springy hair, and dismissed as false the alarm set off in his head by Donal Kelly's last words.

"Why are you getting so thick with Spillane, son?" Dan Kelly enquired quietly over supper. The girls smirked, lowered their eyes, and waited for the answer. Since their father had asked about Caitlin Spillane, they had become very curious about their brother's sudden fondness for Dunane.

"I like him, is all," said Donal. "I know what you said, Daddy, but he's been fair with me. He's good craic in the bar."

"And has he a fine daughter, I wonder?" Dan asked, looking mildly into Donal's eyes. Deirdre giggled and Jacintha admonished her with a frown and a kick under the table. Donal blushed a little.

"He has four daughters," he replied. "Three of them married and one in the convent." There followed a surprised silence.

"Why is he letting you use his horse?"

"Daddy," Donal pushed away his plate. The conversation he was about to have, he had been dreading. "Listen, you have to trust me, OK?" Dan swallowed a mouthful of food and rested his wrists on the edge of the table, knife and fork pointing upwards. "I am moving in with Spillane."

"What?" was the simultaneous response from all three of his family members. Donal went on hurriedly, "It will be easier for getting to work at the school."

"What about work here, son?" asked Dan. "How will we manage here?"

"I've thought about that." Donal looked at his sisters' faces. Deirdre was already losing the struggle against tears. Jacintha had raised an eyebrow and slumped in her seat, her arms folded. Her expression seemed to say, "Here we go again." His father's expression, though, was most heart rending. There was no anger in Dan's countenance, just the emptiness left in someone's eyes when their worst fears are confirmed. "I know a lad – a good lad," explained Donal earnestly, "and he'll work hard. You won't even have to pay him. Spillane will pay him."

"What are you saying, Donal?" Dan's voice was tired. He put down his cutlery carefully, sat back in his chair.

"His name is Pat O'Meara," went on Donal. "He's the youngest of five sons, brought up on a farm out near Dundrum. He'll work hard, Daddy – harder than I do. You'll hardly have to do anything and he'll be here all the time."

"Where will he sleep? In your bed, I suppose?"

Donal nodded. Dan sighed. Deirdre asked if she could leave the table. She got up and went slowly towards the stairs.

"Can I say something?" Unlike her father's, Jacintha's voice was not devoid of anger. "Well, you've done it again, Donal!" Her eyes flashed at her brother. "Dumped us well and truly in the muck and swanned off to please yourself, like you always do!"

"Jacintha…" Dan began to caution his daughter.

"No, Daddy! It has to be said. Who was here when you collapsed on the floor? Who went with you on that horrible journey to the hospital, not knowing if you were alive or dead? Who nursed you, Daddy, and did all the extra jobs around the house and the farm? We did! Deirdre and me! And when Deirdre went back to school, sure who stayed here and held the fort? Cooked and cleaned and gave you your medicine, milked the cows…"

Deirdre stood at the foot of the stairs, sobbing as though her heart would break. Dan bowed his head. Jacintha stood up. She leaned on the table for support but she was trembling with passion. She lowered her voice, stared at her brother. "And where were you, Donal? Huh? When I was giving up school and Deirdre and I were half dead with the work – where were you? Up in

Blackwell, larking around with your friends and teaching and studying in the dry and the warm with nothing to do but read and write!" Her voice rose in pitch again.

"Jacintha, that is enough!" Dan exclaimed, his voice raised. He was afraid of where his daughter might take this outburst. Jacintha turned to challenge her father.

"That's right, Daddy, defend him – you always do! Donal can do no wrong. Well, what if I decide to go? Had you thought of that?"

"No, Jacintha!" Deirdre half screamed from across the kitchen. She rushed forward and threw her arms around her sister's neck, sobbing into her shoulder.

"Ah, come on, Jacintha," started Donal. "Come on, now..."

"No, Donal!" Jacintha turned her body so that she could hold Deirdre but she looked over her shoulder and glared at her brother. "I have had enough! You are not the only one who doesn't enjoy skivvying on a farm. So you can bring your... boy into our house and you can skip off again, but I'm not hanging around to pick up the pieces again – Daddy getting depressed and Deirdre missing you like hell, me with no life, all on my own out here. Fine by me, Donal, if you're replaced." She looked at her father, kissed Deirdre's head. "Let's see if ye can all do without me." And she pulled away from Deirdre's fierce embrace and walked determinedly across the kitchen, went upstairs.

"Don't go again, Donal," begged Deirdre. "Don't leave us again. What'll we do without the two of ye?"

Dan rose to comfort his daughter and she flew to him, burying herself in his arms.

Donal got up, strode across the kitchen, grabbed his coat from the back of the door, and went outside. He was greatly affected by the upset he had caused, grieving already at the prospect of leaving his family. But he had to stay focused. Whatever else he did or did not do, Donal had to get O'Meara installed on his father's farm. He did not have to work the next day and planned to drive

Spillane's horse the almost twenty-mile round trip to collect Pat O'Meara. As he cooled off in the dark February evening, Donal tried to work out when exactly his life had become so badly out of control.

Almost four hours after the doctor had left, Jack regained consciousness. For some minutes he lay still, staring blankly at the space above him, occasionally closing and reopening his mouth. His lips seemed very dry. Caitlin did as the doctor had instructed and approached the bedside, offering him water on a spoon. Still he did not look at her; he responded to the moisture instinctively, like a baby bird, thought Caitlin. She spooned water into his mouth until the cup was all but empty then he turned his head aside as if sated.

"Are you all right?" Caitlin's voice was soft, concerned, but he did not turn his head to look at her. She wondered if he could hear her. "Are you in pain?" she asked. "Will I get you a tablet?" He did not respond at first, but then, as she began opening the packet of aspirin the doctor had left on the cupboard beside his bed, he lifted his right hand in a gesture of dismissal. She did not know what else to say or do.

Suddenly, with a monumental effort, he turned over in the bed. Caitlin jumped back in alarm. Still, he did not look at her. His mouth was open and his breathing came fast and noisily. He moaned occasionally – low, animal moans of pain – but he pushed himself onto his elbow. Shaking all over, he sat up. The blanket fell away from his upper body and he sat – hunched, thin, dishevelled – on the side of the bed.

"I don't think you should be getting up," said Caitlin. "You need to rest, the doctor said…" Again, he raised his hand, said nothing. "Do you want something?" Caitlin wrung her hands in nervous helplessness. Flynn slipped his feet to the floor and, bracing his weight against his arms, pushed himself up from the mattress till he stood hunched over and trembling. The transformation in his appearance and demeanour since the day before was startling. It was as if the incident with Donal Kelly had used up a last reserve of strength or will and he had awoken, like Samson, to discover he was weak.

Like a man twice his age, Flynn turned step by painful step until his back was to Caitlin and he was facing the bed. Then he slowly, slowly bent his knees and began to lower his body to the floor, holding on to the mattress when he reached its height. Caitlin watched, trying to guess his intentions, until he took his right arm away from the mattress and, holding his head and upper body straight, felt blindly about under the bed. All at once she realized what he wanted. She had not emptied it. "Hold on, there," she said. "I'll get that for you." She hunkered down, spied the chamber pot beneath the bed, and pulled it out carefully. Jack closed his eyes as she lifted the pot, half full with cold urine. "I'll empty it. Be back in a jiff."

When she came back, she placed the pot near the bed. "I'll leave you to it," she said quickly, adding, "Can you manage?"

He stood hunched, struggling for breath, hands hanging limply by his sides. As she looked into his face, he frowned sorrowfully and closed his eyes again. A tear was dislodged by the action and his mouth puckered and trembled as though he were trying to fight more. Caitlin left him, full of wonder at the pity in her heart.

CHAPTER SIXTEEN

Pat O'Meara was chopping wood when Donal Kelly pulled into his father's farmyard, scattering chickens and ducks before him. One of his brothers, a burly man with fair curly hair, was wearing a rubber apron and boots and carrying a very large, recently sharpened knife. He stopped on his way across the yard to a shed where he had earlier strung up a large pig by its hind feet, ready for slaughter. The pig was squealing loudly, relentlessly. Spillane's horse, sweating and blowing hard after its long journey, rolled its eyes and snorted in alarm at the sound. Donal got down from the cart and secured the horse as the two men watched him. Saluting Phillip, Donal approached Pat, and the former continued on his way. By the time Donal was close enough to Pat to begin a conversation, the squealing had become a sustained, ear-splitting scream and Spillane's horse pulled at the reins which tethered it to a fence post and neighed shrilly. Donal had to wait some time before the pig's agonized cries subsided, then stopped. "How're you, Pat?" he began quietly. Pat eyed him uncertainly. His hair and forehead were damp with sweat and his shirt sleeves were wet from armpit to elbow from the effort of chopping logs into firewood. But there was a look of fear in his eyes which accounted partially, at least, for the way his chest heaved and the tremor in his hand as he reached to grasp Donal's in a handshake.

"Is it time?" he asked. Donal looked into the young man's clear blue eyes and pitied him. Pat's brother slopped out of the shed in his gum boots, covered in blood, wiping his hands on a rag. He stood, legs apart and hands on hips, monitoring the flow of blood away from the slaughtered pig and into the runnel which led from the shed to a drain.

"Almost," said Donal. "You have to come with me now, Pat."

Pat nodded. "I have a bag already packed, like," he said. "Let me get this wood into the barn, OK?"

"I'll give you a hand." The two men loaded firewood and logs into baskets, swung them onto their shoulders, and balanced them there as they walked the wood from the yard to the barn and threw it onto a large pile in one corner of the building. Pat's brother had gone back into the shed and placed a small tin trough beneath the profusely bleeding pig. His mother always made black pudding with some of the blood.

"I'm away for a while," shouted Pat to his brother through the shed door.

"Are all the logs cut?"

"They are – they're in the barn. There's enough for a couple of months at least, I'd say, now."

"Right so," said his brother, looking up from the blood pooling in the trough. He didn't seem to require an introduction to Donal but nodded at him, then looked back at the trough. He had enough. He bent and moved it away from the wound and the pig continued to bleed into the gutter.

"Can I water the horse?" asked Donal, as he and Pat walked towards the cart.

"You can, of course. There's a bucket over there." Pat nodded towards a metal pail by a pump. "I'll away in and fetch my things."

"Right." Pat emerged having changed his shirt, washed his face, and combed his hair. He carried a holdall in one hand, thrown back over his shoulder. He looked worried but he smiled at Donal as they climbed onto the cart. When they had pulled away and were proceeding at walking pace up the lane from O'Meara's farm, Pat turned to look at Donal and asked, "Do you think we could be killed, like?" Donal didn't look at him.

"Not you, Pat, no."

"Why not?"

Donal smiled and turned towards him. "Ah, now, you strike me as the lucky kind." His smile broadened to an open grin. "Come on there," he urged the horse, and it broke into a leisurely trot. "I'd like to be home before it gets too dark."

"Home? Are we going to your house?"

"We are." Then Donal added, "Don't worry, Pat, all will be revealed. Trust me."

During the journey, Donal explained that Pat would be staying at his house and helping out on his father's farm. Pat would be helping the cause by freeing up Donal to work with Joe on Operation Holiday, and without Pat's help, much of what was being planned would not be possible. But, urged Donal, he must not breathe a word to anyone in the Kelly household, for they all thought he was bringing in Pat to help out on the farm while Donal pursued a teaching career.

"So I am not coming to Buncrana with ye?"

"I don't think so, now, Pat, no," answered Donal. There was a long silence.

"Is it because I am too young?"

"No."

"Not good enough, is that it?"

"Away with you, O'Meara!" chided Donal. "I have told you why we need you. You know, you are supposed to follow orders – no matter what. Did you forget that?" He shot Pat a stern look. The young man coloured. "Just do as I say," said Donal finally, "and you'll be right."

It was evening by the time they got to Golden. Donal saw to the horse's comfort then brought Pat into the kitchen and introduced him to his family. Jacintha had just cooked supper. A steaming pot of rabbit stew stood in the middle of the table and she had cut a fresh loaf into thick slices. There was butter and a bowl of flowery potatoes, their skins split and the steam from them melding with the steam from the stew so the combined aroma filled the kitchen. Donal and Pat were ravenous.

"This is my sister, Jacintha," said Donal warmly, but as he spoke and his eyes met Jacintha's, he tried to hold her gaze to convey that he understood how raw she would still be feeling after the earlier unpleasantness. Pat nodded and smiled, then held out his hand in greeting.

"How're ya?" she said, shaking his hand and nodding briefly in return. She did not hold Donal's gaze or seek to meet it again but turned back to the range and began wiping it down. There was a long pause while Jacintha removed her apron and hung it over the bar of the range. She said nothing. Donal was grateful at least for her restraint.

"Where's Daddy?" he asked at last, kicking off his boots. A sideways glance of disapproval from his sister encouraged him to pick them up and place them neatly on a mat behind the door.

"With Deirdre. One of the cows is lame. They brought her up to the first field so they could treat the foot. They'll be here any second. Sit down. Help yourselves."

A few moments later, Dan and Deirdre came in, flushed from the February chill and talking animatedly about how they had identified an abscess on the underside of the cow's foot. They had sterilized a knife and lanced the black spot on her sole and pus had shot out, then oozed for ages. Deirdre was reliving the moment and Dan was laughing at her graphic rendering of the drama. They both stopped talking when they saw Pat O'Meara's blonde head at their table.

"Daddy," said Donal, "this is Pat. Pat, this is my father, Dan Kelly – and my sister, Deirdre." Pat coloured, turned towards Dan, and extended his hand.

"Pleased to meet you, Sir," he said. Deirdre looked him up and down and raised an eyebrow.

Dan held the young man's hand and looked steadily into his clear blue eyes for a long moment.

"Hello, Pat," he said, withdrawing his hand and smiling. "You're very welcome." Jacintha waited for Deirdre to catch her eye, smiled knowingly at her, and raised her eyebrows. Deirdre feigned confusion, mouthed "what?", but her blushes denounced her as disingenuous.

Pat remembered his lines well. He knew Donal because he was related to one of his friends in Cashmel. They had met when Pat had gone up there for the weekend. The rest was truth. Pat was the youngest of five brothers and would get nothing of the farm. He was not likely to be missed, for though two of his brothers were married they were reluctant to relinquish any entitlement to the farm and worked there every day. There were frequent fights in the yard and around the table about who should get what. And it was hard on his mother cooking for six men and she almost sixty. Since Pat had turned sixteen three years ago, there had been an unspoken and increasing pressure on him to move on.

Donal and Pat slept in Donal's room that night, Pat on the floor. The next morning, Donal got up for work and drove Spillane's horse to Dunane. None of his family was more sorrowful than he as he pulled out of the yard.

It was raining when Donal encountered Caitlin. His heart lurched, and he urged the horse on faster when he was sure it was she.

She was holding her scarf tightly around her face with both gloved hands as she walked, and leaning slightly to her right to balance her school bag where it hung from her left shoulder. She turned as he drew up beside her but looked back to the road when she saw who it was. He kept abreast of her.

"Caitlin," he urged, "get up on the cart. I'll drive you as far as your father's place." She ignored him. "Ah, come on now, Caitlin, 'tis foolish to walk in the rain when I'm offering you a lift – with your own horse!"

She stopped and shouted, "You have no right to that horse and you know it! What do you want?"

"Nothing," he replied, reining in the horse, squinting at her through the rain. "I want to be friends."

"Friends?" She began walking again. "You nearly killed himself the other day! He's terrible sick."

"He was sick anyways from what I hear." The horse walked on again slowly. "I didn't ask him to attack me!" She shook her head. "Anyway, would it be so terrible if he died, Caitlin?" Donal shouted above the rain and the noise of the cart wheels on the stony road. "You'd be free."

She stopped again. "What for?" she asked, as she walked towards the cart, got close enough to look into his eyes. "For you, is that it?" Donal looked down at her upturned face. Even shrouded in a grey shawl and wet with rain, it was lovely. As her eyes searched his and her full mouth fell partially open with the effort of looking upwards at him, he felt a longing in his heart.

"Get up on the cart, Caitlin," he said gently. "I wish you only good." She was surprised at the warmth in his eyes and the gentleness of his voice. She had not heard words of such kindness for as long as she could remember. And his eyes... they were almost a red-brown, warm and liquid as if there were heat in them. He put out his hand and she took it, allowing him to pull her onto the cart. When she was sitting beside him he held her gaze a while before urging the horse onwards to Spillane's yard. Caitlin would not accompany him onto her father's land and got down to walk the last ten minutes to school.

"Tell me," asked Donal before she walked away, "are you coping all alone up there?"

"I'm not alone," she answered. "Pat Maher's wife is helping me. She only lives a mile up the road and they have a pony..."

"So they do," said Donal, laughing suddenly. Caitlin frowned at him as though he had lost his wits. "And do you know how I know that? Because I took the pony back to Maher when you left it in my father's barn!"

"You!" she cried. "It was you... in the barn!"

Donal winked at her and laughed again. "Small world, Caitlin, wouldn't you say?" She could not speak. "I'll see you at school. I hear you're very good at maths. Good luck." He drove the cart into Spillane's yard where he would dismount and lead the chestnut into the barn for a feed. Caitlin watched him till her father emerged from the kitchen. She shook her head in disbelief and hurried on to school. "*Alice in Wonderland* was never in it," she muttered to herself.

A couple of days later, Joe Morgan stood on Mick Spillane's threshold, tall and jauntily turned out in a waistcoat and chequered cap to match. He hitched his thumbs behind the armholes of his waistcoat and smiled, though his eyes remained serious. "We are going on our holidays!" Donal closed his eyes and bowed his head. He had been expecting the call but it could not have been more unwelcome. He had business here to settle now which had become more important to him than trying to frighten regiments of RUC men and troops of British soldiers. He could no longer pin down precisely what the point of it was. "What?" enquired Joe with mock disappointment. "Not excited?" Donal noted Kilty's car for the first time; its sleek cream fenders and chrome bumpers were out of place in a farm yard. He returned Kilty's stern salute with half a smile and a nod.

"What are you doing here, Donal?" asked Joe. "And more to the point, what is Pat O'Meara doing above at your place?" Donal stepped into Spillane's yard and shut the door behind him. Mrs Spillane craned her neck and bobbed her head up to the moment it shut, in an effort to see past him to the strangers in the yard.

"I got a teaching job," he replied quietly, "in Dunane school. I'm boarding here because I can walk there from this house. Pat

O'Meara is helping my father." Joe stared at Donal. "Listen, Joe, can we go someplace else? It's not safe to talk here."

In Kilty's car, driving north-west out of Dunane, Donal leaned forward in the back seat, extending an arm over each of the two front ones, and explained his thinking about Pat O'Meara.

"Listen, Joe…" Donal sounded friendly, earnest. "Let Pat O'Meara off this one, will ya?" Kilty looked swiftly towards Joe, who met his eye and then turned his attention back to Donal.

"Why?"

"If anything happens to me while we're up there, sure there'll be no one to help my father here. Please, Joe – Pat can be blooded on the next operation, can't he? Sure he'll be precious little use to us if the going gets hot in Derry. He's just a snotty kid."

"You were a snotty kid once, Donal," replied Joe. Kilty guffawed. "And not that long ago, either." Donal nodded fast and pulled himself further forward till he was almost wedged in the gap between the driver and passenger seats.

"I know, I know that, Joe. But my first mission was easy compared to this. All I had to do was give McGinty a message. This… this is different. This is war. Let him sit this one out. He can stay with my father while I'm away."

"And what if he talks?"

"He won't! He's not stupid. He already has a story – he knew me from Cashmel days, is related to someone up there. He's fine. What do you say, Joe? I'm desperate here."

"So desperate to help your father you took a teaching job miles away?"

"I knew I would have to leave him again," Donal said sullenly. "This makes it easier." He easily summoned the resentment he had felt the first time Joe Morgan had prevented his returning home for the summer. "If there's no one around for him, it'll kill him, Joe. I think that when I didn't go home… that first time… well, I'm just saying that it might have helped bring on the heart attack." There was silence. Kilty's car groaned with the effort of transporting three men up a steep hill. He changed down a gear.

Joe considered. He had not missed the rebuke intended in Donal's reference to his not being allowed home because of IRA business. Indeed, it was highly likely he would require Donal for further duties. Kelly had the makings of a good soldier: clever, brave, not too principled. And of course, it was true that Operation Holiday could lead to the death or internment of them all. Added to all this, and most salient, was that Joe had had a few qualms about initiating Pat O'Meara at such a level. He had juggled a fair bit with the possible advantages of O'Meara's obvious naivety and the possibility the boy might be a liability under fire. Joe had intended to make Pat travel up to Buncrana with Corcoran, posing as a warehouse trainee learning the routes and routines. If they were stopped, the two made unlikely accomplices in an IRA campaign. Corcoran's lorry would be full to the brim with sacks of sugar. But in the middle of alternate layers would be gelignite bedded in sacks of calcium hypochlorite. It had been easy enough to get the chemicals; calcium hypochlorite was used to bleach linen. One of the lads worked in an industrial laundry business in Limerick. It was loaded on no problem with a consignment of flour at the Limerick depot.

The plan was to park the lorry up close to the barracks and lob a fire bomb in the back of it. The whole thing would go up like the explosion Guy Fawkes intended, taking the barracks with it. Pat O'Meara would know nothing of his cargo. Joe sighed, nodded. "OK, Donal," he conceded. "This once. But only because O'Meara is an unknown quantity and, as you say, this is big guns." Donal looked relieved.

"Thank you, Joe," he said. "I am very grateful."

"I know you are." Joe stared ahead through the windscreen. "And you'll get plenty of opportunities to show it." Kilty stopped the car, turned it around on the deserted Limerick road, and gradually accelerated back to Dunane.

Joe wound down a window and lit a cigarette, passed one to Kilty. "You wanted to know the MO, Kelly. Well, it's this – calcium hypochlorite and gelignite." Donal tried to disguise his horror. Kilty looked in the rearview mirror, watching Donal's struggle to maintain a neutral expression.

"What's the target?"

"RUC barracks, Derry. The others will be going for the Recruiting Office, Belfast." Joe flicked the ash from his cigarette through the open window. "All right?" The interrogative was a challenge.

"Yes, of course," he replied, staring straight ahead and pretending not to notice as Kilty glanced again in the rearview mirror. "Isn't that what I signed up for?"

"It is," affirmed Joe, nodding. "It is indeed."

At Spillane's yard, Donal got out of the car and waved at both men.

"See you tomorrow, so." Joe directed his voice at Donal through the open car window, did not turn his head. "Bright and early," he added. And Kilty's car pulled away, sprays of thick mud churned up by its wheels, spattering its shiny fenders.

"Now that's a very fine vehicle," exclaimed Mick Spillane, crossing the yard towards his lodger, an empty metal pail swinging from his hand. "Who owns a car like that, now, tell me?" He was all smiles and there was that glint in his eye which came when he savoured the possibility of social advantage.

"A couple of friends of mine from my college days," said Donal. "Just turned up to say hello and take me for a spin."

"Is that right?" persisted Spillane. "They've done well for themselves, I'd say." To his disappointment, Donal did not elaborate on the men's fortunes.

They were at the kitchen door. "That is a wonderful smell, Missis!" exclaimed Donal enthusiastically as they stepped inside. "What can I smell? No, let me guess… chicken stew?"

"It is, Donal!" cried Mrs Spillane delightedly, bringing her hands together as though she would clap them. "And potatoes and cabbage, and there's a milk pudding in it for afters."

"Afters?" Donal sounded as excited as she did. "Sure you have us all spoilt, Missis! I'm starving so I am – I could eat a scabby cat."

"Well, it's another of my chickens you have instead," remarked Spillane dourly. "Eggs'll be as rare as money around these parts at this rate."

"Oh, whisht, Mick," rebuked his wife. "Sure there's five hens left and three of us. How many blessed eggs do you want?"

"I'll away up and clean out the pigs after this," said Donal, sitting down as Mrs Spillane ladled a huge portion of chicken stew into a bowl for him. Two of the sows had farrowed and were penned in the barn. "And I'll check on the ones in the field – make sure they're all right." He tucked into the stew, making noises of appreciation so that Mrs Spillane blushed and shrugged her shoulders in girlish joy. Mick eyed him over his own spoon. He raised an eyebrow at the noises; they were not, he deemed, manly. "Delicious," said Donal, apparently unaware of Mick's withering glance. "And then," he added, "I'll clean out the milking parlour ready for when it starts again – make sure everything is spick and span."

Mick could not suppress a smile. Donal Kelly really was an answer to prayer.

Jack Flynn occupied a sort of twilight world in the days after his collapse. He could not regain full consciousness for long. In spite of Herculean efforts to remain awake, he would find hours had elapsed since his last thought and he could not account for them. He was feverish and very troubled in his sleep. Caitlin checked on Jack every morning, brought him tea if he was awake, and held his head so he could sip it. She left water by his bedside and emptied his pot. Mrs Maher agreed to look in each day from mid-morning, when her own family had gone out to work and her kitchen was clean again. It was she who removed Flynn's filthy clothes and washed his body. Once, when Jack fouled the bed, she pushed with all her might to roll him out of the mess and onto his side, cleaned him up and wrenched the dirty sheet from under him before he could wake up and be ashamed. Caitlin was inestimably grateful to her neighbour, for without her help, she could not have gone to school.

Caitlin looked after the horse; she had grown very fond of him. As the evenings had become a little lighter she had taken to walking him around the roads to exercise his joints as Flynn had instructed. She was soothed in his company and loved him for his biddable, gentle nature. At the conclusion of one such walk, Donal Kelly found her again.

After he had scoured Spillane's milking parlour, as he had promised he would, Donal went upstairs to clean himself up, planning to walk down the road to Flynn's farm. On his bed, recently occupied by Caitlin and Maureen, he found an envelope on which was scrawled his name in Spillane's laboured handwriting. There was a hundred and fifty pounds in it, in notes. Donal stuffed the envelope deep inside a compartment of the briefcase he took to work. He had also rolled up a pair of trousers and an old shirt and put them in the briefcase, along with his passport and a few other things he would need on his travels with Joe Morgan. Anything which did not fit in that briefcase, he did not need. When he had had a wash and changed his shirt, swapped his rubber boots for shoes, Donal announced to Mick and his wife that he was "off out" and winked conspiratorially at Mick. Mick smiled behind *The Irish Press*, puffed on his pipe.

"Where do you suppose he's off to now?" asked Mrs Spillane.

"How do I know?"

His wife sat back in her chair, lowered the sock she was darning, and stared into the firelight. They had taken to using the parlour as a sitting room in the evenings since Donal had moved in. Mick wasn't too happy about the extra work and cost involved in keeping it warm, but it was very important that Donal Kelly made it known abroad how comfortable life was at the Spillanes' house.

"What do you want now?" asked Caitlin, more wearied than irritated by Donal's appearance. He ignored her.

"What's wrong with that horse?" he asked. The animal was barely distinguishable from the growing darkness.

"He is lame," she answered simply. "The vet said to exercise him to keep his foot strong." Donal followed her across Flynn's yard and into the barn. It was pitch black.

"This brings back memories," he said, and Caitlin smirked in spite of herself, glad he could not see. She felt for a lamp on the windowsill and the matches always beside it, struck one, and soon the barn was diffused with soft light. She held up the lamp to locate a hook in a beam from which she suspended it. Tethering the horse, she took out a tin of liniment from her coat pocket and hunkered down to apply it to the animal's pastern. "Let's see," said Donal, and, squatting down beside her, he reached for the horse's fetlock and ran his hand down to the hoof. "Ringbone," he pronounced, "but it's not swollen. How old is he?" Caitlin considered, moving further away from Donal.

"I'm not sure. Old enough, I think." Then she added, "He's a lovely horse. Himself says I can ride him if he gets better." She stood up and Donal did likewise. Flynn's sows and new bainbhs snorted and squealed in another part of the barn. The horse pulled at his haynet and chomped contentedly. Reaching for the lamp, Caitlin turned towards the barn door.

"Listen, Caitlin." There was something in Donal's tone which made her stop and comply. She held the lamp away from her face so he could not discern from her any reaction to what he might say. "I like you – a lot, and…"

She cut him off. "Why are you staying at my father's house?"

He walked closer to her, came to her side. "Because it is close to the school."

"And that's all?" There was a long pause. Caitlin hmphed to herself and walked more purposefully towards the barn door, extinguished the lamp, and put it back on the windowsill. She stepped outside and waited for him to exit. As she shut the door firmly she said "good night" and made to go indoors, but he ran in front of her.

"All right," he half whispered in the darkness, "I admit it. Since that morning you showed up in my father's barn, I have thought about you… a lot. Sure how the hell was I to know your father had sold you off to an auld fella… like a… like a sack of grain. I came looking for you, Caitlin." He stopped whispering animatedly and spoke in low tones. "And you were already married. But I couldn't get you out of my head and when I saw you…" He paused again. They could barely see each other's faces in the darkness; he came closer. Caitlin raised her head in instinctive mistrust but she did not move away. "When I saw you… you are beautiful, Caitlin Spillane."

No one had ever called her beautiful. Maureen and her father had mocked her for her vanity, and her mother, for fear of upsetting Maureen, would never have acknowledged Caitlin's beauty. Mrs Spillane was only too aware, in any case, of the superfluity of the attribute in rural Tipperary. It was kinder on a woman if she hadn't it. The mirror, though, had not lied to her. Caitlin knew she was beautiful. But, as with all extraordinary gifts, beauty was no more than a troubling suspicion until it was celebrated by others and became a blessing. The acknowledgment of what she had known in her heart did more to win her trust of Donal Kelly than anything he had hitherto said. Even so, the situation she was in put her irredeemably beyond this man's reach. She may as well have been an apparition or a photo in his pocket. The substance of her was lost.

"It is too late," she said flatly. "This is all… too late." She strode away from him, went into the house, and locked the door. Upstairs, Flynn was coughing, obviously conscious. He would need some tea and maybe a little soup.

Donal left the Spillanes' house next morning in his suit and carrying his briefcase, as though he were walking to the school. Kilty's car was waiting for him five minutes down the road. Donal got into the back seat and the car sped away. Through a passenger window, Donal watched the children on their way to school stop and point at the beautiful car. If they had seen him get in, it hardly mattered. He wouldn't be coming back anytime soon.

"Is this car not a bit conspicuous?" he asked aloud, without taking his eyes from the window.

"Michael here is not coming with us."

"Oh?" Donal was surprised. "I thought he was." He looked at Kilty's heavy set face and Kilty met his gaze in the mirror.

"Change of plan. We need someone back at base, if things go wrong."

"Like what?" Donal sat up, paid attention properly for the first time to what they were about to do.

"Any number of things could go wrong, Donal," said Joe. "You know that. If Michael is ready with transport and papers, we have a chance of getting away clean." The car rumbled its way towards Tipperary and Kilty's enormous farm.

"How are we getting up to Buncrana?"

"You're going with Corcoran, in the lorry. We'll meet him now in Tipperary."

"With the explosives?"

"You're not scared, are you, Donal?" Joe gibed. "It won't be volatile until someone lobs a firebomb in the back of it. And you've been out and about with Corcoran before. There are employment records at the depot with your name on them. It's a good cover. And sure, you could lie your way out of hell, Kelly. You'll be grand."

"Have we clearance to get across the border?"

"All taken care of. Mr Kilty here has some influential friends. Most of the sugar in the lorry is from his beet crops and the North is fierce short of the stuff."

"How are you travelling, Joe?"

"I'm going up with Rourke in a car we have borrowed for the purpose."

Donal sat back and closed his eyes. It seemed to him he was speeding away from anything in his life which had made the remotest sense.

Sister Mary Francis was furious that the junior pupils' maths lessons were uncovered. She had to go in and teach maths herself. As principal, she was not supposed to do any teaching, let alone cover work. Well, Donal Kelly would certainly never get work again in her school, that was for sure! Jim Fennessey shook his head in the staffroom and said he had absolutely no idea where Kelly could be. There was something very shifty about that young man, he pronounced. When Caitlin Spillane turned up as usual for lessons, Jim Fennessey was quite surprised.

Mick Spillane tore up the road from Dunane to Golden in his red truck and screeched into Dan Kelly's yard, crossed it in a few strides, and banged on the door.

"Is Donal here?" he demanded angrily.

"No, he is not," said Dan. "What's the matter with you, Spillane?"

Mick pushed past Dan and went into the kitchen. Deirdre, Jacintha, and Pat were all at the table drinking tea and eating soda bread covered in jam.

"Have any of ye seen him?" he challenged.

"I told you, Spillane," Dan replied, his voice rising in pitch and volume, "he is not here. What is the matter?"

"What's the matter? I'll tell you what the matter is!" spat

Spillane, rounding on Dan. "He's skedaddled off with a hundred and fifty pounds of my money, that's what the matter is!" There were gasps around the table.

"Gone where, Spillane? How did he get the money?"

"I gave it to him…"

"You gave him a hundred and fifty pounds – sure what for, in the name of all that is holy?"

Spillane was burning red. His fists were clenched and he pursed his lips together as though he were trying not to burst.

"It doesn't matter why!" he shouted. "What matters is he's taken off with it!"

Pat stood up and spoke to Mick. "I think you'd better calm down," he said. "It's not nice to burst into someone else's house making all sorts of accusations about their kin."

"And who the hell are you?" demanded Spillane, taking a step towards the younger man. Pat didn't move and Mick stopped before he got too close. "I suppose you're the one whose wages I'm supposed to pay, is it? Well, you can whistle for wages, boy!"

"That's fine," said Dan Kelly, opening his door and standing aside for Spillane to leave. "Pat is family now. Sure we'll manage, will we not, Pat?"

Pat beamed at Dan, and Deirdre smiled, bit her lower lip. Spillane swore roundly and stormed out. Once he had gone, though, Dan sat down heavily at the table and put his head in his hands. "What the hell is that young fella up to?"

Having reconnoitred at Roscommon, the South Tipperary and Wicklow flying columns spent half the night drinking, smoking, and arguing about tactics. Twelve men squeezed into the kitchen of a farmhouse to the north of Castlerea. Some sat on the backs of chairs weighted down by those who sat on the edges of the chairs themselves. Some sat on the floor. Someone even sat in the sink. Joe Morgan and another man from Wicklow, his equivalent in rank, took it in turns to stand on the table and swivel around to look at every man assembled, rousing the columns to patriotic fervour though clouds of smoke.

Donal sat with his arms folded and observed. Occasionally, so as not to draw attention to himself, he raised a fist and shouted when the rhetoric peaked, but his heart was elsewhere. It resided with a lonely girl in Tipperary, betrayed by all she knew. If he could just get through the next two days without being arrested or killed, Donal intended, as soon as it was possible, to take her hand and deliver her from the darkness in which she dwelt.

The following evening, Donal and Des Corcoran rolled into Buncrana along the main Derry road. The one hundred and thirty mile, four-hour journey from Roscommon had been passed mainly in silence. Des had stopped a couple of times so they could relieve themselves and refuel but they had little to say to each other. If Corcoran was worried about his explosive cargo he never betrayed it, even when, as they pulled up to the Derry border patrol at around 7 p.m., the gardai asked them to get down from the lorry. Des smoked a cigarette and laughed out loud with one of the gardai as another checked their papers by torchlight and asked them questions about their cargo. A procession of young women laughed and flounced their way over the border from Derry into Donegal, heading for dances and bars.

Donal stood with his hands in his pockets and smiled pleasantly every time a torch was flashed in his face, but he ached to be as free as the servicemen who tipped their military caps at the gardai and held their girls close against the chill. What he was about to do seemed insane. He had read once, at college, that the measure of a person's sanity was the gap between his reality and what he thought of himself. Donal felt increasingly that his reality was lala land and the safest place to be was his own head.

The back of the lorry was opened up and revealed sack upon sack of sugar. A few were pulled out and one even ripped open with a knife so its contents could be verified, but all that spilled onto the road was sugar. The lorry was so densely loaded it was impossible to climb into it. The paperwork all looked official. After twenty minutes or so, the lorry was waved on, and even then, when they climbed back into the cabin, Des said nothing. Donal wondered what he had laughed at so raucously with the gard, wondered if Des didn't like him, and decided he couldn't care less. It was easier not to talk in any case; talking meant you risked betraying how nervous you were, or worse, any doubts you might have about what you had to do.

They were making their way along Waterside, through the blacked-out Derry streets. Good thing Pat O'Meara hadn't come along in the hope of seeing the sea, Donal thought grimly to himself. The beauties of Lough Swilly and the Inishowen peninsula were shrouded by darkness and a thick fog which had glutted itself over the sea before settling on Derry. British and US naval personnel were everywhere, on and off duty. There were no street lights and many people carried hand torches, shining them downwards to make sure they didn't trip or miss the end of a pavement. The impression Donal had as the lorry moved slowly, slowly towards its target, was of being underwater, a shark nosing massively through shoals of small, shimmering fish.

The ostensible destination of the lorry was a depot off the main Buncrana road, about a mile from the border checkpoint, but the RUC barracks was on the quayside, running parallel with the River Foyle, towards Letterkenny. It had been decided to target the RUC rather than larger US and British naval garrisons, because being Protestant and colluders with the British, they were the treacherous wedge in the door to freedom. And treachery to the IRA – even the sniff of it – was unforgivable; rational thought or changes of mind, revision of tactics in the face of changing political reality were not excuses for it. It was punishable by death and that was that. Also, there was more chance of leaving the scene alive if there was only a handful of policemen to worry about and not a regiment of English- or American-trained military personnel.

Operation Holiday was merely the name Joe Morgan had cynically conferred on the South Tipperary arm of the IRA Northern Campaign which was being mounted across the Free State. It was a coordinated effort which had started in 1942, to get arms and explosives from IRA stashes across Eire to border locations. From there, Republican guerrilla warriors could use them to ambush RUC barracks and plant bombs in various Northern Irish locations. The campaign was continuing where Collins had left off – a sort of homage to the best of his intentions and the bedrock Republican belief that Ireland's unification could not be achieved without armed struggle and blood sacrifice. As there were very few IRA warriors left by 1944, it was expedient that the blood should be someone else's. What sort of god might be appeased by such sacrifice and whether the majority population might like to serve him, was not a legitimate question.

Derry's quays and wharves bristled with US and English naval vessels and submarines which nosed into her like bainbhs suckling a sow. "This is crazy," muttered Donal to himself as he made out the looming bulk of ship after ship along the quay and the lorry parted the crowds of personnel who crossed the Strand Road to and from their vessels.

"It's a hot one, all right." Des echoed Donal's concerns. It was all he said the entire mission but the tone in which he spoke stretched back down the quiet miles and hours of their run from Roscommon. Any talk at all really was a risk. The lorry slowed then stopped.

"Is this it?" Des nodded tersely to Donal's question. They had parked a hundred yards from the barracks, down a side street. Joe suddenly appeared with some other men, but it was impossible for Donal to determine how many in the darkness. Joe had a torch and shone it into Donal's and Des's eyes to ensure their identity.

"Des, you know the plan," Joe whispered sharply before turning so that the searchlight of his torch illumined a huddle of men behind him. "Get in, tie them up – shoot them if you have to." Joe turned back to Des, who looked away to avoid the torch beam. "Twenty minutes from when we set off, drive the lorry down the street till it's outside the barracks. You know what to do then."

"Aye."

"Donal, you come with us." Joe handed him a gun, which Donal swiftly put in his inside jacket pocket.

"Where's everyone else?"

"In their places, Kelly – either close to the barracks or waiting, as back up. There's a few in cars driving round who'll be ready to pick us up and take us to safe houses as soon as we're out. They'll flash their headlights in sequences of three. Jump into any car. Right, come on, boys, clock's ticking. For Ireland!" There were murmurs in response and the men melted into darkness. Joe, Donal, and two others began walking towards the main road. "Act natural," ordered Joe as they turned left onto the Strand Road, his torch leading them into a counterflow of people eager to be home on a cold, February evening in wartime Derry.

Canadians, Americans, Royal Navy personnel, laughing and talking, whistled and jeered at each other as their torches roamed over uniforms, looking for identifying insignia. They split around the four Irish men, brushed shoulders with them, regrouped in catcalls and derisive laughter. Strains of music swirled with the darkness at a couple of street junctions as pubs livened up and dances got underway. *What the hell am I doing here?* Donal thought to himself. *This is madness; this is madness.* His heart was pounding, and though he was aware of the street beneath his feet, the sullen, driven movement forward of his comrades, and how he strode to keep up with them, it was as though he were being transported. Even as he was careful to stay close to the torch which guided them, Donal was distracted by the desperate bid of rational thought which banged in his head for attention, as if against glass.

Within minutes they were at the barracks. Several men suddenly emerged from the night and they were running into the police station. Once inside, there was shouting and men were waving their firearms and yelling to RUC officers to lie down or be shot, calling them names and accusing them of betraying their country. There was an explosion of glass as the men outside smashed widows and stormed the barracks from behind, sweeping through the offices and corridors. A burst of automatic machine-gun fire and several single shots dispelled any vestiges of confusion regarding the seriousness of the situation. Death had slunk in under cover of darkness from his land of distant hills, and shredded the air they breathed with rampant claws, the heart-flailing terror of his roar.

Donal stuck close to Joe, following his frantic movements as if dreaming him. They went into a room dominated by two desks behind each of which a uniformed RUC man lifted his hands in the air. The officer at the desk nearest the door was a sergeant and had been writing, his pen still in his upraised right hand. An incident report? Duty handover paperwork? The barrier in his head finally shattered. Donal's senses returned and he heard with acutest clarity what Joe was saying to the two officers.

"Come out from behind the desks and kneel on the floor – now!" They complied. The one at the desk at the back of the office was much younger and of a lesser rank than the first. He was saying something over and over again in a half whisper. It wasn't until he was kneeling before Donal that it was possible to make out what it was – "Jesus help us, Jesus help us, Jesus help us."

Joe pulled rope from a pocket and roughly tied the younger man's hands behind his back. As he did so, Donal looked at the young officer's face. He was sweating profusely and kept closing his eyes. *This is insane* – Donal's recurrent thought was as clear now as the repeated prayer of the young man at his feet. His lips joined with the words in his head and he heard himself speak them. "This is insane!"

Joe whipped around to fix him with a glare and the gun he was holding pointed at Donal's chest. The older RUC officer, hands clasped behind his head as he knelt beside his colleague, looked up into Donal's eyes. Donal returned the look for a split second but it was enough. He saw an intensity of sorrow in the man's grey eyes which outweighed his fear; imagined, in that moment, how his head must be filled with thoughts of his family, his children perhaps. And what of the young man who could not look up and kept his eyes closed all the time now, muttering his prayers while tears ran down his face? What was he thinking? Of his parents? His girl? His sisters, perhaps?

"Shoot him," said Joe to Donal, indicating the older man with a sharp nod of his head. Donal looked at Joe as if he were stark mad, saw the fanaticism in his eyes, and slowly shook his head.

"No."

"That's an order, soldier – shoot him!" Joe shouted. He stood legs apart before the young officer, pointing his gun at his head, then, when Donal did not move to comply, turned and aimed his gun at Donal. At Joe's command to shoot his colleague, the young RUC man had crumpled and he fell forward, sobbing.

"For the love of God…" the older man said. His voice had a distant quality, a quiet plea for mercy, a forlorn expression of hope. Joe stared at Donal, hatred glittering like splintered glass in his eyes, his chest heaving. He made a decision, focused his attention on the young man crying at his feet, and slowly pointed his gun downwards. Someone shouted, "Come on – get the hell out of here; let's go, go, go!" But in the office, there was a surreal stillness as though time itself had paused to observe events.

"Yous don't have to kill us." The older officer spoke quietly. "Sure what's he ever done?" And he looked into Donal's eyes again. "He's twenty-two years old – your age? He's just a kid, so he is."

"Shut up!" said Joe viciously. He leaned sideways in an instant and hit the older man hard across the head with his gun. The officer fell sideways, blood welling from a deep split in his temple. He crashed against his desk. The younger one began to sob, trying his best to stifle the sound, bending even further forward so his head was almost touching his knees and spittle skeined from his open mouth.

"This is stupid!" shouted Donal. "Leave them be and let's get the hell out of here."

"What's your game, Kelly?" Joe's voice was wrath-filled, unnaturally pitched. "Do you think we're here to make friends? What did you think was going to happen? This is a war! This is what happens in war!"

"This is not war!" yelled back Donal. "This is murder! If you kill these men, that's what this will be – cold-blooded murder!"

"We are all Irish men," said the bleeding RUC officer, pushing himself with great difficulty to his knees again. "Why would yous kill your own?"

"You are not Irish men!" roared Joe. "You are traitors, colluders with the British, stinking, treacherous filth!" Joe kicked the young officer, catching him full in the face, and as his head jerked back from the force, Donal caught the widening of his eyes in abject shock, the blood beginning to pour from his broken nose and split lip.

"Christ be with me, Christ within me, Christ behind me, Christ before me…" The older man now closed his eyes and intoned St Patrick's prayer in a clear, strong voice.

"I've had enough of this." Joe pushed Donal out of the way and stood square before the older officer and aimed his gun, but his finger was not as quick to depress the trigger as Donal's, and time resumed as Donal's bullet sped through Joe's right shoulder. Joe's gun dropped, and Donal kicked it across the office, out of sight and reach. Swearing profusely, Joe cried out in agony and frustration, gripping his wounded shoulder. He shouted at Donal, "You are a coward and a traitor, Kelly! You'll die for this, so you will."

Donal kept his gun and eyes trained on Joe. "Get up!" he shouted, addressing the officers. The older one got shakily to his feet. "And you – get up!" Donal roared at the younger man. When he still remained kneeling, staring at Donal through tears and snot and blood, Donal took a couple of steps forward and, without taking his eyes from Joe, grabbed a handful of the younger officer's uniform and yanked him to his feet. "Go! Now! There's a bomb about to go off will blow this place to kingdom come. Get out. Get the others out."

The older RUC officer nodded his head rapidly in encouragement to his colleague to join him and then they were gone. Donal steadied his gun with both hands. He continued to stare at Joe during the urgent shouts, rapid footfalls, and sounds of doors banging which followed as the two officers gave the alarm, commanding their colleagues to get up and vacate the barracks.

"So, what now, Kelly?" Joe was still clutching his shoulder, blood oozing thickly over his fingers, his face contorted with pain. His breath was laboured and he was sweating profusely. Donal shook his head and backed away.

"You are no better than any man you have gunned down or planned to kill, Morgan, and a hell of a lot worse than most of them, I'd say. You would shoot men on their knees, with their eyes closed, praying for mercy!"

"They are the enemy!"

"They have nothing to do with your stinking war!" Donal bellowed the words. "It is so clear to me now! Those men did not partition Ireland or… or murder anyone! The English are barracked out there" – Donal jerked his head to indicate the street – "but you haven't the guts to confront them because you know you'd be dead in two minutes. But you'd ambush men who can't defend themselves and you'd shoot them dead, because that way you'll live and be a hero, is it? Some stinking hero, Morgan!" Donal's hand shook violently as he continued to hold out the gun, in spite of the support of his left hand. "A child could pull a trigger and shoot a man dead from two feet. What the hell sort of freedom does that get you? And who, in God's name, wants the sort of freedom the likes of you can offer, Morgan? I don't!" Donal was beside himself with a rage he no longer tried to control. "It is stupid beyond my capacity to calculate! Can you not see? The likes of you – and yes, me – is something Ireland needs to run a thousand miles from!" He began to back away. The sirens were loud now.

"Shoot me, Kelly," sneered Joe. "Have the guts to do that at least. Show me what a big man of principle you are. Finish the job." Donal looked at the clock on the office wall. Joe turned to follow his gaze and smirked. "What's it going to be, Kelly? If you leave me alive, you'd better hope to God I don't get out, because if I do, I'm coming after you – make no mistake about that."

Donal sighed, lowered his gun, and looked at Joe with an expression of resignation. "Good luck" was all he said, then he turned and ran as fast as he could from the office, down a corridor to the back of the barracks and the smashed windows. He threw an upturned chair against the wall, leaped onto it, and jumped upwards, grabbing a windowsill. He experienced rather than felt jagged glass pierce his palms. Pulling himself up, he squeezed through torn grilling, falling the ten or so feet to the ground.

He ran for the protective shadow of the rear wall. Behind it, Donal could hear English voices, orders being barked: "Spread out!" "Watch the walls!" Furtive and terrified, he crouched against the cold brick and closed his eyes.

An impression of absurdity overwhelmed him. That everything he had ever done, said, thought should culminate in this moment was ridiculous, and he suppressed the desire to laugh. "If you are really up there," he prayed, "get me out of this, would you, please? I have important things to do." At that precise moment there was an ear-splitting explosion and a lurid orange glow suffused the darkness. Debris and masonry hurtled through the night; the split and crash seemed to go on far longer than the few seconds it took for the lorry to ignite. And then all was screams and shouts and sirens and confusion.

The perimeter wall and the right-hand side of the barracks had been destroyed by the blast. Donal rose and, camouflaged by dense smoke and darkness, stole right, through the ruins, leaping and stumbling away from the flames which sprouted exotically from the rubble. He expected to be shot or apprehended at any moment, but the soldiers behind the barracks had taken cover then pushed forward to the front of the building, missing him by seconds. Donal veered further right, away from Strand Road, making for the side streets. He lost himself in the frantic crowds of off-duty naval personnel and local people who had left the dance halls, cinemas, and pubs to discover the source and effect of the explosion; to discover the nature of this attack which had found their city in spite of the darkness which hid it from German planes.

CHAPTER SEVENTEEN

One Saturday morning in early March, Caitlin was surprised to hear movement from Flynn's room. It was not yet eight o'clock and she was having her breakfast, intending to study at the kitchen table for most of the day. As the sounds of movement upstairs continued beyond those which might indicate he was just relieving himself, she was irritated. What now? She went upstairs and knocked on his door. When there was no answer, she waited long enough for him to make himself respectable, then entered. Flynn was bent over, leaning on his bed for support and clearly very weak. He had managed to dress himself. "What are you doing?" asked Caitlin, quietly. She still feared him.

Flynn straightened up and slowly turned around to face her. He had buttoned up his cardigan the wrong way and he looked painfully thin, his chest heaving beneath the garment.

"I have things to sort out," he managed between laboured breaths. He took a step forward but was very unsteady.

"Hold on." Caitlin crossed the room and offered her arm. With her support, in evident pain, Flynn walked to the door. They could not both go down the narrow stairs. Flynn eyed the sharp descent to his kitchen and almost lost courage.

"You'll have to get back up again," said Caitlin. "Sure, how…" Before she could finish, Flynn reached a trembling left hand for the banister, put the flat of his right hand against the wall, and began the torturous journey downstairs. How Caitlin wished she had gone first! At last, exhausted and coughing, Flynn sat at his kitchen table. Caitlin noted how his heart pounded beneath his cardigan and his shoulders were as sharp through the wool as a cow's hip bones beneath her hide.

When he could speak, he said, "The cows will be calving any day. They need to be brought up from the field, close to the barn – out the back," and he nodded in the direction of the field with the stunted tree, overlooked by Caitlin's room.

"Milking, by mid-March…" he went on, struggling for enough time between breaths to get out the words. "It's hard with calves. Weaning, early April. I need help."

"I can do some of it," offered Caitlin cautiously, for she was very reluctant to get caught up in a milking routine and had no idea how to wean calves. Flynn closed his eyes and shook his head emphatically.

"McCormack's son," he said. "Pay him. There's a brown box above." And he indicated his room by jerking his head upwards. "Money in that."

"OK." Caitlin frowned, nodded. "But which son? Do you mean McCormack the dairyman?"

Flynn nodded, held up two fingers.

"The second one?" He nodded again. It made sense. The third and youngest was only fifteen. The oldest was following in his father's footsteps and accompanying him on dairy rounds, learning about the dairy business. The second was eighteen and had left school, was doing odd jobs around the place to earn a few shillings a week. "How much will I pay him?"

"Three shillings a week."

"Right so." There was a long pause. "Can I get you some tea?"

Flynn nodded, coughed, held a handkerchief to his mouth and closed his eyes against the pain. Caitlin set about filling the kettle. *Why did he have to get up for this?* she wondered to herself, irritation rising again in her breast, for she would not be able to work quietly at the kitchen table now, warmed by the range.

He spoke again. "Something else…" She placed the kettle on the hob, turned to him once more. "Buy a horse."

"What?"

"Bainbhs need to go to market –" He could not go on, had to cough. For some minutes he gasped and wheezed, waited to recover. "You can't crate them up. The horse" – and he indicated the existing horse by moving his head in the direction of the barn – "can't pull a cart to Tipperary."

"I will get my father to take them in his truck," pronounced Caitlin. "That's the least he can do." Her tone and determination made Flynn smile briefly; he looked at her and his gratitude and admiration were apparent. She flushed. "Well, there's no point taking pigs to market to spend everything you earn on a new horse – is there?" And she turned her back to him and made the tea.

"Something else…." As she put his tea in front of him and he spoke again, Flynn lowered his head to avoid her eye. "Get the priest," he said, and after a few seconds' pause, added, "please."

On the same Saturday, Dan Kelly and Pat O'Meara were crossing the yard from the barn to the house, having supervised the births of a couple of bull calves. One birth was straightforward but the second was a huge calf, and the cow's labour had failed to progress so she had needed the men's intervention. Pat had held the cow's head and soothed her while Dan had turned the calf, pulled it clear of its mother by roping its forelegs. All were now doing well. They were about to enter the house when a man on a bicycle turned into the yard and hailed them.

"Kelly?"

"Yes, I'm Dan Kelly."

The man then rummaged in a leather satchel on straps which he wore across his body from shoulder to hip. "A letter for Miss Jacintha Kelly," he announced, then tipped his cap. He had ridden from the post office at Golden as soon as the letter was delivered by van with the papers and other post from the Tipperary sorting office. It had been posted some ten days before.

"That's Donal's writing," said Dan excitedly. He thanked the postman and hurried indoors, shouting for Jacintha.

"I'm here, Daddy," she said, coming downstairs. "I was just putting some linen away. What's the matter?"

"A letter – a letter from Donal – it's addressed to you, here." Dan held the envelope out to her before she had reached the kitchen, flapping it up and down as if he could hasten her approach. She frowned but took the envelope, checked the writing, looked at the postmark. Her father watched her with growing impatience. "Jacintha, would you ever open the letter, for the love of Mike!"

"OK!" Jacintha had never before received a letter. It occurred to her that if it was addressed to her and not her father, there may be something Donal wanted to confide in her. She would have preferred to open it alone. As she unsealed the envelope, she was quick to spot the green edges of bank notes. She left them where they were and pulled out the letter. She began reading it to herself.

"What does he say?" insisted her father.

"Right – he's going away…"

"Going away where? Why?"

"Daddy, do you want me to tell you or not?"

"Yes, yes – go on."

"He says… 'tell Daddy and Deirdre not to worry. I am very well and will be in touch as soon as I can, when I've settled somewhere. Please tell them both I love them. I can't tell you where I'm going because I don't know yet myself. All I can say is that I have to go away. I have no choice. Daddy was right to suspect I was sweet on Caitlin Spillane. But she is married and that is that. I'll probably travel abroad, do some teaching. Who knows? I may study again. I am sorry to leave ye like this but you have Pat. He is a good lad and will work hard. Treat him well and he'll look after you all. Donal.'"

"I knew it," said Dan sadly, sitting down heavily on a kitchen chair. "He's smitten with that young one and he can't have her so he's gone off to get her out of his system." There was a silence.

CHAPTER SEVENTEEN

Pat said nothing, though he had coloured and looked sad. Dan's latest copy of *The Irish Press* featured a front-page article about the explosion in Derry and the attempted planting of a bomb in Belfast.

Several people had been injured by the blast, including a couple of off-duty US naval personnel. Two men, however, had been killed; one an IRA man and the other an RUC officer shot before the explosion. Neither had been named by the time the article was printed and the paper was, of course, already a few days out of date by the time it reached Golden.

No one was more relieved than Pat O'Meara when Donal's letter had arrived. In the short time he had lived with the Kellys, Pat had grown very fond of them. He loved their kindness and how peaceful the house was. Dan was a fair and even-tempered man, unlike his father and brothers, and Pat was flourishing in the praise and gratitude Dan lavished on him. And then, of course, there was Deirdre. She had already won his heart. It was not easy for Pat to deceive these good people by keeping secret what he believed was Donal's real reason for leaving. Yet not for anything would he have betrayed Donal or more deeply hurt his father. And if Dan once suspected that Pat had anything to do with the IRA... it was too horrible to contemplate.

"Is that all he said, Jacintha?" asked Dan quietly. "Why did he send the letter to you?"

Jacintha blushed and took the envelope from her apron pocket. "No, Daddy, it's not all." She pulled out the notes and counted them. "Thirty pounds!" She had never dreamt about, let alone seen, such a lot of money.

"What's that for?" asked Dan, as shocked as his daughter. "Why did you hide it, Jacintha?"

"I'm sorry," she said. "I didn't know how much was there. He says it's for me to..." she paused, considering how to phrase it, "to start a new life, and ten of it's yours, for a horse."

"What?"

"Here." Jacintha passed the letter and the notes to her father. When he had finished reading, he looked at his daughter.

"You know whose money that is?"

"Yes, Daddy, I know," said Jacintha, sighing. "And it'll have to go back to him."

Dan seemed to consider for a moment. "Thirty pounds!" he exclaimed quietly. "Sure that would buy a decent horse and a cow – it's half as much as we get for our milk in a year!"

"Then take it, Daddy," urged Jacintha. "You have it, please."

"I couldn't do that, Jacintha." She looked chastened, nodded. She had never known her father anything but honest. "If Spillane is responsible for the loss of my son, then he can pay for my daughter to start the life she wants. Sounds fair enough to me."

Jacintha looked up and her face broke into a beaming smile. She jumped up from her chair and rushed to embrace her father. Twenty pounds would be more than enough to pay her rent for a few months and set her up in a nice apartment in Limerick city or even Dublin, while she looked for work.

"What's going on?" Deirdre appeared at the door, carrying freshly gathered eggs in a basket. She looked from Jacintha's flushed and smiling face to Pat's.

"Your father is after getting news of Donal," said Pat. And Deirdre sat down with them, crying and smiling by turns as she learned that soon both siblings would be from home and starting new lives. In the end, the news was less devastating than it might have been, she considered, meeting Pat's clear blue eyes through her tears.

"Who did the Spillane girl marry, in any case?" asked Dan some time later. Nobody knew. But Dan Kelly had a mind to find out. Someone in the Spillane household needed to explain to him how it came to be that Dan had no idea when he might see his son again. That evening, as Dan was reading his paper, Deirdre, Jacintha, and Pat were talking and laughing at the kitchen table.

"Pat," Dan said, lowering his paper, "we will go into the market in Golden on Thursday and buy a horse. There'll be several fellas selling them in the main street. There's always a few good ones in it."

"OK," said Pat, delighted to be involved with such a purchase.

"Can I come, Daddy? Please?"

"Haven't you school, Deirdre?" Dan looked over his glasses at his daughter. She stopped smiling and slumped in her chair, folded her arms. Dan went back to his paper. He did not disapprove of the budding courtship between Deirdre and Pat, but he could not determine if he were more pleased they were under his roof so he could keep a close eye on them or if he would have preferred that Deirdre were courting a fella who had to call at the door and have her back by nine o'clock.

Having eluded detection after the explosion, Donal wandered away from the Waterside area of Derry city and walked some miles till he reached an area north-west of the River Foyle where all was quiet. It was still only ten o'clock. He found a pub from which music emanated in spite of the blacked-out windows and, within a few minutes, had rented a small room for the night. Donal told the landlord that he had come up from the South looking for work. If he didn't find any in Derry, he said, he was thinking of getting a train to Belfast and the recruiting office, so he could sign up for work in England. Donal's easy charm and plausible narratives impressed the landlord, who warned him in a fatherly way to be careful if he was intent on going to Belfast; Republicans had tried to plant a bomb outside the recruiting office the day before, but luckily had been caught and arrested. Donal looked suitably shocked and shook his head, said he was despairing of ever finding decent work and that sort of thing didn't help – sure what was the point of that, and it likely to blow to smithereens your own countrymen? The landlord served Donal a pint, told him it was on the house.

"If you're a single man and ready to go abroad, there's plenty of work to be had on the escort ships from Derry harbours," said the landlord. Donal was interested. "If you don't mind living at close quarters with a hundred or so Yanks or Canadians, that is, and waiting till you get to Nova Scotia or New York and back for your pay." Donal sipped his beer. He had a hundred and twenty pounds in his inside jacket pocket. He didn't mind waiting for his pay. "Of course," continued the landlord, folding his arms and leaning on the bar, "you could be blasted out of the water by a U-boat." But sure that was the point, he added philosophically, of the escort and convoy ships – to provide safe conduct for merchant ships used to bring supplies to the allied forces. There'd be no need without Germans. The landlord knew a couple of local lads who had just walked onto a Corvette docked at Lisahally and volunteered their services. They were snapped up, he said. As far as he knew, they should be coming in from their third transatlantic run any day now. They always made for his bar once they'd been up to the Royal Navy base to collect their pay.

Donal spent a restless night in a tiny bed which creaked every time he moved. The mattress springs protruded painfully and so frequently that there was no part of the mattress on which to lie comfortably. But it hardly mattered. His head was so full of fears, regrets, and possibilities that he could not wait for dawn that he might face and explore a few of them head on. At six o'clock the next morning, Donal stole through the hushed streets of Derry to the docks, looking for a ship that flew the Canadian Maple Leaf Naval Jack. The landlord had told him that the Americans and the Canadians had little time for each other and less for the British – that there were fierce fights in Derry on many a Saturday night between the Canadians and Royal Navy Brits in particular.

An officer looked him up and down and told him to walk a quarter of a mile north to where several Canadian Corvettes had docked and were ready to pull out of Derry that morning, escorting an empty merchant ship back home. They were small and grey and heavily armed, explained the officer when Donal asked what a Corvette looked like. They flanked the convoy ships assigned to merchant ships bearing oil, fighter jet engine parts, or ball bearing cargoes to the British Isles, he added. The officer asked Donal if he had properly considered the risks of volunteering for service on a Corvette, given that he didn't even know what one was. Donal assured him he was prepared to accept whatever risks were necessary if it meant he found paid employment. And though the Merchant Marine naval officer shook his head sceptically as Donal walked away, he had no way of knowing that of which Donal was certain – that whatever dangers awaited him at sea between Derry and St John's Port, Newfoundland, they could not be more life-threatening than those to which he had awoken that morning.

By the time Jacintha read her letter, Donal was halfway across the Atlantic Ocean and wearing a Canadian naval uniform. He slept in a hammock ten inches from the next sailor and carried his money and his passport in a breast pocket at all times. In his heart, he carried a sensation which kindled at the very thought of Caitlin Flynn and the possibility he might never see her again.

Several days into his voyage, halfway through a freezing dawn watch duty, soaked, exhausted, sicker than he thought it possible to be, the realization came upon him that he loved her. There were many days in the eighteen-day crossing when the prospect of a German mine or U-boat torpedo seemed merciful. The Corvette would climb a monstrous Atlantic wave until it seemed her single screw engine would certainly fail and she would topple backwards from its crest, be lost in the curl and crush of its mighty fist. Or else she teetered on a crest before plummeting headlong into a trough so deep, destruction seemed certain. As Donal clung to anything he could in a bid to remain upright and on board, it was the thought that he might find his way back to Caitlin Spillane, in spite of the odds, which gave him the strength to hold on. Without any hope he would see her again, he might have uncurled his hands, opened his arms, and embraced the storms and the jealous sea.

On calmer days, or as he lay exhausted in his hammock, trying to ignore the snores of sailors which rivalled in volume and persistence the drone of the ship's engines, Donal attempted to calculate his chances of reunion with Caitlin. Each day he survived the Atlantic might be increasing the probability of seeing her again, but the vagaries of life were no respecters of mathematics; a turkey, a maths teacher had explained to him in the past, would be foolish indeed to calculate the probability of its survival based on avoidance of death on the days leading up to Christmas. Was there, Donal began to wonder seriously for the first time, a God with whom his fate was logged, and, crucially, was he open to negotiation?

For her part, Caitlin tried not to think of Donal Kelly. There was not much in his conduct to recommend him as worth the while. He had seemed to pursue her in spite of the odds, and then, when she had allowed herself to imagine what life might have been like had she met him earlier – just as the seed of the possibility he might be in her future extended a tentative shoot – he had disappeared. Caitlin had no time and less energy to waste on treacherous men – even good-looking ones. Her life had been ravaged by their kind and her focus now was self-preservation. But there were times on long and lonely evenings when Donal Kelly's liquid eyes and the way he had amused her, in spite of herself, crept into her thoughts and she smiled.

Father Kinnealy arrived at Caitlin's request, on the second Sunday in his life that Flynn missed mass. Jack insisted on being up and dressed for the priest. He sat close to the range, a blanket over his knees. Father Kinnealy was unable to hide his shock at the transformation in Jack Flynn when he walked into the kitchen.

"Well, Jack, and how are you?" he asked, though regretted the inanity of the question as soon as it was uttered. Jack nodded and wheezed in reply, smiled weakly at the priest. He lifted his hand, suddenly agitated. "What is it, Jack?" asked Father Kinnealy, pulling up a chair in front of the sick man. Jack leaned forward and seemed to be summoning energy to speak. Father Kinnealy moved to the edge of his chair in readiness.

"Last rites," wheezed Jack. "Can you… hear my confession, Father?"

Father Kinnealy had come prepared. "I can of course," he said solemnly. "I can of course."

Caitlin withdrew from the kitchen and went upstairs, quietly closed her door. Left to her own devices, she had not chosen to attend mass. The prospect of seeing her family was alone a deterrent. When added to the horror she felt at the thought of being gossiped about or quizzed on the subject of her husband's health, antipathy for the service was insurmountable. Now, as she sat on the edge of her bed and contemplated the little tree directly in her eye line, as Father Kinnealy's sonorous tones resonated from the kitchen below, she wondered if she believed in God, and could not decide. As she pondered the question, something in her head was vying for her attention, some impression of difference or alteration to usualness. At last she realized what it was. Getting up and approaching the window, she observed the little black tree. Its branches were no longer stark, but fringes of green like delicate gloves softened their skeletal reach.

"Bless me, Father," struggled Jack in low tones, "for I have sinned." He had to break off to cough.

"Take it easy, now, Jack," comforted the priest. "Take your time." There was a long pause during which Jack recovered sufficiently to continue.

"That night," he whispered hoarsely.

"What night, Jack?"

Jack looked at Father Kinnealy and pleaded with him to recall the only night, the significance of which they had shared. The urgency and sorrow in Jack's eyes were all the aide memoire the priest needed. He knew well enough. He nodded and looked away from Jack's desperate gaze. "Cappawhite. That was…" Jack struggled, tears welling in his eyes in spite of his best efforts to suppress them. "That was murder, Father." The memory and the declaration were almost as uncomfortable for the priest as they were for the confessor. He still did not meet Jack's eyes. Jack continued, "Those men had no chance."

Father Kinnealy looked at Jack at last, mournful and full of compassion. He nodded. "I know, I know."

There was a long pause while each man remembered his part in the Cappawhite killings. Jack recalled out loud for the first time – haltingly because of sorrow as much as difficulty breathing – how he had alighted from the hay cart, having left the Dundrum dance with the other men from the South Tipperary flying column. He had picked up his rifle from the floor of the wagon and descended upon the signal from the driver. He recalled how he had run stealthily, crouching, as if that way the night could afford him extra cover. At last, he and the others had crept silently towards the barracks in which four Black and Tans slept soundly. A deliberate distraction had been created a few miles down the road in Annacarty so that the Irish Constabulary sergeant and his men had gone to the cross to investigate, leaving the Tans alone and vulnerable. The lookout had clearly been too tired, the night too silent and warm, for he had fallen asleep and the next thing he knew was a gun in his face and a command to get on his knees and keep his mouth shut.

Jack related to a pallid and tortured priest how that night had soured his life, weighted his dreams till he dragged them around like shackles through his waking hours. He might, he said now, have tried harder to make something of his life; might even have sold the farm upon his father's death and pursued salvation from grief and loneliness while still a young man, if it were not for the terrible, dragging guilt of that night.

"Did you never wonder," he enquired tearfully of Father Kinnealy, "why I never went up to the altar rail for Communion once in twenty years?"

Jack could still recall the name of the first man to open fire – Dan Mulcahy from Ardfinnan. The shots ripped through the night and made their hearts leap wildly in their chests. All rational thought was scrambled, the training they had received, forgotten. General panic broke out and then they were all firing randomly into the darkness. There were a few short exclamations – cries and indecipherable expressions of anguish in English accents. It was a miracle, gasped Jack now, that they weren't cut down by their own fire, so chaotic was the whole thing. It lasted only seconds. It was impossible to see anything clearly. Although it was a late summer night and there was a half-moon, the barracks were not lit and all was shadows and shifting silhouettes. It hardly even seemed real.

The only Black and Tan still certainly alive was on his knees, pleading for mercy. He kept saying he had a wife and children. He promised he would go back to England – desert that very night – if only they would let him go. Jack remembered that many Tans did exactly that; sick of being ambushed by the IRA, or else having no stomach for the brutality many of their kind exhibited against helpless Irish families, they shed their uniforms and slunk away. If they were not caught and dispatched by the IRA and if they reached a port, they could steal home on a cargo ship or even pay a ferry fare back to England. But there would be no such escape for this one. Whoever had held him at gunpoint throughout the ambush took a step back and pulled his trigger. The man toppled instantly, and everyone, Jack included, ran as fast as they could into the night, taking various routes back to their homes and what was supposed to be normal life.

Three of the bodies, Father Kinnealy recalled afresh, lay together in one room. One had been fifty or so yards from the barracks. Whoever shot him had not killed him outright and he had died slowly, of blood loss. It wasn't likely that Father Kinnealy would ever forget the blood. God knew he had awoken sweating from dreams of it on many a night. On innumerable occasions, he had groped in the darkness for his rosary beads and slipped from his bed to his knees. He had heard a few versions of that night's events in the confessional box.

"This," Jack managed through the outpouring of his grief, "is my punishment. My life was lost that night and it ends here, like this. Please, Father…" Jack leaned forward and looked earnestly into the priest's eyes. "Do you think God can forgive me? Do you think there's any chance of a life at all… after this?"

"Nothing," Father Kinnealy said emphatically, "is unforgivable, Jack." Jack's crying became less intense. He remained bent over, head in his hands. "You are absolved, forgiven, in the name of Jesus Christ, our Lord." And here the priest made the sign of the cross over Jack's bowed head, as he said, "*In nomine Patris, et Filii et Spiritus Sancti.*" He touched Jack's head and closed his eyes. "Your contrition is evident and the grace of God is boundless. Be at peace, Jack, be at peace."

Father Kinnealy heard the remainder of Jack's confession and performed the last rites, then left. He would not sleep that night. How he wished his faith would bring him the peace with which he left Jack Flynn that day.

One evening during the last week of March, Caitlin was surprised by a knock at the door. She was even more surprised to open it and behold a man she had never seen before. She stared at him, waiting for him to say who he was. Dan Kelly removed his cap.

"Mrs Flynn? I am Donal Kelly's father." Caitlin's frown intensified. What was he doing on her doorstep? "Can I come in, please? I won't keep you long. I understand things are… hard at the moment." The man's voice and manner were gentle. He smiled at her. She stood aside and let him in. "I'll get to the point," said Dan, though he turned his cap nervously in his hands. "I have been up to your father's place. I know about... how you were married, and it's none of my business," he added quickly, "but Donal, my son, is why I'm here. You see, I understand that he... well, he..." Caitlin raised an eyebrow; Dan could not continue. Spillane had told him enough – about how he had sold his daughter to Flynn and how, when he heard Flynn was dying, he had hoped Donal might be in line as her next husband. But Mick had also begged Dan not to tell Caitlin of the conspiracy. As it was, he had pleaded, there was enough bad blood between them. "Well, I understand Donal... liked you a lot, Mrs Flynn."

"Would you please call me Caitlin?"

"Caitlin." Dan smiled again, contemplating the girl before him – the spirit in her blue eyes, the way she had folded her arms and stood straighter as he had grappled for the right words. He could see why Donal had fallen for her, and disliked Mick Spillane even more. Caitlin still did not know why this man had come to her house. She waited.

"You probably know," went on Dan, "that Donal has... disappeared. No one knows where he is." Caitlin unfolded her arms and gestured to the table. Dan pulled out a chair, sat down. She did likewise, refolded her arms. In spite of her attempts to dismiss Donal Kelly from her life and thoughts, she was interested.

"He wrote us a letter, some days ago now. He mentioned you." Caitlin could not disguise her surprise. "Yes, he said he had to accept that you are married but that he needed to... distance himself from it all..." Dan was reddening and very aware that there was a dying man in this house and that whatever the circumstances of the marriage, he was this woman's husband. He stopped. Looking earnestly at Caitlin, he suddenly asked for the information which was originally his quest. "Do you know anything of where he is, Caitlin, or when he might be coming back?"

"I know nothing!" she exclaimed. "I barely spoke to him. You've just told me more than I knew."

Dan nodded, looked down at his cap. "I'm very sorry," he said, "but I know you'll understand how worried I am." There was a long silence. The clock ticked as it had through sixty years of nights and days in this house. Dan put on his cap and rose from his chair; Caitlin rose with him. She had been studying his face. She could see the resemblance of Donal to his father but the eyes were very different. She wondered if Donal got his brown eyes from his mother. But instead of proceeding directly to the door and letting himself out, Dan stopped, turned to face Caitlin again, and removed his cap.

"I knew your husband's mother," he said, as if it were a confession.

"What?"

"This is Jack Flynn's house, right? Sean Flynn's son?" Caitlin had no idea who Jack's father was. She shrugged, nodded. "Well, your husband had an aunt. A great-aunt, actually – Maisie, Maisie Kelly. She was my grandmother – my father's mother."

"Why are you telling me this?" asked Caitlin. Dan was very red and appeared agitated.

"Because your husband – Jack Flynn – is dying. Mick Spillane told me he has only days left. I have something to tell him. May I tell him?"

Caitlin was intrigued but wary. "It's not about…"

"No, no, no" – Dan shook his head – "nothing to do with Donal, I can assure you. No. It's to do with Jack's mother."

"I'll go up and see if he's awake. Often, he's not conscious for hours at a time now."

Flynn was sleeping but Caitlin could wake him. She called his name several times, gently pushed his shoulder, and lit the lamp by the bedside. At last, his eyes opened, flickered for a while, and then he turned his head to look at her. "You have a visitor," she said, "a man named Kelly. He wants to come up and see you." Flynn frowned with the effort of remembering. Kelly. Then his eyes became angry, which Caitlin had expected. "No," she said emphatically. "Not him. His father." She added quickly, "He says he has something to tell you – about your mother." Flynn's breathing stopped. His eyes widened as though he was shocked. He began to cough but lifted his head as he did so, gestured to the door, and nodded. Caitlin went back downstairs. "He says to go up," she said.

As Dan Kelly's silhouette appeared in the open doorway, Flynn raised himself on one elbow, trembling with the effort, and peered into the evening gloom to make out his visitor. Slowly, Dan came forward.

"Good evening, Mr Flynn," he said softly. "I am truly sorry to disturb you, now." Dan was clearly very affected by the sight of the dying man. This skeletal figure bore no resemblance to the strapping, surly Jack Flynn he had avoided at markets, whose temper was legendary.

"You know something about my mother?" gasped Jack, struggling for the words between breaths. "What do you know?"

Dan stood close to the bedside. "This is difficult for me – Jack, is it? This is hard. It's a confession of sorts. I never knew how to tell you before. I was afraid to. I hope you can... forgive me, now." Jack could not remain on his elbow. He fell back on the pillow and closed his eyes. His heart was racing so that he could barely concentrate on Kelly's words. The pain in his chest was increasing and soon he would have to cough. He dreaded the agony and this man would see the blood. Jack was desperate for Kelly to say what he had to say.

Dan saw Jack's agitation and was worried. He spoke quickly. "My grandmother was Maisie Kelly of Golden." In spite of the pain and the coughing which had started, Jack fixed Dan Kelly's eyes with a look of sorrow and disbelief combined. "I was no more than a child, now, when this happened, but my father told me later that when your mother… left this house…" Jack opened his mouth wide, trying to breathe over the coughing, desperate to hear. "She walked for a few miles with a child in her arms, and when dawn broke, a man on his way to market in Cashmel picked her up and dropped her off near Golden. She turned up at my grandmother's house, the child wrapped in a shawl. It had been dead for hours." Dan stopped talking. Jack's eyes were overflowing with tears and there was a tiny rivulet of blood seeping its way from his open mouth to the pillow. Every breath the man took seemed to be causing him pain. Dan was terrified he was killing him. "Will I stop?" he asked.

Jack shook his head from side to side on the pillow. "No!" he uttered.

"My grandmother took her in – called the doctor. Your mother was in a terrible state – obviously. My grandmother kept her above, looked after her. I think she had a complete breakdown, like…"

Flynn closed his eyes. The tears found their way out, spilled down his face like ice melting.

"After a long while, she got well enough to try and see you but she never wanted to come back to your father. Anyhow, my father told me that she tried many times to see you but your father wouldn't let her, if she didn't come back to him, like. And although my grandmother tried to fetch you up to the house at Golden, he wouldn't let her bring you there – in case you never came back, he said. My father came here, too, to try and reason with him, but he would have none of it." Dan could not tell how Jack Flynn was taking all this. He kept his eyes closed. Only the tears and the way his brows came together or his breathing changed indicated he was listening. "My father, at the time, was working in Tipperary. We had a house in the town. He was a dairy manager. I had an uncle and an aunt too but none of them wanted the farm. My uncle went to America and my aunt married a chap in Waterford. When my grandfather died, my grandmother sold off acres of the place, keeping only enough that she could manage – a few cows, chickens. Anyhows, your mother stayed with her and together they looked after the place. Then my grandmother got ill." Dan paused. The next bit was the part causing him most difficulty. "Mr Flynn – Jack – I am sorry to say this now, because it does not reflect well on my father or me – but you have a right to know. Especially now."

Jack opened his eyes, turned his head towards Dan, and waited.

"My grandmother – Maisie Kelly – left the house to your mother. She didn't know what would happen her if she did not. My father was not pleased, I have to say. Your mother – the daughter of Maisie's dead sister, I understand – looked after my grandmother till she died. But being in the house on her own, not able to see you… the loss of Maisie. It was all too much. She had another breakdown, and this time there was no one to see her through it. Sure my father lived miles away and our house was tiny. By this time, I had four brothers and sisters as it was…"

There was another long pause. Jack could not speak but his eyes pleaded with Dan for the final piece in this puzzle he had been trying all his life to complete. Whatever this man had to say next was better than the emptiness in his heart.

"My father had her removed to St Joseph's Asylum in Cashmel. To my shame, I don't know to this day if she's alive or dead. We moved back into the house in Golden and my father bought back several acres of land with the money he got from selling the Tipperary house. And there I have been, as the eldest son, ever since." Dan stood, head bowed, at Flynn's bedside. Flynn raised a trembling right hand. Dan looked at the hand then at Jack's face, understood, and moved to tears himself, took the offered hand. Jack smiled at him and nodded briefly. Dan gripped his hand then covered it with his other. "Thank you, Jack," he said. "Thank you. And may God bless you." He held on to Jack's hand a moment longer then laid it carefully on the bed and took his leave.

It was Caitlin who discovered that Jack's mother had died the year before, aged sixty-four and lost in a world more conducive to happiness than the real one. She had been lovely, the nurses assured Caitlin – a gentle soul who smiled and sang her way through most days and had imaginary conversations with children named Irene and Jack. The husband, it was understood, had been brutal, and she had never wanted to go back to him, so no one tried to contact him. No one visited her. There were days when she sat staring at the rain on the windows and cried, rocking and talking quietly to herself. She liked a hug on those days and could be comforted with kind words.

Caitlin had asked Mick to take her to St Joseph's in his truck. On the way back, neither spoke, each lost in thoughts of how senseless it was to bring suffering to your own house when there was plenty of it queuing up from outside to be let in. And Mick's thoughts wandered on to whether or not Caitlin would let him organize things on Flynn's farm after the funeral. It would make more sense to unite the dairy herds in any case. Surely, she would see that. McCormack's lad could continue to help about the place – they could bring the pigs together, too. Flynn's barn was bigger – it would make sense to keep them there. And McCormack's lad could use Spillane's horse to go up and down the lane. And then Caitlin would be back with her family again and the wife would leave him alone. She was driving him mad with the nagging to make amends with Caitlin.

"Your mother is dead, Jack." Caitlin sat at his bedside and broke the news gently. His mouth was very dry. She dipped a handkerchief into a cup of water and ran the cloth over his lips. He blinked, nodded. Then he beckoned her closer.

CHAPTER SEVENTEEN

"Box," he said, and gestured feebly towards the brown box in which he kept cash, the deeds of the farm, Land Act Registrations, other official documents. She fetched it for him, opened it. "Will."

"You want me to find your will?" He nodded. She riffled through yellowing papers, envelopes stuffed with cash and labelled variously "Feed – cows", "Blacksmith", "Feed – Pigs", "Crops". There were immaculately kept ledgers which recorded the outgoings and income of the farm over decades, and finally, there was a white envelope among the brown and yellowing ones sealed and marked "Will 1944". And there were wads of notes, carefully bound by elastic bands. It was impossible to estimate their cumulative worth.

At an encouraging nod from Jack, Caitlin opened the envelope. Another nod and a feeble lift of his hand and she began reading. As she did so, Caitlin thought how neat and effortless was his hand; how incongruous with his character and his life. "I leave all I own to…" – and she hesitated, looked at him, shocked – "Caitlin Flynn, nee Spillane, my wife." She held his gaze for a long moment, frowned in confusion. He smiled and closed his eyes, lifted his hand again. She continued reading. "She may dispose of all fixed and moveable assets as she thinks fit." And that was it. It was dated 8th January 1944.

"Why?" asked Caitlin. "Sure we weren't even… married at that stage."

"After that first meeting… at your house… you said you were a slave. Then you ran away… Spillane said you dreamed of university." He paused, waited till he had enough strength to continue. "I pitied you. I knew I was dying. I could have stopped the wedding."

"Why didn't you?" Her question was not just born of curiosity but profound resentment, which she could never quell. He concentrated on breathing as evenly as possible, closing his eyes as he did so. Then he opened them and turned to her.

"I bought you, Caitlin, to set you free."

There were not many at Jack Flynn's funeral. Caitlin stood pensive and gaunt at the graveside. Her parents stood behind her. The Mahers were there and so were Malachai Brett and his wife. Father Kinnealy said a few words about the sorrows and trials which had beset Jack's life and how short-lived his happiness had been since Caitlin had come into his life. The most memorable thing he said was that Jack Flynn was a much misunderstood man. Caitlin handed Mrs Maher an envelope with twenty pounds in it, "for looking after him so well," she said. Then she pulled her black shawl close around herself and began the walk home. She did not even look at her parents.

April came blue and sweet and full of birdsong. Caitlin was working hard for her exams and the horse was well enough that she could ride him to and from school. She turned him out in one of her father's fields each morning before walking on to school, and brought him in from the field to be bridled and ridden home each afternoon. Always, he neighed and whinnied in greeting when he saw her, and came trotting to the gate.

One sunny Saturday afternoon, Mick Spillane pulled into Flynn's yard, tooting his horn. Caitlin was washing clothes in the kitchen sink.

"Well," he said, and sat down at the table, "is there any tea in it?" Caitlin did not lift her arms from the sudsy water. She blew a strand of hair from her eye as she turned to look at him.

"There is if you make it," she said. Mick sighed, tapped the table rapidly with a forefinger, and began to speak.

"Have you thought what you're to do with this place, Caitlin? Eh?"

Caitlin continued scrubbing, did not respond immediately. She had been waiting for that one.

"Oh, I have," she said at last. Mick frowned, remembering his wife's stern injunction not to get angry or pushy.

"Well," he persisted, "I thought it might be a good idea to put

312

the two herds together, like. It'd make sense. I could milk them below with McCormack's help. The calves need to go to market now. Sure we may as well get on with it as soon as that's done. What do you think?"

"I think," said Caitlin calmly, letting out the soapy water and starting to run cold, clean water over her clothes to rinse them, "that if you pay a fair price for each cow, you can have them."

"What?"

"You heard." She agitated the clothing beneath the running water till there were no more suds, then set about wringing each item separately, placing it on the draining board.

"But sure I'll be doing you a favour!" exclaimed Mick. "What do you want with cows? I'll cut you in on the dairy payment, fair and square."

"I'm selling the cows," she replied, turning to face him and drying her hands on her apron as she did so. "And the pigs. And the house. And the land. Everything. I'm selling it all." She looked levelly at her astounded father.

"What?"

Caitlin smiled. "You heard me well enough, Daddy. As soon as I have my exam results I am leaving here and I am never, ever coming back."

"What?"

"Now, do you still want tea?"

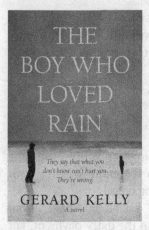

THE VICAR'S WIFE
KATHARINE SWARTZ

"A warm, wonderful, emotional read."
– Sarah Morgan, USA Today
bestselling author

Jane is a New Yorker to the core, city-based and career-driven. But when her teenage daughter Natalie falls in with the wrong crowd at her Manhattan school, Jane's British husband Andrew decides to relocate from New York to a small village on Britain's Cumbrian coast, buying a vast and crumbling former vicarage.

Jane hates everything about her new life: the silence, the solitude, the utter isolation. Natalie is no better, and their son Ben struggles in his new school. Even worse, Jane's difficulties create new tensions between her and Andrew.

When Jane finds a scrap of an old shopping list, she becomes fascinated with Alice James, who lived in the vicarage decades before. *The Vicar's Wife* takes readers on an emotional journey as two very different women learn the desires of their hearts – and confront their deepest fears.

"The Vicar's Wife is gorgeous! Lushly imagined, deeply moving... the perfect book to lose yourself in!"
– Megan Crane, author of *Once More With Feeling*

Katharine Swartz lives in the Lake District with her husband, five children, and a Golden Retriever. *The Vicar's Wife* is the first book in Katharine's new series, *Tales from Goswell*.

ISBN 978-1-78264-070-7 £7.99, US $14.99